THE BACKUP

ERICA KUDISCH

ANGLERFISH
PRESS

Anglerfish Press
PO Box 1537
Burnsville, NC 28714
www.AnglerFishPress.com
Anglerfish Press is an imprint of Riptide Publishing.
www.RiptidePublishing.com

The Backup

Cover art: Jay Aheer, jayscoversbydesign.com
Editor: Carole-ann Galloway
Layout: L.C. Chase, lcchase.com/design.htm

ISBN: 978-1-62649-371-1

First edition
January, 2016

Also available in ebook:
ISBN: 978-1-62649-370-4

THE BACKUP

ERICA KUDISCH

ANGLERFISH
PRESS

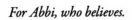

For Abbi, who believes.

TABLE OF CONTENTS

MAY 13, 2011

Departmental commencement is a robes-and-hoods occasion, and it's far too hot for the honor. Hertz Hall is air-conditioned, at least, but it's also packed, and I'm sitting too close to the front and the middle to catch more than the faintest artificial breeze, filtered through five hundred people or so, none of whom are here to see me.

"And one last round of applause for the UC Berkeley Music Department Class of 2011!" the chair commands, and of course he's obeyed. I'm not immune. "Now, for the graduate program, beginning with those who have completed their master's."

The eight master's recipients are packed in on the left side of my row, and filter out into the aisle. They aren't giving us our bona fides today, or even tomorrow at the main ceremony. Photo ops and pageantry, that's compulsory, but the real document comes in the mail in three weeks. I find it amazing that people still do the calligraphy by hand.

Tomorrow will be hours of sitting in the sun with only a ridiculous tam hat for protection, waiting for thousands of undergrads to receive their fake degrees; today *means* something, to me and the people I've toiled beside for the past seven years. Knowing Uncle Paul, he probably thinks tomorrow is the more important ceremony. Then again, he'd texted, *Will contact you on Friday when I arrive*, which is today, and there's been no word since, so it looks like he won't make either. That's the most recent message in my queue. I've been checking for the last fifteen minutes. It's bad enough that I've got my phone in my lap during my own PhD acceptance. I shouldn't check it every five seconds like I'm waiting for water to boil.

The applause never quite dies down, only swells and diminishes for the clearer sound of the chair reading a name, a field, honors or no honors. They're almost through calling the master's. There's a chance that Paul hasn't texted me because he's expecting me to be polite and not answer. He might be here.

"And it also is our privilege to honor four new PhDs," the chair says, and that's my cue. First in line: the alphabet has always been on my side. I hold on to my phone but hide my fist in the billowing sleeve since I can't reach my pocket through the robes, sidle into the aisle, and file down to the stage. "Please welcome, Doctor of Musicology, Anthony Brooks."

The acoustics of the concert hall are built to send sound out from the stage, not up to it, but applause is always an exception. It starts just before I make it to the short flight of stairs up to the stage and ascend. Despite the handshaking and the genuinely proud smiles, it feels like a rehearsal.

My phone buzzes at center stage. Thank goodness it's in my left sleeve, and Professor Taruskin is shaking my right.

I wait until I've made it through the receiving line and the next name has been called to look out at the audience. It's always easy to spot Paul in a crowd like this, where almost everyone else is white or light-skinned. By extension, it's easy to spot when he's not here, and doesn't take me long to ascertain it. He's not.

In the relative obscurity of my seat, I check my phone again.

Work emergency, it says. *I won't make it out tomorrow either. But you have my congratulations and my respect. Call Sunday.*

Well, at least I have other people to applaud for.

The *Rock Band* version of Mozart's "*Rondo alla turca*" cuts out all the repeats that the song usually has in concert performances. It's as jarring to hear as it is to play. Julia's managing to approximate it on the controller, but then, she isn't a pianist. Thank god no one's passed me the guitar yet. I suck.

"Stop brooding, you're making me look like a bad host!" Elise Morgenstern whirls by and sits on the arm of the couch, wrestling with a corkscrew and a bottle of red wine. Her hair—a color that I'm embarrassed to know is *fuchsia* as opposed to just pink—clashes with the gold trim on her master's robes, which she's still wearing, even though everyone else at the party has taken them off. "Everything okay?"

I take the hint and tilt over my empty glass, just in time for Elise to wrangle the cork out and Julia to finish the most difficult section of the song. The applause, canned and live, stacks up with the hiss of the cork. That's vaguely interesting.

Elise pours, first into my glass, then someone else's, then her own, and laughs. "Are you waiting on your turn? I can check if anyone else is ahead of you."

Everyone else, it seems. But she means *Rock Band*, not my life. "I'm not drunk enough."

"Ha-ha, I know I'd be getting drunk too if I was really done." Elise reaches over awkwardly, sets the bottle down on the coffee table, and clinks her glass against mine on the way back. "*Rondo alla turca*" is almost done. Julia's score isn't embarrassing, "Congrats!"

I don't toast, just nod the glass, then drink. This bottle is better than the last. It's an acceptable compromise between brought-by-way-of-thanks beer and are-you-sure-I-can-drink-this tequila. Grad students can't be choosers—then again, I'm not a grad student anymore.

Paul would chastise me for having expensive taste. Paul isn't here. And the wine is free.

"Did any of your family make it out in the end?" Elise asks. Wow. I'm not sure how her timing can be this incisively bad, this consistently. She always seems to know the wrong question to ask. It's as annoying as it is impressive, but what can I say, it's grown on me.

"No," I say. "I heard from Paul on the way over. Work emergency."

"What about your— Oh. Ha. Sorry. Brings back memories." She laughs uncomfortably into her glass. One of the first things Elise ever found out about me was that my parents have been dead since I was ten. It made the Welcome, New Graduate Students Luncheon two years ago weird for all concerned.

She laughs about it. I don't. Par for the course, that. "Mine asked after you, that's all. They wanted to say thanks for helping me with the whole *Boardwalk Empire* thing."

It's tactless to say *You could have thanked Paul for that if he were here*, and I'm not drunk enough to be tactless any more than I'm drunk enough to play *Rock Band*, so I hold my tongue. It's an effort. Maybe if the Ivory Tower wasn't leaning, I'd have something other than that to feel accomplished about.

"Any word yet from New Mexico?"

"They rejected me this morning," I sigh.

Elise winces. "That sucks. But least you still have Indiana and the others to hear back from. Simon hasn't heard back either, so. Yeah. Don't give up!" Before I can answer, not that I'm certain what else to say, Elise jumps to her feet. "That reminds me! I promised to show Chuck and Simon something, just give me a sec," and she scuttles away from the couch to take the *Rock Band* controller. "Sorry everyone! Just trying to make a point, this'll only take five minutes."

Being alone at a party with thoughts of my lack of economic prospects isn't my preferred means of celebration—Well. No shit. I finish my glass of wine in time to deposit it on the nearest countertop, and apologize to a few people on my way into the hall. Elise's apartment is nicer than mine, but then again, she's living outside the city with two other people paying rent. The nearest bedroom is closed, and there's a group of master's students in front of the bathroom pretending not to wait for it, but oddly enough the door to the study is open, and the foamcore soundproofing looks more tempting than it should. It would be quiet in there. I wouldn't have to answer any further questions about where I'm going, or how I can scrape together enough money to stay. I could just spend the rest of the party on the piano and be done with it.

Well, if the door's open, the room's open, and Simon and Elise have given me explicit permission in the past, so that's implicit permission in the present as far as pianos go. The study is arranged with the computer station on one side and the upright piano on the other with a window and writing desk on the far wall. The near wall is covered in mattress pad soundproofing, with an unplugged external computer mic and a keyboard setup disassembled on a shelf. I shut the door just in time to cut off the rush of laughter at whatever's on YouTube, and once I do the soundproofing turns out to be fairly, if not completely, effective. Relative silence. Finally. Silence itself would be better, but doesn't exist, not really. John Cage proved that.

I sit down at the piano, careful not to disturb any of Simon's drafts, and play.

Bach's Toccata and Fugue in D minor belongs on an organ, not a piano. It loses most of its ominous majesty without that requisite screech and sustain. But maybe after having spent most of the morning in Hertz with the pipe organ in view, or maybe since I feel as comically isolated as a villain in a tower—and this piece has been used, or parodied, in every vampire movie ever—that's the first piece that comes to mind and what I settle into playing, whether the instrument is right or not.

It's a hard piece, hard even for me, but Bach is predictable: pattern, math, a perfectly constructed, seamless flow from one tonality to the next. I can't exactly abandon myself in it—it's too difficult—but good luck getting me to think about anything but what my fingers are doing. The prelude ends, segues into a fugue, and my hands follow the old jumps and crosses and skips, three separate voices winding through ten fingers. It really *should* be on an organ. It's harder than it has to be. But it's necessary, absorbing to play.

So the sound of the door swinging open, unknocked, might as well be a gunshot.

"Whoops," Julia says. "Sorry."

I'd stopped as soon as she opened the door, but I don't start again. "It's fine."

She smiles, leans on the jamb. "I heard the Bach, figured it was you. Do you mind if I stick around?"

"All right." There should be a chair for her somewhere, so I don't move from the bench. Julia leaves the door open—whatever was on YouTube is still occupying everyone's attention, so there's no music, just chatter and laughter and one canned voice cutting through the rest—and pulls over the desk chair. Julia is in the habit of wearing impractically high heels even to teach in, and tonight's no exception, so they pitter on the studio floor, and I wait until she has sat down to turn back to the keyboard and start playing again. From the beginning of the fugue, since it's hard to pick up from the middle.

She recognizes the piece, laughs. "You should set up the synthesizer instead. It's got an organ tone."

"It would be rude."

"Maybe, but they wouldn't mind."

I shrug, as much as playing a fugue this brisk allows. Once the left hand takes over, I—Huh, the door's still ajar. And a half-dozen undergrads whose names I don't know are either waiting for the bathroom or listening in. Probably both. I could blame them when I miss the next trill, but it's my mistake at the end of the day. I keep going.

"Are you staying here or going home?" Julia asks, swiveling on the computer chair.

"Here" means in San Francisco. I wish I didn't have to say this, again and again. It gets easier, and easier hurts because hey, failure. "As long as I can," I answer. "I've got enough saved up that I can handle rent for the summer. I'd rather find a job by July though." Thinking about this is entirely counter to the reason I came in here, but there's no point in telling Julia that if she can't already tell.

I do love this part of the fugue: right when it winds to a climax, all the threads coming together to one powerful chord. It feels right to play.

Outside, everyone else laughs at whatever's on-screen. Maybe not everyone else, if those undergrads are still listening to me. Elise's voice cuts through the rest, tells them they have to wait, there's something in the sidebar that she needs to see right now, and fuck, pounding out notes isn't sufficient distraction after all. I can stop soon, even if the next resolution isn't in the right key.

And just as soon as I stop, the television speakers overclock and grate, and I have to wonder if that's supposed to be music at all.

Whatever it is, it's loud enough that if I were playing it in my own apartment, the super would call the cops. There's a guitar under there, winding and discordant, and a bass, drums, a keyboard, coarse vocals so distressed it's impossible to make out the words, and everything is dampened by cheering and pounding feet and the sense that this happened somewhere else and no smartphone can preserve it. I barely remember to cover the keyboard when I get up. I ought to see what I'm hearing.

There's no point in trying to identify who's playing: even blown up on a television screen the video quality and resolution are crap, and besides, the camera isn't focused on the band. It's on the riot in the crowd: mostly naked, some bloody and bruised, but still dancing, and making the mistake of trying to pull the cops into the mosh pit.

For one terrifying moment, I have to wonder if I'd do the same thing if I were there.

No. Never.

"The hell, Elise," someone says. Me, it turns out, since she's looking.

"It's just Nik, sorry!" She fumbles with the controller, but whatever she does doesn't pause the video. Everyone in front of me is short enough that I've got a clear view of the screen, of the focus on the camera choking in and out until it's not on the riot anymore. The lead singer, a skeletal man with black hair, is on the lip of the stage, still singing like there's nothing wrong.

The singer licks his chops. No, not like nothing's wrong. Like everything's *right*.

The video pauses, the screen minimizes, Elise apologizes again and flails and starts going on about a paper topic for next year and how this video ties into it and isn't it great that ethnomusicology means people like Nik exist.

I think some of that song's lyrics make sense. They're only hitting me now. Insidious. "Once you get in there," or something like that. There's a tune to it too. Maybe. I could—

"Quit it with the papers," Simon says. "I've still got revisions to do on my diss."

Elise sticks her tongue out, but laughs. "I'm serious, though. It would be awesome to do a paper on Nik. There's not much work on the rocker persona—"

"Outside of Hollywood," Chuck says.

"—and Nik's so cool. I mean, he's Dionysus."

That statement effectively shuts up about half the room, and the half that doesn't shut up is talking about the latest Giants game.

"Dionysus," I say, at the same time as at least one other person. That's weirdly harmonic. Dionysus, in two parts.

Elise grins. "Yeah. I mean, literally. God of Drunk and Disorderly. And his music holds up to it too."

Oh for fuck's sake. "Have they run out of marketing tools?"

Julia laughs. "Well, David Bowie already took the alien idea."

"And only Lady Gaga can be Lady Gaga," Simon adds.

"Seriously, guys," Elise says, fiddling with the controller. "But yeah. He keeps Dionysus up 24-7 and markets the concerts as bacchanalia, makes everything over-twenty-one only, the works."

Chuck scoffs. "Is that legal?"

Years of trailing behind Uncle Paul confirm that, so I answer, "Yes, if you have the right representation."

That gets a few laughs, and Elise flashes me a smile. "Anyway, I think he might be a diss chapter if I can fit him in."

We've all heard some variation of this phrase out of Elise before, so it means jack-shit at this point. Simon's the first to get a dig in at her though. "Isn't your dissertation on *Battlestar Galactica*?"

She tosses the controller at him, and he catches it reflexively.

"No, I condensed that to a conference paper. I still don't know what my diss is going to be." It's a surprisingly mature answer for Elise. Maybe the MA thesis put her a little more on track. Good. "Besides, comps first."

"No shit," Chuck says, and Julia says "Good luck!" and Simon throws me the controller and says "Hey, Anthony, as long as you're going to play I think I've got Toccata on easy mode."

"No way," I say, and that's the end of that discussion. There are other things to argue about, and maybe *not* dwelling on my lack of a future will make it bearable.

Or maybe playing *Rock Band* will remind me how much I suck at it.

And life.

And until Simon clicks into *Rock Band*, that grinning skeletal face is on the television screen, mocking me from half a world away. "Nik," Elise called him. Dionysus.

I glare right back.

Everything I couldn't part with is at the mercy of the postal system, probably somewhere in Nebraska, on its way to New York City. Baggage fees being what they are, it was cheaper to ship via media mail than to take more than could fit beneath the seat, and as long as I'm throwing myself on my uncle's mercy, I might as well throw the rest on his doorstep.

And right now, I've thrown myself into Uncle Paul's waiting room at Pantheon Talent. It's been refurnished since I was last here, and the sound system is invasive enough that it must be new. In addition to worrying about my luggage, I've been flirting with the idea of putting in my earbuds for the last half hour. Which also means I've been waiting on Paul for the last half hour.

Not blocking out his office soundtrack is an act of politeness that Paul will probably never remark on. But it's better not to give him any excuses, all things considered.

Paul's receptionist taps her heels to the beat of whatever song this is. She must be musical if she can keep it steady on the off-counts for this long. Since I'm still being too polite to put my earbuds in, I notate the song in my head. This particular song's hook is catchy as hell, but there's only just enough flow in the rap to make it interesting. And even on the hook the singer milks that syncopation for all it's worth, but only enough that it might be unintentional. I could do better, maybe. Or at least assemble a song that's not as haphazard. But I've never thought of myself as a composer, not even an arranger, and changing careers takes time I don't have.

"Anthony," Paul says, tripled semiquavers against the beat.

"Uncle." I nod, get up from the bench. It must look more like a casting session or an interview than a family coming together the way Paul leads me into the office, not even a handshake, let alone a hug. And especially since my mother is—was—white, Paul and I have never looked as alike as people seem to think we should, so if the receptionist assumed anything, it's almost certainly wrong.

Paul looks good for his age. His suit's definitely more expensive than the last one I saw him in, and he wears it like he wants the world to know.

"Thanks for having me," I say.

Paul nods, opens his office door. "How was your flight?"

"Flights. I couldn't get a direct so I transferred at LAX."

"I'm sorry I couldn't make it out there to watch you walk."

"It's another color on the hood." I can let it go no matter how much it offended me at the time. Six months of water have passed under that particular bridge. "But I guess you can call me a doctor of music now."

"No more pesky undergrads calling you 'Professor'?"

"No more pesky undergrads calling me *anything*, and you know it." Now that the door is shut, and the Top 40 has been reduced to posters on the wall and files on the desk, I should be calmer. Should be, anyway. I'm not calm, and it better not show more than it already does. "You said you had a job for me."

"I just hope you're desperate enough to take it."

"Which is less demeaning: cleaning toilets or sitting around doing nothing with three degrees?"

Paul pauses to laugh, just once, before he settles into his desk chair. "Last year you'd have said they were one and the same."

"Last year I wasn't sixty-eight thousand dollars in debt."

"Yes, you were. You just didn't have to pay it until you got out."

Is he *trying* to piss me off? If he is, I can't let it work. I've come this far to be professional and polite.

"So I'm out," I say, and shut my eyes, stop my fingers from tapping on the arm of his chair. It's the meter of the rap from the waiting room. It's Bach's Invention in A minor. "And I'm here because you said you had something that isn't cleaning toilets."

"I do," Paul says, "and it does. The trouble with this industry is that some artists are full-time jobs. You have the time for one. I don't."

"Managing?"

"Handling," he corrects. "He has a manager. But he needs someone day-to-day to make sure he keeps his bookings."

"Is this like I used to do?" Paul dragged me on the road with his clients for years, and while I've never worked anywhere in the music industry without him, any summer I haven't been taking courses I've shadowed the bands. He started actually paying me for it when I was seventeen.

"No. This is the real deal. You'll move in with him, take care of his correspondence and his records. You know these creative types, some of them don't know a bank statement from a takeout menu."

"So he needs a butler."

"More than he needs a musicologist," Paul says, and at least he doesn't make an outright jibe of it. "And he's interesting from a musicological perspective, anyway. You might find an article in him."

"I'm not an ethnomusicologist." Shit, there goes that veneer of calm. Honestly, I never thought I'd have to correct my own family on that front, the way I've had to do every time the registrars forward me to the wrong office, ask if I'm familiar with the work of Dr. Akin Euba or whoever else.

"I know," Paul says. "But I still think you'll get some work done with Nik."

"Nick who?"

"Just Nik, and just with the K. You've heard of him, I hope."

Oh. Nik.

Teeth. The graduation party. The cops in the mosh pit. Dionysus.

"*That* Nik."

"You've heard of him. Good."

"I shouldn't be surprised that he can't tell a bank statement from a takeout menu." And I shouldn't be surprised that I'm drumming the arm of the chair again. Stop. Now. "But I am. And I'm surprised he's one of yours. I thought no company would want to be held liable."

"No company does," Paul says. "I took him on privately, long before I started working here. Before he was Nik, even."

"Before he was Nik? So he's repackaged the act? Or don't tell me you buy into his Dionysus bullshit."

"I don't have to buy into it. All I have to do is give you five of the fifteen percent commission I take off all of his profits."

I shake my head no, since I have nothing to lose. "I want all fifteen."

"Ten it is," Paul says. "Ten, for however long you can handle him." There's a contract on the desk, and Paul turns it around to face me without lifting it. The scrape of the paper on the glass is like a bowed bell, almost ominous, and I reach for it. "Take as much time as you need to read the fine print."

I lean forward in my seat, look the contract over. It's all official, but the header's wrong. "Funny, this isn't a company contract."

"I told you, this isn't through Pantheon. His contract with me is private. You won't be on the books here and you won't have to account for it in your taxes. I'll take care of it. It's my pay. I'm just transferring it to you."

"But I'm working for him. His name should be here."

Without a word, Paul stretches across the desk, waves my hand away from the top page, and turns to the last. There, at the very bottom, is one handwritten line, in an angular and nearly illegible hybrid of print and cursive:

Congratulations. You're next. I'm game. — Nik

"Oh, come *on*." I push back in the chair, far enough that if there were a wall behind me I'd probably hit my head against it. "He can't be fucked to use his own fucking name on a contract."

Paul raps on the table. Just once. I've known that signal since I was a kid: *shut up and pay attention*. "You don't talk to me like that outside of a recording booth, and I don't see you on either side of the glass, so watch your damn mouth."

"What am I, twelve?"

"No, you're twenty-eight, and you're still an ungrateful brat."

"It's a legitimate fucking concern."

"You know what's a legitimate concern? How you're going to live when you can't slam your school for handouts. Fact is, you've been getting something-for-nothing for the last seven years, and guess what?

Something-for-nothing only works in academia and welfare, and you're not qualified for either."

For however many seconds I take to register those words, I don't even hear the clock in the corner ticking. I should stop gaping. He actually said that.

"Now, you can bite the damn bullet and sign, because I'm sticking my neck out for you," Paul says, in the same tone he used when I used to pretend I didn't know the rules, "or you can wait outside my apartment until all your books arrive and *then* figure out what you're doing with them."

The *and with yourself* goes unsaid, but it's clear as a bell.

I swipe a pen out of the box on Paul's desk, and take the time I need to read the fine print. The clock ticks, the office soundtrack plays.

I sign, right there under Nik's insulting scrawl.

Being Dionysus pays: Nik's apartment in the East Village, on Seventh between First and A, takes up an entire floor of its building. There's no doorman, and the buzzer is predictably out of date, but after some wrangling with the keys I figure out which opens the front door, which opens the inner, and which triggers the elevator. Two more key tests get me Nik's mail slot, full to bursting, including two outdated package notifications and last month's *Rolling Stone*. None of the mail is addressed to Nik. He's Tenant 8F, Current Resident, or c/o Paul Brooks.

I need my hands free and there's room in my carry-on, so I stuff all the mail in there for now and key up the elevator to the eighth floor. The elevator door opens to another door, which takes the last key, and I brace myself for the inevitable reek of rock star.

Well, consider me surprised. It doesn't stink. In fact, it smells no worse than any other apartment I've lived in, except maybe Paul's first bachelor pad in Harlem. It hasn't been *recently* cleaned, but there's nothing worse than cigarette smoke pervading the air. And it isn't nearly as sloppy as I expected either, at least not in the foyer; not *neat* by any definition, and books are piled in the corners instead of on the shelves, but it's not a coked-out garret or a sty. The hardwood floor is tracked with boot rubber and pinprick spatters of the red-orange paint from the walls, but it's not filthy, and the mirrors and masks on the wall are only slightly askew.

Masks.

A lot of masks. The front hall and the media room it opens to are lined with them: hollow-eyed and, frankly, more unsettling than any stench or wreck would be. Venetian masks and *Commedia* masks with shapeless eyes and curved noses, Greek stage masks with gaping amplified mouths, lacquered Noh masks and feathered French masks and sub-Saharan dance masks with fans of hair. There are over fifty on this wall alone, and if they curve around that corner, there might be more than a hundred.

I set my bag down on the arm of the couch. The nearest mask at my eye level—a gold-plated one, almost featureless except for minute nostrils like a plaster cast—I'm not sure I can place where or when it's supposed to be from, but fuck if it isn't creepy. Maybe there's a label on the other side. The surface is smooth to the touch, too heavy to be plastic—

"Like him?" someone asks in my ear, soft and close enough to create an echo in my skull.

So much for first impressions: it's a good thing I already put the bag down, because I would have dropped it on Nik's foot when I backed into him, and then he might not be laughing. It's a laugh without meter, and my spine tenses all the way up to the base of my skull. The mask settles back into place on its nail in the wall, skittering.

"Hi," Nik says. He claps a hand on my upper arm, turns me around. "You're Paul's kid."

"Nephew," I correct.

"Blood enough," Nik agrees with a shrug.

There's only so much he can look like his concert videos, the way that a piece of music can sound like its score. All of his basic framework holds true: he's tall and attenuated, that Mediterranean mix that may or may not be white, and the hand tightening on my jacket is long-fingered and guitarist-nailed, both sets painted gray. But he's taller than I, which I hadn't expected, and his razor-cut hair isn't black like in the video Elise showed us at the party. It's in loose staggered chunks of red and gold now, colors that would match the paint on the walls if he mixed them.

And he still has a smile that can slice through 360p on an iPhone screen.

"Make yourself at home," Nik says. He moves his hand from my arm to the small of my back, and I'd have shoved him off if he hadn't shoved me off first. "Are you expecting a tour?"

Not if it involves looking at more of these masks. "Are you giving one?"

Nik laughs, that same meterless laugh, and opens his arms. In the fluorescent light, his eyes look more gold than light brown. "You are where you are. You'll know which room's which. What's mine is yours unless you try to auction it off. That's about it."

If I hadn't already had the clearest possible example of Nik's unprofessionalism, I'd probably hit him for this one, or at least call him out. I don't. I've already bounced one check at the bullshit bank: another overdraft fee might wreck my credit.

"Sure." I try not to be sarcastic. I'm not sure it works. "I'll just leave things where they are." I take his pile of mail out of my carry-on, hold it up pointedly for one beat, and set it down on the couch. The paper rustles, a pitchless glissando. "Yours."

"Good," Nik says, grin widening across his jaw. "You can answer it after I buy you dinner."

"What?"

"You do eat, don't you? As long as I'm your meal ticket, I'll buy you a meal."

We still haven't found a restaurant. It's been an hour. Nik's looked at about twenty different menus at twenty different storefronts on the way. We're going to walk clean into FDR Drive if he doesn't choose soon, so I drop a few *this looks all right*s and *how about here*s, which results in vaguely affirmative responses and distracted maybes from Nik.

Is this a test? I thought I gave those up when I got the doctorate.

Whatever. I bite the figurative bullet outside an Italian restaurant on Avenue B. "We're eating here."

Nik just grins ferally and says, "Sure."

Ordering, equally surprisingly, isn't as much of a chore: Nik doesn't even look at the menu, lets the waiter rattle off the specials and says *sounds good* after the entrée sold with the most enthusiasm. I order lasagna. I've never seen a restaurant fuck lasagna up.

"Anything to drink?" the waiter asks.

I'm about to say no, but Nik's already tapping his fingernail on the wine list. He pronounces the name of the wine in appreciable Italian, and clarifies, bottle, not glass.

"What if I didn't want to drink?" I ask once the waiter's gone with the menus and there's nothing but an expanse of table, olive oil without bread, and the restaurant's soundtrack of alternating pseudoclassical and questionably Mediterranean solo guitar.

"More for me," Nik shrugs.

"Fair enough."

"But you do want to drink."

After everything else that's gone on today? I'll give him that. "Yes."

"Good." Nik stretches, tilts his head as if to crack his neck. "So, how'd you get roped into this?"

"Uncle Paul offered."

"Yeah, but you don't take every job offered to you. Unless you do. Do you? What do you do when you're not doing what he tells you to do?"

This is the second figurative bullet I've bitten in the past fifteen minutes. Another chomp and I'll be able to taste gunpowder. "I'm a musicologist."

Nik seems genuinely amused, if not impressed. "So what, you're studying me?"

"No." Frankly, the wine can't get here soon enough. Is he making a joke, or does he actually know what a musicologist is? "I said I'm a musicologist."

His eyes crinkle when he smiles. It shouldn't be attractive. "What, I don't write music?"

"No, but you're still alive."

"So only dead people write music."

"*No.* But I'm not an ethnomusicologist."

"A what?"

A busboy comes by bearing bread and a pitcher of water. Finally. I nod a terse thanks to him for good timing before turning back to Nik. "Someone who studies ethnic musicians."

Nik laughs. "So I'm not ethnic."

"No, but you write popular music. Popular music falls under the auspices of ethnomusicology. I work on Bach."

"Bach," Nik spits out with the backwash. "I thought it'd be something more suited to you."

"What, like Tupac? For fuck's sake, Beethoven might have been as black as I am and you don't see anyone calling him an ethnic musician."

Nik laughs and breaks off a slice of the bread. "They did back then."

It's not the usual response I get when I drop that particular phrase—which I have, several times, to an almost universal *Beethoven was black?* Honestly, he probably wasn't, but it weeds out the chaff. People have been arguing about Beethoven's alleged Moorish ancestry for a century, it's not just a Buzzfeed hoax. If it was true and he'd been born in Georgia instead of Germany, he'd have written working songs instead of symphonies. But any musicologist worth the ink on their résumé would at least know what side he's on.

And Nik does. He's cavalier about it, firmly on Team Alleged Quadroon. Which means Nik *does* think about music, and he *has* the background, and even if he's wrong, he's tried.

I need a drink. There's only water, but it'll do, and the glass is cold. So I drink. And I remember that this must all be part of Nik's Dionysus act.

"Right," I say, deadpan, putting the glass down, "you were there."

"Mm-hmm," Nik says around a mouthful of bread.

"And what were you writing back then, invisible cantatas?"

Nik swallows and shrugs. "I write what I write. Guess you don't want to see the opus numbers."

The waiter brings our wine. Evidently this is a classy enough place that he pours a sip for Nik to savor and approve before he fills up both glasses. Just Nik, though, not me. Guess we know whom the dominant personality is at the table. Then again, Nik's the one who ordered, so I can give the waiter the benefit of the doubt for assuming he cares more.

I hold my tongue.

Nik raises his glass in an unvoiced (but not soundless) toast that's almost a challenge. I just drink. The wine's good, worlds better than the canned orange juice I drank on the second plane. Fuck, I haven't had anything to drink since then? No wonder I'm on edge.

"I don't," I say, bringing the conversation back to where it was. "I'm sure you've put a lot of work into your persona. Ziggy Stardust would be proud."

There's a tinge of wine on Nik's lower lip, and it accentuates the line of his smirk, darkens the left corner as it climbs his cheek. "You don't believe in me."

No, but, "Whether I do or not doesn't matter as long as I get your work done."

"That'll do." Nik takes another sip of his wine. His smile shines through glass the same as it does on flat-screens. "You don't seem too happy about it."

"Just because I'm not happy doesn't mean I'm not thankful," I say, because if I don't turn this conversation back onto a polite path, no one will.

"That's almost worse," Nik laughs. "You know, gods used to kill people for not accepting what they are."

"I'm sure you were there too." My sarcasm's so thick that if I had to eat my words I could swallow it, and this conversation is utterly unsalvageable. Shit.

Nik puts his wineglass down. There's no grace to it, no bracing to protect the stem, and the sound on the tablecloth is the kind that a film score would magnify, would pay an effects team hundreds of dollars to test and augment and get just right. He says nothing. Canned tinny guitar music threads through the restaurant's speakers and into the score in my ears, and Nik drums his fingers on the vertex of the table, like I tend to do but out of time.

I need this job. I need *something*. Putting my future in someone else's hands hurts. So does breathing, but that I actually *have* to do. "I'm not sure I can work for you—for your persona. But I do need a job."

"Fine," Nik says. "You want to work for me, then I'll put you to work. I'll even make a rule in my house for you: don't play your math on my instruments."

"My math?"

"Your Bach. How's that?"

God, that's juvenile. But, "Fine. I'll deal."

Nik toasts again, and drinks. "Sure you will."

NOVEMBER 7, 2011

I'm still on California time, but I'm forced awake at 8 a.m. EST thanks to the magic of smartphone alarms. There's no clock in this room. I take my usual morning run and keep the address of Nik's apartment on repeat in my head in case I get off track while I sprint around Alphabet Soup. Even when I lived in New York, I wasn't in this neighborhood and I had no reasons to come here except the occasional concert at NYU or one of Paul's errands, so thank fuck for street view.

This is new. I find five or six independent coffee shops but no Starbucks, the nearest branch of my bank, the laundromat, and the post office on Fourteenth Street, all of which I'll need to visit again today once I change out of my running clothes. I have an easier time with the keys to Nik's place this morning, and there's no new mail and no UPS notification of the packages arriving from Paul's place, so I take the elevator otherwise empty-handed. It's ten o'clock by the time I get back in, and either Nik's still asleep or the soundproofing in this apartment is exemplary, so I take a shower without interruption. Nik didn't set out any towels, and there aren't any in the linen closet across from the main bathroom, but as long as I'm washing the rest I can appropriate this used one, which smells clean enough. I throw on a shirt and slacks, and riffle through the kitchen cabinets for something that will pass for breakfast.

It's not that there's no food; it's that there are a lot of components but nothing that fits together. Butter and jam, but no bread and no eggs; cereal (nearly expired) but no milk; coffee beans and sugar but no grinder. *Great.* So I pour myself a bowl of dry cereal and eat it while I search on my phone for the nearest supermarket that won't charge me out the ass, and add a visit there to today's errands. Hell, as long as Nik's paying for food, I might as well stock up.

Nik emerges from the studio at about ten thirty, in yesterday's pants and no shirt. He stretches, checks the oven clock (which hasn't been changed off of daylight savings). "Morning, Carl Philipp Emanuel."

"It's *Anthony.*" I could have been less snide, but hey, jet lag. And given the context, being dubbed one of Bach's composer sons isn't meant to be a compliment. I can practically hear the name as *Boring Derivative Mathematician.* "Good morning. What's the wireless password?"

"Your mom."

For fuck's sake. "Are you twelve?"

"No. But I wrote it down somewhere." He takes a glass out of the dishwasher (leaving the rest of them in it), and fills it with water from the sink. "Going to bed. Wake me if you want me."

I thank the dry Frosted Flakes in my mouth that I don't have to answer. I just wait as Nik downs the water like it's nothing but air and leaves the kitchen, yawning. The tattoos across his shoulders and back, a labyrinth of black and rust abstract grooves, seem almost to shift on his skin. That's more attractive than it should be. It's been too long. And he's not my type. And he's probably showing off to fuck with me anyway.

It's ten thirty in the morning, and apparently I have my work cut out for me.

Well, first things first, I should get the lay of the land. All the rooms are on the one long hallway, which is full of masks. The studio's the deepest room in, and Nik's room is next to it, then the bathroom, then my guest room and the kitchen. Presumably, Nik has a bathroom of his own, or a half bath at least, but that's barred to me at the moment, and none of my business anyway. The foyer, its walls lined with more masks and instruments and piles of books, is probably the most prudent place for me to start earning my keep.

There must be about five hundred books on the floor: a perfectly respectable amount for someone who isn't a scholar, and a deceptive amount for someone who *might* be. I'm not surprised to find a few titles I know, some scores I've heard. Nik likes Ligeti. That makes a world of sense. No scholarly journals, but there are a smattering of biographies, and a couple of books I haven't seen outside of music-exclusive libraries. So he's done his homework. That just substantiates what he told me yesterday at dinner.

Nik doesn't seem the type to care about alphabetizing, so categorical shelving is the way to go, and it takes me about two hours. There are more than enough shelves, so some of Nik's antique instruments can stay out here. I gather up any instrument that looks like it's seen action this century to move into the studio. The door is open, and this room is better lit than most of the apartment, enough that I have to shield my eyes.

It's beautiful in here, enviable. Nik's definitely serious about his craft, respectful of his instruments. Everything is well kept, if not necessarily well organized: the electric keyboard has a plexiglass cover, the upright piano is free of coffee stains and water rings, all four acoustic and electric guitars are nestled into their stands and the drum kit is covered in a tarp. Even if I felt comfortable cleaning this place—which I don't—I wouldn't have much work to do except dusting the keyboard and gathering up the stray paper, and I've been around enough composers to know that's a horrible idea no matter how much apparent trash there is. So I only set the instruments from the foyer down on one of the almost-empty shelves next to the computer workstation in the corner. I'll let Nik deal with it his own way later. I could stay in here all day. Well, I could if I didn't have work to do. I haven't played in too long—forty-eight hours at least.

Dry cereal doesn't really cut it, and it's about one in the afternoon, so I take my laptop and Nik's unanswered mail out to a coffee shop and sort it over a sandwich. Fuck, it's as expensive as San Francisco down here. I set up online payments for all the bills I can—Nik's electric bill is exorbitant, which isn't at all surprising—and give the landlord a call just to introduce myself. Nik's wireless password isn't in any of his correspondence, but I'll find it later, after the bank and groceries and everything else.

Fuck, I really am a butler. But the more time I spend thinking about it, the less work gets done.

By the time I make it back to the apartment, it's after four, and there's a new round of unanswered mail, but that's much easier seen to than left undone, and the only real problem is carrying it at the same time as the groceries and keying the elevator. It's not awful, just menial—if I repeat that to myself a couple of times, maybe it'll stick—and by the time the apartment door opens I've convinced myself enough to last another hour—

"What the fuck did you *do*?" Nik's standing in the center of the living room, gaping at the bookshelves.

"My job," I say without missing a beat, sidestep Nik to drop the groceries off in the kitchen. "You've got too many rare books to leave them on the floor."

"But now I don't know where they are," Nik says, and in spite of his low resonant voice, he sounds so much like a petulant child that it's almost comical.

Almost. "They're on the shelves." I unload the perishables into the refrigerator. "Books belong on shelves."

Nik snarls. "Fuck you. I can't find anything."

"I'll walk you through it later. They're just by subject. And if you don't like it, you can move them back."

"But I knew where they were."

I manage to stifle the sigh in my throat, shut my eyes, and crumple the empty plastic bag in my hands. I shouldn't get angry. *I need this job.* "I'm sure you can figure out where they are—"

And I walk into Nik's arm, hemming me in. Is this sudden coil of ice at the base of my spine fear of Nik, or just fear of losing this job? Probably the latter. It had better be the latter.

"Fix it," Nik says. "If you're so good at remembering things, fix it. Put them back where they were."

Of all the fucking things, he wants to make a scene of this? *Fine.*

"Not on the floor," I tell him, around the bar of my teeth. "As long as I am living here, books belong on shelves."

No, that chill was all about Nik. Something in his eyes makes it climb higher, sublimate, slow the world around me down until there's no doubt he's in control of it.

I don't know which I hate more: him, or myself for needing him and this goddamn job.

With one shove of his palm, Nik slams the refrigerator door and stalks out of the kitchen. A few seconds later, the studio door shuts, and maybe the soundproofing isn't as good as I thought because I can hear the strains of an acoustic guitar, an atonal whirl that sets my skin crawling.

Pyrrhic victories aside, the battle's won. I can put my earbuds back in and go about the rest of the day's work without any further trouble. I think.

Posted to asbrooks.com on November 7, 2011

"Ostensibly Safe in New York"

I'm still stealing someone else's wireless since I can't find the password here, but for those of you concerned, I am, as the title of this entry posits, safe. And, as you can also infer, I'm not staying with my uncle, which is for the best.

Instead of pursing my education and the education of others, I've spent the day paying another man's bills, doing his grocery shopping, and cleaning his house, for a percentage of his earnings instead of a fixed salary, and in a position I inherited from my uncle. You can imagine what it looks like. This is the part where all of you laugh in my face.

I know I'm not supposed to look a gift horse in the mouth, and I should be thankful to have a job at all. But is it too much to ask for one that doesn't invalidate everything I've done for the past ten years? That's not a rhetorical question, I actually want to know. If this were the eighteenth century, I'd have maybe fifteen years more to live—if I was lucky. Have I wasted ten of them?

Tomorrow looks like more of the same, but if any of you are in Manhattan and want to get together (or better, have any job leads), just let me know. My phone number's the same.

Comments (0)

Nik's music—not "music, such as it is"; it's music, just not the kind of music I listen to when it's not meant for some kind of analysis—can be described by any number of words, but "pervasive" is the one that I can't let go of at the moment. I'm no connoisseur of progressive rock, and frankly I'm uncertain why they keep calling it progressive rock if it hasn't gone anywhere new in the last fifty years, but *pervasive rock* seems more appropriate for Nik than anything else.

Except, possibly, *provocative rock*. He's clearly trying to provoke me with it. And my earbuds can only go so loud without compromising my future as a musician.

What's the point of soundproofing if you're going to play with the door open? Fuck him.

I shunt my laptop aside, stolen wireless and all, and unplug the earbuds. If not even Prokofiev can drown Nik out, there's nothing to be done about him, and I head for the open studio with buds still dangling from my ears.

It is impossible to tell whether this din is an extract of one of Nik's songs, or just Nik fucking around. He doesn't deserve my attention, but I can't stop the pitches and slides from starting to notate themselves in my head. The rhythm's plain difficult and immeasurable, which lends credence to my *just fucking around* hypothesis. When I get there Nik is so thoroughly engrossed in his shredding that he doesn't even notice me pull up the computer chair. And he must notice my flagrantly obvious disapproval even less, because he just keeps going.

So I tap my fingers on my thigh in steady common time, against the indescribable rhythm Nik is playing.

It takes Nik about a minute to see me. And a minute, in music, is enough for the rules to change completely.

"Cut that shit out," Nik says, and doesn't stop playing.

If he doesn't have to stop playing, I don't have to stop tapping. "Sorry, you seemed to be putting on a show."

"You'll know when I'm putting on a show."

"Guess I will. But right now you're wasting whatever you paid for soundproofing the apartment, so it might as well be a free concert."

Nik scoffs through his teeth, and his fingers flicker over the strings, too fast to match up to the sound they produce. "If you were listening, you wouldn't be trying to keep time like a fucking metronome."

"I'm *not* listening. That's why."

"Maybe you should be."

Nik has cruel teeth. There's a reason that smile works in black light as well as it does in Photoshop. If he looked at me like that at the wrong moment, I'd pull my whole head down into my chest like a turtle. As it stands, my neck is too stiff to move, let alone collapse.

"If you wanted me to listen, you should've said so," I say, because like hell am I letting on how goddamn scary he is.

"Thought I just did."

"Which do you pay me for, settling this month's bills or listening to you?"

"You can't do both?"

I give up, sigh, and clamp my fingers over my knee to stop the tapping. "Consider this a compliment, but I don't think I can give your music the attention and active listening it requires if I'm trying to settle your accounts."

"How the hell is that a compliment?"

"It means I can't listen to your music for pleasure."

"Exactly. How is that a fucking compliment? If you don't enjoy it, I'm just raping your ears."

That's more astute than I'd given him credit for. And awful. "*Exactly.* So shut the damn door."

Nik's hand slams into the wall just over my left ear. It's not quite a punch—though it's as fast and as loud as one, and I can't help tensing from my feet to my jaw waiting for a blow that hasn't landed.

Nik glares, but that's familiar and oddly less frightening, and once my fear subsides to a low caustic burn, I catch his eyes and don't look away.

"Are you starting shit with me?" I'm surprised how collected I sound, at least to myself. Then again, I've put up with this shit for years. Just not from him.

Nik laughs. "Nope." And with that, he shuts the studio door, never mind that I'm still inside. "Free concert," he adds, almost in a trill, and resumes the song or exercise or *fucking around* he was playing before.

I ball up my headphones. "Go ahead. Rape my ears."

"It's not rape if you tell me I can do it."

"Please, let's not go into that."

The way Nik snickers is about as tuneful as the riff on his guitar, which is to say not tuneful at all, but pervasive. Provocative. Complex.

"Do you always do this?" I ask before I can stop myself.

"Do what?"

"Attempt to drive your handlers insane."

"I don't always have handlers," Nik says, working out a complicated soaring riff that's almost like a baroque cadenza, or might have been before the shredding got to it, "and you'd know if I was trying to drive you insane."

"Doesn't answer my question."

"Then ask a better question."

Glowering at him changes nothing, so I swivel in the computer chair, use that creak and gust to keep time on Nik's impossible music instead of my hands. "A better question."

"A better question."

"A *bet*ter *quest*ion," I repeat, just to alter the rhythm and make it my own. "Fine. Which one's yours, Dionysus? Pete from the Street or Phil from the Hill?"

It's a test. Presumably, Nik knows that. Pete from the Street is *Pierre de la Rue*, and Phil from the Hill is *Philippe de Monte*, and only a musicologist would know who they are just by hearing the joke. Well, only a musicologist or an anthropomorphic concept performance artist who's done his homework. And it would take homework to tell the difference, to know that dyed-in-the-wool Apollonian Phil from the Hill played by the rules and Pete from the Street broke them.

"Pete from the Street," Nik says, grinning. "No one's asked me about them for years. Old school. I like it."

And for a minute of music, I'm startled enough to listen.

NOVEMBER 16, 2011

"**A**nthony Brooks speaking."

"Good, I finally found the right number, I can never trust your uncle's handwriting. Nice to put a voice to the typeface. This is Sydney Nerida."

Blame running, but who the hell is Sydney Nerida? I coast to a walk, catch my breath, drown out the sounds of the street, and wrack my brain. Paul mentioned a Sydney, or maybe the name was in the contract, but I'd remember Nerida as a last name. For now, I can give her the benefit of the doubt. Bullshitting 201 was a required course at Berkeley, and letting people think you know who they are was on the syllabus. "Ms. Nerida. Excellent. Thanks for getting in touch."

"I would have kept it to email, but this is faster. And Mrs., not Ms., if you don't call me Sydney."

"No problem." There are benches outside the ice cream parlor on this street, and I prop my foot on the edge of one, and stretch. A million of Nik's people have emailed me this past week. She's probably one of them. "Should I congratulate you?"

"Yes, it's recent. Thank you. How are you handling Nik?"

Well, that's confirmation. Thank goodness I'm too out of breath to laugh. "I think I'm getting through to him."

And then I remember—*Sydney*. She's his actual manager. The one who books his gigs. She's been sending reminders through the company email this last week, not her personal name. Well, that at least saves me from having to lie my way through this.

I go on. "He hasn't missed any of the itinerary, though I can't say he's done it all in order."

She snickers. "He never does."

"I left him at the apartment with the backing band. They plan on heading over to Southpaw together in three hours."

"Are you coming with them?"

"Should I?" I'd planned on catching a recital and possibly doing some networking at Juilliard, but apparently that is about to go down the drain.

"Now that I've called you, yes. And that's why I didn't keep it to email. My partner had a fall at work today, and I'm meeting her at the hospital—"

"Sorry to hear it."

"Thanks. So I need you to cover for me at Southpaw. I've already cleared it with your uncle. He'll transfer you my pay for the night plus a bonus for the short notice."

On the one hand, that'll more than make up for missing a networking opportunity. On the other, "Are you sure I'm qualified?"

"Your uncle is. I don't plan on contradicting him."

I nod, and then remember that I'm on the phone. "I'll do it. And I hope everything turns out all right for you."

"Thank you. Once I get to the hospital I'll send the contact list and concert personnel and everything. And I warn you, it's harder than you think, but just be careful and you'll be fine. And stay out of the pit."

"I'm sure I can manage that."

"You'll be surprised," she says, without any humor whatsoever. I think I like her sensibility. "You don't sound like the kind of person who likes to be surprised."

"What I like has absolutely nothing to do with this job."

Somehow, her lack of laughter is as ominous as the Ride of the goddamn Valkyries.

In my twenty-eight years, I've been to more concerts than I can count. More than half of them were for bands I couldn't stand. That's not something I admit aloud in the circles I walk: the one time I let it slip in the company of my colleagues at Berkeley, a certain annoyingly forward master's candidate named Elise asked me, *"How do you even love music at all?"*

I took a few minutes to explain that music is like humanity: it's entirely possible to hate half of the people you meet without being a genocidal misanthrope.

Elise equated my stance on musical discrimination with racism.

It wasn't a very good party.

It's not the genre of a given piece of music that puts me out; it's the complexity of the structure. I hold Outkast and Metallica to the same standards as Beethoven and Mendelssohn, and if that makes me a snob, then so be it. But I grew up neck-deep in the pop Top 40 and the rap and R & B that crossed over, and I was backstage at rehearsals and recording sessions and concerts when Paul couldn't get rid of me. I was subject to the same four chords over and over; not because the song only needed four chords, but because they were the only four chords the guitarist knew.

So, seeing as I am at yet another concert for a band I can't stand, I will say this about Nik's music: it's gratifyingly complex. Or it would be if I could figure out whether there are rules to it at all.

But the music is not supposed to matter to me right now, even though I can't tune it out because of the backstage headset. This is work. I've roadied and gofered hundreds of shows, and watched Paul hold the reins through all of them. Between that experience and Mrs. Nerida's instructions, it can't be that bad. The rules are fairly standard: keep the backstage clear, keep the band onstage and the audience happy until autographs, and make sure everyone gets paid at the end of the night and nothing illegal happens until Nik's out the door. Easy enough.

Those are a particularly famous set of famous last words, but, *easy enough*.

Onstage, one song ends (distinguishable only by the coordinating eyes of the backing band and the swell of shrieks in the crowd) and another begins. I peek out the side curtain. Nik is faced with the glow of several hundred smartphones the way the old school would have been stared down with Zippo lighters and the even older school by oil lamps and powdered wigs. He basks in it, grins into the microphone like the crowd's approval is tangible and dripping down his face into the creases of his smirk.

Good. He's doing what he's supposed to be doing. That's all I can ask of him. I should stop watching.

Nik's music has a melody the way the roar of a descending plane does, a pace and a rush of wind. It's too loud, and I muck with my headset, blot out the sound as best I can. And the sight, for that matter, the angle of Nik's smile around the vowels; even when I cover my ears I can visualize the tones. And count, tap my fingers on my thigh. There *is* a rhythm to his music, there has to be. But no. Not my job. Not right now.

Is something burning?

It's not the distasteful but expected twinge of nicotine smoke leaking in from the alley or the lobby, or the even more expected pot stench that's endemic to concerts. Smoke, as in where there's smoke, there's fire.

I grab the nearest stagehand by the shoulder. "Do you smell that?"

"Huh?"

"Never mind." I shut my eyes again, concentrate for a moment. It's not coming from the crowd, thankfully, but it's definitely there.

Nik keeps singing.

I shouldn't listen. I *can't* listen; I have a job to do. I shoulder out of the backstage area toward the loading dock, put a few layers of concrete between me and the sound so I can isolate the smell. If no one else has noticed it, it might just be in my head, but it can't hurt to have a look, and I squint through the generator-red darkness, check all the corners.

Yes, there's fire. A few sparks, breaching a tangle of wires and electrical tape, along the concrete wall.

There are about five hundred people at this concert, another fifty backstage or working the bar. It would be entirely worthless to pull the fire alarm, and New Yorkers are conditioned to never listen to it anyway. I go back inside, grab a passing roadie by the shoulder, and demand, "Nearest fire extinguisher."

"Under the corner exit," he says, a little softly, almost dazed. But he doesn't ask why, and I don't thank him.

The music goes on, swells like a storm cloud. I pry the fire extinguisher off the wall, check for and find the C that marks it okay for electrical fires (thank you, Paul, for leading by negative example), and take it to the loading docks without anyone remarking on it. I blast the corner. Sparks die.

There. Done. No one heard at all inside, and no one has to go home. I probably won't even mention it to anyone unless I'm asked. They *will* ask, I'm sure, and there'll be cleanup to do, but that's after the concert, not during, and that's what's important.

My clothes crunch. Shit, I'm covered in carbon powder, or whatever this crap is. I swat it off, as much as I can with the fire extinguisher in my arms, and lug said extinguisher back inside.

Once it's up against the wall, ready for whoever checks it later, I wipe the sweat off my forehead and scalp. There's carbon powder there too, and on the headset. Great. So fuck the headset. There's nothing backstage to clean it with, not that I can see anyway, so I leave it, find the bathroom, and get all this crap off my clothes.

This is not what I got three degrees for. This is what I got three degrees to *avoid*, yet here I am, cleaning up other people's messes, putting out other people's fires.

"Fucking ridiculous," I say, though only my reflection is listening.

Well, backstage is taken care of, at least for now. I'll check the rear of the house, get a closer look at the crowd. By the time I've forced my way there Nik has shredded a strain to end the song and asked, "How'd you like that, New York?"

Their cheering echoes in my skull. *Fuck, that's loud.* I lean against the wall, shut my eyes to block the sound out. It's not even applause. Just endless shouting and shrieking, unintelligibly positive.

"Bet you'll like this even more," Nik drawls into the microphone; the cheering hasn't died down before his voice damn near comes out of the walls and the floor. My bones ache, like the last stretch of a too-long run. Nik starts off with one hard, dissonant chord, then another, then the first in tremolo, and whatever the fourth chord is, it's blacked out completely by the crowd clamoring for more.

They know this song. I think some part of me does too. Maybe I've heard him practice it. Maybe it's the one from that video back at Berkeley. Right, it goes—

Fuck. The dance kicks off and goes straight from zero to one-forty. I flatten my back against the wall just in time to stop from getting swept into the pit. It's almost as if the floor is boiling, as if the shifting surface of hair and skin only breaks to let out smoldering air.

The word isn't *frenzy.* Or *orgy.* Or *gestalt.* The very idea of *words* is absurd, inadequate. If there were a rhythm to their movements it might be a dance, but there isn't. I remember, a long time ago, finding a raccoon at the side of the road, teeming with maggots. I poked the carcass with a stick, back then. This is how the larvae moved.

Once you get in there, you can't drag us out.

They dance. They tear at each other's hair, clothes, flesh. They mouth Nik's words, cheer his name, breathe his music: an autonomic process, irregular but sound.

And dozens of smartphones still shine in the dark. Some crunch underfoot, trampled and cracked.

The song echoes in my head, spreads a chill through the hollows of my skull.

I can't watch, but I have to see where I'm going, so I get the basic trajectory and fumble through the crowd, hands over my ears. Sharp elbows and a height advantage get me almost to the bar before I have to look again. Once I get there I make eye contact with the bartender and shout my order. The bartender's wearing earplugs, bright pink in the black light. Smart. A note for next time, I guess.

There better not be a next time.

Over her shoulder, in the near-darkness behind the bar, I catch a glimpse of cash changing hands. Well, that looks like it's got nothing to do with the bar. *Great, just great.* I pay for my shot, down it quick, then cut across the front of the bar lines to intercept this fucking drug deal before either participant gets out of sight. I remember the first time I saw Paul do this; I must have only been twelve. He broke the dealer's jaw. No one pressed charges. He didn't have to lecture me on drugs after that.

Obviously my distaste with this situation isn't evident on my face when I get there, because the one with money still in his hand looks me in the eye and says, "You want in?" just loud enough to be heard over the music.

I grab him by the collar and shove him into the wall.

"Listen," I say straight into the dealer's ear, "take it outside, right the fuck now. I don't care what you do the rest of the night, but *not in here.*"

"It's a free country."

"Yeah, but it's not a free concert. Go. Now. Or I'll tell the bouncers, and they're not half as nice as I am."

"Fine, let go of me, asshole."

I do, and step back, put my hands up to show I've still got them. Paul'd be proud, maybe. The dealer pats down his pockets and hisses through his teeth in my direction—a choice racial slur that's only half true—but he goes. I follow him toward the main doors, and make sure they shut behind him.

Fires. Drug dealers. Provocative rock. I wonder if this is a good night.

I could go back through the crowd to the side door, or I could chance the alleyway. The latter is probably best. But in the time it takes me to decide, someone slams into my back, and a wall of sound finishes the job and lays me out flat to the concrete.

Once, when I was six or seven, back when people were still allowed to board planes on the tarmac, I'd let go of Mom's hand and rushed out of the line on the runway to watch another plane come in. The sounds hit me first, the groaning of engines, the hiss of gears turning and slats opening, the slice of its wings through thick summer air. The wind blasted me like gunfire, passed through me like my body was nothing but paper and ash. And then the heat, both the literal haze of a plane only ten feet away and the fire of fear and embarrassment and certain death, snapped up through my bones and told me I wasn't *there*. Empty. Gone. Alone in the dark, when the shadow of the wing blacked out the sun. By the time Mom and airport security caught up to me, I was curled on the concrete, clawing at my face and bawling until my throat and eyes were the same blazing red.

They're that red now, with Nik's music in my ears.

My bones aren't mine anymore: they're swollen, aching to burst out of the muscle and skin that surrounds them. The pulse of Nik's song has climbed inside me, irregular and demanding, has taken over my heart and every hollow place in my body. The crowns in my teeth, the sockets of my eyes, the ball joints in my shoulders and pelvis and the hinge of my knees, they're all resonating with fire and sound and the rasp of Nik's voice, and I could scream if my lungs still belonged to me.

They don't.

And if I keep listening, they never will again.

Fire, he sings, everything sings.

The third—fourth—time I tell my hands to rise and plug my ears, they obey. My mouth warps on lyrics I've never heard, and Nik's voice is in my throat, *Break it down, burst it open, once we get in there they can't drag us out, once we get in there they can't drag us out—*

I can't breathe. My mouth and throat are ready for it, but nothing comes in or out. I brace for pain I can't control. There's a door; I can get to it but not fast enough, fuck, my feet are still dragging in rhythm, and it *is* rhythm now: there's a beat, fifteen-eight, six-eight, eight-eight, and then seven. Seven. Somehow *I'm* broken into septuplets against eight and it's writing itself on my skull like a curator would with a microdrill if I'd been dead a thousand years and not just forty-five seconds.

I'm not dead. I'm not done. *I'm not dead. I'm not done.*

That gets me out the concert hall door.

It shuts of its own accord when I'm on the other side. Heat rakes through my throat, and I catch my breath—*force* my breath—once the sound is dammed and bunkered behind metal and insulation but not gone. It's not gone. It's not in my head anymore, but it's still going on. Sight returns to me a moment later, when I notice that the bouncers are dealing with the dealer I kicked out. That's good. That's something to focus on. Something to notice. Something that's mine, not Nik's, not music. I did my job. I hate my job.

"Tony?" one of the bouncers asks. His voice echoes, whirls.

"Throw him the fuck out," I say. I can't blame myself for the gravel and blood in my voice. I blame the music.

NOVEMBER 17, 2011

"Paul Brooks speaking."

"Good thing you're speaking. I want answers."

"Anthony. Good morning. Is there a problem with your payment? That was the amount you discussed with Sydney, wasn't it?"

If this phone wasn't my fucking lifeline, I would throw it at the wall. Maybe if I threw it hard enough it would break one of those fucking masks. That'd be a blessing in and of itself. "This isn't about the money."

"Good."

"Unless I have to make bail or something." The masks don't find it funny either.

Paul's sigh, which has always been more like a growl, cuts through the iPhone static. "You won't be held responsible for anything that happened last night."

"Are you sure? There was nothing about orgies in my contract. You know, the one Nik didn't fucking sign."

"Watch your mouth."

"If you subject me to that bullshit, you're going to talk with me like a fucking adult."

"Fine. Then get your head out of your ass, boy."

I grip the phone so tight that it nearly slips from my palm.

"You read it. You signed it. And you knew enough about Nik and what Nik does to make that choice. No one's coming after you. That's why your contract is with me, not him. I can protect you. He can't. So did anyone die? No. Did anyone get robbed? If they did, it's not on your head. Take your money, and back out if you really want out. But it won't be enough for a plane ticket back to California, and there's no other way I'm keeping you around and waiting for the IRS to get you."

This is the same as when he told me, years ago, that if I didn't want to go into foster care I'd have to live by his rules. Not the best thing to say to a kid who just lost both his parents at once. "I'm surprised no one's come after you for extortion."

"It's not extortion if there's nepotism involved."

I trap the intended *Fuck you* behind my teeth before he can hear it.

A good thing, too, because Nik chooses this precise moment to stroll into the living room, stretching. He catches my eye, and there I am, back at the concert, in the swarm of the dance floor. The image fades as soon as I spot last night's groupie, a young Desi man with thick curly hair and a dark spread of hickeys on his neck. The groupie waves awkwardly from the hallway.

Fuck Nik.

"Never mind," I grit into the phone. Fuck, I hope I sound resigned instead of terrified. "Sorry to bother you. The numbers are fine."

"Good," Paul says, and at least he sounds like he means it. "This won't be the last time you have a problem with something he does."

"No," that's for damned sure.

"When you have a *real* problem, then we can talk about extortion. Any luck finding a teaching job?"

The groupie disappears into the kitchen, and Nik cracks his shoulders, then sprawls on the couch with his legs dangling over the arm. He swipes a magazine off the coffee table, perches it on his chest, and thumbs through. Somehow the scantily clad pop singer on the cover is less appalling, less sensuous, than Nik ignoring me. *Fuck him.* Then again, said scantily clad pop singer wasn't at the front of a roomful of her fans while they had a violent orgy in her honor and *recorded it for posterity.* Or maybe she was.

"No," I say instead of everything I want to.

On the phone, Paul gives a faint "Hmm" that probably accompanies a nod. "Keep looking. Anything else?"

The answer is yes, but that's not what I say. I just give him a "No. Later," hang up, shut my eyes, let my hand fall slack to my side.

This is my life now. Orgies and extortion. I am sixty-eight thousand dollars in debt and I can't work my way out of something I never wanted *in* to: I have to take what handholds I can get or I'll only have myself to blame when I fall. And it's going to happen again. That creepy cultist fuckery is going to happen again.

On the couch, Nik turns a page. Papercuts make that sound.

"Yes," he says.

"Yes what?"

"You're trying not to ask if that usually happens. The answer is yes."

Maybe I'm just being too obvious. Either way, there's no point in talking about this now. I indicate the groupie in the kitchen. "Is he even over eighteen?"

"He signed a waiver." Nik shrugs into the pillow. "What, not your type?"

The answer to that is no, but like fuck will I let Nik know I think about sex at all. Let alone sex with him. Fuck this, I need to play something. "Are you using the studio?"

"Do I look like I'm using the studio?"

"Touché." I shove my phone into my pocket, turn for the hall—

"Don't play your math on my instruments," Nik says, almost sings.

The No Bach Rule. Of all the childish bullshit. "Fine. I'll try my luck in Midtown. Call if you need me."

"Only if you'll pick up."

I won't. "Then text."

Walk-ins at this rehearsal complex cost $12 an hour up front; worth it as far as I'm concerned. A trip to the movies costs more, after all. The rooms here aren't soundproofed, which is annoying as hell with a clumsy soprano singing excerpts from *The Marriage of Figaro* next door, but it's no worse than being at school. Honestly, I miss school, more than I probably want to admit, even to myself. Then again, I'm trying to get back in. At this point I'd take a postdoc. Hell, at any point, I'd take a postdoc, so I didn't have to be here, steering a rock star's ridiculous life.

Why am I even giving him space in my head? He's got more than he deserves.

I settle myself at a piano. How many of my colleagues are having just as hard a time as I am? Simon's a struggling composer, but at least he's got a few commissions in LA and Elise to share his apartment. How many of the others are taking what they can get, like me?

No, this doesn't deserve space in my head either.

I warm up first. It's never a waste to do scales and études, especially not if I haven't played for about a week—and *that* is plain unfair, but I'm not letting Nik intrude on this place. B-flat minor trips me up as usual. It's almost refreshing—no, it *is* refreshing. I wish I could put my thought in my hands instead of in my head, but as long as it's impossible to empty everything out, I can fill my world with things I appreciate.

After ten minutes of scales, I calibrate the stopwatch on my phone and launch into Carl Philipp Emanuel Bach's *Solfeggietto*, twice. The first time I clock the piece at one minute, seven seconds; the second time, fifty-four seconds with a couple of missed notes. Not bad. My knuckles throb. Good. Now I can relax. Easy pieces, easy memories. Bach.

I start through the Two-Part Inventions, one right after another.

The best thing about Bach (and a thing Bach passed on to his sons, in a limited capacity, including Carl) is that the rules lay themselves plain in the opening measures and hold true on every musical level. They're easy to memorize, no surprises, no unexpected transitions. The construction isn't unsubtle—if it were, I wouldn't have been able to finish my dissertation—but it's cohesive, perfect, clear. It's *honest*. Forthright. Bach makes a choice, and stands behind it, from the tiniest gesture to the piece as a whole, even to the entire compilation if you squint hard enough.

So when my hands dance from position to position over the keys, they always know what the steps are.

People would never claw each other to ribbons to the tune of a Bach invention.

. . . I never wanted that mental image. Thanks, Nik.

I flatten my fingers, grit my teeth, stop playing. The vision is inextricable. I don't consider myself a visual person, but it's there, clear as film behind my eyes. Hundreds of people, clustered together like flies in the eye of a corpse—and the rest, I can't bring myself to articulate. Sex and blood and the cops in the mosh pit. A cult. It's a fucking cult.

It's not as if I haven't seen people hurl their underwear at the front men, or simulate sex on the dance floor, or brawl with security. Once or twice, I've seen all three at once. But I've never had the sense that it's all part of the same thing, the same worshipful gesture, directed out of hundreds of eyes and mouths at the same man. At Nik.

They believe him. They believe *in* him. That's almost as disturbing as the orgy.

I lift my hands from the keys, brace them against the side of my head. Nothing hurts, but sound chases the image and burns behind my eyes. Not Nik's music, I don't want to remember it and I'm not sure I could if I tried, but the sounds of the crowd, guttural and shrieking, without meter. Like Nik's laughter in a thousand mouths, without meter.

If thoughts could be scalded or painted away, I'd do so now. I can't. But if I can't have a clear head, at least I have music. Real music. Bach, with structure and glory and rules.

Invention 13 in A minor, my favorite of the études. That's what I need to play. I hit it faster than I mean to but steadily, like I'm racing across a rail instead of dwelling, balancing. The rules are clear, counterpoint and exchange, and I give myself over to them, let *this* music, *this* sound be what defines me for now.

Invention 13 in A minor only lasts a minute. But it's a calibrating minute, and by the end, I'm counting and breathing the way I mean to again.

I could keep playing for a few more minutes, no problem, but someone knocks, nearly in rhythm. I wouldn't mind, if a second later she didn't open the door without my permission. "Sorry, we're next in this space and— Holy shit, Anthony. Anthony Brooks, right?"

The young woman in the doorway—well, not so young anymore—is small, round, white, and artificially blond, with big loud earrings and a voice to match. There's a short list of people in my memory like that so it takes a minute, but I do remember, from college. "Lisette . . . Madden, right?"

"Yeah!" She leans on the jamb of the open door, tilts her head, and grins. "You look great. What happened to your hair?"

"I got rid of it." It's the stock answer I've used since shaving it all off after undergrad. Razors are less expensive than good shampoo.

She nods, and frankly, if she tells me it suits me I won't believe her, not with that look on her face. "Cool. So what brings—"

"So what have you been up to?" I ask quickly.

"More than I can handle right now, ha. *Manon* today."

"Singing?"

"Conducting. I'm with Dicapo these days. Doesn't pay as much as the summer festivals, but it's a good tide-over."

Lucky asshole. I close the piano lid and gather my things so I have an excuse to turn away from her. She doesn't deserve to be the target of my frustration when she's only working the system better than I am.

"So yeah," Lisette says, already showing me the literal door. "Show goes up the week before Christmas. Are you still going to be in town?"

"Probably," I say, and hope that's enough.

It isn't. "Good. So where are you working?"

At this point, I wish I could roll out my stock answer like a cartoon red carpet. "I just finished up my doctorate. You know how that goes. I'm taking some handling work until a job opens up."

"That sucks," she says, wincing but still bright-eyed. I'm sure she doesn't mean to gloat; she's just a conductor. Professional self-centeredness is in the job description. I'd be the same. "Well, if you want a few accompanist gigs, I can hook you up! I'll friend you on Facebook later, okay?"

"Sure."

"Great. See you around!"

I nod, because telling her, "Sure, at a Wagner concert in Israel," would just be plain rude, and it's better to end the conversation without emasculating myself further.

It takes a moment alone in the hall, breathing and counting, for me to get my bearings. The soprano next door is still mangling *"Deh vieni non tardar."* But as long as I divorce her voice from the melody, and think of the tune as an instrumental refrain instead, there are much worse songs to have stuck in my head.

And it remains stuck in my head the entire way back to the East Village, since I force it back in every time I refuse to think about my future.

My phone pings just before I key up the elevator: *you said to text*

Well, yes. I did. I hold the key ring on my finger while I thumb back, *I did. Are you in or out?*

both soon, Nik texts ten awkward seconds later. For fuck's sake. Also, he's evidently disabled his autocorrect. Who does that? *wine shipment at post pick it up on your way*

I'm already here. Let me drop off my stuff.

closes in five so go now

I need the package slip.

no i called ahead go fetch

I type *Kiss my ass* but don't send it. Of all the condescending bullshit— But no. It's my job. So I put the keys in my pocket, shoulder my bag, and shove right back out the door, phone still in hand. Running is easier than thinking. Nik keeps texting, but I ignore it until I'm in the inordinately long just-before-closing line at the post office.

youre still not letting yourself think about it

it wont work

once it gets into your head you cant drive it out

come out and say it

youll be happier

Since I won't be able to text and carry a case of wine at the same time, I have a legitimate excuse to throw off a quick *On my way* and leave it at that. The phone doesn't ping anymore en route, or in the elevator, thank God. And this case of wine is exactly as heavy as I expected it to be.

Nik is precisely where I left him hours ago, legs over the arm of the couch with the magazine open, perched on his bare hip bones. Same magazine too. The groupie's gone, as far as I can tell, but Nik still hasn't put on a shirt.

He grins at me with half of his cheek but all of his teeth.

I let my bag hit the floor. It's heavy enough to rattle the masks on the wall. And that's nothing compared to the sound this case of wine will make when I throw it at Nik's head—if I do that. Which I won't. But I do let the box clatter on the coffee table like a traffic accident.

"I am not your fucking butler," I say, because *for fuck's sake*.

Nik laughs. "Nah, you are. I thought you read the contract."

The case of wine clunks again when my knee smacks into the table. It hurts, but I won't let him see that. Or any of this. "I don't fucking believe this. It's down the damn street. You could have gone anytime in the last three hours—"

"But it's not my job." Nik shifts the magazine down so that the spine's between his thighs. He stretches, cracks his jaw, and looks simultaneously about as bored and amused as a house cat. I could hit him. I might if Nik says anything worse.

"It's not my job either," I say. And regret it.

"Yes, it is." Nik swerves so that his legs aren't over the arm of the couch anymore; they're propped up on the wine case, close enough that his bare toes brush against my crotch. I back off. Any sane man would. Then again, a sane man would have punched him two weeks ago. Or not gotten into this mess in the first place.

Why do I need this job? Why don't I live in a world where I don't need this fucking job?

"I'm a creator," Nik proclaims, as clearly as a philosopher about to guzzle acid. "It's my job to create. You're a musicologist. I don't even know what your job is."

As far as I'm concerned, the *Oh right, you don't have one* is implied. "Fuck you."

"Not sure that's in your contract." In hindsight I should have expected him to say it, but the rest of that hindsight is remembering Nik's mouth over the microphone and a roomful of people *reveling* in his music and no, *no*, that's the last thing I want to hear right now.

"Funny," I say, but it isn't true, and doesn't stop the red flood behind my eyes.

"Fact is, *Johann Christian*, your job is to make my job easier for me." Another Bach son, another name I wouldn't consider an insult from anyone else. "That's what you signed. So give in or give up."

The empty eyes of the masks on the wall stare me down, just like him. I entertain a brief vision of prying open the wine case, breaking the first bottle I touch, and gouging out Nik's eyes so he matches. The thought's disgusting enough that I can't look at him, so I turn away, and listen because I have to.

I didn't set out to hate my life.

"You're not saying it again." Nik laughs, does something to the couch cushions so they creak. "Are you saving your thoughts for a special occasion?"

I sigh, find a mask on the wall to glare at instead. That's not much better. "Look, if I didn't need your money, I would have left on the first day."

"I know. That's not what you're trying not to say."

"I'm trying not to say something that'll get me fired."

"Who says I'd fire you?" Something taps my knee, and I look down just in time to realize it's his foot. "You signed the contract. Either you leave because you can't take it, or I keep you around until I get bored. That's how it goes."

If he wants my honesty, he can have it. "Fine, I'm trying not to say that you're a sanctimonious asshole and a charlatan."

Nik tilts his head back and laughs to the ceiling. This time, there's almost a beat to it. "No, that's all pretty clear. That you think it, I mean. That's still not what you're not saying."

Well if it isn't that, then I'm well within my rights to remain silent. I glance out the window, listen to the chatter and car horns and construction seven stories down, build it into notation, a drone between my ears like the pedals of an organ in church.

Something gusts over my ear; Nik is standing far too close. "If you can't put words to it, create something. That is, if there *is* music in what you do."

I turn. From his tone I expect Nik to be smirking, but there's nothing like that on his face. Challenge, yes, but almost earnest. Almost.

I say nothing. And that's when the smirk flares up, climbs Nik's face like light when the blinds have been cranked. "Come on." He claps a hand on my upper arm and steers me away from the window.

I wouldn't have let him, but it looks like I don't get a say in that. "You're a musicologist. *Logize* about music at me."

"You know—"

"Why wouldn't I know what that means?" He pulls, and I stagger after him, down the hall toward the studio. "It's words. Music, words. You explain music in words. That's what you say your job is. But I don't see you doing that at all, so I guess you're the charlatan here, not me."

I never thought I'd actually feel like an unstrung marionette. It doesn't amount to feeling much at all, really, just a cold impotent rage and a heaviness in my limbs. He yanks me into the studio, presents me the piano like a cat that's just dragged a whole pigeon onto the welcome mat.

"Play," Nik says, with a sinisterly childish lilt to his voice. "Create something."

The piano keys gape at me like slavering teeth. Seven floors down a car alarm blares, cycles through its sirens. The track transcribes itself in my head, endless repeating glissandi, and my hands do nothing.

The piano didn't look nearly as threatening two hours ago, Midtown, when I could play on my own terms. I will not give Nik the satisfaction.

"Play," Nik says again, and this might be some kind of delusion but he seems confused, genuine. "Why don't you play?"

"Which is it?"

"Huh?"

"Which is it?" I repeat, louder this time, because the last time sounded far too much like the snap of a twig. "Play or create?"

"Same thing." Nik shrugs. "Just play something. Not math. Music. Put your hands on the keys and play." He tugs my arm, sits me down, like one of my very first teachers when I was too keyed up to practice. "Come on."

My hands only make it as high as my lap. "No math," I say. He made that rule for me, he said. It's been a taunt all along. "What, do you want me to bang on the keys like a five-year-old? Is that *creation* to you?" I cut Nik off before whatever he plans on saying takes on meaning. "I'm not your fucking butler, and I'm *not* playing just because you tell me to."

"It's because you can't, isn't it."

No. I shove back the piano bench, and if it hits Nik's knees, so be it. "You think that reverse-psychology crap's going to work on me? What the fuck do you think I am?"

It takes looking Nik in the face for me to see that maybe what Nik last said wasn't a taunt. He's not smirking, not gloating; more curious than confused, with the shadows that frame his mouth as dark as his tattoos.

He's still playing the god. He's still putting on that show, even for me.

"I can play," I tell him.

"No, you can't," Nik says. "I get it now. You don't play, you just read."

"I am not having this conversation."

"You read." Nik tilts his head, regards me the way most people regard relics in a museum or inconvenient homeless people in doorways. "You read other people's art and you push it around like the clay isn't dry."

"Will you stop already?"

"Why? It's true."

"And that's so alien to you?"

"Alien? No. Just pathetic."

"This is part of your act, isn't it." I stand, shut the piano lid with more reverence than I thought I could, given how close I am to breaking his face. "Fine, pity the poor shit who knows he's better at analysis than he'll ever be at production."

"Good analysis is creation too. But if you were as good at that as you say, you wouldn't be working for me right now."

"Go fuck yourself."

Nik laughs, leans an elbow on the wall, just about blocks my way. "Go balance my checkbook. Go fix my bookcase. Go make dinner and measure everything like you're making a bomb. Go stuff those dead men with wigs in your ears. It's not going to work."

The only thing I can say with my voice instead of my fists is, "Get out of my way."

"I'm not in your way." His smile says precisely the opposite, clear as the car alarm seven stories down.

I shoulder past him, face the masks in the hall. At least their smiles don't have teeth. "Fine. And after that, I'm going to a concert."

"Anyone I know?" Nik asks just before the studio door shuts in his face.

"Chopin and Liszt, mostly." It's about music, not about me, thank fuck—and then, another test for him, "Chopin or Liszt?"

"Chopin," Nik says, with enough of a lewd turn to his voice that it's audible through the door. "Liszt was insufferable. Waste of good hands."

A strange wave of vertigo hits me, and I lean against the wall. I'm going to spend most of the concert watching the recitalist's hands, aren't I.

NOVEMBER 21, 2011

My packages arrive at Uncle Paul's apartment uptown on an inconvenient Monday afternoon, when I'm bogged down and hungover (from a candidate concert at Juilliard and my requisite attempts at ingratiating myself to the faculty). But the number of the counting shall be three: the price his apartment's concierge quoted me for having someone else oversee the transportation is more than I want to burn, Paul won't keep the boxes in his foyer for more than a day, and I flat refuse to call in any more favors. So, U-Haul it is.

I haven't driven in about a year and a half. By New York State law, my license is set to expire in two months.

Well, what traffic doesn't know won't hurt it.

The apartment in question isn't the one I grew up in. When Paul adopted me, he was living in a bachelor's one-bedroom in the low 160s on the West Side, in that nebulous area between Harlem and Washington Heights; a year and a dozen successful musicians later, it was a three-bedroom in Hell's Kitchen, not that Paul spent much time there. He probably doesn't spend much time in this one either, since the doorman has to check his name and add an "Oh, right, 17B, let me see if anyone's there to let you in."

There isn't. But apparently it's safe to leave boxes stacked outside your door in apartments on the Upper East Side. Either that, or Paul doesn't care.

But as far as I can tell, nothing's missing, and the doorman's staff even help me load the first few boxes into the truck. I hope I have enough cash for a tip. The concierges certainly make more than I do anyway.

And just as I've wrangled box number three into the back of the U-Haul, a cab pulls up right behind it, close enough to make the truck shudder.

The cab driver leans his head out the window. "Watch where you're parked!"

Asshole. "Funny," I shoot back, "it's supposed to be 'Watch where you're going.'"

"This isn't a loading zone."

"It isn't a stopping zone either, and you don't see me stopping you."

"He's just trying to do his job, Anthony." Paul emerges from the cab and shuts the door.

Shit. I hold on to the frame of the truck. Paul pays the cab driver in cash and sends him off.

"He'd better not have dented this," I say, just in case I don't look stupid enough.

"It's on his head if he did; I've got the license plate." Paul doesn't smile, but does lend me a hand on my way back down from the U-Haul. "How many more boxes?"

"Five."

"I thought you'd be here earlier."

"I did too. I had to deal with a travel agent this afternoon; it took longer than I thought."

"Where's Nik going?"

"Seattle." Though for all the time it took to hunt up his bona fides, he might as well have been going to North Korea. "Scoping out a venue to see if it's worth stopping there on the tour next year."

Paul raises an eyebrow. "You should have gotten the ticket online."

"I did. Nik was out all last night, probably still is, and for once I know which hotel, but he didn't answer his phone. And then the travel agent called *me* because Nik's information doesn't stack up." Because he's lying on about half of his documentation and even his permanent address is under Paul's name, because he's fucking ridiculous, because *this is my life now* and all I can do is deal.

But Paul just shrugs, nods at the doorman on his way to the elevator. "Don't let anyone tow that truck." The doorman damn near salutes a *yes, sir.* As if the address wasn't impressive enough. I lower my head, wait for the elevator to close around us both to say anything resembling what I mean.

"You've come a long way," I say. It's a compliment. We both know it.

"A long few blocks," Paul agrees. "Thank you."

"About Nik's information—"

"If anyone gives you trouble, send them to me. Air travel screening's hard to get around."

"It isn't if you give them your real name and SSN." And there, that's what I couldn't say where anyone might hear. Not in a building like this. Not in polite company.

The elevator door opens, lets us out on the seventeenth floor, in perfect view of the boxes that still line the hallway leading up to Paul's door. "Come inside," he says. He used to use that tone to tell me *Not now, go find someplace else to play*. An order.

He unlocks the door. Hardwood floors and glass windows that might as well be walls shine into my eyes. Seventeen stories up, you can afford people looking in on you in your underwear, it seems. Nearly everything is glass or white or clear, more like a render than reality. I shield myself from the glare and step into the foyer, make a move to take off my shoes before Paul coughs.

"Don't. We both have places to be. I just wanted to tell you in here, not out there." Paul shuts the door.

I sigh. "You really do buy into his Dionysus bullshit, don't you."

"Like I said," Paul goes on, ignoring me except to glower up at me just like the blazing glass walls, "if anyone gives you trouble about Nik's personal information, you go through me. Not him, not Sydney, not anyone else. If it means chartering a tour bus instead of taking a plane, we can deal with that. But don't ever use your own information in place of his, and don't make stuff up about him."

If this were the kind of floor I could spit on, I might well, tsking this hard. "Am I in the mafia now?"

"Funny," Paul says. "No. But it's not a bad analogy."

"How does he sign a lease if he won't give anyone his name?"

"The lease is in mine."

My jaw won't close. It's like my breath has suddenly turned solid, a row of expanding foam filling a crease in a cheap wall. This place is magnificent: quality shining through every frame on the walls, wrought-iron chairs, a service that cleans them all to such an aggressive shine. He said he wouldn't help me with college, and bought up his image instead. And Nik's.

"I am sixty-eight thousand dollars in debt," I manage to say, "and you own his apartment."

I have seen that face on Paul many times in the last eighteen years. It's as enraging now as it's ever been. Paul never seems to display overt disappointment in anyone but me.

"*You* are sixty-eight thousand dollars in debt," Paul says. "And I control Nik's finances, so I know he makes his rent. Don't act like I'm giving him anything I should have given you."

"You control his finances." My fists are going to start shaking any second now if I don't curl them soon—so I do. "All his accounts are yours. How illegal is that?" And how long has it been like this? How much have I missed?

"Less than you think," Paul says. Less illegal, not less missed. He can't get inside my head, never could. At least that's mine, for all the good it's done.

"For how long?"

"You wouldn't believe me if I told you."

"I don't believe any of this." Maybe I should be less worried about my fists shaking and more about them flying into the nearest shelf of picture frames. "Fine. Guess you drank the Kool-Aid."

"Don't say that."

"Why shouldn't I? It's true, isn't it?"

Every time in my life that Paul's hit me, I deserved it. I'm not sure I do now, but if he did, I'd hit back. He doesn't, but he grabs my wrist and wrenches it before I have a chance to dodge, holds me still enough to stare down, like I'm seventeen again and somewhere I'm not supposed to be.

Like here. Like in this life.

"I don't worship him," Paul says, "and if you can stop believing that, you stop believing it right now."

"I can't believe that's the part you take offense at."

Paul scoffs through his teeth. "It is. I make it easier for him to be here. That's all."

Fine. If that's all I get today, that's all I get. I pry my arm out of his grip, and he lets me. It doesn't hurt much. It won't stop me from playing later.

"How long?" I ask, because the other options will cut more ties than I can afford to part with.

Paul's voice drips caution and consolation. "Since nineteen seventy-four."

"Bullshit." That's not possible. That's before I was even born. Before Paul was my age.

"I told you you wouldn't believe me," Paul says. "Next time, don't ask."

"Sure." My lips are almost too tight to get it out. "Yes, sir. Anything else, sir. What else can I do for you, sir."

"You can get your boxes out of my hallway." I bet this door's too classy to hit my ass on the way out.

"Nice place," I say so I don't have to look at him.

"I mean it," Paul says. "Come to me if you think you have to lie for Nik."

"Right," I drone, "you're the expert."

"I'll see you for Thanksgiving."

"Fine."

The door clips shut behind me, and I stoop to get the next of the boxes into the elevator.

It turns out, downstairs, that I have just enough cash on me to tip the concierges.

It matters less when I get back downtown. Nik's out or asleep—out, I think, practice—and so much the better, even if it means unloading everything into and off the elevator on my own. I bring each of the boxes to the guest room—my room, now, I guess, *fuck my life*—plug in my phone to charge it, and let my laptop play the music instead even though the speakers suck, and unpack.

Considering Nik's apparent aversion to bookshelves, I'm not surprised the one in here—IKEA circa 2004—is on fraying pegs and tilted slightly to the left. I shove it closer to the corner and unpack the books first, in the same order they rested on my shelves in California. There's enough space for everything but the scores. I stack them under the end table for now. There are still far too many. Great. So they'll stay in the box.

"I thought you said books belong on shelves," Nik says, overhead.

I could have sworn I shut that door. Either way, he's creepy as hell, but I should be polite. Maybe he'll go away. "Sorry if I woke you."

"You didn't." Nik steps over the boxes in the doorway, sits on the edge of my bed, and turns the Tchaikovsky on the laptop off.

"That's not yours."

"It's not yours either; it's Tchaikovsky's."

"Ha." I stow a stack of sweaters on the ledge in the closet. Brisk as it was in San Francisco, I'd need more winter clothes, and soon. "Fine, turn it off. Your house. Your life. Your lack of rules."

Nik grins, runs his finger over the trackpad, scrolls through my iTunes collection. "It's not all math," he says, like he can't believe it.

Fine. Let him do what he wants. I continue folding my clothes. The relative silence is awkward, but better than arguing, at least right now.

"You're giving up?" Nik asks, in a smaller voice than I've heard him use yet. Silence, it seems, doesn't suit him.

"I'm moving in," I sigh. "Does that look like giving up?"

"I meant on the math."

"Whatever you say." I don't mean a syllable of it.

Nik laughs. "Okay, you're not giving up."

He *hmms* deep in his throat, then a little decisive sound like a huff, and flicks his fingers on the trackpad. A William Bolcom piano étude creaks out of the laptop's tinny speakers. It's peppery, modern, a piece I learned more for credit than pleasure, but it's not terrible. Nik could have chosen worse. I let it slide.

I should probably get the ridiculousness of this living situation out of the way now, before it makes my life any worse. "My uncle told me he owns the apartment."

"No, he didn't," Nik says. "He told you the lease is in his name and I sublet. That's not the same as owning it."

"Guess you're not just immortal, you read minds too."

"No, but I do have a phone."

"You answer when he calls, but not the travel agents?"

"I was busy when they called. I wasn't when he did."

"Fair enough." I finish with the sweaters, start hanging the pants and jackets. Everything I own is still school-ready. For some reason that seems less appropriate now. "How long has he been in on this?"

"This place? Three years. He put me up in Tokyo before this for about ten, London before that." Nik cranes toward the ceiling, scratches behind the collar of his shirt. He's changed his hair, I'm not sure when; maybe that's what he was doing today: it's all red now, no more gold. It has a strange effect against the tarnished color of his skin, distinctive but not exactly flattering in the room's yellowed light.

Then again, I'm looking.

I shut my eyes. "How long have you known him?"

Nik shrugs. "He picked me up in Johannesburg in the seventies."

I nod, first, since the seventies part just confirmed itself—and then the rest of it hits me in a lull in the music. "Johannesburg? In the seventies?"

"Nice rephrase. See, you do know how to play."

"What the fuck was he doing in *Johannesburg* in the seventies?"

"Obviously something that allowed him to get out alive."

There are jackets to hang. I resolve to bring this up, later. With Paul, not Nik.

"Just meant to say," Nik says, like he intends to be reassuring, "that he hasn't given me anything that's supposed to be yours."

It *is* supposed to be reassuring. Nik's tone has all the hallmarks: steadier, softer, damper consonants. And it still sounds like Nik, not like he's putting it on or coming out of nowhere with genuine sympathy.

So I let my shoulders unknot, just a fraction, and say, "That's good to hear." Not "thank you," since it didn't work, not really, but it's better than nothing.

Nik grins, wide enough to nestle the doubts back in my head, but all he says is, "Great."

I sort a few more hangers, let the music play, and listen to Nik breathe just barely out of time. It's almost bearable. I can get through this. I—

"You need another bookshelf," Nik says.

Yes. I do. "Should I just take one of the ones from the living room since you'd rather not use them?"

"Nah, now I know where everything is again." Nik says it more to the laptop than to me—apparently something up in my tabs has caught his attention. There's nothing compromising there, as far as I know. Job applications. Calls for papers. "Put one on my card, have it delivered. You missing anything else?"

"A job in my field," I tell him, seriously.

"Can't get you that. Try a new field."

"Too late."

"What do you mean, 'too late'?"

"I've already committed myself to this one."

The sound Nik makes, tuneless as ever, is somewhere between a scoff and a full-on belly laugh. "So you think you've put in your time."

"Time, money, blood, sweat." *The tears are compulsory*, I don't add. "I haven't got time to be anything else."

I'm looking Nik in the eyes right now—which may be a mistake, all things considered—and the expression on his face develops and cycles, from confusion to amusement to something too much like pity. I stop looking after that, get back to work, compress these jackets more. He didn't choose this apartment for its storage capacity. I didn't choose this apartment at all.

"How the hell did you get so old?" Nik asks, and the question's almost as infuriating as the pity.

"You're one to talk." I'm out of jackets to hang. I open the next box: T-shirts, socks, underwear. There's no chest of drawers here. For fuck's sake. I start transferring them from the cardboard box to an open suitcase.

"I'm not old, I'm just ancient," Nik says. He stretches over the corner of the bed, reaches into the box, grabs a rolled-up pair of my socks, and tosses them back and forth between his hands. I swipe back the socks mid-toss. Let it not be said that I learned nothing on the playground. Nik preens at me, the smile as cutting upside-down as right-side-up. "See? You're old."

"You tell me I'm old, and you tell me to get a new field." I roll my eyes, sit on the floor with my back to the mattress, and deal with the box. "Pick one."

Nik doesn't choose, not aloud, and there's no need to care what he thinks. I sort out the T-shirts and socks, make a mental note to listen to the Bolcom again, this time without Nik in the room, and pick up the scores from the NYPL if they have them— Wait, I can't. Interlibrary Loan is closed to me now that I'm not enrolled at any institution. Shit.

This may be the last fucking straw. Water towers have been climbed for less.

I tighten my fists around the pair of socks I'm holding and can't unclench them. Bolcom's études play on, rhythmically strange but metered at least. I can concentrate on that instead. Music. Music, source of all light divine. Fuck, that's Handel. I need to focus.

Then Nik scratches me on the scalp, like a cat.

I duck, swerve to the side. "Are you trying to brainwash me?" My words are quieter than I mean them to be, weaker, enough that one piano on the laptop's tiny speakers nearly drowns me out. But Nik evidently hears.

"No," Nik says, on the heels of a little huff that might be a new kind of laughter. "Why would I want to?"

Seconds pass. The laptop stops playing. The near-silence that follows isn't silence at all, between the flicker of Nik's fingers on the laptop—guitarists have weird fingernails, and now my skull knows it—and the faint whirr of the computer's drives, winding on with nothing to do.

I let the socks tumble into the suitcase. "Is Bolcom one of yours?"

Somehow, I get the sense that Nik's hands can smile just like his teeth. "He doesn't suck," Nik says. "His heart's in the right place."

"Hell?"

"Michigan."

In spite of everything, including myself, I laugh.

A moment later, Nik's selected something else in iTunes, and it's not nearly as generous a choice as Bolcom's études.

"Bookshelf, dresser, clue," Nik laughs, uncoiling himself from the bed and sidling out the door.

"I can't put a clue on your credit card."

"I'll give you cash."

I sigh, resume unpacking, and forget to turn the new music off until the third song.

Posted to asbrooks.com on November 25, 2011

"And a Fat Load of Thanksgiving That Was"

I should probably preface this with a note that I know, somewhere, someone had a worse Thanksgiving than I did. I'm certain of it: there are homeless, hungry, and otherwise unlucky people in America, or stuck outside it. And I've definitely had worse Thanksgivings myself in the last eighteen years, and stranger ones (the one I spent stranded at SeaTac comes to mind). I'm in no way saying that my figurative stubbed toe was worse than anyone else's gangrenous foot. But it was a fucking inconvenient stubbed toe.

Somehow, in the last ten years of being graciously invited to other people's homes for Thanksgiving, I forgot what Thanksgiving with my uncle is like. We don't have any other family: he's never married (as far as I know), all of my grandparents are deceased, and, well, the rest. The first year after my parents died, my uncle and I went to Thanksgiving and then Christmas with my mother's extended family, and we haven't been back since, which speaks for itself.

I really shouldn't be complaining. It's a holiday about celebrating what you're thankful for, and he's thankful for his success. His new apartment (new to me, he bought it four years ago) is beautiful, his job is stable and lucrative enough to maintain it, and he's become exactly what he set out to be. If that's not something to celebrate, I don't know what is. And I should be thankful for his support.

Instead, I'm reminded that I don't have his life. If not for his sufferance, I'd have nothing. I've always been aware of that. But now he's gloating. He's never approved of my choice of graduate school or the prospects in my field. I used to think it was because he wanted an heir or something, but it doesn't pan out that way in his industry and he's worked against nepotism all his life. When I was a child he insisted that I could be anything. That he'd support me because no one else would.

Setting me up as Nik's handler is his idea of supporting me. He's made that abundantly clear. And I spent Thanksgiving being reminded that even that support comes with a price.

Also, the food was predictably awful. My uncle likes to think he can cook.

A happier Thanksgiving to everyone else. I have a concert to deal with tonight, but if anyone's in town for the holiday weekend, please, let me know.

Comments (5)

EliseMorgenstern
Wait, the musician you're working for is Nik? *Last Against the Precipice* Nik?

> **ASBrooks**
> Clearly this is what it takes to get a comment on this blog.

> > **EliseMorgenstern**
> > I'm serious, are you or aren't you?

> > > **ASBrooks**
> > > Yes.

EliseMorgenstern
OH MY FUCKING GOD

ARE YOU SERIOUS

I CAN'T EVEN

NOVEMBER 25, 2011

Sydney's excuse this time is just as acceptable as the last: because of her wife's injury, they took a plane to their Thanksgiving destination, namely Buffalo, instead of driving, and travel back was out of their control and, thus, delayed. Sydney alerted me to the possibility before she left, and when it became clear that she'd be spending the night in the frozen wild she texted me with two words and a file attachment:

Plan B

The Bowery Ballroom is a larger venue than Southpaw, less concrete, more pit, with iron railings around the second floor. It feels like a theater, not a concert space, complete with curtains that the crew's since torn down. But out there in the house it's the kind of floor an audience of noble French courtiers would be comfortable on, if they had enough room to galliard in their enormous skirts and wigs.

The fans aren't galliarding right now. And they're not wearing much of anything.

I pull back into the wings of the stage, scratch under the ear of my headset. My scalp is sweating enough that the device can't keep its grip over my ears. At this point, I'm considering spray adhesive. Or maple syrup. Or something. Anything.

I hate my job.

Nik sings. The audience rails. I grit my teeth, check my watch, and the headset slips down my scalp.

"Fuck," I say to the nearest stagehand, not that she seems to care. "I'm getting a drink. Are we comped?"

"Don't know," about four people say at once, in damp and passionless voices like the cult they probably are.

"Great." I sigh, swipe off the headset and wipe my scalp with my sleeve. No one ever warns you about this shit when you decide to go bald. "Use my phone; it's on vibrate," I tell the stagehands, since they're apparently sharing a brain right now, and leave the headset slung around my neck on my way out the stage door—

—when I'm promptly shoved back in by the crowd.

Fine. It's easier, not to mention safer, to go outside through the back and in the front door. I should check in with the bouncers anyway. So I cut through the loading dock to the alley (and past the three people making out against the brick wall since thanks to a past lecture from Elise I know it's none of my damn business as long as no one's screaming for help), then around front. The music isn't nearly as loud out here, just a distant rumbling. Then again it could still drag me back in. And it will. Work.

"Hey, Tony," the larger of the bouncers says, and the other just cocks his chin up at me, *'sup*. "They tell you about the kid who tried to get in without a waiver?"

"No," I nod back, "so I assume you handled it."

The other bouncer laughs, scratches one of his nails down the zipper of his hoodie. "I took his phone and called his mom, told her where he was."

I huff out a laugh. "Let me get you guys a drink. What are you having?"

"Ha, just get me a Coke, it's cool," that one says.

The larger one adds, "I'm sticking with coffee, we know your old man's rules."

"You got it." I make my way in. "I'll have someone bring those out."

It's the first I've heard of a rule about no alcohol for the bouncers. It makes perfect sense: they can't be expected to deal with drunks if they've had much themselves, but I thought there'd be a standardized statute from the venue instead of a company clause. Still, it's smart, and the rule sounds like Paul, and it's definitely for the best at a concert like this one.

Back inside, I put my earbuds in to serve as plugs, and set the headset on top of them, slippery or no. I ignore the ground level the best I can and head up to the second floor. I'm right, it's less crowded up here—it only takes me two minutes to fight my way up to the bar area instead of five. The instrumental passage Nik's on now is garbled enough by the dancing and shouting that it doesn't demand I listen to it. I can even focus on the crowd enough to shoulder my way through and not trip over anyone. There's a rhythm to the shouting too, in a sense, but between my forced focus on getting from point A to point B and the dulled sound thanks to my doubled ear protection, I'm good to go.

At the bar, I flag down a shot of tequila—I've been here before and the beer is crap—and call over the barback to take a Coke and a coffee to the bouncers. The increased cheering in the house must mean one song's over and another's beginning, though I resolve not to pay attention to that until I've had this drink, and the bartender has enough to deal with that I can't begrudge her the wait. They must make bank on nights like this.

How fucking desperate am I for money? Right. Desperate enough.

Nik's lyrics briefly become intelligible: "Climbing vines against the gate, winding up my skin, bare the barbs and shoot them in." I can't help a shudder, my back teeth settling over each other like the grooves don't quite fit. The bartender hands me my drink and the barback signals that he's taking the bouncers' stuff downstairs, so all's well. Since I'm still not sure if we're comped or not, I put down my cash, toss back the shot, and set the glass on the bar. The burn sets in a breath and a half later, on schedule, and the grit in my jaw subsides. There, things should get much easier to deal with in about ten minutes.

The chatter on the headset and the noise of the crowd blur together into something almost like a buzz, a sound designer's dream. It's like white noise, an island of false silence—maybe I could find something similar to block out the world when I work on papers. I shoulder out of the bar patrons' way, work mine out toward the stairs and the iron railing. Someone, wisely, has gotten rid of the ironwork tables and chairs that usually line this balcony, but even without seating the crowd isn't as thick as the morass downstairs. I peer over the rail like it's far more than one story high, briefly hear Bernard Herrmann's score for *Vertigo* in the back of my mind, and laugh. It *is* that kind of moment, a precipice. Wait, no: it's actually in the music. Herrmann's arpeggios are in the keyboard and the rhythm guitar of

Nik's song right now, not the exact augmented chords but the same sense of dueling scales, crisscrossing and spiraling down.

And some idiot about ten feet away has had the equally brilliant idea of illustrating that musical gesture by climbing on to the iron rail. No, not on to it: *over* it.

"Get down from there, you fuck-head!" I'm already shoving my way through to her. And apparently I'm using a voice people listen to despite music, because the crowd nearest me stops dancing and lets me through. Good. I make it to the edge, skid on something underfoot, and reach.

For one terrifying moment, the soles of her sneakers hover above the iron rail, with enough space for my hand to pass beneath them.

It's equally terrifying to watch her fall.

There's no slow motion. There's nothing cinematic about the arc, no illustrative scoring, no zoom or flash or succession of cuts. My fist closes on nothing in the same real time as my breath, and the girl falls without the delicacy of editing. I don't hear the impact. I doubt anyone could.

I can't even hear my own heart right now. It might have stopped for a second.

Nik doesn't stop playing. Most of the floor doesn't stop dancing. There's a knot where the motion has slowed and spread to accommodate the body on the floor, but it's not even a ripple in a pond: it stills at the edge of the knot. People brush themselves off, look down. No one screams any differently than they do for Nik's song.

Fuck.

I bolt downstairs, without giving a shit who I shove aside. I yank the headset down and rip the earbuds out, barrel through the people congregated at the base of the stairs and yell at anyone else in my way. Why is this my job? No, someone's just tried to kill herself, now is not the time to worry about *my* life. I'm not the only one pushing. Security's here too, thank fuck, and by now there's enough of a commotion that I know where the stillness is. Nik keeps playing. *Asshole.* I shout, "Out of my way, don't move her!" more than once, and give up on the second half of that when only the first gets me anywhere. I need to get through. I might be the only one here who knows what to do.

By the time I make it over, the crowd has drawn its own police line, a ring of smartphones and questions. I get in there, kneel next to the girl, stop myself from touching her. In this light it's impossible to tell if she's breathing, even with her shirt pushed up over her midriff. That means she might not be. "Don't move her," I snap at one of the idiot fans trying to reach in, "not until the ambulance comes. Who's called it?"

I must not be speaking loud enough. Not even security seems to hear me, and they're an arm's-length away.

Headset. Right. I threw it off. I should be yelling at someone to pull the plug on Nik first, and I can't without the headset. Well, too late now.

In a silence that's only mine, I finally get a good look at the girl. Younger than me, white, hair straight and dark, so dark I can't see if there's blood in it. Tall body, broad shoulders, smart enough to wear sneakers instead of stilettos to a place like this. Skinny jeans. Belt. Impractical shirt for November.

Nik keeps playing.

People reach forward, and I have to shout again, "Don't move her!" Security makes its calls. The floodlights snap on. The dancing still hasn't stopped, neither has the music, but there's an island of stillness around me, us, cordoned off with phones, angled down, taping everything.

"Assholes," I say, louder than I want to, but under the music no one can hear me anyway.

The band falters, one instrument at a time. Nik's voice soars, unintelligible, at least to me. I stand up, let security and the smartphones bracket off the girl and glare at the stage. This is what Elise showed us months ago, isn't it. It goes on. The show goes on.

Well, not on my fucking time.

I reach out to Nik since words aren't working even now. My hand has to take care of *stop* instead.

There's a pocket of silence, or nearly, like a screen taking a blink too long to load, like the moment before your ears pop on a plane. Nik meets my eyes and laughs into the microphone.

I point down at the girl.

To Nik's credit, he looks like he considers her for a moment. Even twenty feet away across a mass of lights and shadows, the shift of his eyes, over the crowd and back to me, is clear, gold, evident. Then he shakes his head, makes a wide sweeping gesture with the handle of his guitar. *Everyone else*, he means.

It may not be silent, but it's quiet enough for me to tell him, "*No.*"

It's also quiet enough for me to hear someone start panicking. "Dina! Dina, oh shit, oh god, oh my god—"

Forget Nik. I have to deal with this now. One of the security men is holding on to a frantic girl, and it's pretty damn obvious to me that it's *her friend* bleeding on a concrete floor, even if none of the people recording this on their phones seem to care.

I know my rules. Calm her. Get the insurance card. I stretch out my hands to her, make eye contact. "Hey, sorry, if you know this girl, I need you to get her information. Did you come here with her?"

"Oh god—"

"Look, this could save her life, just calm down. I need you to get her insurance information, anything she brought with her, do you know where it is?" This is easier than it should be. Relief is uncharitable.

The panicked, choked noises creaking from her like tears aren't an answer.

I grit my teeth so that nothing comes out but, "Please."

The girl clings to the arm of the guard restraining her. "She just wanted to dance. Nik just wanted her to dance, oh my god. Oh god. Oh. Shit."

Some part of me files that away for later. But over her shoulder, another smartphone sweeps in from the side, trying to get a better look at Dina. Smartphones. Recording. Instead of helping. Instead of caring.

That's *it*.

"If you've got time to do that, you've got time to fucking call 911!" I make a grab for the guy or the phone, either one works, and although I get neither the point is made. The guy backs off, lowers the phone so it's not seeing anything but shoes.

The girl that security's holding on to hangs her head. "Sir," she heaves, "sir. Sorry. Her stuff. It's in the coat check. Her stuff's in the coat check. Wallet too."

I shut my eyes for a moment, nod quickly, and once they're open I gesture to the guard that's holding her. "All right. Let him take you there and make sure you get everything. You should go with her when the ambulance gets here. Did you two come alone?"

"No, there are four—three—four of us."

"Good. What's your name?"

It takes her a couple of breaths to say it. Her eyes are blasted red. It might only be from tears, it might not. "Gabrielle. Gabrielle Stuart. Sir."

"Go get Dina's stuff from the coat check, Gabrielle. And get her some water," I add to the guard taking care of her, who nods and ushers her off. The crowd's not dispersing, not at all, but it parts for Gabrielle once the guard makes it clear that there's a goddamn hurry.

I wish someone had been this courteous with me when my parents died.

Nik's still up on the stage, leaning on his guitar the way a knight might lean on his sword propped up on the battleground, surveying the audience. This place is big enough that the section nearest the stage is still confused, shouting Nik's name, and "Play, play, play."

Eventually, the sirens drown the shouting out. I'm not sure if they're cops or ambulances.

NOVEMBER 26, 2011

I wake on schedule, and run on schedule, and return to the apartment on schedule. Nik isn't awake, though he is actually here, not out with groupies like the last few shows. I made him come home. The kitchen is the way I left it yesterday, only water glasses left unwashed. I eat breakfast, make coffee, check my email, all on schedule. Sydney, still trapped upstate, apologizes as if she knows. She probably does. I get the feeling we're supposed to put nothing in print. Anything we say can and will be used against us in a court of law.

I shoot off a quick text to Lisette, of all people, for sore throat remedies that don't involve tea. The only people I can think of who might be awake at this hour and in this time zone on a Saturday are singers and athletes, and she's both.

I stare at the comments on my blog for about ten minutes. They've proliferated in the night, like roaches.

They'll still be there after I do everything else I need to do. I can put them on hold, like the rest of my life. It's getting much easier to pick and choose what takes up space in my brain. I shower, shave, get dressed on schedule. I order the bookshelf and dresser online, set a Monday delivery. I can't put a clue on a credit card. I'll assemble the furniture myself. Nik is slated for two Skype interviews today, both in the early afternoon. If he isn't awake by then, I'm prepared to cover for him and reschedule both. His rent is due next week. I could make the check out to Paul instead of the landlord. I'm not that much of an asshole. The temptation is fleeting.

At 9:02, my phone rings, a New York area code but seven more digits I don't know. I set the laptop on top of an as-yet-unshelved pile of new books, and answer the call. "Anthony Brooks speaking."

"Good morning, Mr. Brooks." No one knows to call me "doctor." I get the feeling I'll only be seeing that on wedding invitations. "Sorry for the early hour."

"It's fine."

"This is Bradford Wilson, I'm on the legal team at Pantheon Talent. I work for your uncle."

This calls for shutting the laptop, so I do. "This is about last night?"

"Yes. You need to make certain you get the reports to your uncle as soon as possible. Dina Marshall died in the ambulance, and he's put us on Nik's case. We've already been dealing with calls this morning."

"I thought Nik wasn't a Pantheon act."

"He isn't. I have a nonexclusive contract. I'd rather not go into that here if you don't mind."

"It's fine."

"You have the incident report forms?"

"Yes, Mrs. Nerida sent the PDFs."

"Who?"

"Sydney."

"Ah, right, right. Good. Just have them to us by noon, earlier if you can."

"I will, thank you."

"Have the police been to the apartment?"

"Not yet, and I've been up since six. But I gave my witness statement last night and they have my contact information."

"Did they speak to Nik?"

Not as far as I know. "He hasn't said anything. He's still asleep."

"You don't know whether the police spoke to him last night?"

"With all due respect, Mr. Wilson, I had my hands full."

Laughing matter or not, Mr. Wilson chuckles. The phone accommodates it in bursts. "Fair enough. I take it he didn't stay out last night."

He didn't fight me about going home. Much. "I said he's asleep. I meant here."

"You don't have to cover for him if he's not."

"No, he's really here. Asleep."

"Alone?"

My cab arrived last night a little later than his van. When I came upstairs, the door was shut but the light was on. "I think."

"Good. When he wakes up, ask him whether he told the police anything. And have him call your uncle ASAP." Wilson pronounces it "a-sap," not "A-S-A-P." I wonder if he's ex-military. Maybe only officers' kids have names like "Bradford."

"I will," I start, but a knock at the front door might have drowned it out. I get up, head for the door. "Anything else, Mr. Wilson?"

"Yes. When you fill out the report, be as clinical as possible. It's a synopsis, not a narration. Don't ascribe motivation to anyone, just write up what happened."

Before I can quite react to that, I open the door, and UPS is standing there with an electronic pad thrust in my general direction. "Sign for this?"

Paul's warning flashes through my mind, but I pick up the stylus anyway. It's not signing for Nik, it's signing for a package. I scrawl a digital X on the line and take the box. It's dimensional enough that it's awkward to carry under one arm.

"Mr. Brooks?" Wilson asks in my ear. "Are you still there?"

"Yes, sorry. Had to get a package." The door shuts behind me, and I go on talking. "I heard what you said. And I understand. I'll be clear and won't add any details."

"Good. And I'm sorry you had to deal with that last night."

I set the box down next to the laptop, shut my eyes. "So am I. Thank you." It's the first anyone's outright apologized to me. I hadn't thought I needed it.

"Of course. Save my number. I'll call again when we've received the incident report."

"All right." And with that, I end the call.

There are things to take care of before the incident reports: budgeting, balancing, emails to shoot off. I still take a few minutes to get started, scroll absently through the spreadsheet toward the infinite corner, rows and columns I'll never use. Dina Marshall. Marshall. I'm not even sure I heard her surname at the concert. I don't remember Gabrielle's either. She's probably wrecked, somewhere. I hope she's not dealing with this alone. I remember what that was like. It's not my place to call her, and I'm sure it's the last thing she wants, but she said she and Dina were there with a couple of others. I hope they're dealing with it together. God, I can't do this.

I listen down the hall. Nik's breath is faint, but that's all the sound there is.

Lisette texts back at 9:38 a.m.: *Salted caramel! No joke. That, and the usual gargle. You okay?*

Fine, thanks, I lie through my thumbs.

Last night's check triggers my PayPal alert at 10 a.m. sharp. The money won't clear until Monday, and even when it does I've already withdrawn my five hundred dollars this month, but there will be more than enough in there for a loan payment. I could get a card to lift the PayPal ban so there's no cap on how much cash I can transfer. It's another thing to do. It's another thing to do that isn't this. I don't want to do *this*. *I never wanted to do this.*

By eleven, I've added the concert revenue to Nik's accounts, written the rent check and balanced the spreadsheet, emailed the bouncers and security guards to check in on last night's write-ups, and added a few application deadlines to my Google calendar. Seven floors down from here, New York breaks out of its hangover haze with traffic and chatter and the phenomenon of city wind, and I realize that I haven't put my earphones in all morning, that there hasn't been music. Not while I was running, not over breakfast, not even now, with a dozen computer tasks. It hasn't been silent, but I haven't tried to fill the world with anything else.

I close the laptop, set it aside, and listen.

My throat aches, the dry and slow sort of pain that means strain instead of rupture: the blood is close enough to the surface that I can hear it. It's mine. I have to remind myself, it's mine.

There are six incident reports to file. Two fights, one resulting in injury; two dealers; one for the three people getting it on in the alley, but only because a passerby called 911 assuming that someone hadn't consented. Let it not be said that New Yorkers are completely heartless. I thought, last night, that I'd find it funny in the morning. I don't.

The last report is for Dina Marshall.

No. Not yet.

There's still time. It's not as if I don't remember what happened, even the details they don't want. I reach over to the package, check the label. No manufacturer, a return address in what looks like Greek. I open it.

There's a new mask, wrapped in plastic and buried in foam. I draw it out, try to place the era. I'm no art historian, but I've taken a few electives, and with what little I know I can guess the mask is modern, maybe even contemporary, with workmanship so smooth it must be industrial. The expression is ecstatic: blown eyes and a bar of even teeth, a mouth so wide that if the mask were to be worn it would look as if the wearer had two smiles. The base is veined like marble, but not nearly as heavy, a rich horn color at the forehead and chin tapering to a darker flush across the nose. There are no nostrils for breathing.

Well. I have to find out where Nik keeps the hammers and nails anyway if there's a bookcase to build on Monday. And anything's better than dealing with last night. I leave the computer behind and the mask on the table, check through the logical places for hardware in the apartment until I find a hall closet near the studio with folded music stands and spare chairs and a wall of tools. I take one of the hammers and a box of nails, since there aren't any picture hooks, and try to find a space on the hallway wall for the new mask.

There's another knock at the door. I have no idea why this place bothers with a keyed elevator if anyone can just walk in.

I answer it.

"Detective Judith Lansing," one of the three people waiting says, badge out, "FBI."

I tuck the hammer behind my back. The last thing the FBI gets from me this morning is a black guy with a weapon.

"You're not Nik," Lansing says, peering up at me. She's not particularly tall or broad, and is wearing flat shoes, but she still manages to make me feel about six inches shorter with that look.

"I'm his handler." Shit. The FBI. Wilson didn't mention anything about this. No one did. No one *would*. *Assholes.* "Please, come in. Should I wake him up?"

"Not just yet. I assume you're Anthony Brooks?"

"Yes."

"Then I have some questions for you as well." Lansing strides in, right past me; there are two younger agents behind her, also in plainclothes, and they file into the apartment after her. One stands by the door, but the other takes the seat on the couch that I offer him and Lansing.

I am so fucked. My life is so fucked. "Can I get you anything? Water, coffee?"

The junior agent looks at Lansing as if he'll defer to her, but she says, "No, I've brought my own," and takes a bottle of water out of her purse. She wrinkles her nose, presumably at the lack of coasters, and pulls over a magazine to set the bottle on instead. "Thank you. Get whatever you need for yourself, Anthony. We'll be recording this conversation. I assume that's all right with you."

I am so thankful that I have my back to her while I set the hammer and nails on the counter next to the coffeemaker. "It's expected," I say, which isn't an answer.

As long as I'm in here I'll refresh my coffee and try not to jump out the fucking window. When I return to the living room, the agent by the door is looking uneasily at the wall of masks—I don't blame him, they're creepy as fuck—and Lansing and the other are watching me. Their eyes don't leave mine at all as I sit across from them. I set my mug down on the coffee table and slide the laptop farther away from the condensation on Lansing's water bottle.

"This is, of course, in reference to what happened at the Bowery Ballroom last night," Lansing says, with a measured tone that indicates we're already being recorded. "In specific, the death of Dina Marshall. I understand you were responsible for keeping the area around her clear until the EMTs arrived."

Something's not adding up. "Aren't you supposed to read my rights first?"

The corner of Lansing's mouth quirks. "No one is under arrest, Anthony. This is an interview. We're not searching the apartment, we're just trying to get your picture of the incident and clarify some of what we've seen in other accounts."

"I haven't filed the formal incident report with Nik's legal team yet." *Why the fuck is this my life?* "I'm sure you'll be able to request a copy of it for your investigation."

"I plan to. But there's a lot more to this than one girl's suicide. How long have you worked for Nik, Anthony?"

It's a harmless enough question, one I shouldn't be worried about answering without a lawyer present. "Less than a month. I arrived in New York on November sixth."

"And how aware were you of Nik's history?"

"History," I repeat.

Lansing glances at the junior agent holding the recorder, then squares eyes with me. I finally get a long look at her: late forties maybe, white but dark, a woman who dyes to cover the gray, and tans against her better interest. Nails with clear polish. Hard gray eyes. Something's off, but then, she's an FBI agent and maybe they all act like they wouldn't care if I got torn to shreds right in front of them.

"This isn't the first time a kid's killed herself at one of your boss's shows, Anthony," she says.

Outside, down at sidewalk level, someone shouts, "Get the hell out of the street."

"I had no idea," I say, for the record and for the sake of saying something at all.

Lansing doesn't smile. "Does it surprise you?"

There's too much of a cloud in my head for me to stop the words from coming. "Should it?"

"Well, it would surprise anyone else, considering how well your uncle's kept it out of the media."

Oh so it's *that* kind of conspiracy. At least it makes me less afraid to speak. "Guess it takes a white girl."

Never mind if the recording device picks that up: Lansing certainly does, and she huffs a disapproving gust out through her nose. "Dina Marshall is not the first white girl. And if you want me to talk about George Young Jr., who OD'd at one of Nik's shows last March in Philadelphia, we can talk about him instead. Twenty-two years old, already accepted into med school. Or Jack Walsh, who disappeared after a concert in Boston in June 2010. Or Yosuke Nakamura, who threw himself off a balcony at Nakano Sun Plaza when Nik was performing under his previous alias. We'll talk about them all you want, after you tell me your perspective on what happened to Dina Marshall last night."

Engines roar in my ears. "How many?"

"We're investigating Nik in connection with more than twenty incidents over ten years. Some are missing. Most are dead."

"I had no idea," I say again. I mean it more this time.

Apparently satisfied, Lansing picks up her bottled water and uncaps it. "Please tell me what happened to Dina Marshall last night, from your perspective."

I'm going to have to write this up anyway. Clearly this is the universe's way of punishing me for not taking care of it first.

"It's the same as I told the NYPD," I start, trying not to visualize it any more than I have to. It doesn't work. "I saw her climbing on to the rail and didn't make it in time to stop her. She jumped. I didn't see her land. I went downstairs to see if she was all right, and she wasn't. I kept people from moving her, identified one of her friends, and told her to get Dina's wallet and go with her in the ambulance. Once the ambulance got there I helped Bowery security keep the path clear and gave my statement to the police. After that I had to deal with clearing the space, since some people didn't care and wanted Nik back."

"Did Nik come back onstage?"

"No, not until wrap-up."

"Where is Nik now?"

"Asleep in his room. I saw him home at two in the morning, and I've been up since six."

"On a holiday weekend?"

"I run."

"All right. So you tried to stop Dina from jumping?"

"Yes."

"How?"

"I ran to her and yelled at her to get down."

"What were you doing on the second floor?"

"Getting drinks for the bouncers. The downstairs bar was too crowded."

"Drinks?"

"Coffee for one, Coke for the other." Paul's rules. Now I know why they're in place. I am so fucked.

Lansing nods, takes a drink of her water. "There are already numerous videos on the internet of how you handled the crowd after she jumped. You said you've only been working for Nik for a month?"

"Less."

"Where did you learn procedure?"

Uncle Paul. Years of Uncle Paul. Summers handling. Not enough. "Isn't that what you're supposed to do when someone might be paralyzed? You leave it to the specialists."

"It is. It's good of you to remember. What did you do in school, Anthony?"

"I'm a doctor of musicology."

"Of what?"

"Musicology. Music history."

"So you're not a medical doctor; you have your PhD."

The "just" is implied. "Yeah."

"Why are you working as a handler?"

I don't care what the recorder picks up in my tone; I am *not* answering that question. "Do you have any more questions for me, Detective Lansing?"

She doesn't laugh at me, doesn't smile, and lets it go. It's about the most decent thing she could do, I think. She screws the cap back onto the water bottle, replaces it on the magazine. "Can I expect your cooperation as this investigation develops?"

"This wasn't on the schedule," Nik says from the hallway, leaning on the wall in the gap between the masks.

So I don't get to answer, and get an eyeful instead. "Put some pants on, Nik, this is the FBI."

"Oh." Nik shrugs, shoulders past the first agent, and puts a hand on the back of the couch between Lansing and the second. I try to keep my eyes above his waist; thank fuck he's the right height that as long as he stays on the other side of the couch I can pretend he's got anything at all on. Fuck this. Fuck everything. Fuck *him*.

"Here," he says, "have a waiver."

He drops a paper, which wafts like a feather and drapes itself over Lansing's leg. She picks it up by the corner, gives it a glance and a sneer that shows she's seen these already, and hands it off to the agent beside her. "You evidently don't care that a girl killed herself last night."

"You don't get to tell me what I do and don't care about," Nik says. "Get a warrant or get out."

"We're not here to search the house," the agent by the wall says.

Nik turns, looks him up and down. The front of the agent's pants visibly distends, and he adjusts the panels of his jacket. Nik grins. "Looks like you've already found something you like."

I speak up somehow. "Nik, cut it out."

"Are you done talking? I am. I've got lawyers for that. If you've got the money, you can use them too." He flashes that same smile at me before he turns back to Lansing, and repeats, "Get a warrant or get out."

"Or what?" Lansing asks.

"You won't get me to say."

Lansing folds her fingers around the water bottle, taps one on the cap. The agent against the wall is still squirming, knees pressed close in an uncomfortably familiar posture. Maybe it's just Nik. Maybe there's something really *wrong*, other than *everything*. "You can't bury this under red tape and consent forms forever, Nik. Sooner or later, you have to take responsibility for what you do."

"I take responsibility for one thing," Nik says. "I make music. How you listen is your responsibility, not mine."

"I suppose that includes telling me to get a warrant or get out."

"Can't call the cops on the cops, I know. But if you want to talk to *Anna Magdalena*," he flicks a hand to indicate me, (and great, I've gone from Bach's sons to Bach's wives), "you can do it on the street. And only if he's stupid enough to keep talking without a lawyer."

He's right.

I tense my hands around the arms of the chair. The decision's not in them anymore.

I'm not sure when I shut my eyes, so I'm not watching, only listening, when Lansing stands up and gathers her things and associates. "Do you have anything more to say, Anthony?"

"He's right," I say aloud this time, still not looking at her. "I should file my report first and consult with the lawyers. I'm sorry, ma'am."

"I understand. If you want to learn about the other cases, please don't hesitate to give my office a call." When I open my eyes, Lansing is setting a business card down, in the ring of condensation her water bottle left on the magazine. "You did very well last night. Thank you for trying to help Dina Marshall. I wish it had worked."

"Get out," Nik says.

No one shows the agents the door, but they all leave. I stay in the chair, watch the light shift through the eyes of the masks as the shadows waver from the hall to the foyer. Nik sits on the back of the couch, looks down at the open package.

"You signed for this?"

I don't answer that. "You have a history of people killing themselves for you?"

"Yeah." Nik shrugs. "I'm going back to bed. Don't let them wake me up without a warrant."

"Paul said to call him," I barely remember to say.

"Figures. I'll call him from bed." He stands up, indicates the mask again. "Did you sign for this?"

"I put an X on the line."

"You hang it up, then." And with that, he leaves me alone in the living room.

The masks on the wall stare blankly down at me. I still haven't counted them. I get the hammer and nails out of the kitchen and add the new one in a slightly-too-small space near the door, between a blue feathered half-face mask and a red one with deep wrinkles and spikes through the cheeks.

The FBI just came to the apartment I live in by sufferance to question my involvement in the suicide of a teenage girl.

This isn't my life. That's the answer. I'm subletting someone else's. If this were mine, I'd have left it long ago.

I let my feet take me down the line as I look the masks over. Some have clear expressions: the squashed eyes and bared teeth of anger, the narrow triangles of arrogance, gaping sockets of fear; others have that schooled neutrality of workmanship and nothing else. For a moment, I think there's no joy on the wall, but I prove myself wrong not once but twice: two exuberant masks, one in the commedia style and one that must be Southeast Asian or Pacific. And a few others have, if not joy, a kind of peaceful acceptance, relaxation without resignation. But their number is relatively small compared to the dozens of others either contorted into rage or fear or polished into blankness.

By the time I've reached the door to Nik's room, I've stopped counting, stopped looking. Nik's door is open a crack, enough that

I don't feel guilty about checking on him until a second after I've done it.

Nik isn't alone in bed.

I remember. Gabrielle's last name is *Stuart*. It takes the sight of her face.

I shut the door and decide to reschedule both Skype interviews. As long as Nik's not too troubled by what he does to his fans, he might as well sleep. Someone should. I won't.

In the comments to the entry posted to asbrooks.com on November 25, 2011

LaurentTErikssen
You're working for someone famous? If so, congratulationss! I know it's not your side of the stacks buthat would be fun for anyone. So who is this guy?

EliseMorgenstern
Definitely famous. <u>Here's his wiki</u> and <u>here's the official site.</u> I'm surprised you haven't heard of him, Laurie, he's totally up your alley. If you need a paper next year maybe Anthony can build that bridge!

Basically, Nik's a neo-progressive rocker, but he's got a hook. He's the Dionysian spirit in music. "All the creation and all of the passion and all of the magic but none of the rules," that's his motto! And he keeps the persona up 24/7 from what I know. You can't even edit rumors into the wiki entry. His watchdogs are practically federal.

Anyway, yes, he's definitely famous. I've never been to a concert but I've crowdfunded a couple of his projects, bought an album, caught clips on youtube and stuff. I'm not one of the scary fans, I swear. Hey! Anthony! Is he coming out to California anytime soon?

juliamei
Seconding! He's a match for you Laurie. I just remembered that party and checked the wiki and he sounds like a hell of a project.

LaurentTErikssen
You're right, that's a good avenue for me, at least re: this summers Music and the Moving Image paper. Anthony, if you're up for it, can you get me an interviw?

Eusebius
Nik's a hack. But at least you're making money, Tony, so that's something.

EliseMorgenstern
Careful, Chuck, I hear the last time someone said this he got ripped to pieces.

jk

Has anyone taken Florestan for a name yet? This thread needs more Florestan.

Eusebius
You sound old.

Black Friday still has its chokehold on New York City on Saturday night. The Met Opera Shop is having a blowout, same as the rest of the city, and it's packed with people who aren't here for *Rodelinda*. The celebrity soprano singing the title role tonight has energetic interns out hawking every CD she's ever recorded. When I abandon the shop level to make my way to my seat on the top floor of the opera house proper, her book is out on tables—$40 unsigned, $100 signed—with relics and costume jewelry on display like some kind of postmodern yard sale. But I'm not here for her swag—or for her, for that matter, though I'm sure her performance will be as authentic and effective as reputed. I present my ticket at the topmost entrance, the one that leads to the score boxes house left.

It's not about Fleming, or Blythe, or Scholl, not to me; it's about Georg Friedrich Händel. And even if the money from last night is taking a hit, it's worth it as far as I'm concerned: music, real music, is worth anything. And the more of last night it drives out of my mind, the better.

With ten minutes to go and the grand chandeliers still lowered, I settle into my seat. It's my first time all the way up here, though I've been to the Met Opera House a few times before, and I'm a little surprised to find I'm not alone in the score box: an old white woman with an enormous shearling coat and glasses as thick as my little finger has the other seat at the lectern. She smiles up at me. No harm, no foul, so I tell her, politely, "Good evening, ma'am."

"Is there a problem?" she asks, shifting in her chair as if she can't quite rise.

I try not to assume fear or malice, but old white ladies can be assholes, so I sit down in my seat, to her left. "No, ma'am. I just wanted to know if you would rather turn the pages."

"Oh! Oh, I'm sorry, dear, I thought you were one of the ushers." That figures: no malice, just ignorance. I can let it slide. She goes on, "No, take the score, I'm only here to listen." She smiles, pats the arm of her chair. "Go ahead, scoot forward if you need to."

I do as she says. "A little expensive, just to listen."

"It's always better live," the old woman says. "I could go to those, what are they called? When they play them in the movie theaters."

"Live in HD."

"Yes, that's right. Live in HD. I suppose. But there's nothing like hearing Handel in a proper house. I can't see so well, dear, so I oughtn't deprive someone who wants to see everything of an orchestra seat. So I sit up here. It's worlds better than playing an old record."

It is one of the most beautiful things anyone's ever said to me, and just what I need to hear after last night. "I know exactly what you mean." I touch the corner of the score, thumb the pages. "Putting it in your ears is one thing, having it surround you is another."

She beams, tilts her head toward me, puts a hand against the ruffled collar of her blouse. "Oh, you sound so much like my first husband. He was a cellist. Such a snob, really, about everything else, but he was right about live performance. I remember, once, we got stuck in traffic in London, and he was so upset that we wouldn't make it to one of his friends' premieres, and his violist was in the car with us and said it was fine, they were recording it. My husband was so hopping mad we almost got rear-ended! Not that I think you'd do that, young man, I apologize, but he said almost the same thing."

"I don't mind." Well, maybe that statement would piss me off too. But it's more about being there to support the performers, in that case. He was probably mad about something else.

"Are you in the arts?" she asks.

"I'm a musicologist."

"Oh, that's lovely, dear! Are you studying Handel tonight?"

"I usually work on Bach," I admit as the lights dim and the chandeliers begin to lift toward the ceiling on their hydraulic wires. It's strange to see them coming closer as they disappear. "But tonight, I think I just need to hear this kind of sound."

From the score boxes, it's almost impossible to see the stage, let alone the pit, but I still applaud for the conductor with everyone else. The overture begins, and then the opera, and I'm more or less alone with the full orchestral score, following along with each part and each aria as if they're coming out of the page. Between the stately processionals, the sparse orchestrations around light and agile voices, and the frayed and yellowed edges of a score that, while not as old as the opera, is certainly older than the chair I'm sitting in, I let myself disappear. There are notes on the page, and they resound just as much as the voices and strings that ring off the acoustics.

I turn back the page for the return of *"Dove sei, amato bene?"* and I could swear, for a moment, that Scholl's ornamentation is printing itself on the score right in front of my eyes, as clear as it is in my head. There's a hum of approval in the crowd, as if each person here has given the music more surface area to reverberate on. It's exquisite, pervasive, that sense of the hollow parts in my skull filling from the inside.

Wait.

The music may not be as loud, and the effect not as pronounced, but it hits the same places as Nik's.

When the audience applauds for Scholl, my hands remain apart, one on the corner of the score and the other on my knee, both too tense to tremble.

"It's as I said, young man," the old lady says, applauding for a performance she can't even see. "This never happens with a record player."

NOVEMBER 27, 2011

On schedule, on schedule, on schedule. Never mind not having slept, everything else happens on schedule. I run, make coffee, check my mail. No word from the bouncers at the Bowery Ballroom, no word from the Feds, no word from Paul. I shoot off a quick message to Sydney asking whether she's back, and if she responds I'll ask if thirty-six hours is too long for Nik to be asleep. Five hours definitely wasn't enough for me.

"*Dove sei*," that aria from last night, is stuck in my head. Earphones laden with Bach and Britten don't quite get it out. Isn't the popular English version of "*Dove sei*," "Art thou troubled? Music will calm thee"? If it is, I'd like to punch that translator in the teeth.

I sit at the kitchen table just after nine in the morning, staring at a Sunday Times article online while my coffee gets cold.

"We have any food?"

"Presumably." I don't look up. I have no idea how long he's been there. For all I know, he's in my head.

Nik laughs, drums his fingers on my scalp as he strolls to the refrigerator. I swat at him and miss. Fine, he's real.

And awake. Guess I don't have to check—another item off the butler agenda.

I gather what little presence remains at the frayed forefront of my mind, shut my laptop, and swivel toward the fridge. Nik is rooting around in the crisper, comes up with a bunch of carrots and a jar of tomato sauce, and sits across from me in the same fluid motion. He opens the tomato sauce jar, grins, dips the back end of an unwashed carrot in and takes a bite right out of *Looney Tunes*. *Disgusting.*

"It's Sunday," I say.

"I know," Nik says, licking a curl of tomato sauce off his lower lip. "When am I supposed to do all the stuff I missed yesterday?"

"I pushed both interviews back to next week. You already had the *Tell All Your Friends* Skype scheduled for five tonight. *Now This Sound Is Brave* is at one in the afternoon next Saturday, *Alter the Press* next Sunday at three, and you've got practice tonight at eight but I don't know where."

"Here, I guess."

"It's *Sunday.*"

"Yeah, I know. Are you trying to make a refrain out of it?"

I sigh. "No, never mind, I'm sure your neighbors are used to it."

Nik dips the carrot again, brings it up, bites down. "There aren't neighbors."

"Don't tell me my uncle owns the apartment below this one too."

"No, they left last year and no one's stepped up since." He shrugs, works a kink out of his neck, leaves the half-eaten carrot propped against the bag. "Landlord's market."

"Or maybe people don't want to live under someone who plays loud music at all hours."

"So it's music." Nik smirks and leans in with an elbow on my closed laptop.

I try to hide my inevitable grimace with a sip of coffee. "I never said it wasn't music."

"You didn't. But you were thinking it, and you were trying not to think it, and now you know you're wrong."

The coffee is cold, but I fold my hands around the mug. I level my eyes at Nik, exhale hard enough to rustle the surface of the coffee. "What was that?"

"What?"

"At the Bowery Ballroom."

"Now you're wrong again."

"No, I know it was music, I just—"

"You don't know what music is."

My respective percentages of exhaustion and frustration are at just the right levels for me to only *say,* "Fuck you," not shout it.

And since I only *said* that, Nik smiles, takes another Bugs Bunny bite of his carrot, and shakes his head. "You shouldn't have to think about it. You already know it's true. Stop trying to take it apart until you find *why*. You don't need the why. Music just is."

"Right." I drone the party line, "'All of the passion and none of the rules.'"

"You make it sound like a bad thing."

"You have rules. Your music has rules."

"But they don't rule me, and they don't rule it."

I set the coffee mug down, and belatedly make sure to put it far away from both the jar of tomato sauce and the laptop, because that's a disaster in the making. "So that's all. Just music."

"Worked for you at *Rodelinda* last night."

Yeah, it's a disaster in the making, especially if he says anything that makes me twitch like that again. "I thought you said you didn't read minds."

"I don't. You brought the playbill home. Good show. About time they figured out Handel's tempi. Fleming's getting boring, though."

I can let it go. I should, since there wasn't an accusation. Smugness, yes, and an uncomfortable smirk, but no accusation. It's actually easier to deal with than the way Lansing looked at me yesterday. *Fuck, the FBI is after him, and I need a paycheck.* "What do you mean, it 'worked for me'?"

Nik wipes his mouth, takes a gulp of my coffee before I can stop him, and sets the cup back down on the wrong side of the computer. "'*Dove sei, amato bene?*'" he sings, an octave lower than Scholl sang it last night, without the smooth timbre of a professional but on rhythm, on tone. My shoulders chill. "'*Vieni, l'alma a consolar, a consolar.*' Odds are, that song worked for you. Handel wrote it that way. Scholl's as good as Senesino was, even if he still has his balls, and he understands the music. With a song like that, if you understand the music, you can share it with everyone else. That's how music works."

For a moment, I shut my eyes, as if that could force out the vestiges of Nik's song carved into my skull. It doesn't work, of course, but it does calm me out of saying half of the things I want to, none of which are acceptable now. *Your music kills people* would get me fired. *New-age bullshit* is pointless, since he knows and doesn't care.

I settle on, "So that's what you say you did," and even that doesn't sound right, because I can predict the answer down to the laughter.

But I can't predict just where Nik's laughter works its way into me, and echoes, and stays.

"It's what I am," Nik says, with the last traces of that laughter still threaded through the words.

I shake my head no, and move the coffee cup to the other side of the table, empty or not. "No. I'm sure you've gotten it right more than once, and I know what effect you can have. But Handel created reverence. You create—" I can't finish that. *Riots. You create riots.*

The part of me that is playing this for points knows, in this moment, that I've scored one. Nik's stillness is as terrifying as his manic audience: placid but not silent, never silent. If not for the glare on his face, which could peel paint, he could be asleep.

"And you create nothing," Nik says, all spite, no amusement at all.

This is done. This has to be done, now, and I should get up and shut myself in the shower and call the conversation over. But the part of me that hasn't slept more than three hours in the last two days and the part of me that's despaired of being what I should be ever again and the part of me that has "*Dove sei*" and "once we get in there they can't drag us out" still ringing in my eye sockets, those parts rule me now, and they speak first.

"What kind of god are you if you can't create reverent silence?" I ask, and don't have the energy to regret it.

I've seen people tear into each other at Nik's concerts. There aren't hands on my skin now, but I feel it peeling off all the same, like the curling edges of burning paper. There's a slight red and copper stain around Nik's teeth. His eyes match it. They're more gold than brown, even without Photoshop.

Deer really do stall in headlights. I'd know. I am one right now.

I should move the laptop off the table so Nik doesn't throw it. Then again, it might startle him like a mad dog—

"Five," Nik says, getting up. "You said five?"

". . . Yes," I say, more breath than words. "*Tell All Your Friends* at five." He's not going to do anything. Not here. Not today. He could, but not today.

"Got it." Nik leaves the carrots and the jar of tomato sauce where they are, turns his back on me on the way out. His skin shines around the labyrinth of tattoos. "And what are you doing until then?"

Applications for jobs that aren't you, I don't say. I don't have to.

It turns out not to matter, since Nik goes after that, and the sounds of a running shower taper through the hall half a minute later. Well, as long as Nik's throwing my schedule off, I might as well get started on what I need to do.

I check the clock five minutes later. It's moved and I haven't.

In the comments to the entry posted to asbrooks.com on November 25, 2011

LaurentTErikssen

You're right, that's a good avenue for me, at least re: this summers Music and the Moving Image paper. Anthony, if you're up for it, can you get me an interviw?

ASBrooks

I can try. It would have to be before the tour, but he's usually fine with Skype. I won't make any promises.

LaurentTErikssen

I am still in Finland now and then I am going to Korea until February and don't know if thereis reliable internet. Is it possible for me to interview him in person when I get back to Berkeley? When does thhe tour come through California?

ASBrooks

May 17th through Memorial Day he's in the state, NorCal first, and then until June 1st he's in Vegas. I'm not sure about the venues yet. I'll have to check with the manager, and I probably won't be with him on the tour to make that introduction, but if we work something out beforehand you should be fine. I'll bring it up with him later. And let's take this to email, I don't want to give anyone the wrong idea.

LaurentTErikssen
That"s just fine, thank you! It's cutting close to the conference, but I will still writehe paper, or a different one after I see the concert.

EliseMorgenstern
I want to know the INSTANT the tickets go on sale.

ASBrooks
Of course you do.

EliseMorgenstern
Why doesn't Nik have a Twitter?

Eusebius
Maybe because he can't keep the persona up in 140 characters or less.

ASBrooks
This isn't his blog, it's mine. Cut it out.

DECEMBER 2, 2011

Tonight I will make like the bouncers and stay the hell away from the alcohol, for liability's sake if nothing else. I will keep my earplugs—not earbuds, actual plugs, the strongest I could get without a prescription—in at all times. I will remain backstage as much as possible, as lucid as possible, and as uninvolved as possible, because even if I'm standing in for Sydney for the third fucking time (through no fault of her own, anyone would get sick after being snowed in at an airport in Buffalo for two nights, and she's lucky it's only the flu and not some kind of anthrax), it's not my place. It's only my job.

And I will spend most of the concert in persistent terror that all these precautions only give strength to Nik's claims.

The earplugs are only for protection. The lack of alcohol is only sensible. The music is only as powerful as the people make it, and every fight that breaks out is caused by drugs or hype or sheer fucking stupidity. I have a mantra: only this, only that. And I convince myself, in this remarkable sobriety, that if Nik can make everyone crazy, I can make them sane. I can make them sane. I can make them sane.

It's easier to lie through my thumbs than it is to lie through my ears.

DECEMBER 3, 2011

"Anthony, good to hear from you."

"Mrs. Nerida. Is this a bad time?"

"I'm still sick, so we should probably keep it short, but no. Any reason you'd rather not email?"

"Several," I say, "but the main one is that the network I've been stealing from at the apartment finally got wise to me and I still haven't found Nik's wireless password. I can't do everything on my phone."

"Ha. Make him let you use the desktop and go straight through the router."

"I will when he wakes up."

"Still under?"

"It's only noon." At least there's no groupie today, as far as I know. I settle onto the couch, ignoring the way the nearest masks catch the overhead lights—well, evidently I can't ignore it. Noon or not, it's slate-gray outside, the sort of concrete sky a subway poet would spend an entire poster describing. No wonder the pleasantries hang in the air: it's too thick for them to be anything but awkward additions. "Does Nik usually sleep for a whole day?"

The sounds Sydney makes on the other side of the phone aren't quite laughter, or if they are I've missed the joke. Maybe that's how she coughs. "It depends. You'd have to ask Paul. I've known him to be more likely *to* sleep after they play, but if there's a pattern I guess you could say that he sleeps after good nights."

"So three arrests is what you'd consider a good night."

"Three arrests is a night. I wouldn't measure good and bad by what happens to the fans."

Whether they die or not, she means. Morbid curiosity can only keep me in this game for so long, right? "What would you measure it by?"

"How many fans there were. I do this for the money, Anthony, not the love. Even the ones who get arrested already paid for their tickets and aren't getting that money back. If you want to quantify the quality, ask the critics."

It occurs to me that, based on Sydney's tone, sick and harried as it is, she finds this funny. I don't. I probably never will, scare chords and all. But I can snark back with as much cheer as she deserves. Laughter is, after all, the best medicine. Maybe if I start seeing the fun in this I can get out. "And if you go by the critics, everything he does is without fault."

"Not everything— Sorry, give me a second." She sneezes magnificently. The iPhone transmits the sound such that it's like being in the room but thankfully not getting sprayed. Technology is truly a marvel.

"Gesundheit."

"Thanks," Sydney says around a sniffle. "Anyway, no, not everyone either. He has detractors. They just tend to say what they say and stop after that. Most people work on the principle that no press is worse than bad press as far as Nik's concerned."

"Unless people die," I say, aloud this time. "Then no press is the only press."

"Do you really want to know what effect that press would have on him?"

"You have a point." This conversation is doing nothing for my headache. I lean forward elbows to knees, switch which hand the phone is in. "But three arrests, Mrs. Nerida."

"And six last week. And I've been at concerts where they've posted so many cops outside that it makes Occupy Wall Street look like a parade. They go with the territory."

"But what do you *do*?"

"Exactly what I told you to do. Keep your head above water, keep the band playing, keep the audience happy."

"They're not very happy when they get dragged off by the cops."

"No, but Nik is, and he's priority one."

"He must think exceedingly highly of his fans."

"His fans get hauled in for enjoying him too much. I think Nik thinks higher of them than you do."

"You're right, I don't think highly of people who wreck their résumés on Nik." *Or their lives.*

This time it's easier to tell that Sydney's laughing before she starts coughing. And the coughing goes on for a minute or more, peppering all the false starts until she gets through a sentence. "You don't think highly of many people. But yes, some of Nik's fans are pretty pathetic."

This position does nothing for the headache either, so I double back into the arms of the couch. Nik's schedule for the remainder of the day is up on my computer. I should deal with that. *I'm his fucking butler.* "To tell you the truth, I don't think highly of him either."

"He knows," Sydney says.

"Well at least it amuses him."

"Nik can find amusement in just about everything."

"Right, right, Dionysus."

"No, I think he'd enjoy this whether the rest is true or not."

Well, that's a hope spot for the headache if I ever heard one. "You don't believe? Thank fuck, finally there's someone sensible about all this—"

"I never said that."

I switch the phone back to my right hand.

"Managing Nik's career is my job," Sydney says, "just like managing his day-to-day life is yours now. I've got enough distance to deal with him as an artist, nothing more. So whether I believe in him in, ha, in the Greek sense, doesn't matter. I believe in his work, I believe it's worth promoting, and I believe in his ability to sustain the reception that comes with his promotion of that work. It's true, none of the other artists that I book for have to contend with this much . . . Nik. This many incidents. But that's part of how Nik has decided to market himself. And all I deal with is the marketing standpoint, so whether I believe or not isn't my concern, or his. Just the work."

I wait until she's done coughing again to say, "And you believe in the work."

"I believe his work is good enough that he should have a manager in order to keep producing it on the scale he's producing."

"But you don't think I can afford that distance."

"You're the one who has to live with him. I only managed that for six months."

"Six months," I repeat. "If I'm lucky I'll be out before the tour."

"It's that bad," Sydney says. It's not a question.

"Yeah," I answer anyway. "I know part of it's me, not him, but yeah."

"I'll give you the same advice I gave you about the pit, then. Head above water, Anthony."

"And what about the rest of me?"

"You can only keep your head above water if you're using the rest to tread."

The desktop in the studio has two flat-screen monitors attached, and the Skype window is already waiting on one while Nik works on the other. I really would have appreciated him using headphones while he samples, since if there is one thing more annoying than hearing half-finished music you don't like, it's hearing half-finished music you don't like at one-fourth speed one track at a time. But I have an ink cartridge to install in the printer because I am his fucking butler, and I am subject to his bullshit.

At one o'clock sharp, an incoming call window pops up in the middle of the Skype screen. Nik, apparently, doesn't notice, so after half a minute passes I remind him. "*Now This Sound Is Brave.*"

"Not yet," Nik says, and if I wasn't sure he was doing it deliberately, I'd wonder if Nik was lost in the tracks.

"No, they've already called. Hit Accept."

He blinks, leans back in the chair, and swivels it a little too far at first, forgets the mouse. Maybe he really was absorbed. But he clicks into Skype without a problem. "Hey."

"Hey there!" The interviewer is a cheerful young woman, white, with dark hair in that vintage Rosie-the-Riveter style and a lip ring. She notices me over Nik's shoulder, so I give her a quick wave to be polite, then go back to work. I can't believe I'm doing this with three degrees. "Thanks for rescheduling and everything," she says to Nik, though I was the one to reschedule.

"As long as you still want to hear me, any time's fine," Nik says.

The interviewer laughs. I am impressed with but not surprised by the quality of Nik's computer speakers. "Definitely. I'm sad it's taken so long to get a personal interview up on the site. I caught one of your shows when I was visiting New York two years ago. Why have you waited so long to do a stateside tour?"

Nik grins. "Travel arrangements take more time than they're worth."

Especially when you're being tailed by the Feds, I think in his general direction, as loudly as I possibly can. He doesn't flinch. I guess it's proof that he can't read minds.

"Right, right, I can imagine." The interviewer takes a long drink of bottled water on her side of the screen, then sets it down out of sight. "Okay, so we have to get a few bureaucratic things out of the way before we get started. I sent over the consent form and you scanned it back, but you forgot your signature."

"I don't sign things."

"I realize that, but in order for me to record you today and publish your interview we have to have consent."

"My signature isn't consent. My word is consent."

I look back into the innards of the printer.

The interviewer's laugh is less easily picked up by her computer's microphone this time, and the static enhances her nervousness. "Okay. Uh. Well, if you don't want to give us a free autograph, I can respect that. Should I just put an X on the line?"

"You can put whatever letters you want on the line," Nik says.

Correction: there are at least *two* things more annoying than music you don't like, and one of them is the sound of uncomfortable laughter across state lines and two computers.

"Okay, sure," the interviewer says. "I'll just do that right now." And she riffles through the stack of papers on her desk, comes up with Nik's faxed consent form, and holds it up to the camera, blocking everything else out. "Do I have your permission to sign this on your behalf?"

"I thought you said you just needed a signature."

"The *yours* was implied."

I remember what he wrote on mine. *Congratulations. You're next. I'm game.* It's bullshit. It's all bullshit. He's a scam artist and a charlatan, and I'm his fucking butler.

Nik leans closer to his computer's camera, and even if he can't see the interviewer, it's pretty clear that she'll see him, daring and glowering like a Hot Topic Homicidal Maniac. "You have my permission. You can use this interview however you want. But whatever you put on that piece of paper isn't my signature. If the verbal agreement isn't enough for you, we're done talking."

"Can I . . . have your word on that?"

"I thought I just gave it to you."

"Okay," the interviewer says, and then again. She pulls the paper away from the camera and sets it down on the desk, worries at her lip ring, then takes a pen and scrawls a quick X at the bottom of the page. "It's enough for me. I hope it's enough for the admin, and if it's not I'm sorry."

The previous ink cartridge is staining my fingertips. Shit. I really should concentrate.

"All right," Nik says. "So let's get started."

"Well, since we just ran into a hurdle about your persona, let's dig into that first. What made you choose to present yourself this way?"

"This way how?"

"Ha, you've got a point. I guess it's better to ask you why you are the way you are."

"Because that's how music is," Nik says, leans back in the chair, and swivels it slightly. "If you ask a song why it is the way it is, all you get are notes passing through time. I don't think that's what you want to ask me."

"No, it's fine. And that's a fine answer. Um. In that case, do you choose anything about how you share yourself and your music with the world?"

"Of course I do. Sound without choice isn't music."

The computer screen has enough of a reflection to show Nik's looking right at me, and if there were hackles on the back of my neck they'd be standing on end. So this is his argument. Great.

"People like to use that logic to try and take me down a peg," Nik says. "They say that music needs rules to be music. It doesn't. You can have music without rules, without form. But you can't have it without choice. Choices turn into rules when you make them too many times. So, yeah," he goes on, turns back toward the computer's camera, eyes as gold as they were when last I looked, "I make choices. I'm making choices right now. I could have gone easy on you about the signature, and I chose not to. I choose my chords, my tunes, my lyrics. I even choose to use the same ones again, in the same songs, sometimes," he laughs. "Things don't spring fully formed out of my head. That's someone else's technique."

The interviewer laughs too, less nervous now. I envy her that. And the fact that she's doing what she loves, as far as I can tell. "So how would you describe your technique?"

"Distillation."

Fuck, I almost caught my fingers in the printer's gears.

"Seriously?" the interviewer asks.

"Distillation," Nik says. "You asked."

"Can you elaborate?"

"I take what I want to say and I filter it through what I am."

There. The empty cartridge is out, without too much of a clatter and no ink anywhere but my hands. No, I'm wrong, the interviewer's looking at me now, over Nik's shoulder. I wave her off. *It's fine. It's none of my business. It's not my job.*

She fidgets with her trackpad. "Can you maybe give an example?"

"What, my music doesn't speak for itself?"

"It does, but talk about a choice you've made in, say, 'Last Against the Precipice.'"

"Song or album?"

"Song. Talk about the lyrics. I've always loved the classical symbolism in your lyrics."

"What symbolism?"

"Well, I've always thought it was an allusion to the myth of Prometheus. 'Last,' like last in line, and 'last,' like last forever, chained to the rock."

"I just thought the words sounded good together."

"Ha, really?"

"No," Nik says, opens his arms almost like he's stretching his smile with his fingertips. "I know about the wordplay. And I'm sure it means something if you take it apart. But what the lyrics mean is going to change anyway, so why does it matter what I meant when I wrote it?"

"What about the instrumentation? Why'd you design the electronic track the way you did?"

"Because it's what was right for the song."

"Okay, okay, your process is your business."

"No, you can go ahead and analyze it if you want to. I can tell you want to. I'm just telling you why I did what I did. If you want to figure out why it *works*, I can't tell you that."

"Why not?"

"Because if it works for you, it works."

Bullshit. I wedge the printer cartridge into place. It's bullshit. *Not after what you said about* Rodelinda. If Handel made a piece that worked, he knew why it worked. Bach too, Bach more. Bach especially. It works because of counterpoint, progression, instrumentation. It works because of knowing what expectations your audience has and either playing to them or subverting them.

"Something to share with the class, Wilhelm Friedemann?" Nik is leaning over the back of the chair, looking at me the way a bat or a possum might.

Possum. Definitely a possum. A possum with nothing better to do than eat and fuck groupies and continuously throw around the Bach family composers as if I should take offense. "Do you recycle your dead cartridges?"

"That's up to you."

"Get out, your name's actually Wilhelm Friedemann?" the interviewer asks.

"No. It isn't." I shut the printer lid and ask Nik, "Is it safe to leave you alone with her?"

"Safe as anything else I do."

It's not an answer, but I'm done with this shit. I take the empty cartridge and the packaging for the new one and crumple them both in my fist on the way out.

"So tell us about the upcoming tour," the interviewer says, and Nik starts laughing just as I shut the studio door.

"It'll be exactly what you expect it to be."

DECEMBER 4, 2011

(to be) Posted to asbrooks.com on December 4, 2011

"Well, Fuck"

Last night, because I was absolved from shepherding Nik, I attended a candidate recital at NYU. In order to make certain that this entry is unsearchable, I will not cite whose recital it was, or what famous people were conscripted to play the material in question, or whom I spoke to afterward. Let it not be said that the performers weren't talented, or that the compositions in question were, if not necessarily to my taste, not meritorious in their contribution to an otherwise half-dead field. There wasn't anything wrong with the evening itself, because there's nothing wrong with music, unless it isn't music, and whether aleatory, chance-music, and improvisation constitute music is a debate that has been going on for far too long for my opinion to be worth shit.

It may be music. It may not be. Frankly, it's none of my business. But whether a program consisting entirely of aleatory and improvisation is acceptable for a DMA in Composition's dissertation *is* my business, because the equivalent in my field would be putting quotations and score excerpts on the wall, throwing eggs at them, and seeing what sticks. I wouldn't have been published if I tried that, and neither would any of you, and to hear this DMA candidate praised for his lack of work was, to put it bluntly, offensive.

But I probably shouldn't have said so aloud.

Speaking of chance, I should have checked whom I was conversing with at the reception after the recital. I don't have anyone to blame for that but myself. I'm supposed to know who the luminaries are at that school and I did think she looked familiar. Yes, she's the kind of person I see at the AMA. Yes, I said some things I shouldn't have to someone on the dissertation committee of the recitalist.

Yes, people *do* say, "You'll never work in this town again."

So that's it, I guess. There's no point in making contacts at NYU anymore, at least not among the faculty, because any time my name comes up I'm sure they'll be alerted to the presumptuous, self-absorbed peripatetic scholar who criticizes his betters to their department heads. Which basically means that if I don't find a tenure track position before word makes it back to the West Coast, I am about as fucked as a surfboard salesman in Alaska.

The internet is down.

The *stolen* internet is down. Again. The apartment internet appears to be in perfect working order, not that I can access it.

On the one hand, it's for the best, because actually posting that blog entry means nothing but trouble, mockery, and the probable lack of comments regarding anything but Nik, Nik, Nik.

On the other, it's the principle of the thing, and at this point I don't have much left aside from my principles.

By the time I barge down the hall to the studio, not even my principles matter. The studio isn't locked, and Nik isn't in it, maybe not in the apartment at all. Good. So I sit down at the desktop, bring up a new browser window on the left-side screen, and look up the modem directly.

The wireless password, it turns out, is 4G4V3BR00K5. Forgave Brooks? No. Agave. Agave Brooks.

"What's the wireless password?"

"Your mom," he said. Fucking hysterical.

As long as I get off the computer now, I can just tell Nik I looked up the password personally and not get into trouble. I'm not sure he'd care anyway if I was in here, but it can't hurt to be cautious. I close the browser window, push back the computer chair—

—right as the Skype Accept button pops up on the right-side screen.

It's Sunday, three o'clock. *Alter the Press* is on the line, and it's eight o'clock in the evening in England, and they have places to be and things to do that aren't sit and wait, and Nik isn't here.

I click Accept.

"Afternoon," the caller says. "It's afternoon where you are, right?" Over the computer speakers, I can't place where in England the interviewer's accent comes from. The camera reveals him to be a little younger than I and a lot darker. "Sorry, did I call the wrong person?"

"No, Nik's supposed to be here," I say. "I think he stepped out. There's probably subway trouble on the way back. But I can reschedule you with him again if you need me to."

"Oh, you're his minder," the interviewer says. "Thanks for rescheduling us earlier. Nice to meet you. I'm Frank."

"Anthony."

"Cheers. So what do we do now?"

"I can keep this up for a few minutes in case he comes back, and if he doesn't, we should use that time to reschedule if you're available."

"We should. The head keeps having trouble with his info. Could you clear a few things up for us?"

Of course they're having trouble; everything's fake. I drum mirrored arpeggios on the arms of the desk chair. "Sure." I'll tell them what they need to know. I might figure something out in the process anyway.

"Great," Frank says. "Give me a bit, I'm bringing up the file . . . There. So, his real name?"

Well, that answer's easy. "I don't know."

"Even you don't know?"

"Yeah. Nicholas or something, I guess."

"You mean he keeps it up even with his help?"

He seriously just called me the help. Well, he's English. It might not mean the same thing over there. "He keeps it up, and it's annoying as hell."

"So, what, does he order off menus in Ancient Greek?"

"Ha. No. But you're not the only ones that have trouble with his paperwork. He's cagey about everything that isn't his music. The last interview I saw him give, he wouldn't even talk about his process."

"That's a pity. That's most of what we want to ask him."

"You're going to get shit," I warn. "Sound bites and shit. That's what he deals in."

Frank laughs, startled, and types a quick note. "Well, if you don't think we should reschedule at all, I can appreciate that—"

"No, go ahead and interview him if you get the chance. You'll make bank in ad revenue." *Unless someone dies.* Which happens far too often. Fuck, this is my life. *Then you'll just get shut down.* Why hasn't Lansing followed up on Dina Marshall's death? Wait, stupid question. Because the legal team is running her in circles. They know what to do in case of suicide.

They probably know what to do in case of mine. I'll bet there's a chart.

"Maybe I should get the *Daily Mail* on him, then," Frank says.

It's clearly intended to be sarcastic, but I take it seriously, because that's what Nik deserves. "I'm sure he'd find something to do with it. What would the headline be, 'Crazy Yankee Thinks He's Dionysus, Starts Orgies at Concerts'? It would sell."

Frank's jaw hangs. "*Starts* orgies? I mean, I've seen the stuff on the internet, but he starts them himself?"

I refuse to say, *Yeah, with his music.*

"Anyone coming to a concert has to sign a waiver absolving Nik of any legal responsibility for their actions," I say instead. I need to stop grinding my teeth, it's making the headache worse. "It's more like an invitation."

This time, Frank's laughter crosses over from uneasy to uncomfortable. "Is that legal in the States?"

"Fuck if I know. But I'm not convinced he's concerned. People get hauled in for what they do at his shows and Nik's record stays clean. Sure, they're idiots, but it's still his fault."

"Does it carry on after the concerts? I mean, is he the partying type? Wait, stupid question, of course he is," Frank says, rapping himself lightly on the head, "he's Bacchus."

"He's dangerous." Something in me *gives*, and the headache's gone for a couple of blissful seconds. I finally said it. I finally said it, and something in my head is quiet and at peace. "He's a scam artist with a cult, and if one fewer person in the world buys into him by the end of the day I will consider my job *done*."

And he's leaning on the doorframe right now, exhaling an audible breath through his teeth. His mouth glares as harshly as his eyes.

Fuck.

I hold tight to the arms of the desk chair. Frank's next question is only sound, not words, prattling on in the background like the static that frames it.

Nik stalks into the studio, rounds the guitar stands, rests one hand on the top of the monitor. No one has looked at me like this since the man who mugged me when I was fifteen.

"It's not Nicholas," he says in a low growl that sets off every alarm in my head, all at once, "it's Nikos."

I keep my mouth shut. This isn't a victory. This is a tactical retreat. This is my life. I push back the desk chair to stand and leave. Nik doesn't touch me on my way around and out.

"Oh good," Frank says on a computer screen I can no longer see, "now we don't have to reschedule."

I wait in my room for an hour, earbuds stuffed in my ears. The Bach harpsichord concerti aren't loud or chaotic enough to drown out the world, so I switch to rap and try to focus on the rhythm. There's a lot of it. There should be a lot of it. It doesn't work. Nothing works. Nothing works, and I have nothing, aside from the certainty that I've ruined an already wasted life.

The simple fact is that none of the recordings are loud enough. None of them cut to the heart of the music. None of them make me the music. If I were the music, I wouldn't have to be *me* now.

Fuck this. Earbuds out, phone down. The house is quiet, not silent but quiet: the heater thrums in the corner, electricity buzzes in the walls. The sweat on my feet leaves prints on the hardwood floor, and once the footsteps cut through the air the space closes around the sound like a storm cloud. The studio door is open, the lights still on, and if I'm going to leave the apartment, I should turn them off. I don't. I go in.

I sit down on the piano bench, level my hands over the lid to shut it. They slip, and settle on the keys instead.

If I could transcribe the ridiculousness in my head right now, it would be on level with the most complex polyphony ever written; Stravinsky's, Xenakis's, Berg's. *Nik is a liar*, in the bass and the timpani.

You're going to end up on the street, a patter ostinato in the middle strings. *You never should have tried to make anything of yourself, they're right to not support you*, two contrapuntal, lyrically dissonant melodies in the winds. And if all of those themes are tonally and melodically related, the completely incongruous *Go ahead, he can't hurt you* and *This will calm you down* and *He doesn't deserve your help anyway* plane through it all, a rhythmically steady focal point in the chaos. *"Don't play your math on my instruments,"* Nik said. That's not just a theme, that's the pedal, the cantus firmus, the rule.

He doesn't get to make the rules. *I do.*

Invention 13 in A minor begins in my left hand and spreads to my right. The melody is simple, straightforward, and the counterpoint is a precise echo and support and sequence. Action passes back and forth between my hands, an intricate choreographed dance. Establish the key, charge into the theme, step down one hand at a time until the tune unwinds into a countermelody that isn't *counter* to anything, it's perfect, it's *easy*, and I'm a part of it for the minute it takes to play the piece too fast. It, and nothing else.

"I told you not to do that," Nik says behind me.

I'm too drained to be startled. It's the second time today, after all. I don't even turn around. My hands flatten on the keys, and they sink but don't sound.

"So what," I say. "So fire me."

Nik's breath is more like a scoff than a laugh, but not really either, and he grabs me by the neck and spins me around, shoves me onto the keyboard shoulders-first. All the white keys in a row behind me crunch and resound, and I have to wonder, distantly, if "fire me" isn't the wrong idiom and "set me on fire" would have been more appropriate.

Guitarists have weird fingernails. They're not as weird when only one set of them is biting into my scalp. Why am I not as angry as I could be?

"You break my rules, fine, I'll break yours," Nik says, or sings, or something between.

There is a song in my head.

It's not a song I've heard before. If I'd heard it before, I'd have asked after the unequal temperament, the alternate scale, the unmetered rhythm. I'd remember. It's not noise—I know it isn't noise, it's too *planned* to be noise—but it has the ease and spontaneity of birdsong or shattering glass.

It's untranscribable.

Nik is gone, Nik's been gone for the last hour at least. I've been sitting at the piano for most of that time, scratching at my throat until I force myself to stop. There aren't any bruises or scrapes on it, or on my scalp. I've checked in the window and the computer screens. I should use a mirror. I haven't. I don't.

Nik's piano has been recently tuned. A440 standard tuning is in effect. It's the same on the keyboard. I know this because I've tried and failed to find the starting note of this fucking song several times now, and it's closest to A440, higher than the G-sharp below it but not equally between. It isn't a quartertone or a blue tone. It's also not *wrong*. It's the exact right note for the tune to start on, just like the note it moves to is the right note to succeed it, and the turn after that and the figure after that and the overall contour, a macrocosm of itself but not, but warped, twisted, and overgrown, larger and organic and rhapsodic.

There is a song in my head. It has no motif. It has no meter.

This is ridiculous. I shouldn't be sitting here puzzling it out. Sunday or not, there are things to do: jobs to find and writing samples to truncate and Nik's practices to schedule if I care about that, which I'm not sure I do. I should. I don't have anywhere else to go, and Nik hasn't fired me.

Nik. *Ha.* Trust him to keep the act up even now. I could laugh about this, might someday when I'm a little less rattled. No bruises, no hurt, no threats. I expected to have to fight back but there wasn't anything to fight, just words and a touch and that slaughtering smile, and then Nik patted me on the head like a begging dog and left me here. And once I could catch my breath again, there was the song.

I abandon the studio, take my phone to the living room and grab the laptop, ignoring the masks. I access the apartment wireless. The password is still 4G4V3BR00K5. It's still a bad joke. And I have no idea how he knows my mother's name, because Paul doesn't talk about my family at all, let alone her. I delete the blog entry I planned on posting without even rereading it. There are better things to do with my time than complain to the ether. I bring up my résumé and edit the header to reflect this address, though I might change it to Paul's or something if I can move out. Soon. Or now. Now would be best.

Once I get in there— There is a song in my head. I'm typing to its rhythm.

Fine. If I can type it, I can transcribe it, right? I set the laptop aside, get some staff paper and a pencil from the studio, bring them back to the living room, and spread the paper out on the coffee table. The first note is longer than the next, but they're not divisible, the ratio's not there at all, or if it is, it's irrational. Messiaen would have a field day with this. I sketch the tune out, what's long and what's short and what's in between, time it with the second-counter on my watch. There's math, there, but it's not in base ten or base eight or base seven or anything that can be broken into pieces of a reckonable size.

I put the pencil down, leave the notes and numbers where they are. It's pointless. It shouldn't matter. There's work. Applications. Revisions. Calls for papers. But the rhythm still comes out of my fingers, unplanned, unsustained.

I shut the computer.

Fuck. If I can't let it out, I'll drill it out. I put my earbuds in and let Bach take over. A steady stream of sixteenth notes at standard metronome allegro floods my ears, settles on the inside. I force myself to count along like I'm twelve again and learning this piece for the first time, like I don't even know where to put my hands but always, always I know how to count. I know how to count.

The notes slur, bleed, tangle. The Invention isn't in A minor anymore. Or any minor. Or any key at all.

There is a song in my head, and not even Johann Sebastian Bach can get it out.

Forget it. Forget this, forget everything. If music only feeds that fire, I'm turning it off. I rip the earbuds out, and the music keeps playing—on the phone. I turn that off too. I can't listen. Or, more accurately, I can't *not* listen. Because *there it is*, in the rhythm of my thoughts and the exasperation of my breath. The hiss of air escaping the couch, the scrape of my shoelaces through their eyelets, the cranking of the elevator gears: they're part of it now. They illustrate the song. They bolster it, accompany it.

I walk into the streets. The crowd from the avenues has bled out this far, even on a Sunday night, and for a moment there's the respite I crave, because there's noise out here. Traffic and trucks and overflowing restaurants and people yammering into their phones, wheels on concrete and tar, and feet on rubber and metal: *noise*. Noise too thick and too present for me to have a song in my head. I breathe as if that could take the sounds into me, fill my head instead of clear it. There. Better. And as long as I'm here I should take care of something, anything, groceries or winter clothes or printer paper.

I forgot to zip up my jacket in the elevator, so I do it now. The song climbs out of the zipper teeth.

My mind tries to take the tune apart, as autonomic as the neurons firing to make me breathe, blink, walk.

By the time I reach the corner of this block, I have music instead of a heartbeat.

DECEMBER 7, 2011

There is a song in my head. It's been playing for over two days. I breathe to its rhythm. I blink to its articulation. I can't chew food or swallow water without restarting the phrase in my head. If I sit around and do nothing, it loops like a car alarm, which means lying in bed with my eyes closed is the worst of all. I'm not exaggerating, even if this sounds like a load of melodramatic crap. I've lost sleep over less than this. I'm losing sleep *now*.

But my alarm goes off at 6 a.m. like any other day, and I run.

Forgetting the phone isn't a mistake, it's a conscious decision, one I force myself to make, because plugging up my ears does nothing when the song is already between them. I run, and breathe, and if my feet pound the pavement to someone else's rhythm, I try to ignore it.

I can't drag it out.

I can't. It's there.

South is a mistake. I go anyway. It's louder on Houston Street, even more so when I cross it, with engines grinding and radios blaring and the metronome ding of a pictorial Don't Walk. They're still the song. They're all still the song. It's still in my head, and everything feeds it. I run. I turn a corner onto a street with a name instead of a number. The font smears into a white haze on the sign. I try to home in on that. Color. Words. Anything that isn't music, that isn't putting the song to words. I spell out the names of the stores I'm passing, count how many times my feet hit the pavement. How many times? Twelve. Sixteen. *How many times* in a beat as steady as I can make it, regular as a racing heart. I can't keep time. I can't force the song into time. I can't force myself into time.

Even my feet move to the song.

Fine. I'll stop them. I'll stop everything.

I stop everything three quarters of the way across a two-way street, against the light. If I'm lucky it'll be silent on the other side.

Incongruously, I remember when I was fourteen, on tour with a band Paul had only just started representing. The bus ran over a deer. It was after midnight, and I was up in the front trying not to bother the driver, probably failing. I saw everything. Deer really do stall in headlights.

The truck that's about to hit me is an artificial green. Headlights aside, I can see my reflection in the silver grating over the hood.

Someone grabs me by the neck, sends me hurtling backward. No, the impact's supposed to come from the front. Things should be bruising and destroyed and quiet. The song is still in my head even if everything else has stopped and *I want it out*. But everything hasn't stopped. *Nothing* has stopped. My back is flush against something solid but not as solid as pavement. The world is still vertical. I'm on a traffic island in the middle of Delancey Street and some Good Samaritan is shouting at me and it turns out there *is* a Starbucks this far south in Manhattan, and everything is fucking hilarious.

And the laughter brings the song screaming back.

"Fuck you," I say. It doesn't work. No one hears me. *I don't hear me.*

I wake in bed—a bed, my bed at Nik's, can't think of it as mine but it is, isn't it? I stare through the darkness toward the ceiling. The song's not gone. I'm on top of the covers, my running clothes caked to my body with sweat. It's disgusting. What day is it? Probably still Wednesday. It might not be. I have so much shit I should be doing. I'm not sure I care. My fingertips are drumming on the mattress. My eyelids scrape through a hard crust at the corners. Yes, they're both the song.

Nik is sitting on the edge of the bed. His eyes shine, but he's not smiling. I expected him to smile. It's his fault.

"It's not gone," I say. It's not a question.

"No," Nik agrees. The sliver of his teeth flashes, just once, around the vowel of the word.

I breathe. It's about all I can do. Nik's breath, softer, is a counterpoint, a pulse under mine. Mine's still ragged, still running. I'm still running.

"What do you want?" Nik asks.

There's only one answer to that. "Get it out," I whisper. "Get it out. You put it there so get it out—"

I didn't think we were close enough to touch, but here we are, and I'm babbling into Nik's mouth. It isn't a kiss. It's my head held in Nik's hands, my body pinned to the bed, my mouth opening and closing on words that Nik laps up and swallows. The song floods me, reds out my eyes like a nightmare.

What the fuck.

That's the clearest thought I've had in two days. *What the fuck.*

"Can't get it out if you don't let it go," Nik says, and the words have a taste.

"What the *fuck*?" I manage, aloud this time. My lower lip catches on Nik's when they flare apart after the *f*. Heat gathers in my jaw. *What the fuck.* This is a dream. It's not the first time I've dreamed of an asshole I'd never let touch me in real life regardless of whether I want him or not. I'm still running. I'm roadkill on Delancey Street.

"I thought you wanted to." Our faces are too close to tell if Nik is confused or sarcastic.

"You don't read minds."

"You said you want the music out. Let it go."

I would laugh if the breath for it were mine. It's not. But I stretch my mouth like the laughter could come, and nothing comes out; Nik's tongue comes in. If it wasn't a kiss before, it is one now, even if my eyes won't close and Nik's hair stings them, mines them. Nik is clearer in the new red heat than anything else in this room. Clearer than the window. Clearer than the dark.

The lack of sleep has finally gotten to me. That's it. I'm dreaming. Or high. Possibly both. Nik probably isn't even here. But the song is gone or it's drowned in something else, so it's a good enough trip that I'll take it and stay, and all the hollows of my skull ring with near-silence, all the cracks between the fused bones around my brain.

There's no music in this kiss, just pace and pulse and choice, the swipe of Nik's tongue and the scrape of his teeth, the beat of the bed against the wall. My eyes and ears fail me so I hold on, and a white void fills everything, a terrifying relief. Skin swells in and under my fingertips. Regret is pointless.

I've wanted silence for days and fuck, I almost have it. Even Nik's heavy breath is muffled like my ears are packed with cotton, and everything else *feels*, without sound at all. Swathes of heat climb up and down my neck, chest, arms. My palms sting as if the muscles are asleep so I keep wringing them, tearing at Nik's shoulders—he deserves it. It's impossible to describe the taste in my mouth, but it doesn't matter, I just drink it and breathe it and scrape my teeth on Nik's long, rough tongue. *Smoke*, maybe. Wine. Whatever it is, it tastes too hot and too good. I'm out of my head and the vertigo should slow me down like every other high I've had, but the thrill moves with my blood, shatters and spreads from one joint to the next.

I could play. Hell, I could sing if there was nothing to play.

Euphoria is such a strange word.

Nik wrests his arms out of my grip, reaches down between us to tear my shorts off.

I choke, on whatever this is, and the sound echoes off Nik's teeth. It's the first thing I've heard in the past two days that doesn't flip a switch in my mind. It doesn't even reach the inside. Nothing reaches me but sensation now, searing skin alongside mine, one tight fist wringing us both.

This isn't what I would have chosen. I won't deny I've thought about it, more than I'm comfortable with. But right now, real or not, it's *working*, and that's what matters.

Isn't it?

I hold on to Nik's back like I could carve him new tattoos. The blood rushing under them is just as fast as mine, just as driven. Nik's nails scrape somewhere far too sensitive, and I shout into his mouth, struggle to get a hand down there too and show him how it's done. It's a very human mistake for a god to make. Unless he did it intentionally. He probably did. Asshole. *Yes. There. Faster. Now.*

I can't blame the music when I come. There isn't any.

After, Nik kisses me again, mouth stretched around a smile. He cracks his shoulder, pries his hand out from between our bodies and settles atop me, our legs interspersed. His right hand, still slick and then sticking, swipes at my scalp, gives it a quick scratch. I flinch.

Once you get in—

"It's not gone." Shit. It's not gone, just dampened, muted. I'm still dreaming. I have more to say than that. *It's not gone. It's your fault. I want my life back.*

"No," Nik says, and I feel the voice where I'm drained and sore. "You didn't let it go. But it's better. It won't bother you like that anymore unless you want it to."

"You're sure."

Nik makes a deep purring sound in his throat, a kind of approval. "You said it yourself, I put it there."

Something tightens in my chest. It doesn't let go either.

I could be afraid. I probably am. Good trips gone bad do that. This one wasn't even good to start with, just passed through it on the way back to *this is my life.* Fear creeps in, like exhaustion, like fragments of melody when an orchestra is tuning. Self-consciousness kicks me in the head a second later.

I breathe, and the pace is mine, finally. It works. I do it again. My heart races, but the pattern of my breathing slows it—I've gotten enough control back for that at least. I can worry about *how* later. When I wake up. When I sober up. When I come down.

Nik sleeps, his pants undone around his knees, his thigh still nudged against my groin. It should be too much pressure and too much mess, but it's not, and I sink into the mattress, shut my eyes. My head is silent except for the static buzz before thunder.

DECEMBER 8, 2011

My alarm goes off at 6 a.m. Nik's gone, if he was ever here, but the walls shudder with the music that breaches the studio's soundproofing.

The next time I check the clock, it's past seven.

I haven't missed a morning run in months, and even then only for illness and hangovers. The similarity of my current state to a hangover is blindingly clear, complete with worse-than-usual headache, congestion in my joints, and the blistering assurance that I did something reprehensible and embarrassing last night.

I should get cleaned up. Anything else can be dealt with when my fingers aren't half-stuck together with cum.

Fuck. The thought turns my stomach enough that if this was a hangover, I'd probably get rid of it the time-tested way. I rush to the bathroom, wait a few minutes to ascertain that, no, I'm not going to throw it up, then just get in the shower and scour myself clean.

But putting things together is impossible if the things themselves are too abhorrent to think about.

There was a song. That, I remember. An impossible song. But it's not that creeping back, just the taste of Nik's tongue, the pace of his blood, and the weight of his swollen skin in my hand. The shower's just hot enough to thicken the air, impress steam on the walls of my throat. Nik and I did something. Or I dreamed we did, and got off on it.

The only thing I hate more than my life right now is my subconscious.

But the memory is an image, not a song. That's something. And once I'm clean and dressed, since I'm certainly not running today,

I can take care of the rest of this hangover bullshit. I need breakfast. An enormous, protein-heavy breakfast. The walls still thrum with the music from the studio, but I put my earbuds in and drown it out. Lully's *Ballets du roi*, interestingly enough, make a good accompaniment for frying eggs, slicing chorizo, grinding coffee, negotiating toast.

Circumstances aside, maybe a leisurely morning is exactly what I need, maybe even deserve, after two days of hell. But making that decision doesn't shunt the circumstances aside, and here they are at the forefront again, concerns that must be immediately addressed.

I might have just fucked up my life more than it already was. And even if I didn't, there's damage to repair.

Someone taps me on the shoulder, and I damn near throw the eggs out of the skillet. And almost burn my hand bracing myself on the stove, for that matter.

"Smells great," Nik says, eating Frosted Flakes right out of the box.

Looks like one of the eggs will be over medium instead of easy. I get clear of the stove, pry the earbuds out, let them dangle. He gets the worst glower I have to give. "Cooking costs extra."

"Good to know." Nik gathers up a handful of cereal, munches around it, licks his fingers. There's nothing pointedly lewd about it, but it's evocative all the same, and I turn to the stove to deal with the eggs and hide the color rising in my cheeks.

They're cooked far too soon; this place has an enthusiastic stove. But I keep my back to Nik while I put the plate together, pour salsa on the eggs, and butter the toast.

I'm not going to discuss last night unless Nik does first. I'm only eighty percent sure it *happened*, let alone whether I agreed to it. And that's a certainty I can't afford.

Nik's not at the table when I finally turn to face it; he's leaning on the refrigerator. He must be feeling the weather, since he's wearing a shirt for once, a claret oxford that looks vaguely familiar. It's not mine, I look awful in that color, but Nik must have worn that shirt at a concert or something. The sleeves are pushed up but the collar is fully done. I almost wish it weren't. I'd like to ascertain whether I left marks on Nik's skin. Whether, and where.

Fuck, no. I put that thought down with the plate on the table. Between the sound of Nik's crunching and my slicing, there should be enough to keep my focus where it needs to be. Enthusiastic stove aside, two out of the three eggs turned out well. I polish off the bad one first.

"So," Nik says, over my shoulder like a cartoon disseminating bad advice. "What am I supposed to do today?"

It's one of the better questions he could have asked. "I'll check right now." I bring the calendar up on my phone. Lully is playing though the headphones that are still dangling around my neck, and the light hiss of the speakers swells and nags, but I don't turn it off. "No interviews, no deadlines, no gigs. Your webmaster has a deadline tomorrow; he'll probably email you. Tour dates are finalized next week."

"Good."

And as for my schedule, it's not nearly as empty, but that's not Nik's business unless he asks. So I put the phone down, focus on breakfast again, and make my way through half of the next egg and a piece of toast. I can leave the chorizo for now.

"You'll like the tour," Nik says.

"I didn't think I was going."

Nik pulls out a chair, sits, holds the box of cereal between his knees. I look only long enough to ascertain that I shouldn't look. His pants are inhumanly tight. "So you're holding down the house?" he asks.

"If I haven't found a better job entirely, yes," I say. "At least, to my understanding."

"You won't find a better job." That's also not an innuendo, though the fact that it's *not* an innuendo creates the same blip on my radar.

"Maybe not." *Thanks for the vote of confidence, asshole.* "But I can at least set myself up to get one. I've been published three times in the last five years including my dissertation. If I work on a few more articles I can build up credibility even if there's nothing available for me right now. I can't do that on tour."

After a moment long enough for me to finish my eggs, Nik asks, "What was your dissertation on?"

Well. Of all the things I've heard Nik ask and seen Nik do, that's the one that makes me almost choke on chorizo. I never expected Nik to care.

It takes a couple of coughs to clear my throat, but I grit out, "Bach as a teacher," then wash the fragment down with a hard gulp of coffee. "On the role of his dissemination of easy and intermediate pieces to secure his position among his contemporaries and his eventual longevity. Because he wrote so many good teaching pieces, he was always part of the canon. Even during periods where his work wasn't considered stylish, people still learned him and respected him."

"Because he gets you while you're young."

"Exactly. Even though his work is stylistically baroque, he wrote pieces that encouraged artists to develop their skills regardless of the style."

Nik smirks. "Math."

"People learn math to get by in life," I say, on the heels of a scoff that he definitely deserves. "I had to sit through two years of calculus back in high school and I never use it, but I don't mind. Math teaches you how to think about things you can't immediately understand. Why shouldn't it do the same for music?"

"Because music you *can* immediately understand." Nik rolls a flake of cereal between his fingers, walks it on his knuckles like a magician. "You know what music is doing the first time you hear it. Once you start taking it apart it's not music anymore. You wouldn't break a sunset into pieces to see why it's beautiful."

"I would."

"No, you'd break it down to see why it's a sunset. That's even worse."

I stand up, clear my plate, go to the sink to wash it. "So, what? I should just accept everything the world throws at me and not ask why?" *Or whether it happened*, I don't say, *or what the hell you did to me*, but again, like hell.

"Not everything," Nik says, "just music."

"How progressive of you."

"You didn't ask me why."

If my hands weren't mired in dishes and soap, they'd be curled into fists. All right, so this counts as Nik addressing the issue. An issue, at least. There are others. I let the water run, wait.

Nik's fingers trail up my neck, sticky with sugar from the cereal. I don't turn from the sink, don't drop the dishes, don't think.

"I know you know what music is," Nik says.

"No," I say now, because I couldn't then, "I don't."

By the time the dishes are clean, Nik's gone, as if he were never here. But the walls ring with heat and the floor shifts with footsteps, and the masks in the foyer rustle on their nails, tilt toward the door on outlines of shadow.

DECEMBER 11, 2011

Posted to asbrooks.com on December 11, 2011

"As for whether I will be on the spring tour"

The answer, as far as I can tell, is no. I've gone over my contract and there are no provisions about accompanying Nik, and numerous ones about how I'm supposed to maintain his apartment and correspondence. Besides, I can't keep looking for a job and networking if I'm following him around the country, and all the parties involved know I don't plan on doing this for the rest of my life.

So here are the tour dates you asked for, courtesy of his website, all bookings subject to Nik's whims unless his manager says otherwise. I may be flying out to check up on him in LA and Chicago, but other than that I'm keeping his house like the help I apparently am. Then again, based on the concerts I've been to, I'd rather be humiliated here than there.

Comments (13)

juliamei
And Canada. Following him around the country *and Canada.*

   ASBrooks
   Sorry.

juliamei

It's cool. My sister and her friends at UT are calling for tickets right now.

ASBrooks

I hope they still have clean records after the show.

juliamei

You're assuming their records were clean to start with.

ASBrooks

Good point.

EliseMorgenstern

HA! Well played!

LaurentTErikssen

So you will be able to make the introduction after all. Ihope so!

ASBrooks

I haven't mentioned the possibility to him yet.

LaurentTErikssen

Please do. And feel free ot give him my email.

Florestan

Actually I kind of wish you were going on the tour, at least that way we'd get to hear about it.

(It's Yuki btw, Chuck talked me into renaming the account to mess with Newcomb's head.)

Eusebius

Not just Newcomb's. First we take Vienna, then we take Paris!

EliseMorgenstern
Somewhere, Schumann is rolling in his watery grave.

DECEMBER 12, 2011

U ncle Paul's receptionist is hanging Christmas decorations. She's standing on a stepladder with a staple gun in one hand and a trail of gold tinsel in the other, and her skirt is far too short. I pretend not to notice.

"Just go on in, Anthony, he's expecting you!" she says, bracing the staple gun against the wall. At least she's taken her shoes off. Between the tiny skirt and the boots with heels that are clearly not only intended for keeping her out of the snow, that spells disaster upon recoil.

Even though Paul is expecting me, I knock. There are a few muffled excuses before the doorknob turns, and Paul opens the door still talking on his cell phone. "No," he says, not to me, "if he's not providing his own Fresnels I don't know where they're getting them from. Do you even have a rig?—I didn't think so. Tell him if he thinks he's big enough for a light show, then he's big enough to front the lights and make it back from sales . . . Are you kidding me? You can get a fog machine at Kmart for ten dollars marked down since Halloween. Someone ripped him off . . . No. No, I am not your bank." He pauses for a second to mouth to me, *Sit down*, and rounds the desk toward the windows.

I settle into the same chair I sat in last time and put my earbuds in. This time, I have the excuse that they're my first line of defense against "Jingle Bell Rock." It's surreal, watching Paul work and gesture and enunciate his words like they're so hard he could chew but not swallow, while I'm hearing Toru Takemitsu's flute suites. The motion and the music interact oddly but not unpredictably, like a half-rehearsed chorus. Paul even hangs up the phone at the exact moment one movement ends and the pause begins. I forget to turn it off for a second though Paul's obviously ready for me, extending an envelope across the desk.

"Here's November." He shakes the envelope once.

I accept it. It's far too thick to be a check, and sure enough, inside is a printed statement, signed and dated, and a wad of cash too small to consist entirely of twenties. I count before I even look at the invoice. That's more money than I've *seen* in a while anywhere but Nik's ledger.

"You're not on the payroll," Paul explains, in an undertone. "There's no point if you're still filing taxes as a student."

"Thank you." He's probably right. And I'm still counting. "That's about to save me a lot of taxes."

"I know. How's the hunt?"

I set the first thousand in cash aside on the end of the desk. There's more.

"Not going well," I admit, though like hell will I bring up what happened at NYU two weeks ago, never mind what may have happened the other night. "I've resigned myself to doing what scholarly work I can under these circumstances and trying my luck on this spring's market."

"With this spring's graduates."

"If I keep publishing I still have a chance."

Paul nods. He waits while I count out the second thousand dollars, and start a third pile for the next, which looks like it will be mostly twenties. I can't call the pay unfair, unsettling as it is. Twenty-two hundred a month before taxes is ten percent of Nik's profits: no wonder Nik can afford that apartment, even if he only sees half of what he makes. If I made all that Nik does, I could pay my loans off in two years. Maybe less.

The twist in my stomach is envy or disgust, and I'm not sure which I'd prefer.

Two thousand three hundred and twenty eight dollars. I put the cash back in the envelope, stow it in my bag, and look over the invoice. The number is correct, rounded up to keep coins out of the paper.

"Have the police been in contact with you?" Paul asks.

"Not since the night after that concert."

"Good, they're keeping things where they said they would. If they do call, remind them that there's nothing you can tell them that the lawyers can't."

"I thought you said Nik wasn't signed to Pantheon."

"He isn't. Neither are you."

"You have a point." I thumb the flap of the envelope. He's protecting Nik with company staff; there's got to be something fishy going on. I could tell Lansing. Her card is still in my wallet, right at the back of the pile of useful people and blocked ways out.

"We can do this on PayPal next time if you'd prefer," Paul says. "Or I can write you a personal check. You said the withdrawal limit was a problem."

No. If it's going to be off the books, I'd like no record of it whatsoever. Just in case I need to dodge my loans in the future. "I did. But cash is fine."

"Great."

"Is this considered a good month?"

"You're asking if you'll still be paid this much during the tour."

"Yes." Because it's better to think about that, than this. Than everything.

"You'll make a lot more. I'd save as much as you can if you plan on doing this all year. He makes less when he's recording."

"I don't plan on doing this all year."

"Then you'd better be saving anyway."

Obvious or not, I nod.

Paul lowers his eyes, folds his hands on the desk mat, a plateau over his discarded phone. "You really think you have a chance to get back into school."

"I do," I say, as much to myself as to him. I need to hear it. "I have to. I've already started looking overseas."

"And how long will it take for you to give up?"

I manage not to hang my head like a shamed dog on the internet. "That number changes every day."

"And how long before Nik drives you up a wall?"

There's no humor in the question, just honesty. I answer the same way. "Not long enough."

I could ask Paul how he's dealt with Nik through the years. I could ask just what he's covering up with legalese and snarls of red tape. I could, and probably should, ask what passed between them, what Nik meant by *picked me up in Johannesburg in the seventies*. And, awkward as it is, I should ask if Nik ever tried to break Paul with a song, or if there are any rules between them that Paul didn't impose.

I don't. And I get up from the chair without being dismissed.

"Wait," Paul says, and reaches into his desk for another, smaller and thinner envelope. Another contract? "*The Messiah* at the New York Phil," he says. Tickets. I should have known. "This Saturday at eight. Sydney has Nik that night. Don't worry, I won't let her get out of it. Merry Christmas."

"Merry Christmas." This is touching, honestly. Usually he just sends money or saves gift cards. I haven't gotten a gift with any thought in it from him since I believed in Santa Claus. "Thank you."

"The other ticket's mine unless you find someone to take."

Even though his tone is lighter than before, Paul doesn't smile, so I don't smile back. But I can't think of anyone else to go with, and it will be good to take him, so I say, truthfully, "No, it's yours."

"Good," he says. "It's been a long time since I've been to a concert without amplification."

I put the envelope into my satchel, up against the cash.

"I'd deposit that right now if I were you. You need to know where the nearest bank is?" he asks.

"I'll find it on my phone."

"Good. And get yourself a winter coat."

"I think I'll deposit the money first." This sounds shady as hell. But beggars can't be choosers, and I leave off the part where it's starting to be strange that Paul cares. I turn for the door, get my hand on the knob—

"Be careful," Paul says. "Don't let him tear you up. I know what he does."

My breath stalls in my chest. "Do you."

The door is open a crack. Out in the hall, *all* Mariah Carey *wants for Christmas is you.* I tighten my fist but can't pull the door shut, not yet. He knows. He knows what Nik does.

Paul rounds the desk, his soles scraping the carpet. "I offered you this job because I think it can't happen to you. I might be wrong. So be careful."

"You might be wrong." I can't believe this.

The doorknob slips from my hand, and the door slides open without me there to hold it shut.

"Yes," Paul says.

"Wrong about what?"

"About what kind of person you are."

"About me."

"About what he can do to you if you aren't who I think you are."

"Let me get this straight." I'm still halfway out the door, with holiday pop and chimes flooding my ears, and I can't breathe. The world is a headache. "You believe in him. You support him. You agree he's dangerous. You believe in him and you gave him me."

Paul says nothing. The song outside cycles through a verse and a chorus. The receptionist struggles with her staple gun.

"It's a good thing I haven't drunk the Kool-Aid," I say and shut the door behind me.

But I can still hear Paul say, faintly, "Yes, it is."

DECEMBER 14, 2011

Posted to asbrooks.com on December 14, 2011

"Charity"

I attended a recital at Juilliard last night. It was a good program, but I'm not going to mention the performer's name because this isn't about the performance itself.

At the end of the concert, he got up from the piano and asked for donations.

I'm not saying he shouldn't have. I'm impressed with his confidence. There he was, in a tux, facing a room full of people who had already paid to be there, asking them to drop checks in the convenient program envelopes. As if their prior support was insufficient.

I've seen musicians with GoFundMes and Kickstarters asking for help to continue their education. I don't begrudge them that either. They're just asking better-off people to make up the difference and meet the demanding standards our industry sets out. And people get to decide whether to donate or not, and to whom.

But something still annoyed me about his asking *at* the concert. About asking the people who'd already paid. And I thought, then, that maybe I should give my uncle the benefit of the doubt because I'm doing the exact same thing as that guy in the tux.

Don't look a gift horse in the mouth, after all. Or try to get blood from a stone. Or some other trite metaphor.

Anyway, the moral of the story is that if it pisses me off when other people do it, I shouldn't do it myself.

Comments (0)

DECEMBER 18, 2011

Messiah runs long, even for itself, even though this isn't the kind of production where people sing-in. Afterward, we ford the figurative river of people bound for the nearest 1 trains and wind up on the corner of 68th and Amsterdam, just out of sight of Lincoln Center.

It's hard for me to thank him, but I do. Paul nods, pats down his winter coat, and splits off to hail himself a cab. I remember when we couldn't afford that. I wait for the next, working my way down to 59th Street on the opposite side of most of the concertgoers. It's brisk but not freezing, not with a thick coat and a hat over my scalp. The cabs miss me for about ten minutes, but hey, what else is new?

Eventually, I get one, take it down to Nik's. This cabbie isn't playing music, but I've got my own, and right now it's all Handel. So many of my colleagues—former colleagues, I guess—complain about their inability to subject themselves to too much Handel at once, with terrible puns to that effect. I've never had a problem with the baroque. If anything, the concert's put me in better humor than I've been in since I got here. *Messiah* is still unwinding in my ears when I pay the driver and key myself upstairs.

It's one thirty in the morning, and Nik isn't home. The masks shine in the dark, but I know my way to the closet without the lights by now so I don't have to fumble for them. I hang up my coat, stuff the hat down the sleeve, skip my room, and take to the studio.

Nik's not here. I *know* he isn't here.

I sit at the piano, loosen my tie, then steady my hands over the keys. No neighbors: no one downstairs to protest me playing at all hours. A niggling impulse at the back of my mind flares up with the remnants of that maddening song, *not Bach, anyone but Bach.* Fine. I can play someone else.

I've accompanied *Messiah* before, in college and at Berkeley, and heard it enough times to run almost any song. I'm not surprised when the first one to come to mind is "Behold, I Tell You a Mystery" with "The Trumpet Shall Sound." The bass who sang it while I coached in undergrad needed more rehearsal than I was prepared to give. The trumpet part translates easily into my right hand, and then the bass melody, an octave higher, like I did when I had to help the singer along. It's different without a score: there may be a few wrong notes, but it's still fresh in my mind, transcribed from this evening's performance, and flows as simply as something I've practiced for weeks, muscle memory at work.

The next song choice comes as clearly as that, more half-remembered extracts from *Messiah*, other Handel I recall off the top of my head. Every time I consider switching to Bach those excuses smooth the urge over. It's still Nik's place. Even if the song was never there, there's no point. I made that rule.

"*Dove sei,*" I play, "*amato bene?*"

Rodelinda. Well, I'll go with it. It was beautiful when I saw it at the Met, an island of calm, of *music,* in this sea of *everything else.*

This time, I don't illustrate the singer's line, just play the accompaniment: I conclude the introduction, and there is a remembered voice in my head, singing along. It's not Nik's untrained baritone; it's a clear alto like Scholl's but not quite, brighter, warmer, like a child's. I listen, follow, imagine the piano as a harpsichord, roll the chords when they aren't meant to be in the strings. The orchestra is at my fingertips, and the voice is independent of that, and whoever is singing in my head creates ornamentations for me to mimic and support in that orchestra. Turns, silences, ascending patterns where the score descends: new music that illustrates the intentions of the song until the outro, where the score returns to thwart the singer—

"See?" Nik says, "You can play."

I will never get over him sneaking up on me. I wish I could.

I slip my fingers off the keys after the anticipation of the very last chord.

Nik, draped in the doorway like a garment on a dressing screen, is nearly glowing. He hasn't taken off his coat since coming in, a light-gray trench open to his knees, and underneath it his stage wear is plastered to his skin, black even blacker with sweat and spilled water. His hair is different too, all gold now instead of all red, shorter than it was when I met him but still hanging over his forehead.

"Don't stop," he says.

Fuck you, I already have.

Nik sighs, deep and ringing, and pulls up the guitar stool, sits beside the piano bench. "You know, Handel started riots too."

"Not with his music." I know what he's talking about: price riots when Handel was in England, two hundred and fifty years ago. "With the politics surrounding it. Context isn't the composer's fault."

Nik laughs, an untranscribable echo of that untranscribable song I may never have heard. "You're so close. It's right in front of you, and you're fumbling at it like a blind man in a strip club."

"Thanks for the mental image."

"You're welcome."

I draw the piano lid shut—or start to, when Nik covers my nearer hand and stops me. His skin is feverish, hot and dry and shining, almost shaking from underneath like a purring cat's. I shiver, pull my hand away.

"I said don't stop." He pushes my hand again, and there's nothing for me to do but keep the piano lid up, a trick of physics and potential energy. "Play."

"For the last time, I am *not your fucking butler*."

"It's not the last time, and yes, you are." His fingers fold over my knuckles, between and down.

It's not blood under Nik's skin. It's sound. It's the amplifier blast that rustles curtains and blows back the hair of the dancers in the front row. It's the rumbling inside the body of a cello when bowed at full volume, the sympathetic vibration of a voice on the piano's strings, the patter of breath through a reed.

"Play," he says again, and the shiver in my bones stops completely.

"And what?" I shove back the piano bench, already on my way out, gone, not here, not now. "Drop the act. I know exactly what you're doing. How was the concert? Plenty of people fry their brains for you?

Lots of worship? Glitter in your hair, spoon up your nose, everything else in order? And then instead of partying with your groupies you come home to the one person you can reach who doesn't think you're a god and say, oh look, there's a poor unbelieving shit with insecurities I can exploit until he either caves or gives up, why don't I fuck with his head. Well, you're fucking with it. You fucked with it good, are you satisfied?"

"No," Nik says, but it's only an anticipation to what I say next, an appoggiatura right out of Handel and Bach.

"No, because you won't be satisfied until everyone bows and scrapes at your nonexistent altar. I know how it works, Nik, I've been doing that my entire fucking life. It only matters when the ones that hate you and the ones that don't believe in you come around and give their support because *that* means you have power, *that* means you're as good as you say. Well, guess what? You're not. You're not as good as you say because I say you're not good. You hurt people. You fuck up their lives if they live at all. And you can do whatever the hell you did to my head last week until it drives me in front of another truck, but I will die believing you're nothing but an egomaniac who's read too much Nietzsche and gets off on people destroying themselves for you. And until then, I will answer your fucking mail and keep your damn house, and that's all the worship you'll get."

Finally. It feels almost too good to say, like I don't deserve it. Like something will give.

That's probably why I make it to the end of the sentence before Nik shoves me against the doorjamb.

I'm not surprised enough to stand there without punching back. My fist connects with Nik's jaw, splits his lip. His blood stings my knuckles, hot in the dry winter air. That feels even better.

"I told you so." Fuck, this has been a long time coming. "I should be the one telling you to give up."

Nik straightens to his full height, flicks out his fingers like a spider's legs. There's blood on his coat too, smeared on the lapel. He doesn't lick his lip or wipe his mouth, just lets the trail drip down the curve of his chin.

I don't mean to stare. That I don't mean to means I am.

Nik grabs me by the collar and hurls me to the floor, drags me close enough to spit at and shakes me like a toy. *What the fuck.* "Unsay it. Now."

I will not take this. I grab his wrists, pry them off, choke, "*Unsay* it? Are you fucking k—"

"Now. Take it back now."

"Or what?"

—or I shouldn't have worn a tie with this suit.

Pressure. On my throat. He's pulled the tie tight and red fills the corners of my eyes, but Nik is clear and shining in the center, teeth bared and stained bronze. I throw all my weight down on Nik's wrists, twist toward the floor, anything, anything to break out of his grip. It doesn't work, doesn't do more than choke me. I try to knee him in the gut. I miss.

Blood drums in my ears, encroaches on my eyes. I get free enough to put my feet back on the floor, hold Nik in place, and bash our foreheads together.

He lets go—fuck, finally—curses, and reels back into the guitar stands, knocks one over on the way down. There's blood on the cuff of my suit, Nik's blood. I'll take it to the cleaners tomorrow. He'll pay. Oh, he'll pay.

Nik's knuckles are blinding white when he picks up the fallen guitar and rights it. His forehead is pink, and if there isn't a bruise there in an hour I'll eat shit. Blood still rings the curl of Nik's lower lip, stains that perfectly cruel smile. He bruises and blushes and bleeds.

And the blood in my mouth is the same color.

Nik pounces on me like a fucking tiger, lays me out flat with a kiss harder than any punch, sharper than any knife. I stagger back into the doorjamb, then down when he takes my shoulders and pushes me to the floor. His hair is heavy, soaked with sweat. It's softer under my nails. His swollen lip tastes like heat, not blood. My shoulders and head crack against the planks, and then Nik's hand is there instead of the hardwood, cradling the base of my skull, tilting me to take more.

Maybe I hit my head as hard as I hit Nik's. It's the same madness as the song, but in my mouth and my groin instead of my ears.

It's too much, too good, to lie down and take it. The next thing I know I'm not on the floor anymore, I'm on Nik, bearing down with all my weight and tearing into his mouth. I could rip his lip off in my teeth, get his laughter and make it mine. Like his hands. Like his voice. Like his throat, under my tongue. Like his breath—he's got enough for both of us, I want mine back. If he can take mine I want it back—

It's mostly laughter. His breath is mostly laughter. The way our bodies are tangled, I feel it where I'm hard.

Fuck. *No.* This is the last thing I want. *He* is the last thing I want. I don't care how good it feels, how right it feels, this is not my life. *I am more than this.*

But once you get in there—

It's pointless to cover my ears when the song is on the inside. I do anyway. I *stop* this, clatter back to my knees, over Nik, let go of everything I can. Cold overcomes me where I'm not touching him. I hold my head, force my eyes open. I did this. I almost did this.

They're both true. Nik cranes up to me from the floor, works his fingers past my palms to caress my cheek. His smile isn't cruel now; it would be damn near beatific if not for the traces of blood still threading his teeth.

"Don't stop," he says, the same cavalier command as before, in the same low urgent voice. "You're almost there. I won't force you, but it'll be worse if you stop now."

There are dozens, hundreds, of things I could say to that. About half of them are questions, and the rest are pleas and threats with the same words rearranged.

But Nik's blood is caked on my lip, dried quickly in the cold December air, and panic silences any rational thought except one:

This chaos ends here.

I hold Nik by the hair and wind up. This time, I'll aim for the eyes.

—Or I would, if the song didn't overtake me first.

Sound, no, *music* floods me from every angle, every direction within and without. Nik's fingers are on my eyelids, closing them. Like I'm dead.

I'm not.

It's worse.

DECEMBER 19, 2011

There isn't an error on my phone. It's Monday the nineteenth, and Sunday's messages and missed alarms have flooded my call history.

This ringing isn't even my 6 a.m. alarm. It's noon, and it's a phone call. And despite the bile rising in my throat, I have to answer it. Someone had the unexpected courtesy to leave my phone plugged in to its charger. It takes two tries for me to grab it.

It's Sydney.

"Mrs. Nerida," I say, by way of a greeting.

"Afternoon, Anthony. Is this a bad time?"

She's not here. She doesn't have to see me with two days of growth on my cheeks and head and someone else's dried blood on my lip, still in bed and sore enough that even picking up the phone sends *stop don't no* signals through my bones. "It's fine," I lie. "What do you need?"

"I don't know if you've checked your mail, but I sent you a request for a meeting yesterday. I just got done talking with Paul, though, so the point's moot. I'm not going on the tour. My wife's recovery isn't going as fast as we'd like, and I've negotiated a leave of absence. He suggested that so I could maintain some income, you and I switch places, and when the tour starts in February I'll check up on the house and do his correspondence while you proxy for me on the road."

It's worse. This is my life.

"—*What?*"

"Sorry, there's construction going on across the street. I was just saying that I'm not going on the tour, and your uncle suggested—"

"No, I heard you." I try to sit upright. No, that's not happening. I get most of the way up and lean against the wall. My nails scrabble on it, and I almost drop the fucking phone. "What did Paul say about this?"

"He said it's your decision. Nik's enthusiastic, though."

"He would be."

"Sorry?"

"Nothing." Shit, my filter's broken like my damn skull. "Nothing." I brace myself on the edge of the bed, touch my feet to the floor. It's freezing. Someone's removed my socks and tie, but not my pants or either shirt. They're both wrecked. Everything's wrecked. "I'll call Paul later. That's something I have to think about," *and I can't think right now.*

"Oh, of course," Sydney says. "It's an enormous commitment. You'd need a new contract and everything. But if you do turn this down, I'll have to call someone in or train someone up, which means I'd like to know before Christmas."

The floor's almost warm enough to walk on but I can't get my knees to cooperate. "Nothing like a gig for the holidays."

"Exactly. And this one won't be so bad, since all the bookings are already taken care of. Just get back to me soon, whatever you choose to do."

They want me on the tour. They want me to follow the man I just either fucked or clotheslined—or both—around the country and peddle his snake oil.

"So I'll let you go," Sydney says.

Oh. She's still there. How long did I just sit here staring at nothing? "Thanks," I cover quickly and hang up before any actual good-byes begin. The phone feels so heavy in my hand that when they thud down to the mattress together nothing bounces.

My head's a mess and so am I. I missed an entire day. This is the second fucking time. At least I know most of what happened. I played some Handel. Nik was an asshole. I hit first. He kissed me. I kept hitting him. Somehow he still won.

It takes me a half hour to get to the bathroom to shower. The hot water makes me so dizzy I nearly keel over retching. I get myself clean, shaved, feeling vaguely human until I clock that there's no way to cover the goose egg on my head and the razor does jack-shit for the pain.

But thank fuck the shower loosens my limbs enough that breathing and walking no longer hurt, and once I'm dressed—I'll run in the afternoon instead of the morning, I guess, because I'm damned if I'll miss two days in a row—I've put as much of *that* behind me as I can.

There's a gift-wrapped box on the kitchen counter, right beside the stove with a note taped to the outside.

Gone to Tokyo until the 26th. Paul arranged it, you were out, it reads, in the insulting jagged scrawl from the contract at the very start. *Stick your suit in with my dry cleaning. Enjoy this. Merry Christmas. — Nik*

Tokyo. How the hell can he go to Tokyo with an FBI investigation on his tail?

I put coffee on first. That's priority one. Then I open the box. It contains, in a display case, a crystal bottle of Gran Patrón Burdeos tequila.

It's bait.

I take it anyway.

Uncle Paul's receptionist is roadkill to be ignored on the way in, listening merrily to the latest boy band cover of "The Little Drummer Boy." I don't even give her the chance to wave me through, just glare and dare her to stop whatever call she's on. It's surprisingly effective.

And Paul is startled enough to stand when I barge in.

"Sorry I missed the meeting," I say, and don't mean a word of it.

"It doesn't matter."

"Guess it doesn't." I sit, pull the chair closer to the desk like I could trap myself between, like I have to or else I'll explode. "Does it really matter what I decide?"

"If Sydney told you it does, it does." Paul sits back down as well, braces his elbows on the desk mat, turns off his ringer. "Why would she lie?"

"I'm not asking if she'd lie, I'm asking if it matters to you."

"It does. I want you to go."

"Why?"

"Because I don't want to train anyone else," Paul says, folding his hands in front of his chin. "Because he wants you to go. Because you've got a good enough handle on him and you need the money."

"I've got a good enough handle on him," I repeat, and then again, and it's not quite a question either time. I point at my forehead. The bruise can explain itself.

Paul, to his credit, actually looks, and a brief wave of assessment and concern washes over his face. "I take it you didn't get that shelving books."

"Show a little fucking empathy."

"I am. I also know Nik didn't hit you first."

Shit. Strike one. I tighten my fists on the arms of the chair. "So you know."

"You think I never got fed up enough with him to clock him?" There's almost, but not quite, a smile on Paul's jaw, dampened by the resignation in his eyes. "I've broken my fingers on his thick head."

"Before or after you drank his Kool-Aid?"

Paul doesn't answer that.

My fingers patter on the chair to a rhythm even I don't recognize. "Why don't *you* take the tour?"

"I've done my time, Anthony."

"Not like this, I'll bet."

"When I was with Nik, there were street riots," Paul says. "Police. Water cannons. Don't come crying to me just because some girl tries to crowd surf and you can't take it."

No. No, he *doesn't* know. He doesn't know, or he doesn't care. Or he thinks it's all violence and no sex.

Either way, I'm not going to tell him.

"How much of his shit have you covered up?"

"Watch your mouth."

"That's not an answer. Nineteen seventy-four, right? How many people since then have tried to crowd surf? How's he keeping it up without you? He can't, can he? That's all you. How many?"

"You think I'm going to tell you anything when you're making like you want out? Go ahead, throw your lot in with the FBI, I'm sure they'll give you something to settle for. I hope your record's as clean as you think it is."

The bruises from two nights ago swell on my skull. There's a bottle of tequila on the kitchen counter that costs about five hundred bucks. Nik knows I drink it. Nik knows I drank it at the show when Dina Marshall died. Lansing doesn't know, but she will, and we both know what it looks like. I know what *all* of this looks like, what it means to handle Nik's correspondence, sign for his packages, keep his records. I've made mistakes everywhere. One little mistake is all they need.

One little mistake is all anyone needs.

*And once you get in there—*I refuse to laugh—*they can't drag you out.*

There really is nothing else I can do. Dr. Anthony Brooks is in the past.

Well, if I'm going Faust, I might as well make it worth Hell.

"Fifteen percent," I say, hands on the desk now. Music laughs in my blood. "Fifteen percent, *and* Sydney's commission. If I'm doing her job, I want her money."

"Fine." That's all it takes.

"And I want him to sign the same contract I sign."

Paul pauses with his hand on the half-open desk drawer. "I can't make him do that."

"Fine, if you can't, I will." I reach into my coat pocket, pull out Nik's note from that patronizing Christmas present. "I've got all the letters I need to forge his signature right here. That's the first name, isn't it? Nikos? If he is what he says he is, just about any last name will do. I'll just *make one up.*"

Paul snaps the desk drawer shut. "Put that down."

"Not until you guarantee me some protection from your client."

"Stop talking crazy and put that down."

No, you won't get off that easy. I give the note a sharp wave, just in time for "The Little Drummer Boy" outside to stop his puerile *parumpumpumpum.* "Am I really talking crazy? I don't think it's so crazy to counter extortion with extortion."

"It is if you don't know what you're asking for."

"Then tell me what I'm asking for and maybe I'll withdraw my request." I don't withdraw the note, though, keep it firm in my hand, thumbnail creasing the paper. "And I want the reasonable explanation.

No gods, no magic. Either you tell me what big secret you're keeping for him or I show you how little I care."

"You wouldn't believe me," Paul says. "I don't want you to believe me."

"Then lie."

"I can't."

Out in the waiting room, the herald angels sing, and the song in my head responds in antiphony.

I can wait. I can wait all day. Paul sinks into his desk chair, and it swivels, just once to the side. He glances out the window behind the desk, at a cloud-white sky that sucks in any reflection he could cast, then turns back to me with eyes as low and precise as his tone.

"I have a contract like yours," he says. "The difference is, it's with him and he signed it. I've broken the terms and paid the price, more than once. Those breaches of contract are the reason I live the way I do. I've made my peace with that. But now you're a term in that contract. Don't lie for him. Nothing good ever came of it for me, and it won't come for you."

I tap the point of the note on the desk to the beat of the song outside. "Is that the part you want me to believe, or the part you don't?"

"Put it down, Anthony." Paul sighs, still turned almost as much toward the window as toward me. "I'm not the one you want to control."

It's true. It's abhorrent, but it's true. It's *Nik* that I need something over. Not Paul.

I slide the note back into my coat pocket, slow enough that it doesn't feel like a retreat. Still a threat.

Paul turns the chair toward me, opens the desk drawer again, takes the new contract out. "He's back from Japan in a week." He slides the contract across, folded into envelope thirds. "Take this back with you. Look it over until you decide. If you find another job before then, take it. If you don't, give the tour serious consideration. You could make enough at it in six months to support yourself for all of next year while you do what research you need and try to get where you want to go. If that's what you want out of this arrangement, I will do everything I can to make sure you get your money and get out. Believe that."

I do. Mostly. I tell him so.

"And the rest?"

I could ask what color the whites of Nik's eyes are supposed to be. I could ask *Johannesburg, nineteen seventy-four.* I could ask why weeks later there are still fragments of a song in my head with no meter, no determinate pitch, and whether the madness that comes with that music always ends in suicide and sex.

"Nothing," I say instead. "I've already told him I'll die thinking he's nothing."

DECEMBER 24, 2011

On Christmas Eve, alone in Nik's apartment, I send a two-word text to Sydney:

I'll go.

SET
TWO

FEBRUARY 4, 2012

Posted to asbrooks.com on February 4, 2012

"Afterword: Bowery Ballroom Kickoff, 2/3/12"

My predecessor in this trying vocation told me once that three arrests is a night.

Last night was a night. I can't say I prevented any of them. In fact, I'll go on record to say I enabled them. I can't help but have the sense of Groundhog Day, since my efforts to impose order on Nik's gigs are either misguided or downright pointless, but if someone has to do something, it might as well be me, and if I can put more assholes out of Nik's liable misery I will consider it a public service.

We leave for Pittsburgh on Tuesday. Nik's packed, I'm not. I'm taking care of that after I finish this entry. I'm exhausted and we haven't even started yet.

I know most of you will tell me this isn't a mistake. I respectfully disagree. If I had gotten a single paper accepted to a conference this spring, I wouldn't be going. I'm willing to believe that this is the necessary course of action given my circumstances and the state of the field and a thousand other excuses. But I'm not convinced I'm doing the right thing for my career, let alone my life.

Those of you in Western PA, feel free to text. I won't have as much time as I'd like, but I do at least have the mornings and afternoons free, and I plan to take advantage of that.

Comments (19)

EliseMorgenstern
My ex-roommate is coming to the Saturday show. Be gentle!

ASBrooks
I am the least of her problems.

EliseMorgenstern
Then pass that along to Nik. Tell him Johanna is not to be harmed!

ASBrooks
As if he would listen to me.

####### EliseMorgenstern
I guess that would make you the man behind the man!

Eusebius
I'm in the camp of not thinking you're making a mistake, at least from the financial perspective. I probably should have taken time off between degrees myself. This might be just what you need before you sell your soul to the Ivory Tower for good.

ASBrooks
I thought I made that transaction long ago.

CrossBridge
Hi, you don't know me, but I found your blog through a friend of a friend of yours at IU. I run one of Nik's unofficial YouTube archives and when you mentioned that you helped make the arrests last night I figured I should ask either your forgiveness or

permission. <u>Is this you?</u> The bald one doing the hauling, I mean, not the one getting hauled.

ASBrooks
Yes. That's me.

CrossBridge
Okay, 1, do I need your permission to keep that video up, 2, you're hot, and 3, want to meet up in the line before the April 6th Chicago concert?

ASBrooks
1) If you don't need Nik's permission, you don't need mine, and since it's already got 15000 hits I don't think taking it down will make any difference.

3) I'm not sure, since as you said I don't know you. But thanks for the courtesy.

Florestan
You didn't answer question 2!

ASBrooks
I don't need to answer it if it isn't a question.

Florestan
You need to get laid.

ASBrooks
What a tactful thing to say on my blog.

CrossBridge
Fair enough! I'll keep you posted in advance for all the videos I can. And sorry if I was forward. I'm Henri, nice to meet you. Hope you change your mind.

juliamei

Wow! Who'd of thunk you were a badass?

ASBrooks

Thanks, I think.

juliamei

I wonder if anyone's ever written a paper about bouncers. To JSTOR with me!

FEBRUARY 6, 2012

The driver of the tour bus is a woman named Louanne, and she will tolerate no bullshit. The bus has AC and wireless and plenty of outlets in the walls, which mitigates most of the issues I've had with tour buses in the past, and a driver who will not take crap from the passengers erases problems I didn't even know I had.

I remember how excited I was to be on my very first sleeper bus, fifteen years ago. None of that fascination remains, but at twelve years old there was something magical about a bus with bunk beds and a VCR. Paul was managing a hip-hop girl group back then, Li-A-Sone. They would travel by plane between concert sites and sleep in motels, but their backing band and dancers took the bus, and I followed them around like a ghost, snuck into other people's bunks, and even found my way into the cargo hold a couple of times. It scared Paul half to death. He said, once, that he got his first gray hairs on that tour.

Good thing I'm staying bald.

But Nik's traveling with us. I shouldn't be surprised. He's certainly rich enough to take his own transportation, but considering the hassle of booking him on planes without a social security number, let alone renting him a car without a driver's license, *surprise* is the incorrect response.

It pisses me off that Nik's traveling with us.

There. That's truer.

I take one of the bunks near the front, in case Louanne needs me to enforce her antibullshit policy. Then Nik takes the bunk underneath mine. Of course he does.

Aside from the occasional absolutely necessary words, we haven't spoken in person in about a month. It's surprisingly easy to avoid him even though we share an address. I've gotten into the habit of taking my laptop out after my morning runs, communicating by text message if I have to, and I don't come back to the apartment unless I'm sure Nik will be somewhere else. It doesn't always work, but Nik can apparently take a hint if he wants to, so he's been avoiding me back.

Right now, he doesn't want to take a hint.

"Nostalgic," Nik says. "You pick the same place Paul used to."

"It's sensible." There's a television monitor here, like on a plane. I unplug it and let my cell phone charger take over. "People who sleep less should sleep in the front."

Nik smiles, hurls whatever it is he's stowing onto his bunk, and leans against the divider. "You'll sleep more than you think you will."

"So you're immortal and prescient now."

"Call it a hunch."

I ignore him. I have emails to catch up on, anyway.

Well, Nik evidently doesn't give a shit. "So, no more morning runs." He kicks his feet up onto the lower bed and disappears under me until he's just a voice through curtains and plastic. "How are you going to turn yourself off?"

"However I can." So it'll be three days a week instead of seven, whenever we're in one place long enough and I can be spared. Harder sacrifices have been made. *Fifteen percent plus Sydney's commission* is a fairly effective conciliatory mantra, and if I play it in my head enough, I might just convince myself it's okay to let certain things go. *Fifteen percent plus Sydney's commission. Loans paid off, application fees for postdocs, plane tickets, time for research.* I can do this.

Nik tsks, a soft vibration like the engine. The bus is louder than I want it to be, and Nik louder and nearer than that. Someone, somewhere, is playing Radiohead on an iPod, close enough for me to track the specific buzz of Thom Yorke's voice. That's strange. I can't usually pick out music on other people's headphones, but that song keeps playing, stirs up another—

No. Not today. Not ever.

"We're supposed to arrive in Pittsburgh in six and a half hours, accounting for traffic," I say, to fend off bullshit with the shield of policy. "You have one promotional interview tonight while everyone else is setting up the venue. Nothing to do until then."

"Not nothing," Nik corrects. "Just nothing to do with you. And you don't have anything either."

Funny, I never heard the first shoe drop. I shouldn't be waiting for the other to.

I missed a spot shaving the base of my scalp. It itches. "Nothing to do with you," I tell Nik, "unless there's something I don't know. And if you laugh ominously and tell me 'There's a lot you don't know,' don't expect me to take you seriously."

"You don't take me seriously enough," Nik says. "I thought you'd appreciate the warning."

"I know how seriously you want to be taken. I just don't care."

Nik laughs, but it's not the ominous chuckle I didn't want to hear; it's almost joyful, clearly amused, like a schoolyard bully getting off scot-free. "I missed you."

"Missed me?"

"You took a month-long vacation up your own ass."

I refrain from punching the mattress, even though I could probably hit it hard enough to crumble it onto Nik's face.

"So I'm glad you're back," Nik goes on, "even if you aren't."

Fine. He can have this round. "At least I can't 'play my math on your instruments' while we're on the road."

"No, they're still my instruments. And you wanted that rule until you broke it."

"Are you glad I broke it?"

Shit. The question escapes me before I have time to bite it back. Whether the answer is yes or no, it's going to take root in my mind, fuel for the music. I don't want him to be glad. I *never* want him to be glad. But it's going to be worse if he isn't.

"Not as glad as you'll be once you let it go," Nik says, which is *even worse than that*. His smugness permeates layers of plastic and batting and flesh, and thank fuck no one can see my face up here, because hell if I know what's showing on it.

"Once I let it go," I repeat, dismissing him as vehemently as I can. "Someone has to maintain order. Someone has to deal with you like you're not a god. It's my job now, and my pleasure, and I'm going to do it no matter how hard you try to win me over."

"It's not your pleasure," Nik says.

"What, if it was you'd know?"

"Yeah. I'd know. You don't enjoy not believing in me."

"But I do enjoy you doubting your shit." I delete the last of the spam in my inbox and snap the phone into its charger. "Call it reciprocity. I've been around plenty of people in my life who gave me hell for one thing or another, and you're just like them. You don't want me to feel confident in my work, or comfortable with my skills, and you want to benefit from me more than I do. Fine, I'll play that game. You need me to keep you on track, I'll keep you on track, but I can do that without fawning all over you like your fans, just like you can use me without actually treating me like a person."

"I do treat you like a person."

"That's rich, Nik. Thank you. I appreciate your consideration. I guess I should get my life in order before someone comes to lock me up."

At least Nik doesn't laugh. He reaches off the bunk, clasps his hand around my thigh, more testing than rough but I still don't want it, and he still doesn't let go. "The Feds don't get that all those people who die for me do that to themselves," he says. "I create what I create. I play what I play. They handle it how they handle it. Blaming me for that would be like blaming Paul for you. Wait. You *do* blame him." Now he laughs, and it's just as hateful as I could ever expect. "You blame other people for everything that's wrong with you. No wonder you expect me to take responsibility for my music."

He's not holding me so tight that I couldn't just walk away. I could just leave, fuck off to the galley or the lounge or talk to the driver or take an imaginary phone call or something, anything but taking this.

But even if I can't quite will myself to leave, *staying here* and *taking this* are not the same thing.

"You have no idea what you just said, do you." The words fall from my lips as if my mouth didn't have anything to do with their creation. "I won't ask you to take it back if you don't."

Nik says nothing. It isn't silence, and even if it were, his voice would still be ringing in my bones.

"Excuse me." I pry myself out of Nik's grasp, brace a hand on the wall of the corridor, and head for the stairs.

"This is exactly what I mean," Nik says.

"Fuck you."

"Yeah," Nik says, "you did."

Shit.

I stop cold, shut everything out.

So we did. My throat's dry enough that I have to try and ask twice. "The first or second time?"

Nik huffs through his teeth. "The first. Why would I bother the second time? You were dead weight."

"And the first time I thought I was stoned."

"No, that was just me."

"I don't remember saying yes."

"You said yes when you broke the rules." Nik shrugs like it's nothing but a tic in his shoulders, and *that's* what makes me hold the handrail tighter. "I told you not to."

The handrail doesn't break. It doesn't even give. But it slicks under my palm, and I'd leave prints, and there's no way out now. I'm in. I'm complicit. I'm responsible. I should never have taken this job—but I'm the one who took it, after all. I could have turned it down. I didn't.

This is fucked up. This is beyond fucked up. If Nik said that to Julia or Elise I'd call the cops. And I would never blame them for something Nik did. But I can blame me.

And I do.

"Like fuck I'm letting it happen again," I say, and the *again* is the part that stings the most.

"Your loss," Nik says, with the same shrug.

"I don't think you get it. That is not happening again. You can ask until your fucking tongue falls out, but if my head isn't clear, the answer is no. Do you hear me?"

Nik laughs. "Your head's never clear."

"Then I guess I can't ever say yes to you."

"Okay," Nik says, and shrugs, as dismissive as before. "New rule. Let's see how long before you break this one."

There's a door at the bottom of the stairs, and a driver at the top. We've barely left Manhattan. I could demand to be put off here. Now. Before this gets any worse.

Fifteen percent, I repeat, like the song in my head, *and Sydney's commission.*

I stay on the bus, and I-95 stretches out before me like the road to Hell, paved with truck stops and good intentions.

FEBRUARY 10, 2012

Someone once told me that Pittsburgh is a drinking town with a football problem. Based on the past two hours of drunken revelry and the five or six people who consider Steelers shirts concert attire, it's true of this representative sample. No wonder they love Nik even more than the fans in New York.

I need prescription earplugs.

This venue used to be a warehouse, and it shows, from the bare brick walls to the rust-encased ceiling to the utter lack of paths or layout. I keep to the back of the house near the bar, watching the bouncers out front take care of their shit. There's another clue that the football problem joke has a kernel of truth in it: both bouncers look like they'd be right at home on a defensive line. Yet, after they've turned someone without a waiver away from the door, one turns and waves at me, about as intimidating as the sidekick in a romantic comedy, and I throw him an acknowledging wave back. It's my best Paul impersonation, complete with *are you kidding me* eyebrows. I can't tell if the bouncer gets the joke or not. Probably not.

It doesn't matter. What matters is that Nik keeps playing and the fans don't kill themselves. There aren't any balconies here, thank fuck, but there are still plenty of stupid things Nik's horde can do, and whatever his insistence that he can't be held responsible, I can be. I am.

It disgusts me to think of this concert as tame, but it is, so far. The fifteen or so people down to their skin? Perfectly normal. The dealers patted down and turned away at the door? Excellent work on the part of the bouncers. The slowly brewing fight in the house-right corner? Easy enough to contain, once we have to. Increasingly useless earplugs aside, it's better for me to step back and assess the potential damage.

The wall of iPhones documenting everything? Compulsory. It's risky as hell to get confident, but I don't think it's hubris to say I'm getting *better* at this, if not necessarily *good*.

I can afford exactly one stupid cocky mistake a night, and looking up at Nik on the stage is probably it. Nik pulls away from his microphone for a complicated riff, grins down to his fingers, lips curled in a Joker grin. He catches my eyes, and the stage lights play across his teeth at the same flashing rhythm as his nails on the guitar strings. Yeah, that's my mistake for the night. Done.

I shut my eyes. But when I open them again, Nik's still on me, eyes bright gold, singing words that the earplugs don't muffle enough.

Once again, this is my life.

At least there's a cheering crowd to drown him out. Once Nik's basking in that instead of passively tormenting me, I turn away from the stage, escape to the front hall, and shut the double doors.

One of the girls at the box office waves me over and speaks, still somehow audible through the earplugs. "We're at capacity!"

"Great." More money. *Fifteen percent plus Sydney's commission.* I ask the remaining bouncer, "How many still outside?"

"None with tickets," he says. The other, the one who waved at me earlier and didn't respond to my imitation of Paul's expression, must be out dealing with that.

"All right. If someone claims to have one, tell them to wait until someone else leaves. It's not like we're going anywhere. Is tomorrow's venue bigger?"

"The Altar Bar? Yeah, it's bigger."

"See if you can persuade the ones outside to wait in line for tomorrow's in advance, that'll clear some space."

The bouncer laughs. "Soon as Jonas gets back, we can do that."

"Jonas is the other bouncer?"

"Yeah."

"Okay. You two need coffee?"

"Nah, he's taking care of drinks right now, we're good."

Great. It leaves me less to do and less to screw up.

"At capacity" looks more like "slightly over," but that's typical enough. These earplugs really need to be replaced: if it weren't for the crowd's voices and feet to distract me, I'd be having the same trouble as last time. And once that gets— No. Not dealing with that. I have shit to contain.

There's Jonas at the bar, like the other bouncer said, waiting on his drinks. I nod at him, head to where he can hear me. "Just so you know," I project over the music to make sure I've got his attention, "once you get back out I need you to clear some of the squatters in the front."

"Got it," Jonas says. "This is a good gig."

"Looks like."

Jonas puts some money down on the bar for the bartender. He's got a cup of coffee in one hand, sure enough, but whatever's in his left is at least 70 proof.

Looks like I'm not the only one who goes straight for the tequila in this business.

He grins after he's done the shot, waves in the general direction of my shoulder. The way he's smiling suggests he's certain he's done nothing wrong, and at his size and in this city maybe he hasn't. But I'm no slouch either, and one shot's still a liability if something *does* go wrong, and it could come back to bite him in the ass. But I say nothing as he passes, and Nik's music surges against my ears, forces itself through the cracks in the plastic.

I also need a drink. But I'm not going through that again, so I flag over a bartender for water and down it as soon as I close my fist on the cup. There are worse things to worry about than a bouncer breaking rules he might not even know are in place. Like the spat in the corner that hasn't quite come to blows yet, or the straight couple sliding into third base against the wall.

I'll take the one I'm more qualified to break up and hope Jonas has his eye on the fight. It's hell getting through the dancers, but I keep my chest out and my elbows high, undeniably filling the space. Mace would be great right about now. Or bullhorns. Or the water cannons that Paul mentioned.

There are enough people with smartphones out recording the couple on the wall that I can't cover them all up with my hand. I shoulder through, give the nearest amateur pornographer the kind of glare I usually reserve for Nik, and tap the exhibitionist on the shoulder before he can get the girl's jeans down her hips.

I can't hear what the guy says over Nik's music, but he's about as angry at being interrupted as I'd expect.

I just point at the smartphones.

The effect isn't as immediate as I'd like, but it filters through the glaze over their eyes perceptibly, like the carbonation leaving soda flat. The girl's the first to get it, and she slaps the guy before she even bothers redoing her fly. To his credit, he takes the slap and launches into barely audible obscenities at the nearest asshole with a smartphone. I hold out an arm, don't say a word, and hope they take the hint—and wonder of wonders, they do.

The girl fumbles with her pants, storms through the crowd: the guy follows a moment later, around a swell in Nik's music that signals where one song ends and another begins. I check my phone. There's still about another three songs in this set, so fifteen minutes, maybe twenty before I have to be backstage again, which means I should start making my way now. I head in the opposite direction of the storming couple but keep to the wall, avoiding the pit in the center like it's contagious.

Jonas is in the pit.

Jonas is the figurative island of *linebacker* in the pit. For a moment, I'm relieved; this might be the safest measure I've never thought of.

But no, the figurative island is moving. *Dancing.*

I remember this. I remember how this feels. And I know the risks.

Never mind the music threading through me; an indignation stronger and slower than I've felt in years wells up, drives me into the crowd unheeding of what they see, do, care. The song's over halfway done by the time I get to the worst of the pit, and Jonas is still dancing, as much a part of this body as his fingers are to his hands. The sweat in the air is so thick that I almost choke on it when I shout, "Get your ass out front!"

Jonas hears me. He even turns to look.

And he laughs in my face, keeps dancing, and tries to drag me into the dance.

He misses. His palms are about as big as my face, and he swipes through the air, gives up, goes back to dancing, and puts a wall of bodies between himself and me, oblivious.

Onstage, Nik is singing as he watches us, as amused as a cat with a ball of string.

Fuck propriety. I break up the dancers in front of me and knot a fist in the back of Jonas's jacket, give him a yank. It's like moving a monolith, but at least this monolith has nerves and cognitive functions and might take the hint and move itself.

—or it might attempt to slug me in the face. *Fuck.*

If it had been a real premeditated punch instead of a careless swing, I wouldn't be standing. My shoulder throbs, but nothing's dislocated, and Jonas doesn't seem to give a shit. He's still trying to *dance*, but arms out and off-beat like a puppet.

I get around him, under his arm, shove the nearest poor shit out of the way and take hold of Jonas's jacket again. "Outside," I yell, "now—"

This time I see the punch coming, thank fuck, and dodge.

The dancer behind me isn't so lucky.

Once, when I had just moved in with Paul and still wasn't used to taking any bus that wasn't yellow, the crosstown I was on got into a pileup just off Herald Square. Never mind that I was already terrified of accidents: there was a particular kind of panic that happened then, when the world exploded around me and had nothing to do with me, when the ambulances came for people who weren't me and I still had to check, *Am I still here? If it's my fault, why am I still here?*

Someone else hits the floor in a mosh pit, on my watch, on my responsibility, and the panic is precisely the same.

I take Jonas by the collar and shove him out of the crowd with everything I have.

It's a mistake, and I know it, but it's the *only* mistake to be made, the only thing to be done. Jonas isn't dancing anymore, but his arms still arc wide. The crowd around him disperses, spreads and staggers, and I would be thankful if only I didn't have to dodge fists the size of rotisserie chickens.

About the only advantage I have right now is that I'm more afraid than angry.

Jonas takes another swing at me, on the same arc as the bass. He's big, but not slow, and I grab for his wrist and get nothing. I have to fall to one knee to duck the next punch, tearing my slacks on the concrete, and I shouldn't have time to worry about that when my fucked-up life is on the line.

Paul said he broke his fingers on Nik's thick head. I have to wonder if he hit anyone else during his time.

I sock Jonas in the back of the skull on the way up, and it stings like a bitch. Jonas doesn't go down, but he staggers—too close to the people on the edge of the fight, and like hell I'm going to let anyone else get hurt tonight because of Nik's fucking music.

I shake out my ringing knuckles and the song in my ears, and land an uppercut on Jonas's temple. It doesn't knock Jonas down either, but it affords me the time to hit him again. Then twice more. The fourth time, apparently, is the charm.

Jonas hits the floor. The lights of a dozen smartphones wash over his face, highlighting the blood and spit. Onstage, Nik keeps playing.

I turn to the first fan I see with her phone out. "Stop taping this fuckery and call an ambulance. Now."

Five or six of them obey.

FEBRUARY 11, 2012

In the comments to "Nik's new manager breaks some guy's face" (youtube.com/watch?v=to5c4-h0b4j) on February 11, 2012

<u>Top Comments</u>
I love how Nik just keeps playing through all this, he's a total pro.
oklaho (+37)

i'd hit it back
bleekerstreet14 (+23) in reply to junojunononono (Show the comment)

<u>All Comments (116)</u>
<u>Sign In</u> or Sign Up now to post a comment!

HAHAHA check out the chick at 2:32.
82heymickey82 (+4)

asbrooks.com Found him!
junojunononono (+2)

Dude, where'd Nik pick this guy up, the WWE?
hescoming (+1)
NIIIIIK <3<3<3<3<3
ohahanmeansfriend (+22)

Nik's concerts are THE BEST. THE END.
lastagainst (+19)

lol that poor shit
dhingiskhan088

totally going to one of these concerts when I turn 20 next year!!!!
nik is so hot!!!!
degrassi95 (+21)

u can have nik i want the mangaer
dhingiskhan088

This looks like an ad for iPhones, jfc.
lucyTcluy (+10)

mmmmmmmmm all to the tune of This Side
that song is so fierce
DreamsOfSiriano (+14)

This has been flagged as spam show
justthisguy

This has been flagged as spam show
justthisguy

This has been flagged as spam show
justthisguy

ew that bouncer is so big ad sweaty guess he liked nik tho.
XXsoraXXXXrikuXX (+1)

9/10
Zooooooooey

Cut the crap, Nik's real! REAL REAL REAL. Stop spamming you douche!
twinstar14 (+15) in reply to justthisguy (Show the comment)

I'd hit it!
junojunononono

February 11, 2012

The hotel wireless hiccups, and the next page of comments doesn't load. Morbidly fascinated as I am, it doesn't—shouldn't—matter. I shut the laptop and leave it on the end table.

It's five in the morning, and the bedside clock broadcasts that fact at me with artificial insensitivity. The urge to catch up on sleep on the bus is increasingly desperate, nags my eyelids open despite the grit at their corners.

Two concerts in, and already *this*.

I am fucked. My career is fucked. My life is fucked. It's 5 a.m. in Pittsburgh and my death is playing out on the internet at ten hits a minute.

Sleep has already decided it's not happening. I extricate myself from the covers and shove my feet into the nearest pair of shoes, then throw on a sweatshirt. There's a piano in the hotel lobby and like fuck I'll let anyone tell me I'm not allowed to play it. Or *play my math on it*, for that matter. Fuck Nik. Fuck Nik and Nik's rules.

But before the elevator doors open, I can already hear the piano at full tilt. Someone is playing Rachmaninoff's Prelude in C-sharp minor, and not poorly. A little too expressive with the swells and tempo changes, and maybe the articulation's heavy, but it's not incorrect. Even good. And it's more impressive that someone's playing it at all, so I make my way toward the lounge area, my fingers already chasing the notes through the difficult triplet passages. I know the piece. Even if this pianist doesn't share, at least he'll be constructive to listen to.

. . . Of course it's Nik. Nik, in a gray T-shirt that clings to his back with sweat despite the pervasive winter chill, bowed over the keyboard, hands easily meeting the demanding octaves. When I first learned this piece, I was sixteen and still growing, and I had to roll the larger chords in the coda. I'm not sure which is more compelling and annoying, Nik's big hands or the unhindered interpretation coming out of them.

Neither. It's Nik's smile. Because from this angle, behind the lounge couch, I can see every curve of it, and Nik is putting on a show.

"Rachmaninoff," I say, the same game we played months ago: *which composer is yours?* Nik winds into the soft coda, not softly enough for my taste but then, why would he.

"Great for drinks," Nik says. "Less boring when he's had a few."

"Shostakovich?"

"The opposite. More boring when he's drunk."

I sit down. I'm not sure when this game became *Which composer have you fucked?* but again, I'm not surprised. The couch, a thick brocade that must have been in this hotel for at least ten years, scrapes the back of my sweatshirt, just loud enough to mask Nik's chords. "Tchaikovsky?"

"Almost mine."

Like Dina Marshall, I'll bet. "Suicide?"

"Cholera." Nik laughs, pats the keys now that they aren't sounding anymore. "Not that he didn't think about it. As if cholera wasn't romantic enough."

I roll my eyes. "You know, you could settle a lot of questions in the musicological world if you gave a shit."

"If I gave a shit," Nik repeats, rephrases with that same edge of laughter. "They lived. They died. I know why they wrote what they wrote. Either they're mine or they're not. What more shit do I have to give?"

"Right," I say, "you'd have to substantiate your claims."

Nik turns on the piano bench, leans back with his elbows on the keys, letting the dissonant clusters ring. The song in my head wells up against the back of my eyes, as much fire as sound. I hate this. I put a man in the hospital tonight, and I hate this. And Nik.

"Does it hurt?" I ask, more sincerely than I meant to. "When I don't believe?"

"Only when you're an asshole about it," Nik says, cracks his neck. The piano interior vibrates sympathetically, a cloud of sound like a distant swarm of insects. "Does it hurt when I try to convince you?"

"What do you think?"

Nik scoffs through a smile, props up a hand to beckon me over. His elbow slides higher on the white keys, a half glissando, illustrating everything and nothing.

I stand, come nearer. It's not obedience, it's curiosity. The lie is far too convincing.

Nik only gets up from the bench when I'm at his side. I avoid the arc of his arm on the way up. "Play."

That sounds like a horrible idea. "Are we starting this shit again?"

"No," Nik says. "Play whatever you want. Music, math, I don't care. Just trying to make a point and it's easier if you play. So play."

I sit. The bench is residually warm. So are the keys. "You going to fuck with my head?"

"Yeah."

"Why should I let you?"

"You shouldn't."

The way Nik says it, it's almost funny enough to smile back to. Almost. "I told you that reverse-psychology crap wouldn't work on me."

"No. But putting pressure on you does. I like that. It makes you more fun."

"More *fun*?"

"Play."

I set my fingers up on the keys out of unadulterated spite.

For some reason I gravitate toward the same piece Nik just did, Prelude in C-sharp minor the way I learned it was supposed to be played. Soft, steady, melodious chords towering in their scope but fragile because of human nerves and failings. Over my shoulder, Nik laughs, low and insinuating.

"You're reading," Nik says, and so does the song in my head that I can't drive out. Lyrics. It has lyrics now, and that's part of them.

"I can't be reading if the score isn't in front of me," I murmur just as I start the triplet section.

"You're *reciting*. You memorized it and you're reciting."

Fuck. I falter at the half cadence, but play on through, take the *fortissississimo* reprise as loud as I've ever taken it. Nik tsks overhead, and I can't quite ignore his heavy presence at my back, but I try. The chords line up the way they should, plangent and dark, and my knuckles snap around air too thick to breach my skin. It's good. It's better than Nik did. It's good *and* right.

As my hands spiral toward the coda, Nik leans over me onto the stand, like a teacher circling a mistake. His fingers trail down my left arm, warm even through the sweatshirt. I can't swat him off. "You're good with the spreads. You don't cheat."

"My hands are almost as large as yours," I say, too absorbed in the chords to thank him.

"I remember."

So do I. And I miss the next pedal. *Shit.*

"Rachmaninoff was an asshole about that," Nik goes on, his hand still settled on my forearm. "He meant what he wrote, for the hands to intersect in the middle. He said it made the octaves stronger. So you're playing it the way he wants."

"Thanks, if that's supposed to be comforting."

Nik laughs. It's decidedly not comforting.

Neither is the way his other hand frames the back of my head.

can't drag us

No. *No.* Never mind finishing the song, I swing my legs around and get the hell off the bench. That doesn't stop Nik from grabbing me by the hood of my sweatshirt, but I swat him off, break for the elevator.

"No," I say. I should have said it before. It echoes on the strings. "Not this again."

"Not what?" Nik asks, and that *doesn't* echo on the strings, it fills my head, counterpoint to the song. "Not something I did?"

"I don't know what the fuck you did—"

"But you think I did it."

The elevator call button is dark under my hand. My fingertips hover, shake to a beat not my own. I put a man in the hospital tonight. It's my fault. Not Nik's. As long as it's my fault it means it's not Nik's.

"You asked if it hurt when you don't believe in me." Nik's voice and his footsteps are in the same counterpoint, slowed down by an order of magnitude, wheels on gravel or wind in a grating. "It hurts you when I don't believe in you, right? It hurts when I tell you you're wrong, when I take something from you, when I remind you you work for me. Why shouldn't it hurt me when you're just as much an asshole about it as I am?"

"Because you're lying." I don't turn. I can't look at him.

Nik laughs. Untranscribable, inerasable. "Aren't you?"

"No."

"You're not what you say you are. You call yourself a musicologist, and that's not what you do. You call yourself a scholar, and you don't have a place to study. You say you can play but you don't. And you treat me like you believe, and you do believe, and then shit like this comes out of your mouth. You know how it feels. You're feeling it now. It hurts, doesn't it?"

I press the elevator call button. Sparks fly and gears turn, inside the walls, where I'm not supposed to hear. Numbers flash overhead, descending, decreasing, not fast enough.

"You know I did something to you," Nik says. "You wouldn't be afraid if you didn't believe I could. That's how doubt works."

The elevator opens, rings and scrapes and grates on my skull—and then Nik holds me against the jamb. I shove him off, but Nik darts in before the door can close, blocks the way out and the wall of call buttons.

It's worse when he doesn't smile.

"You stopped someone from worshipping me," he says. "You did it out of spite. It wasn't like the first few times when you thought you were saving them. You broke him out of it even though you yourself believe. If it weren't so fun, I'd be much angrier than I am."

"*Fun*," I breathe.

"You like hurting me, don't you?" The earnestness in Nik's voice is more terrifying than his music. "Why shouldn't I feel the same about you?"

The elevator demands I choose a floor or get off.

"I can find pleasure in just about anything," Nik says. "And I'd rather be pleased with you than pissed off."

I shake my head, *no, no, a thousand times no.* "Drop the act."

"Exactly." Nik grins, and the elevator opens, and the sounds line up pitch-perfect. "Keep trying to stave it off. I can enjoy you either way."

"Get out. I'm going upstairs."

"You're going upstairs to lie awake and box up all your thoughts about me. It hasn't worked since you started believing, and it won't work now. Why fight me? Paul believes, and he's happy—"

I ram Nik out of the elevator, shoulder-to-sternum, and send him flying into the mirror on the far wall.

I hit the call button for my floor, hold the Door Close button down. The whirl of electricity floods the elevator, pulleys and wires and compressed clean air.

Nothing blocks Nik's laughter, not even four hotel floors.

Even though I don't recognize the number, I know exactly what call this is. I still let it ring twice, finish a long gulp of necessary coffee, since there's no other way I'll get to drink it before it gets cold. And I still answer the phone without a presupposition: "Anthony Brooks speaking."

"Good morning, Anthony. This is Detective Lansing."

I was right. The small sliver of hope that I was wrong tilts at its last windmill in my skull. "Good morning."

"This conversation is being recorded." She doesn't have to tell me *hanging up would be unwise.*

I fold my hand around the mug and slouch over the table, glad that no one else is at it. No one else gets to hear me talk to the FBI. This is my life. "I thought as much."

"Anthony, we've already received a fax of your incident reports pertaining to last Friday, Jonas Walker's in particular. We've also reviewed statements from the Pittsburgh police and UPMC. There is nothing the lawyers can tell us that we don't know."

"Then they should have told you that I was defending myself."

"I don't doubt that, Anthony, and I don't doubt that it will stand that way on the record. I'm more interested in a comparison of your experiences."

"They couldn't be more similar, Detective. And I shouldn't talk without the legal team here."

"I thought you might say that. But I consulted with the team at Pantheon, and they revealed that you aren't on the books. You aren't legally an employee. As such, they don't represent you."

The coffee doesn't chill; if anything, it's reciprocally warmer, since all the blood just stilled in my hands. "I thought this was about Nik."

"It is, in the long term. But Nik didn't fracture Jonas Walker's skull. You did."

Fuck. Fuck. Fuck. *Fifteen percent and Sydney's commission* just found competition in my head. *Fuck.* "In self-defense."

"Yes, YouTube's made that clear," Lansing says. "We have multiple accounts of the incident including your own. And I am sure Jonas will give his own when he wakes up, *if* he can and *if* he does. What the accounts don't tell us was why you felt compelled to approach him in the first place."

"He was supposed to be working. He wasn't doing his job."

"I see. And what were you supposed to be doing?"

I shut my eyes. It doesn't make the words come any easier. "Keeping my head above water, keeping the band playing, keeping the audience happy."

"Are those the tenets of your contract?"

"That's the advice of the woman I'm filling in for. Sydney Nerida."

"Yes, I've been in touch with Sydney. I only had to make one trip—she was already at Nik's apartment when we arrived."

We have a warrant, she doesn't have to say.

I hear it anyway, in the fragments of the song laughing in my head until it's hoarse. "Jonas didn't have a waiver, did he."

"No. Furthermore, he was in the employ of the venue and unconnected to Nik in any way. I don't need to tell you what may happen if his family decides to press charges."

"Self-defense, Detective."

"I'm sure you'll win. They may still sue. Lawsuits cost time whether you win or not. Knowing your uncle and his affinity for red tape, I am sure he'll draw this out as long as possible on your behalf."

Fuck this coffee. Fuck this table. Fuck this job. "What can I tell you that you don't already know, Detective Lansing?"

"About Nik."

I should have known. Maybe I knew. That doesn't make the song in my head any less pervasive. I'm not just fucked, I'm *collateral.* Dead and expendable.

Lansing's words are almost part of the goddamn song. "Is Nik killing those kids?"

It takes two breaths for me to answer. "I can't tell you because I honestly don't know." I don't. He insists they die for him. That's not the same. If it was, he could count me among them.

"Then find out for me," Detective Lansing says, in a tone that brooks no argument. "Find out for their families."

There's not much more to say after that, just *yes* and *thanks* and *I know*. It still feels like a lifetime before I hang up.

I take another gulp of coffee. It's tepid.

FEBRUARY 15, 2012

Whoever booked the winter leg of the tour through Rochester was an idiot.

The snowbanks on the roadside have probably been there since October. For all I know, so have some of the cars. A trip that's supposed to take five hours is instead *still going on*, and I have no idea where precisely on I-90 we are because the snow has taken out the bus's wireless and the GPS on my phone.

Three bunks down, someone is using white-noise headphones. All the way in the back, someone is using the bathroom and having trouble with the toilet. A floor below in the galley, the backing band is watching old episodes of *South Park* and singing along. Apparently Louanne's antibullshit policy is void in the event of snow.

I put my brand-new prescription earplugs in, and nothing changes. How the hell has my hearing gotten *better* while I've been working rock concerts?

The hooks of my curtain rustle, the bus wheels scrape on cold concrete. Maybe the darkness just makes the sounds worse, or maybe they really are that loud. Either way there's nothing to say about it, and nothing to do but stare at the ceiling and try to sleep.

Even the reading light makes noise, like a cloud portending rain.

I sigh, press my ear into the memory foam. Bored and awake enough to test Nik, it seems.

"Pergolesi or Scarlatti?"

"Pergolesi," Nik answers from the bunk under mine.

Right. "Robert or Clara?"

"Robert."

Right. "Fanny or Felix?"

"Neither."

Interesting. "Reich or Glass?"

"Reich." Nik turns a page of whatever he's reading. The paper sounds too rough to be a magazine—apparently I hear the difference. Downstairs, the backing band has launched into a drunken rendition of the next *South Park* song. Even at this volume I can tell their voices apart: Lorenzo, the keyboardist, who can definitely carry a tune; Thierry, the rhythm guitarist, who can't; Genevieve, who runs the mixer and does a good Mr. Mackey impersonation; Deon the bassist, and Mona the drummer, who is spending too much time laughing to sing.

Sleep isn't going to happen.

I arch back into the memory foam. My spine uncoils and air snaps through it, and I can't help the groan that follows. "Think they'll kill me if I ask them to keep it down?"

Nik snickers, turns another page. "Yeah."

Figures. "What about you?"

"What, will I kill you or will they kill me?"

"Either."

"No."

"You could have just said that."

"I wanted to know what you asked."

"Fine." I sigh and shut my eyes again. No, it's still too loud down there for me to sleep. Someone opens a beer can—fuck, how can I tell it's a can and not a bottle this far away? "Can you? Keep people quiet, I mean." It would make sense: if Nik can drive me nuts with music and noise, he can probably take it away. God, I wish I could.

Nik doesn't answer. That doesn't mean it's quiet.

A minute passes, at least: a real minute, ticking by with unasked questions.

Fine, I'm getting nothing out of him. I can't believe Lansing wants me to spy on the guy. "Is Cage one of yours?"

Another page turns, loud enough that the corner must have creased. Nik groans, more under his breath than on it. "John Cage is almost as frustrating as you are."

"I'll take that as a compliment."

It's surprising, confusing even, that Nik doesn't laugh. Then again, I didn't either.

"Great ideas," Nik says. "Endless ideas. Sometimes even the right ideas. And then he wraps them in rules and systems and takes the music away."

I nod, turn onto my side. The pillow dampens some of the sounds from the galley and the engine. "But that was his point," I say. "Silence is music."

"Cage didn't create silence."

I listen.

"'Four minutes and thirty-three seconds' isn't silence," Nik says, and the sharp edge of his tone is almost as fascinating to me as the words around it. "If anything it's the opposite. It uses silence to show there *isn't* silence. He tells the players not to play, and the audience listens. It's breathing and snickering and shuffling feet. It's not silence."

You hate him, I don't say. I don't have to; it's clear. "So you have to use music to create silence, which means there's no silence at all."

Underneath me, Nik shuts the book.

I win this round. It shouldn't feel so good, but then, nothing else has lately. "Simon or Garfunkel?" I ask.

"Fuck you," Nik says.

I settle into the mattress, and don't quite smile.

FEBRUARY 20, 2012

Nik is late.

It's unfair. Everyone else is already on the bus (or at least at it—Mona and Thierry apparently need cigarettes at 8:37 a.m.), and I even cut my morning run short to get back down here on time. Not that it's pleasant, running through Rochester in February in the dead dog-walk hours of the morning, but it's the principle of the thing, and Nik isn't answering his phone.

No one was hurt last night. I hope it's still true.

I double-check with the others what room Nik is supposed to be in, and *gladly* tell the front desk to spam his suite with wakeup calls until he answers. Once that figurative gear is turning, I head up to the room in question and bang on the door. After the first three tries, I stop being courteous to the neighbors. Over five minutes later, I go back downstairs, inform security that he isn't there, and call Nik's phone again.

Someone answers this time, on the fourth ring. "Yeah, sorry. Hello?" The voice is too high to be Nik's.

I ask, "Where the fuck are you?" anyway.

"Eastman," she giggles. "Oh wait, is this my phone? This isn't my phone. Ha-ha-ha, this isn't my phone! Luke, check it out, I'm on Nik's phone!"

"No shit." I grind my teeth. Fucking groupies. "And this is Nik's manager. I'd rather talk to him than you."

"Oh shit, it's the bald guy!" She sounds far too excited to be scared. "Luke seriously, it's the bald guy! The bald guy's calling me!"

"I'm not calling you, this is Nik's phone. Put him on, now."

"I can't. He's asleep."

"Then wake him up."

"But that's rude!"

"Do I sound like I care?"

"Ha-ha, fine. Luke, Cory, come help me wake him up!"

By this time, I'm almost out the hotel doors. I hear the girl's partners in accidental kidnapping agree to start waking Nik up. Good. He might be here in half an hour, or we can pick him up on the way, and we'll be on the road to Albany only a little behind schedule.

Then I hear just how these Eastman students have decided to wake Nik up.

The revolving hotel door hits my ass on the way out. Literally.

The level of aural clarity between our phones is commercially distressing. I hear all three groupies' voices as distinctly as the trebles in a string quartet, and when Nik's unsteady breath unravels into amused laughter and a distinct "that's fine, come here," well, there's the fucking cello.

"Nik," I shout into the phone to make this digital connection mutually uncomfortable. "Nik, I know you can hear me. Tell me where you are."

"Eastman," Nik says. Either he's projecting or the phone is very close to his lips. He laughs, low and heady. It's the latter. He's on the phone with me while groupies are going down on him. This is disgusting. I wish it wasn't also arousing. I hate him. And my life.

And I need to end this call, *now*. "At least tell me which section of the dorm."

"Don't remember." The tail end of that word tapers into a faint moan, a hissed intake. "And I'm not getting up to check."

I could throw the phone onto the concrete, but I don't have time to get it replaced. "Fine. Then call me when you're done."

"No, stay on the line. It's just the three of them. Maybe when one gets off they'll feel like telling you."

Fuck this. Everyone else laughs. There's a room a few blocks away where three Eastman students are taking turns giving Nik head and *laughing at me*.

I stay on the line. It's my job. "We were supposed to be on the road to Albany half an hour ago."

Nik's laughter is slipping, increasingly breathless. "Guess so."

"I suppose you don't care."

"No, I care. I just also, mm, care about the people right in front of me."

I brace myself against the side of the bus. I can't help listening. One of the boys corrects Nik, *right on top of you, not right in front,* and they're all still laughing. I remember that night back in New York, how Nik's skin shifted under my hand, how quickly his pulse ran, more sound than motion. I'm hearing it now.

And if I listen for more than a minute, maybe the rules will change.

"We're leaving the hotel," I say, as evenly as I can. "We'll pick you up at the Gibbs entrance at nine thirty sharp. If you keep us waiting any longer than that it won't just be fans disappointed in you, all right?"

"Sure," Nik says. "That mean you'll stay on the line?"

Someone comes.

I hang up.

MARCH 3, 2012

Boston is tamer than Cambridge is tamer than Albany is tamer than Rochester, and only the first is surprising. Every other time I've been to a concert in Boston I've come out of it with a headache for the ages. At this point, I'd be thankful for just the headache, but I've now had a headache *and* an eyeful, and it's still less than what I've dealt with since Pittsburgh.

I've shown the video of me punching Jonas out to the bouncers and security guards at every venue since. It's accrued eight hundred thousand hits in the last month. I was pretty disgusted with myself at first for making that the first thing people know about me, but honestly, it's worked. The payoff is worth it. I haven't had to raise my fists since.

The rules are the rules, and they're holding true, at least for now.

By the end of the second set, most of the pit is topless. I pay it no mind on my way to the stage. Until someone starts getting publically fucked, it's not my place to defuse it. That feels like an increasingly arbitrary distinction. Dozens of breasts and upper arms bounce when the fans jump and cheer. Maybe I should get a blindfold to match the white-noise headphones I liberated from the bus.

Sure. Like that would help my liability for all this fuckery.

Since the No Alcohol rule doesn't apply to the band members (though it possibly should) I take a six-pack backstage with me. For once, it's *not* my job, but the barbacks are running ragged and it's on my way. I glance at Lorenzo, sprawled behind the keyboard setup in the back. Lorenzo has the least work of any of them since Nik doesn't always score for keyboards, but he's still getting paid almost as much as the staples. I should be grateful that somewhere, out there, pianists are getting the priority pay they deserve, but it doesn't matter since I'm not one of them. And once you get into that business—

The song in my head whispers against the shell of my ear. It's better to keep it in than to let Nik in beside it, live. I'm not sure when I started personifying this bullshit.

How long will the white-noise headphones work before I'm inured?

Once the applause and dancing have died down, I shoulder past the backstage crew to the edge of the stage, break a bottle out of the carton and wave it toward Mona, who's nearest. I can't hear her reply, but she looks thankful enough, and reaches over her kit to take the six-pack. I read a *thank you* off her lips and mouth a *you're welcome, good job* back.

Something tugs on the bottle in my hand, pulls me into the light, and kisses me.

It isn't Nik. There are no bones about how it isn't Nik. Whoever it is is shorter, broader, and doesn't make my head immolate or sing. He also has substantial stubble on his chin and a wide jaw and either an extremely hard pelvis or a wall over his hips. It's the latter. It's a bass guitar. It's Deon.

Deon's not a bad kisser.

I thought he was straight. Then again, I never asked.

The fans haven't stopped whistling. They haven't stopped phone-taping everything either.

Shoving the other guy off when you don't want to be kissed is a perfectly appropriate response, and if I'm a little forceful about it, I'm sure no one cares. Deon grabs the beer out of my hand with a grin on his face that says *no hard feelings*.

Nik laughs into his microphone. "My manager, ladies and gentlemen!" he says, with a wide arc of his arm that sends the words clear through the plastic and white noise, sets them echoing in the crowns of my teeth.

Deer do stall in headlights.

"Come on," Nik says. "Play."

He says it just like every other time, but now his mouth doesn't have to move for me to hear it.

MARCH 4, 2012

Posted to asbrooks.com on March 4, 2012

"Afterword: Boston and Cambridge concerts, 3/2 and 3/3/12"

In light of the recent developments in amateur videography that have led to my increased presence on YouTube, I am instituting a policy, effective today. I don't expect any of you to follow it, I just want it known. Think of it as my equivalent of Nik's waiver.

I am Nik's manager. This is my job. As far as I know the position is temporary and I will thereafter return to my pursuit of my intended career—which as anyone reading this blog knows, is the kind of career that requires tenure—and the sensationalism inherent of this unexpected memetic popularity is not the type that will help me secure that career.

Whoever linked this blog with the videos of the incident last month in Pittsburgh: I hope someone, someday, does the same to you. I'm sure that the people who might otherwise have hired me will be thrilled to watch me send a guy to the hospital, because it's extremely relevant to my musicological pursuits. I understand that Nik is a public figure with a stage persona and a policy that no press is bad press. I'm not Nik.

Therefore, because I can't stop you from taping me, I won't try. But everything that happens at Nik's concerts stays at Nik's concerts. Everything that happens to me there is in no way relevant to my work as a musicologist, past or present. I maintain that I am not under any influence, and not deliberately seeking attention, and just doing my current job. What I do for Nik at Nik's concerts has nothing to do with my professional aspirations.

So here's the waiver. Any documentation of these activities is without my consent. If you post in ignorance of that, I can't stop you. If you post willfully, you're an asshole. And I hope it reflects as poorly on you as it does on me.

Comments (67)

Eusebius
Kind of oxymoronic.

> **ASBrooks**
> There are other reasons that I can't talk about here. But these people don't need or want my permission. It's not about permission.

> > **Eusebius**
> > Fair enough. It's still awkward though. What happened this time?

> > **ASBrooks**
> > You'll hear. I won't talk about it here and give confirmation either way.

Dekultuur
hi there.

youtube.com/watch?v=4din4-NE8n0

youtube.com/watch?v=5CaRm-1g70N

> **ASBrooks**
> I know where they are.

Dekultuur
oh okay. u can try to get them deleted tho.

ASBrooks
Thanks. I'm not sure if that would just make it worse.

EliseMorgenstern
hugs I'm so sorry there's not a good way out of this, and I'm sorry if my encouragement has contributed in any way. I know how much this part sucks.

ASBrooks
Really? Thanks.

EliseMorgenstern
Yeah. I know you don't want to talk about it here, but I've had important things get out before I wanted them to too. We can talk about it on the phone if you want.

ASBrooks
Sure. We're on the road tomorrow. I'll call before we cross the border. Honestly, thanks.

EliseMorgenstern
No problem. Hang in there!

CrossBridge
I hope this policy works out, and I'm really sorry for linking you with the blog in the first place.

ASBrooks
It's fine. You didn't think it was going to get this far either. I could always have denied it.

CrossBridge
If it's any consolation, I don't think any university hiring committee is going to hold what YouTube people say against you.

ASBrooks

I've been on hiring committees. I know they do.

CrossBridge

You could always stick with Nik instead. You're good at it, you know. Maybe there's a career to be made there?

ASBrooks

I know you're trying to be helpful but that is the last thing I wanted to hear.

CrossBridge

Sorry.

ASBrooks

Just let it go.

kingssingersFTW

JSYK you sound really entitled. Be thankful you have a job and stop telling people what they can and can't do.

ASBrooks

In my capacity as Nik's manager, it is my responsibility to tell people what they can and can't do.

kingssingersFTW

Nik lets people do whatever they want. That's the point.

ASBrooks

I'm not Nik.

kingssingersFTW

If you stop policing his gigs we'll stop policing you.

ASBrooks

Keep threatening me. Go right ahead.

kingssingersFTW
That's not a threat, that's a promise.

ASBrooks
I hope I get there in time to stop whatever happens to you, just so your parents have to thank me.

kingssingersFTW
See you in Wichita, asswipe.

Florestan
Hang in there!

ASBrooks
Thanks.

CraneWife3
What's so bad about kissing the bassist? Why would you want to work for people who aren't okay with who you are?

ASBrooks
That's not who I am.

Just because you and the rest of Nik's fans don't care who sees what you do with other people doesn't mean I'm the same. Who I involve myself with is none of my employers' business and should be within my control to disclose. Nothing like that had ever happened before, and I wasn't expecting it. I'm sure you think it's romantic. It's not. It's a hassle.

I'm glad that you seem to enjoy a world where you'll be financially taken care of regardless of what stupid decisions other people make for you.

beautifulgeese
wow, your a jerk

ASBrooks
I'm a jerk for wanting some control over my personal life.

beautifulgeese
no, your a jerk for answering her like a jerk. she just thought people should treat you like a person and anyone who hires you should be okay with who you are.

ASBrooks
You seem to know who I am better than I do.

beautifulgeese
guess so cause your an asshole.

juliamei
I know you're coming from a place of concern and hope, but the reality is that it's difficult to get hired as a teacher if you have easily accessible personal material that is in any way controversial. It sucks, but it's true, and Anthony's within his rights to want as much of his personal life under his control as possible.

beautifulgeese
what he did shouldnt be controversial. how hes acting right now should say more about him than any of those clips.

juliamei
I don't disagree with you. But his potential employers probably do.

beautifulgeese
then he shouldnt work for them. nobody should.

ASBrooks
I wish.

DontFret
Hey! Didn't know you were blogging the tour. Hope you don't mind that I'm keeping up now.

Just want to go on record and set it straight. It was just a kiss, I started it, I'm not even gay, it was a good show and I was just really thankful for the beer. Take it with a grain of salt. I guess that's as much for anyone who needs the disclaimer as much as for you. You're a sport.

ASBrooks
You're posting from the galley, aren't you.

DontFret
Yeah. We need a fourth for Guitar Hero. You in?

ASBrooks
Give me ten minutes, I have to call Sydney.

Eusebius
Fair warning: he sucks at vocals.

DontFret
Everyone sucks at vocals. That's why we play drunk.

(Go to Page 2)

MARCH 5, 2012

E lise doesn't wait for me to call. She never does. In this case, she calls right when customs is asking everyone on the bus to wave their passports around. The Mounties aren't the kind of sticklers I expected them to be, but then, I've never been to Canada and nearly all of my foreign experience is in Germany and Austria, where they really do care if you're American.

I don't know where the hell Nik is, let alone whether he's going to get caught, but at least if I'm on the phone it looks like it's not my fault if anything goes wrong. For once, I have plausible deniability.

"Sorry if it's a bad time," Elise says.

A little late to be sorry, but it's not as if it matters. "We haven't crossed the border yet." It's true enough.

"But it's been way too long," she says, whether she's heard me or not, "and keeping up online is one thing but it's not the same as really knowing what you're up to. I mean, you've got to be cagey, and I bet it's exciting enough that there's no real time to deal with people who aren't there."

"You put it better than I would."

She laughs. "I'm writing more papers than you. I'm in shape, I guess!"

I know she doesn't mean to rub it in. She never does. It still stings. "Guess so."

"But your modern music muscles must be getting a workout! Have you crossed over to the dark side of ethno yet?"

This is not the time for an argument about just how ridiculous and potentially offensive that turn of phrase is. "No. I'm not doing an academic study of him. Laurie will be, once we catch up with him in California, but—"

"But you're too close to get the view you need."

"And I don't want to. I think that's more important."

"Right."

The pause is as awkward as any on the phone can be. And not silent or private: not with breathing and coffee shop chatter on her end and Canadian border guards loosely patrolling mine.

"So," we say at the same time—and I yield. Elise goes on, "About what I said about secrets."

I'm honestly relieved. If she thinks she has a comparable experience, I'll take what I can get; misery loves company. "Right."

"You know," she says, "I was out at school before I was out to my family. But I was really, really out—GSA board and kinky film club and pride-float committee and everything. And since I still had a boyfriend for most of college, even though we were both bi, I never had to explain anything to my parents, and I had no idea what they'd think, so I didn't try to. Milo was okay with that and said it was my choice and everything, so he didn't bring up how we met or who else we slept with together or anything.

"But then we both started getting serious with Audrey, and Audrey wasn't really . . . what's the word? Scrupulous? About that. And didn't like being introduced as anything other than what he was because Audrey thought everyone should just accept you for what you are.

"So my parents came down for my thesis presentation, and they invited me and Milo out to dinner after, and Audrey said that there's no reason to leave the rest of the relationship out and told my parents right there. And was a real jerk about it."

No shit. And that kind of drama is one of the reasons I never came out to Paul. He took me in: I didn't need to be even more of a burden on his charity. And I knew I would be, because the only gays that cross Paul's path are costume designers, club kids, or on the down low. Better for him to think I just don't think about sex. Like him.

I don't have anything good to say to her, but it's Elise, and I *should* say something so she knows I'm still here. "What an asshole."

"Yeah, he was, I guess. I mean, I know why he did it and maybe everyone was kind of at fault for not drawing the lines clear enough, but that was seriously cold. And it really ruined my parents' visit, and they spent the whole time grilling me and Milo about whether things were even safe—you've met my parents, we're not exactly the most progressive family out there, and they said some seriously gross things to Milo, and we decided to take a break that night and that break turned into breaking up." She laughs. I've heard Elise frazzled, and heard her laugh at herself, but it's never hitched like this. "If my thesis hadn't gone well, I think that would have been the worst day of my life."

It startles me enough that I laugh too, and the border guard nearest to me raises his eyebrow. I wave him off, and lower my voice. "Don't take this the wrong way, Elise, but I'm glad I'm not the only one." She doesn't have to know why. She can sleuth it together, if I know her at all. I can say a lot of things about Elise, but she's an excellent scholar, and a better friend than I probably give her credit for.

"Ha, I know what way you mean. It's fine." The time she takes to pause is still awkward, but more because I know what's coming. "Your uncle doesn't know, does he?"

Bingo. I nod, even though she can't see it. "I've never brought anyone home. He's never brought it up."

I'm sure she nods too: there's a faint switch in the reception. "Well, like you said, Deon kissed you. If you still don't want your uncle to know, you can hang on to that for a while. But if he hasn't asked before, do you think he's going to ask now?"

"He may not," I agree. "He's got enough to deal with." I can hope.

"Yeah, and with all that's happening on the tour, who knows? It might just get lost under everything else you both have to deal with. But if it doesn't, well. I guess not being alone is something."

There's nothing to say to that but, "It is."

Elise laughs, and the border guards file off the bus. Whether they checked Nik's passport after all or whether they never saw him doesn't matter: no one checks with me about it. And I have an alibi, for this at least, if something turns up later. That I have to think about that at all disturbs me. If I'm lucky, nothing will get in my way until we cross the border again.

Wishful thinking.

"So! Enjoy Canada!" Elise says. "I forget, have you ever been?"

Nik speaks to the waiter in French. He's all the way at the other side of the table, but I still hear him clearly, and his diction isn't Québécois, it's metropolitan, as neutral as a newscaster.

I should figure out what I'm ordering. Which means I should stop listening to Nik.

Not that anyone's in a hurry. Most of the band are still carrying on conversations despite the presence of the waiter, which Paul drilled out of me years ago. Lorenzo reveals that he took French in high school and then shares the story of the incompetent and insulting administrators that went with it, and when the waiter gets to him he asks for more time. More time for him is more time for me though, and by the time the waiter gets to my side I've decided. Brie, ham, and arugula omelet. I miss fresh eggs. All the hotels serve scrambled from the carton.

"Good call," Mona says, "that was my second choice. Half of yours for half of mine?"

"What are you having?"

"A mushroom burger."

"Sure."

"Switch seats with Gen, that'll make sharing easier."

"Hey," Genevieve cuts in, "how about asking me first?"

Mona gives Genevieve's chair a shove. "Like it matters?"

"Ha-ha."

Thierry snickers into his coffee. "Who gets a hamburger in Quebec?"

"Americans," Genevieve says.

"I don't know," Mona shrugs. "The kind of person who wants to see what they think a burger is maybe?"

"A burger's a burger." Thierry taps the menu. "That's the point of a burger."

"That's like saying wasabi's wasabi in America. It's not even made from the same horseradish."

Genevieve and I switch seats, which puts me right in the thick of the band, across from Deon, about one tier closer to Nik at the head. Between the band and the techs that have joined us, there are enough people here for a Last Supper parody, and the line of pushed-together tables doesn't help. If Nik is Jesus, I just moved up from Simon to Matthew. It's hilarious. I don't laugh.

"Since when is wasabi not wasabi?" Lorenzo asks, interrupting his own story.

"Ask Nik." Mona shrugs. "He's the one that lived there."

A coordinated glance at the head of the table confirms that Nik's still chatting up one of the waiters in French. Fucking groupies.

Mona laughs, and a few others join in, and she turns to the group. "Ask him later, I guess."

Deon asks, "When was he living in Japan?"

I, apparently, will be the one to answer, because no one else speaks up. "About ten years ago, he said. Until 2007."

"And he was just there before the tour too, I remember," Lorenzo says.

I would rather have not remembered that. I wonder if my ludicrously expensive tequila is enjoying its shelf life back in New York.

"Cool," Deon says. "Think he'll take us there next?"

"If they still like him, maybe," Mona says.

Genevieve asks me, "You ever been to Japan?"

I shake my head and reach for the breadbasket a table over before Thierry gets the last section of baguette. "Just Europe. I did research in Germany and Austria, kept to that general area for a year."

"Bach work?"

"Yeah."

"You know, forget Japan, Nik should take us on a Euro tour," Mona says.

"He doesn't have a passport," I remind them. "It was hard enough getting him into Canada."

"How'd he get into Japan?"

"Fuck if I know."

"He could get into Europe the same way, they're less strict there," Lorenzo says.

Thierry nods. "I'm sure the boss will take care of it. He had trouble with mine too. I think it's still expired."

"It's not like you need a visa if you're only spending a week in each country," Mona says.

Wait.

Wait, something's wrong here. Busboys deliver drinks. Baguettes are replenished. No one at the table has questioned Nik's lack of identity. There it is.

"Don't artists get special rules?" Deon doesn't seem to ask that of anyone in particular, but I get the directed eyes after no one answers.

Nik is now flirting with both a waiter and a waitress from another corner, still in French. Our orders probably haven't been entered into the system at all. *Fucking groupies.*

I could say *I don't know*, which is true, and let the conversation take off to wherever from there.

Instead, because it's Deon, and because Detective Lansing needs an excuse if I'm ever to be exonerated, I give this a shot. "It doesn't bother you, does it."

"That Nik's a god?" Deon glances at the lighting fixtures. "Does, but it's true."

A faint swell of laughter blocks out the music, and not all of it is outside my head. I fold my hand around my water glass, lower my voice, and lean a little farther across the table. "Why do you follow him?"

Deon doesn't laugh. He doesn't appear to give the answer much thought, but he doesn't act like I'm nuts either, and that's refreshing. "The music's good. It's scary as shit to play, but it's good, and it's real, and so's he. I don't know how else to explain it. You wouldn't say the sky wasn't blue. It's like that."

I check the head of the table sidelong, just to make sure Nik's not listening in. It's pointless and I know it, but I do it anyway.

"Look," I say, low, "you're not crazy, and my uncle's not crazy. But Nik *makes people crazy.*"

"I know; I've seen it. I've been there."

"How long?"

"I've been playing for him about three years now."

"And you don't care about the people you're letting run wild?"

A busboy reaches over Deon's shoulder, sets down coffee and milk. Deon looks up, thanks him, and starts mixing them together. "I care," he says. "And yeah, there've been a few who go too far. But I'd be going too far too if I was down there instead of up here."

"And since you're up here?"

"I'm making his music."

I take a long, careful look at Deon's face, and line it up with the ones I've broken. The similarities are entirely superficial: no bright mad eyes, no smile to speak of. Deon could be counting off time.

"You've believed in crazy things before," he tells me, "all of us have. So all of us do."

At the head of the table, Nik lets the waiter and waitress go. He eyes a corner of the ceiling, at a speaker switching from one song to the next.

A busboy refills my water, in an absence of music but not in silence.

MARCH 16, 2012

No, Elise, I haven't been to Canada. I've been staying in a hotel for five days and it's still hard to say I've been here. I turn corners on avenues with French names, sprint down streets far too cold for March, have run out of Canadian dollars in band petty cash and have to convert more at a disadvantageous exchange rate, and, yes, Canadians do end sentences with *eh* and *non* in equal measure, but *no, Elise, I have not been to Canada.*

One might even go so far as to say I'm *not* here, as in *not all there*, if one was a sanctimonious asshole.

Either way, I finally have the freedom to run. It's the wrong time of day, and the streets are more crowded than I'd like, but "beggars can't be choosers" is fast becoming the motto of my adult life. It's almost eight at night, the band doesn't have a gig, and Nik doesn't have an interview, and I don't have any immediate shit to take care of. So I run.

I don't bother with headphones since I'll never be able to drown everything out on a street this busy. There's barely any sidewalk, but running along the shoulder of the street is apparently legal here and no one blinks. There's probably a park where it would have been less hassle to run, but, birds, stones, killing. I shouldn't think about that. I shouldn't think about anything. I should run—I might as well pretend I've experienced the glory of Montreal. Pretending doesn't make it any easier *to see* the city, but I'm sure I'll be back. After all, my passport is entirely legitimate.

Speaking of assholes, who let him out?

I skid to a stop on the street corner opposite his side of the street. The cars stop a second later. There's an open-air market, the kind of place with crepe stands and buskers who leave their violin cases open.

But it's not a violin case, it's a guitar case, acoustic, turned on its small side, and Nik's propping one foot on it like Washington crossing the Delaware.

He could be a look-alike. Plenty of guitarists ape his style. This is Canada. No one's watching him but me, but that's almost certainly because he isn't playing yet. I wonder if the laymen know who he is.

He grins, at no one in particular, and strums, just once.

Of course I hear it, traffic and all. Cars rev, and people chatter, fremescent and French, but six simple notes cut through the bluster. It's Nik, just fucking around, like back in New York, like so many times on the bus. Practicing. That's all. The tents are coming down and stands are being wheeled away; they must be closing the market for the night, which means no audience, which means Nik isn't here to busk. Passersby still stop with their hands on their purse zippers and the market seems trapped in slow motion as soon as Nik's fingers touch the strings.

I should stop him. This definitely isn't authorized. Sydney doesn't know. Paul doesn't know. There's nothing on the schedule; it may not even be legal in Montreal. Aren't there supposed to be lyres in the subways and lists and rules, just like there are in New York?

Nik sings, a low hoarse whisper over the traffic.

Right. Right, there are no rules.

The lights change, first red, then green, and this time the cars don't start again. The tents come down, but don't roll up. The crowd congests, thick enough to spill out into the street, murmuring and asking and singing along, and Nik keeps playing, just him, no band, no artifice. I remember insulting him, telling him he creates nothing but riots.

The cars a block away start honking, stalled, too far from here to hear him. But I'm not. I can. Someone dances into the street, green light and all, but the cars don't move. Someone else laughs, joins her. Overhead, people lean out of their buildings like they're watching a parade, open their windows, tap their fingers on the sills to Nik's beat.

How can they stand it? I know my ears are fucked up, but theirs aren't. They shouldn't be able to differentiate between twenty angry commuters and a crowd of hundreds to hear one man on one unamplified guitar. They shouldn't. They *are.* They believe.

Fuck. So do I.

MARCH 17, 2012

The noise-canceling headphones have lasted two weeks. At this point, they're at the *better than nothing* stage. I bet they'll be completely useless by Seattle, if not as early as Chicago. Traces of the song in my head are echoed in everything Nik plays now and half of the things he says, in how the cuff of his jeans scrapes the mic stand and the pattern of his nails on the strings and the humid crackle of hair plastering his neck. I'm all the way across the venue with a world of bodies and speakers and smoke between me and Nik, and every sound that Nik's body makes is as clear as an alarm.

I watch, with my hands and back pressed to the concrete wall. No one else in the crowd is still. A missed patch of hair on the nape of my neck splinters, stings. I'm not sure whether I've fucked up in the past, present, or future tense, but that's definitely the right verb. Maybe it's in that awkward state of adverbial hell. Subjunctive, continuous, complete with AAVE. *I be fucked.* It sounds uncannily like *I believe.*

I leave for the front hall and refuse to categorize the act of leaving as more or less difficult than it's been in the past. The shock of cold air in the lobby is almost exhilarating, dry enough to know it's a difference in humidity, not temperature. Some roadie hands me a stack of waivers, and I take the white-noise headphones off just in time to catch, "—about thirty whose IDs didn't match up."

"Where are they now?" I have work. I work for Nik. Nik is a god. It's really starting to add up. It's the only thing that makes sense. He's a god, he's fucked with my head for half a year, and I can't convince myself that either of those statements is false. Not anymore. Not in the face of overwhelming evidence.

He told me that my head's never clear. If that's true, how is it so easy to see him in it?

"The kids?" The roadie waves dismissively at the front doors. "We scared them off. Anything inside we should call the police about?"

"Not that I know of." They'll believe too if they get close enough. Nik can do that. He did it to me, and I don't have a clue what else he wants, now that he's got that. "Are you going in?"

"No, I'll man the lobby."

I nod, give her back the waivers and tell her to check in with security. She does, and I don't watch. It gets easier. It's an ostinato alongside the song in my head, an incongruous steady counterpoint to the chaos above it. Without the white noise, I can hear Nik through the walls.

It's the song that possessed me at the second show, *once we get in there they can't drag us out.*

Believing gets easier too. So does the state of being fucked. He told me that I can't give it up if I don't let it go.

Fine. I'll let go. I can't fight the truth.

The words disappear entirely: the electronics track and the lead guitar soar up and eat through them like a grease fire. I lean against the door like it could ground the sympathetic vibrations in my bones, and it can't. Sound suffuses them, melts my joints, and weighs my eyes shut. Euphoria is a strange word. But that's what this is, isn't it? So I listen, unclutter the corners of my mind that the sound has to pass through like I'll never hear this again—

—like I'll never hear anything again—

Nik. The shift of his skin under my hand; the half-awake, half-alive, paralyzing pleasure of fighting him, fucking him, both, neither. *"Almost there,"* he said, the second time, and that he wouldn't stop me. All along, he's just wanted me to listen, like everyone else he makes so happy. I do, and it feels like walking off a limb that's fallen asleep, like pushing past pain until everything is just sharpened clarity. Like the third hit of Adderall the night before exams.

A body slams into the door from the opposite side, hard enough that I take the recoil.

That's a cue to move, and move fast, and I shove the white-noise headphones on in the same frantic motion that opens the door. One person topples onto her back, and the second falls on her knees, and the state of their clothes and their position leaves no illusions about what they are doing. Aside from a glance at me and a giggle, they don't stop either.

I stagger into the room, trip on someone's discarded boot. Those two are far from the only ones.

There are at least seven hundred people in this room. Most weren't all that dressed to begin with and over a third are naked now, or baring enough skin that it shines in the stage lights. Clothes litter the concrete floor, bunched up under bodies that might still be dancing by an ancient definition. Twos and threes and fours tangle together, and I hear every gasp, see every hitch.

Nik is a beacon. Even his voice beams. The song has no words anymore. Neither do I.

Our eyes lock.

I straighten, fix my arms at my sides. I can't turn, can barely breathe. The floor isn't even: my heels catch on glasses, shirts, phones as I back away, one excruciating centimeter at a time. For all that I'm trying to leave, I'm still here. We're still connected. I'm still listening. Nik's voice seeps through the cracks in the headphones, like a vacuum crushing a body in space. I remember that market, just him and the guitar, stopping traffic. The ones who couldn't hear him, trapped in their cars and red lights and rules. The ones who could, leaned out their windows and danced and were happier for it. I could be happier, or at least less trapped. I could give in.

I believe. That's all it takes.

Even after the door shuts between us, I see and hear nothing else. That's it. He's it. There's nothing left to fight, because he is what he is and I can't hold off the truth anymore. It's not my job. It's not my place. And I can tilt at all the windmills I want; they'll still be windmills and impossible dreams, and a life in which Nik isn't a god is an impossible dream. The sky is blue, the earth is round, the job market is oversaturated, and Nik is Dionysus come to earth. And it is my job to keep him here. I signed that contract, and I'm reaping those benefits, and I can't bite the hand that feeds anymore. There's no point.

The sirens outside come as a complete surprise.

I reach up to my ears, fold my palms over the headphones. They're useless now, and I know it, so I peel the band back along my skull, drop them onto the floor. They don't bounce. The roadie from earlier is already running toward me, and I understand what she's saying before I hear it, if I hear it at all.

I could let the police in. I probably should. They would break this up, destroy the concert, charge in here with cuffs and nets and seven hundred Drunk and Disorderlies. I could do my job.

Which part of this is my job?

"Officers," I say as soon as I meet them outside, "what seems to be the problem?"

Canadian police wear their vests over their coats. The officer nearest me glances at the other five over his shoulder—and the cars parked on the street, lights still spinning—then looks me up and down like he doesn't expect competence. "We've gotten multiple reports of illegal activity. Are you in charge here?"

I don't address that last point. "What illegal activity, officer? Are we above the noise ordinances?"

"No."

"Are too many people out in the street?"

"No."

"Is anyone hurt?"

"We've had no reports of—"

"Have the bouncers let in anyone they shouldn't have?"

"Not that we—"

"And no one here is underage." I swipe the folder of waivers right out of the roadie's hands. I hold it up in the cop's face. "Everyone in here is over the age of twenty-one—excuse me, twenty, this is Canada—and everyone signs these. It presupposes consent and absolves both our agency and the venue."

I speak to the rhythm of the song in my head. I'm in. They can't drag me out.

"Anyone we give you, you can have," I say. "The rest belong to Nik."

And so do I.

MARCH 18, 2012

I t is four in the morning, and like fuck am I running in two hours. I disable my phone alarm in the elevator, and swear I can hear the information snap out of existence on the screen into a blank striped wall. The elevator lets me off on the sixth floor, and I key myself into my hotel room—I know exactly when to pull the card out and thus have no trouble with the reader.

I drop my bag on the floor, turn on the lights, hang my coat in the closet, and shut the mirrored door.

Nik's reflection is silent, even if Nik himself isn't, sitting on the edge of the bed like his room isn't two floors down. His stage wear smells of red cotton and chilled sweat and fresh beer. He breathes, steady and slow but not regular, an augmentation of the words I'm about to say. I believe him, and I want him, and I hate him.

"The door was locked."

"They gave you two keys." Nik holds the other up between his fingers, keeps it there even after I turn away from the mirror, and extends it to me. I take his so I'm holding them both. His is warmer. So is his hand. So are *both* of his hands, first on my wrist, then my shoulders, then the sides of my neck.

"You son of a bitch," I whisper, just before our mouths connect.

There's no laughter this time, but I taste it all the same. I trap Nik's lip between mine, bite, lick at the chapped corners. Nik's mouth is stretched taut, like he's grinning, like there's more than just a tongue to take in. There probably is. I'm not sure I care. I'm not sure of anything right now, not even what I'm doing, not even the beat of my own heart. Nik cradles my head, coaxes me closer and open, and certainty hits me like lightning.

We're doing this. And we're doing this on my terms, this time. No ambiguities. No excuses. As long as it's going to be my fault, it'll be my way.

I grab Nik's wrists, pin them to the bed. Nik's gasp isn't laughter, but amusement wells up in his eyes, drowning out the faint glimmer of surprise. The whites are shot red, the irises still gold, just as terrifying as they should be. As this should be.

One kind of fear subsumes another and buzzes behind my eyes like a dying bulb. I let go of Nik's wrist only to pin it with my knee instead, yank Nik's belt until the buckle gives. Nik arches up from the bed, a challenge as much as an offer. If he wants to challenge me, fine, he deserves to lose. I get Nik's pants down just enough to jerk him off.

My terms. My way.

Nik is stunning, as frightening as his music, chaos unraveling into motion and sound. He strains to touch me back and I hold him down, fix him to the mattress, keep him where I can listen and see, where Nik has to show me what he is. And it works, too well to tear myself away from: the hitch of Nik's breath, the groan of the mattress, the snap of his hips, and the beat of his blood, all of it is music.

I tell him, "Now," and he listens.

He digs his nails into my forearm and knee, the only places he can touch, and comes with a rattle in his throat. Something in me echoes, tenses everywhere, sympathetic vibration, and when Nik sinks down to the bed I still can't relax. He's beautiful. He's stuck in my head.

I can't back out now. A part of me wants to, the same part that's not sure I wanted this in the first place. But I did it. And this time, at least I meant to. That has to count for something. To justify something. To justify *this*.

There's everything more to say. The words swell on my tongue, breathless but not soundless. I bring up my hand, focus on it instead of Nik's face. It says the same thing as Nik's sated smirk. We did this. I did this. I shudder to hear it. See it. Either. Both.

Nik hooks his knee around mine and flips us both over. I try to shove him off but only smear my hand on Nik's shirt before he grabs my wrist, lifts fingers to his lips, and cleans the rest off with his tongue. The walls of his mouth tighten around my fingers. It's a preview, and I know it and can't say a thing either way, not with how quickly Nik moves down my body, unfastens my pants, and poises his mouth over my cock.

I once thought that smile could slice through 360p on an iPhone screen. It probably can, like it's sliced through everything else I've built up between us.

Nik's teeth flash, just once, before his lips curl to cover them, and he surrounds me, takes me in and down. Any protests I could have made wither in the heat of Nik's tongue. I grab for his hair, get his collar instead—fine. As far as I'm concerned it makes no difference. He's too damn good at this, searing and tight and practiced and *fuck*, words mean nothing, only color and sound and the patterns Nik's mouth makes around me.

Words, recriminations, *get a condom, I don't trust you,* are trapped in my throat, and nothing comes out but curses. I hold on, shove up, *remember*, tangle my fist in Nik's hair when the collar of his shirt warps too much to hold. Nik doesn't choke—of course he doesn't choke, he *laughs*, the walls of his throat slick and easy and fluttering. Tremolo. Flutter tongue. My fingers waver against the nape of Nik's neck in the same rhythmless pattern. It's real, and here, and maybe he's not a god after all, just an extremely talented psychopath and I'm not in as deep as I think I am—

—and then no. And then I'm not here anymore. The pattern on the ceiling spins. The creaks of the mattress come split seconds too late, then early, then aren't creaks at all. My skin crawls like the surface is burning, like the creases between my fingers are climbing up my hands like vines. Light has a sound, a buzz like pain and drunkenness and fire, and it fills me, then empties me all at once. I thought I was high, last time. I didn't know how right I was.

I don't warn Nik before I come. I can't. I can't do anything but collapse and give in, fuck his face and *fuck my life*. But for what feels like the only time since I walked into his apartment, it's *good*.

Nik swallows like there's more. I wouldn't be surprised if there were. But I'm sore, dry, aching and oversensitive, and thoroughly wrung out, and Nik pulls away too slowly to ignore.

My terms. My way. But my terms don't matter to a god. Like whether I wanted it didn't matter. Like whether I want it now. It's done. I did it.

The heater rings out by the window, clatters to life. Curtains rustle, and springs strain, and terries of carpet twitch and melt in the onslaught of steam and sound. I catch my breath a moment before Nik. I think it had stopped completely. Nik props his chin on my hip bone, tilts his head sideward, prompts me for thoughts that won't sort themselves out. My head isn't clear. I broke another rule. I paid the price. I wonder if it will ever be clear again.

I don't think it will.

"About time," Nik says, mouths the words right into my skin.

I know that if I say, *Fuck you*, Nik will come back with something like, *You just did* or *Give me half an hour*. The song in my head clicks like an engine trying to start.

"I can't take it back," I say instead.

"No," Nik agrees.

He peels my pants the rest of the way down, rests his head on my stomach, his arms wrapped around my legs as if there aren't pillows two feet away. His uneven fingernails are stranger on my thighs than they were on my scalp. A human mistake, scratching me there. He's not human. He's a god and he's chosen me, and I don't have the energy to fight that. Nik can have what he wants for now.

It's all his anyway. Isn't it?

If I were going to run, I'd get out of bed now. There's no alarm, no wake-up call from the front desk. I'm awake, I think, but not enough to move, or at least not enough to leave.

I ask Nik, "Wagner?"

"No. He was barking up the wrong tree."

"I'm not surprised. Beethoven?"

"For a while."

"Stravinsky?"

"Let's just say the *Rite of Spring* riots were real."

"Taruskin says you're full of shit."

"Taruskin wasn't there."

"Fine. John, Paul, George, Ringo?"

"John," Nik says, almost a sigh against my cheek. It's as romantic as it is perverse. I'm not dreaming. This is fucked up.

"What about Yoko?"

"Her too."

"That must have been interesting."

I feel the faint impression of a glare, a tightening of skin beside me in the dark. "I wanted to keep him," Nik says.

Despite the heat—of the room and the covers and Nik's body stretched alongside mine—a chill crosses my shoulders, settles at the base of my skull with the song. *Keep him.* Something is inherently wrong with that. The tattoos on Nik's upper arm blur in the shadows.

"Did you?"

"Keep him?"

"Yes."

"No." Nik chuckles into my shoulder. "Some musicologist. Everyone knows he's dead."

"Fuck you, I know he's dead," I groan.

"So that means nobody got to keep him," Nik says. "He might have let me. You never ask about the ones I keep, only the ones I had for a while."

"Most of the ones who've succeeded can't be yours forever."

"Depends on what you mean by success. I might keep a couple from the band. They'd all think that's successful."

The chill flares into fire, forces my eyes open, wide enough to burst.

"You're off the hook, though," Nik goes on, with a smile that couldn't be any less reassuring, not even with a second row of teeth. "Can't keep you unless you want to be kept."

Posted to asbrooks.com on March 18, 2012

"Afterword: Montreal Concert, 3/17/12"

Odds are this update will coincide with a bevy of unauthorized videos of last night's concert getting their approval on YouTube.

I'll edit the links in later if they manage to adequately capture the experience, which they seldom do. No, I didn't take any of my own. I was too busy insisting to the police that the incidents which will almost certainly go viral were all part of the show.

I'm reminded of the rather infamous riots centered around Stravinsky's *Rite of Spring* when it first premiered in 1913. Memes are no new thing. Scandals and taboo used to sell a product are no new thing, and when even our god-among-musicologists Taruskin insists that the riot was staged, one has to take that into consideration.

Nik says the riots were real. Stravinsky's, I mean. Yesterday's orgy (for lack of a better term) may or may not have been. I wouldn't know. As I said, I was talking to the police, and Nik, while far from tight-lipped, is letting the music speak for itself.

Comments (4)

Florestan
If he says the Rite of Spring riots were real, you should bring him to meet Professor Taruskin. That would be an entertaining debate to watch!

Eusebius
That won't happen. If they meet, Taruskin will recognize Nik as whatever rogue musicologist he really is, and out him.

EliseMorgenstern
Maybe Nik IS Taruskin! Or Taruskin is Bruce Wayne!

ASBrooks
Please no.

When is a good time to call you?

"**F**or fuck's sake," I snarl into the phone, then end the call, pull up my contacts, and call Sydney. The wind whips around me almost on cue, an unsubtle reminder that I'm in Chicago and the gray sky doesn't necessarily mean the pressure is low. I wait with the phone cradled against my ear for two, two and a half rings, tapping my heel on the sidewalk.

Some things have gotten easier since I gave in. This isn't one of them.

Sydney picks up. "Anthony, any reason this isn't a text?"

"The opening act isn't here. Did you book it?"

"Shit. Yes. Good reason."

"I've called and emailed every number their manager gave me. What do you have that I don't?"

"I don't, I don't think. Let me get my list together and send it to you to cross-reference. Give me five minutes."

"Fine. Thanks." I sigh. Five minutes is too long, but hey, better than not trying. "I'll keep trying and text you if I hear anything." Though between the wind and the lengthening line of Chicagoan fans spilling out of the Metro and around the block, I'm not sure I'd hear my phone if I didn't keep it out. Clearly the wind doesn't bother the natives as much.

I sign off the call and pace the sidewalk redialing. The first call yields nothing. The second goes straight to the answering machine. Texts go unanswered. I may well thumb all the way through the screen if I have to dial one more time.

Someone in the line is taping me, grinning in the light of a smartphone.

I tell her, with no uncertain terms, "Cut that shit out." She does, but not before giggling with her friends, hiding behind one of the larger ones and peeking around her like I'm the goddamn bogeyman. I shouldn't be used to this.

Fuck it. I'll make the calls inside.

"—Anthony? Anthony Brooks?"

I don't know the voice, but I stop in my tracks, lower the phone. I don't turn around even though the person is behind me. "Yes?"

"Oh good, I thought it was you. It's Henri. CrossBridge," he corrects, "sorry, from your blog."

Well, that turns me around. And then I have to look down a long way to find Henri grinning up at me. In addition to being short and mixed East Asian (I'd guess Korean and white, but I won't presume aloud), Henri turns out to be possessed of a trilby and scarf in mismatched patterns that would have looked right at home in the Bay Area. He doesn't get out of the line, just taps one of his friends to hold his place in the knot, and comes to the edge. "I recognized your voice before your face."

"Sorry I didn't have the reference for yours." It's not as if it's the first time I've met someone abstract in person, but it's certainly the first time I've heard that, though I imagine I'd say the same to Sydney if I ever get to meet her face-to-face.

"It's cool. You look good scruffy." Henri doesn't wink or anything, but his open appraisal is, well, open.

But *scruffy*. I check my cheek, and sure enough. "Shit. Just forgot to shave."

"Right, I completely get you're busy. It does look good, though! Did you get in from Detroit today or yesterday?"

"Somewhere between." It must have been about three in the morning. I had shit to do even then, so someone else took care of unloading my stuff from the bus, and I didn't sleep. I don't even know what room in the hotel I'm in tonight. It doesn't matter. Nik probably wants me anyway.

The thought is disgusting. I hope Henri can't see it.

"Sucks. Do you have much time in the city before you leave for— What's next? Winnipeg?"

"Minneapolis first. And yes, we're here through the eleventh. Nik has interviews."

"Good, you're still here Tuesday! Uh, well. This is going to be forward, but you can totally say no. I have an internship at the Joffrey Ballet and because of the regime change we get free tickets to the Phil and the CSO sometimes. There's a famous Russian pianist playing the CSO this weekend—Monday and Tuesday too. It's a Rachmaninoff and Strauss program. It's not Bach, I know, but I promise you I didn't pay anything for the tickets, and I thought you might want to go. As my apology for, well. That." He points.

The line is stalled because of the four or five people on smartphones, filming this very conversation.

I don't glare at them. Much.

Henri grimaces, shrugs, and the gestures together make a wince. "I really am sorry about this."

"It's not your fault," I say, because it's mine. "I'll think about it. I've got some shit to get through tonight and tomorrow." I lift up my phone, and see no one in the opening band has tried to call. It figures. "Give me your number."

Henri does. "Put me under Henri Mock," he says once I key it in. "Spell it like the verb, not the cookware. I know your last name, so you should know mine. And if it turns out you can't make it to the concert or anything, at least let me buy you coffee?"

I nod. If I'd met him back at Berkeley, I'd probably have taken him up on it with no reservations, so it's worth a try now. "But I'll try to make the concert. Thanks."

"No, it's my pleasure, I promise." Henri tips his hat, backs toward the line with a little dance in his step.

I text him on the way back inside, just *This* so the number goes through. I get an *Added!* in reply, and that's that. It's refreshingly uncomplicated.

The opening band shows up ten minutes later in a succession of cabs, stammering apologies about "the fricken Loop" and "lack of reception" and a whole lot of things I don't believe. But I don't have to believe. I just have to make the show go on. So I do.

The CSO plays in one of the roundest halls I've ever been in: everything is elegant ivory curves, from the floor to the arrangement of the orchestra to the chandelier. Henri's internship has gotten him—us—seats in the front of the highest gallery, and Henri turns out to be the type to use little brass binoculars.

"My boss gave me these." This time, he almost winks about it, flashes a quick toothy smile.

"At the ballet?"

"Yeah, they're compulsory there. If you sit back in the sticks like I always do, I mean. They don't usually let me film, just perch next to the cameraman in case he needs to spot something else. But the dancers hate it when you use the big techy binoculars, and I don't blame them. And besides, these are more stylish. So I take them to the symphonies too. Not that the music's not enough on its own, but I like watching the people. Especially the soloists. Helps me know what they mean, you know?"

I nod. "Is that why you film Nik?"

"Part of it, I guess? I got started with it because he did something at my first concert, and I can't remember what it was. I'm not sure I do it to find meaning. With classical music I sometimes don't understand it the first time, you know? I'm so used to working with dancers and singers and people who move and tell you what the music means. With straight-up music it's harder." He flips the binoculars back and forth on their stem, tilting his head in counterpoint. The movement's out of synch with the orchestra tuning four floors beneath us. "Though I guess the whole point is that it means what you think it means. If there's no director. Well, even if there is a director too. You know?"

"I think so." I do understand; even if that hasn't been my experience with classical music, I've dealt with it enough from Nik. The lights buzz, then dim, and fragments of melody eke out of the pit before the conductor enters. I applaud politely, and watch Henri watch through the binoculars.

Don Quixote has never been my favorite piece, but I don't want to look this gift horse in the mouth. I have no complaints about the playing, so far, and settle back in my chair, shut my eyes. Frankly, if Strauss hadn't named the piece *Don Quixote* and presented it as a symphonic poem instead of just a symphony, it would still be interesting, absent of a narrative. It's not the perfect experience of *Rodelinda*, or even as personal as being alone with a piano, but right now it's close enough to what I need.

I need practice. I'll admit that to myself, if not to Nik. Having Lorenzo's keyboard around and staying in hotels with pianos has kept my hands in shape, and the hotel pianos aren't subject to Nik's insulting rules about math, but it's impossible to focus with the constant sense of Nik over my shoulder. At least there's the occasional impromptu jam session in the galley. I was surprised that Thierry could keep up and improvise on guitar when I played Mozart. The first time Mona requested "Free Bird," it was cute and I obliged. The second time, I played "Flight of the Bumblebee" instead, and Deon switched the keyboard to Stadium Organ mode right in the middle. It was predictably ridiculous. It should have cheered me up.

Nik agreed, it should have cheered me up.

get in there

Don Quixote tilts at windmills in the orchestra. I open my eyes. I'm here, there's music here, and the song in my head isn't all I have to listen to right now. Henri lowers his binoculars, looks up at me, and mouths, *You okay?* I nod, maybe too quick, and Henri accepts it but not without an uncomfortable little shrug.

This music should be enough. It should be easier. It should fix something, and it doesn't.

The symphonic poem concludes with the cello's glissando of a quiet death, and after a long moment the audience applauds. Henri's one of the first, clapping around the stem of his binoculars. The lenses flap on their hinge, an extra hand, and it rings distinct from the applause. No one stands, it's not that kind of performance, but the applause sustains itself through the soloists' and the conductor's bows, and people only start to leave for intermission when the orchestra itself does.

"Whew," Henri says. "I still think it would make a better ballet."

I nod, more politeness than actual agreement, thumbing at the edge of my program. There *is* a *Don Quixote* ballet, I think, though I'm fairly sure it's not to Strauss's music.

"Fifteen-minute stretch," Henri says, already on his way out into the aisle. "You want anything to drink?"

"No, I'm fine."

"Okay, sure. I'll just grab a cigarette out front, left street corner. Catch up when you're done with whatever you have to do?"

"Yeah. Thanks."

Henri has an easier time sidling out into the aisle than I do, and an even easier time navigating the crowd as it filters up the stairs and into the upper lobby, but mostly because I lag, looking down. It's a well-attended concert. There are at least as many people here tonight as have seen Nik in the last two days. The thought's more comforting than the music itself. Nik is what he is, but music is music, and it doesn't have to be Nik's to be music.

Echoes of *Don Quixote* thread through my ears on the way to and from the bathroom. Most people are still talking about it, in one way or another, this moment or that, this understanding or that. A passing couple debates the conductor's tempo in German. A group of high schoolers is subject to their teacher's lecture on symbolism. Three old ladies with walkers and seat canes compare this version to one they heard twenty years ago, in this very hall. Related themes in counterpoint, civilized, stately. Exactly what I need to hear.

The drink prices are exorbitant, and something twinges in the base of my neck when I consider buying alcohol, so I just lean against the bar, listen to the patrons, wait for the lights to dim. I could go down and join Henri, maybe. I'm pretty sure that he's going to ask me out for less expensive drinks after this. I'll probably say yes. I owe him that much, and anything else that happens will be up to us both, later.

Someone echoes Henri's sentiment from earlier, "I still think it would make a better ballet."

It's a tall white woman with dark hair, a little older than me, an obvious dancer from the protruding collarbones. Her companion, who merits the same description except for being only average height, scoffs into the lip of her bottled water. "Yeah, I think the Dulcinea sequence would be really exciting. More than Petipa's, anyway. And the corps of sheep."

They both laugh at "corps of sheep." I don't. I shouldn't be eavesdropping, but try telling that to my increasingly recalcitrant ears.

"It's just so much better when you can see the story," the tall one says. "I mean, with a song like this, you know there's supposed to be a story, and the music half tells it, but I kinda need the pictures. Wouldn't it be cool if, like, they broke up the episodes and actually made it a ballet? It's long enough."

"Someone's got to have done it before," the short one says. "It's too good not to use. At least some of it's got to have been used somewhere."

"I guess the problem is that it's, you know, Don Quixote, not Don Juan. He'd have to be a pantomime dancer and no one likes pantomime anymore."

"Yeah, sucks. What if you put together *Faust* and *Don Quixote* or something?"

"Ha, that, like, misses the point. Maybe you could have a primo do it anyway and just act old. And then just Sancho Panza could be in pantomime. That would fix the music, since all his stuff is funny."

"Yeah, and the corps of sheep! What were they doing to make that sound?"

"Flutter tongue," I answer, even though they never asked me.

Both dancers stop what they're doing and look straight at me. The taller one, in heels, is about my height and doesn't have to look that far. "Flutter tongue?"

"The brass trill their tongues against the mouthpiece while they play," I explain. It's an extended technique, one not all players do and no one knew to codify it until Strauss's time. "That's what made them sound like sheep."

"Cool," the short one says. Her brow knots, and it might be skepticism, might be something else, but either way I notice.

I shouldn't have interrupted, even if they wanted to know. Maybe I'm just missing school.

"I still think it's not enough, though," the tall one says. "I wouldn't have known they were sheep if it wasn't in the program and stuff."

"It doesn't matter." I shake my head, look over the tall one's shoulder toward the stands. This is a bad idea. It also doesn't matter. "If you could still listen without the program, it would still be music."

The tall one wrinkles her nose. "Not if it's supposed to be about *Don Quixote*. If he wanted it to just be music, he'd have called it Symphony Number Whatever. If he says Don Quixote's important, he's important."

"But it's there in the work. If you'd read *Don Quixote*, you wouldn't have to ask if the flutter tonguing was supposed to be sheep."

"Are you calling me stupid?"

"No." I try to back off a step but crash into the person behind me instead. "Sorry," I tell the one I bumped. This isn't just a bad idea, this is *strange*. The song buzzes. I wish it would just go the fuck away.

"Look, if music can't just be understood, it isn't good music," she says. Clearly she's had a good coach for dramatic expressions—I'm sure I could see this sneer from the back of the house.

"Then why do you think it should be a ballet?" My head aches. "Does that mean the music isn't good, or does it mean you can't understand it without the pictures?"

She slaps me. Not that I don't deserve it, but it's surprisingly hard. Somewhere between the initial smack and toppling into the cluster behind me, I can't help thinking that it makes perfect sense for ballerinas to be much stronger than they look.

I raise my hand to block her if she tries to hit me again. I should never have said anything, and neither should she—

Everyone around us shuts up completely. No, not just everyone: every*thing*.

Through my spread fingers, the ballerina is still shouting at me, but I hear nothing. Her mouth moves, clear and crisp and mute. Silence. Silence, *finally*, everywhere but inside my head. I can't help the relief that washes over me any more than I can help the fear that comes down after it.

I see the exact moment she notices. She stops shouting, and tries again, but nothing comes out.

A moment later, shoes scrape, and glass shatters, and overly expensive wine fizzles on overly expensive cloth. Her breath is silent. Her flailing hands are silent. Her hot angry tears are silent.

She gapes down at me like I'm a monster. I think I might be. At every last one of Nik's concerts, there has been a moment like this: potential energy humming, the eye of the figurative storm exploding into chaos and noise and hundred-mile winds, blasting through my unprotected ears.

Nik isn't here.

She launches herself like she's going to tear my eyes out, and I roll out of the way, because like *fuck* am I hitting a white woman even in self-defense. But she doesn't have to hit me to start a scene, and by the time I scramble to my feet someone's already holding her back. And no matter how much she thrashes and tries to scream, no one hears it. But they don't have to hear her to see she's blaming me, and here I am, looking guilty as all hell.

I'm not sure why I put up my hands again. Maybe because I'm used to having to push crowds of dancers out of the way. Maybe because I'm dead certain they're all going to come at me at once. Maybe because I have no idea what the fuck else to do.

But I do it.

And they shut up. No—this isn't the quiet of people rubbernecking at a train wreck, it's the vacuum of space.

As it becomes clear that it isn't just her, all hell breaks loose, like a disaster film without a soundtrack. I never thought I'd see anything more disturbing than Nik's concerts, but this takes the cake. It's the same violence, all that chaos, in a vacuum of utter silence. It's a circus of blame and hatred but all silent, except the song in my head and my own hard breath. This is Nik. It has to be. It's just like the street fair, the traffic, the Pied Piper of Montreal. He's here, or I fucked up, or both, but not neither.

I force my way out, trip down the first couple of stairs. Someone's body skids on the carpet, and I have to get out; I can't be blamed for this. Someone's glasses crunch underfoot. The steel pegs in someone's walker rupture and break. Someone spits teeth, and the flecks hit my face, and I keep moving.

I should be more afraid than I am. But instead, I feel like the eye of a storm, white noise and all.

Henri is at the bottom of the stairs, flattened to the row of street-side doors, phone out, capturing the chaos before the police inevitably arrive. I can't let that happen, but I can't let on either. I fold my palm over the iPhone's screen, pluck it out of Henri's hand like I could crush it.

"Nice try." How did I get so calm? "Erase it."

He hears me. I might be the only person in here who can speak. He does as I say.

When I kiss him, he tastes like heat and fresh nicotine; not as good as Nik, but then, he's not supposed to. Henri mouths *Holy shit* against my lips, over and over, until his voice comes back and the sirens start.

It's easy to notate police sirens. It's canon, a round, the same theme staggered.

The song in my head plays on and on as we run, into an alley and out onto the next street.

A bassist lives in the apartment above Henri's. He's still practicing at midnight. He's also really into lo-fi and has been working on the same riff since before Henri and I started having sex.

I point out the unsolicited soundtrack. Henri laughs and ties off the condom—I tried but my fingers kept slipping. "Seriously? Wow. Guess it's got to be perfect."

There's a buzz in my ears that the bass riff hasn't driven out, an ache at the back of my skull that isn't a hangover. My throat is parched, but it's definitely working. We never drank anything; there wasn't time while running, then kissing, then making it here, and it doesn't look like Henri has room for a liquor cabinet. He doesn't leave his camera equipment lying around. The apartment is neat, except for the bed, which is a mess, and the coatrack keeled over in the hall. Henri laughs at that too, on the way to the bathroom.

The bassist plays on.

Henri comes back, framed in the doorway, wiping his hands. "So . . . I guess you don't usually do this."

I think he was asking me. I should probably ask him back. "Do what?"

"Start riots in concert halls."

Henri either thinks it's funny, or is nervous enough to laugh. I'm not sure I wanted the confirmation that the riot was real. And if the riot was real, the silence was real, and that's even more insane than the rest of my life. But the safe answer is, "No."

"But the rest?"

The rest: racing through the streets, shoving a man half my size through the door, into the wall, onto the bed, forgetting to untie his scarf before it cut off his air. Wanting to pull it tighter. "Yes." Yes, the rest I've done. Not all at once, but one or two pieces at a time.

Like sound returning to the world.

Henri leans in the doorway and smiles. He looks good naked. It's different, after as opposed to during. "I see why you don't want anyone bringing it up online."

This is almost normal. If it weren't for how we got here, it would be. There's no haze behind my eyes. No anger, at least not at Henri. No question that I did this because it felt right.

When did normal become strange?

"Do you want to stay tonight?" Henri asks, at the edge of the bed now, a little tentative, like it's mine, not his. "When do you have to be back at the bus?"

"Eight in the morning." I answer. "But I should stay."

"Great! Guess that means I can call you if you pass through here again? Or if I see you in New York. I think I'm going this fall. So that's good."

It is. It's easy. But something's still wrong, and not with Henri.

I stay anyway. And when the bass player finally stops, the sirens down the street keep me up for hours.

The bus would never have left without me. It certainly won't leave without me at seven in the morning when they're still loading luggage on and the band hasn't had its collective coffee. As I walk up, Deon waves, Mona gives me a bleary hello, Lorenzo asks where the hell I was last night, and I blow all of them off.

Nik is at the loading van, leaning into the back with one arm on the door. I wrench the other almost out of its socket to turn him around and hammer my fist into his jaw.

God, that feels good.

Nik thuds against the drum kit, unseating the packing job. The van shakes; the roadies scatter. One of the drums, presumably the snare, falls onto his head. I don't laugh. Nik does. A lot.

Every drum and every cymbal twitches in time with his voice.

"Good job," he says.

I brace myself on the back door so I don't hit Nik again, even though I want to so much I can hear the synapses firing. "You were there." Just like in the streets of Montreal. He was there.

"It's on the news."

"Fuck." I could punch the van instead. But it would hurt even more than punching Nik, and won't be nearly as satisfying. I hold the doorjamb tighter. "Fuck. Was that you?" It had to be. I can't do that. I couldn't even have *believed* in the possibility of silent riots until I started believing in this divine asshole.

"You," Nik says. "Who else would it be?"

No. No, that makes no sense.

The drums rustle and topple as Nik climbs out of the pile, rubbing his jaw. He doesn't set them to rights yet, just perches on the lip of the van with one leg between mine. Fuck, I want to rip that leg off and beat him with it. I back off but can't let the door go.

"So they didn't catch you?" Nik tilts his head to the side, eerily concerned.

It was me. He's saying it was me. He hasn't lied to me yet; for everything else he's done, he's never lied. It was me. "Fuck. *Fuck.*"

"That's not an answer."

"I thought you said it was on the news."

"It was. You weren't."

Okay. Good. I wasn't there when they rounded people up so they may not be looking for me. There may not even be cameras. Henri will speak on my behalf if he has to speak at all, but he won't. I hope. "I didn't run. I just left."

Nik tilts his head the other way, grimaces around the bruise forming at his jaw. "No cameras?"

"If they didn't show me, they didn't see me. Does it matter?" I can play this cool, at least. I can pretend it never happened. No one else will believe it anyway. No one important.

Except Lansing.

once you get in

"Not to me. But it matters to you." Nik slides closer to the lip of the van, raps his ankle against mine to get me to move the rest of the way out. I don't. "Do you feel better?"

My hand slips off the door. "Better?"

"Better," Nik says again, leaning back into the van, propped on his arms, an offering.

"Better." I could laugh. Could. Might. Maybe should. Maybe it would let out everything that's building up.

I can't.

"You know what," I say, and can't muster up the inflection to turn it into a question. "Whatever. Whatever you want, Nik. I've got calls to make. If they try to arrest me, it's my fault, not yours." *And they will. They want to. They just want you more.*

It might be the haze, or the red bruise spreading on Nik's jaw, but he looks genuinely confused. "You're miserable," he says, lips knotted, strangely round in the angles of his face. "You had fun, you had music, you got laid. Why are you miserable?"

"You're the god of pleasure." I know exactly when I stopped adding *supposed to be.* "You figure it out."

I leave him there. This is too much bullshit for one morning, and I should make sure someone got my luggage out of the hotel room that I never bothered to use.

APRIL 25, 2012

O n the road between Winnipeg and Calgary, Lorenzo has a
breakdown in the galley.

It's a very subtle breakdown, and I'm not sure I was even supposed
to notice. I might not have, if I hadn't been at the keyboard at the
time, stealing some practice in the middle of the night. Invention
in A minor is steady, regular as ever despite the easier action of the
keyboard. It's so easy, and the headphones are on so high in my ears,
that I don't see Lorenzo sitting across from me until just before the
cadence. I have no idea how long he's been sitting there.

"Does he know?" Lorenzo asks. His face is half-shrouded in the
light-green dark of the bus and his hooded U Michigan sweatshirt. I
remember stupid jokes about William Bolcom living in Hell. Hell is
in Michigan, literally. I should ask Lorenzo.

Somehow I don't think this is the right time.

I let my hands off the keys. They click into place, more computer
than piano. "Does who know what?"

"Does Nik know you can play?"

"He says I can't."

Lorenzo nods, which pulls the hoodie farther down his face.
Something shines on his cheek, and I try to ignore it. Lorenzo's
fidgeting makes the cushions hiss, let out the air they've gathered
since everyone else has gone to bed, except us and Louanne and,
presumably, Nik. Nik's going to want me later. It doesn't matter, I
probably wouldn't sleep anyway.

"Well he says I can," Lorenzo says, "so he's gotta be wrong about
some things."

I've heard this part before: half-envious musicians who can't play
classical, who skived off their lessons one time too many when their

fingers were forming, who don't sight-read or maybe don't read music at all, but who still have careers when I don't. Lorenzo at least has the grace to look sheepish, like he knows the question's touchy but not as touchy as it really feels. "Reassuring you that you can play costs extra," I say.

Lorenzo tsks through his teeth. "Yeah." He could be smiling, but it's honestly hard to tell by just the sound. "I mean it. I can't. I can't play tomorrow."

Well, it's my job to know. I make a note of it. "Something I need to know about Winnipeg?"

"It's not Winnipeg; it's me."

I'm not sure if I should have sympathy. Whether I should or not, I don't. It hits in a strange, jealous place, but I'm not sure I'm jealous either. Just accepting. Not for, not against. "If you're sick, I can call someone in to cover your parts."

"Yeah," Lorenzo says, with a mad little laugh and a flicker of shadow. "Yeah, I'm pretty sick. I've gotta be sick to do this."

"If you're being serious, I'll get someone."

"You can't. It's gotta go through Nik. And he knows it's starting." Lorenzo laughs again, pulls back his hoodie to fidget at his ear like he's got a rash or a zit, but it's still too dark over there to see if something's wrong with his face. I turn off the keyboard, gather myself out from behind it, listening to the engine churn and the staggered snores and breathing of everyone upstairs. Lorenzo follows me with his eyes but doesn't make a move closer. "Guess I'm using the wrong meaning of 'can't.'"

I need a straight answer. "Which will help you more, practice or sleep?"

"Neither," Lorenzo says, "but I want to play."

I nod, stand aside and let him. Lorenzo passes close to me, taking his hood down on the way. There's nothing off with his face at all. His eyes even seem clearer than usual.

I've been subject to far too much weird shit this year. Tricks of the light are compulsory.

When I make it up to my bunk, Nik is in it instead of his own, reading my copy of *City of Night*. Naked. He tilts his head toward me, one guileless cheek pressed into the memory foam. Tattoos crawl up and around his shoulder like lines of ants through the veins of a farm.

I resigned myself to this weeks ago. He doesn't have to go through the trouble of seducing me. And he looks ridiculous.

I sigh. "Fine, I'll take yours."

"No need," Nik says.

The curtain rings chatter on their rail. I dart my eyes at them, as if that could make them, or Nik, stop. Neither does. "There's no room."

"There is with one of us on top."

"You really just said that."

Nik shrugs, grins, and tucks the book away. He flattens himself against the mattress, shifts his hips. It's meant to be accommodating. It's not.

I undo my shirt without rolling down the sleeves, and swing myself up. Fine. What the hell. Better me than everyone else.

MAY 10, 2012

I'd heard Seattle rain was a design feature, a perpetual annoyance. This storm is neither. It's the kind of weather newspapers talk about for days when celebrities aren't getting divorced and no one wants to bring up global warming. I've had flash flood warnings screeching on my phone all morning. If anything flooded, I didn't notice. There are, as always, more important things to deal with.

This umbrella, for instance. It doesn't work.

I shout at the roadies to make sure everything's zipped up tight. They scramble to obey, but with their dripping-wet hands it's almost pointless. Some strip off their shirts to wrap up the amps, the kits, Lorenzo's keyboard, which isn't as protected as Nik's back in New York. I make a note on my phone, *Next time, tarps and tape.* Water streaks across my iPhone screen, blown in off the umbrella spokes. The roadies scurry, enveloped around their cargo like it's worth more than they are, which it is, and a gust of wind whips their asses toward the door, knocks some of their soaking shirts off the cases.

I stoop to pick them up, clear the path for round two. Fuck tarps, next time there should be a flat-out tube from the vans to the stage door. It's probably in the budget, exactly as much trouble as it's worth. The knee of my slacks soaks through the instant it touches the ground.

"Anthony," Paul says.

For a moment, I'm convinced I can hear all the way back to New York City. It's not true—there he is, four parking spaces away with a black golf umbrella that actually keeps the water off him, even standing still. Only his shoes show a light stippling, beaded on the oil of a fresh airport shine.

I stay on my knee for far too long. "Come to check up on me?"

"Not only that," he says.

"Then thanks for taking time out of your schedule."

"You didn't inconvenience me." So it's at least half-true. I suppose it would have been an inconvenience to come out to see my PhD acceptance—he was dealing with Nik. I know what that's like.

I stand too quickly, back up with my heel in a puddle. *Shit.* "Who else is here?"

"The opening act. It's interesting."

"To you or to Pantheon?"

"Let's get inside before you ruin that suit."

I exhale through my teeth. There isn't enough energy for my breath to become a laugh, not even a sarcastic one. I start inside without waiting for Paul, letting the umbrella down on the way. He didn't say hello. Then again, he never does. Rain drums on my head, catches on the faint stubble along my scalp. This time it's not there because I forgot, it's there because my electric razor is broken and like fuck will I ask any of these clowns to lather up and take a flat one to my head.

Once inside, my pants cling to my ankles. Paul shakes off his umbrella, but I just band mine and leave it by the door. The roadies left trails and puddles behind, and I follow them toward the stage, leaving Paul to fall in line. There is a pointed difference in the echo of our shoes, and the song in my head taunts me with counterpoint.

"I'm glad you're holding up," Paul says.

I throw the armful of wet shirts at the nearest shirtless roadie, and don't bother to check if they're caught. No, still can't bring myself to laugh. "Do you even know what band is opening for him?"

"All I said was you didn't inconvenience me. That doesn't mean you're not the reason I came personally."

"Good, maybe you can fix my PayPal problem. I've already hit my withdrawal limit. Am I on the books yet? The FBI wants to know." Like they want to know about Nik. And riots. And the bouncer who's still in a coma back in Pittsburgh.

Paul doesn't answer, so I stop walking and turn around. Clearly he's found something more important to look at.

Namely, Nik. Who is swinging himself around the pole of the nearest amplifier, extending his hand to Paul in the same fluid gesture. Paul takes it, gives Nik a firm shake and an equally firm embrace with their hands clasped between their chests. Paul's skin is darker than mine, so it shouldn't be surprising that Nik's hand looks paler framed by it. I can't suppress a shudder anyway, from the skull down.

Jealousy is pointless. It's also more present than everything I've felt in the last few weeks, except irritation and fear.

"Sticking around for the show?" Nik says, over the top of Paul's head, eyes on me.

"At least the opening," Paul says. "You know how that goes."

"Yeah, I know you." Nik grins, then steps back, looks between me and Paul like all of those ignorant people in the past trying to find a family resemblance and coming up with nothing—at first. His searching is more personal than theirs, and I hear it in the snicker echoing off Nik's teeth. "I like him. He can stay."

"I was afraid you'd say that," Paul says.

Petulant as it is, I don't stop myself from reminding them, "I'm standing right here."

But all Nik does is grin wider and wink at me. "I said you can stay."

Deon and Genevieve walk by with energy drinks in hand, wave hello to Paul, and get quiet nods back in return. I watch them disappear into the wings, but the sounds linger, warp in the hollows of my ears.

Nik gives Paul's back one more thump before he pulls away, backs through the stage door. "Do the old-man thing, I'll do mine. See you out there."

"Take care of yourself." Paul backs off, almost to my side.

I don't ask, don't reach out, don't say anything. Roadies scurry by, dripping water onto the tile, at odds with the rain. It's not my place.

I know my place. My stomach lurches at the thought, but it comes concretely all the same.

Paul asks, under his breath like I'm seventeen and drunk all over the kitchen floor, "What did you do?"

"My job." I turn up my palms, barely a shrug. "You gave me a job, and I did it."

"You—" Paul bites down on whatever words would have come next. I find I don't care what they could have been.

"I drank the Kool-Aid." Does it count as sarcasm if it's one hundred percent true? "Aren't you happy?"

"That's not what I wanted."

"Well, it's what worked. You should have told me what you wanted."

"I did tell you. I told you to trust me and keep him in line and keep your head down."

"Bullshit." I count everything wrong with those words, drill my fingers into my palm like the orchestra is full of idiots. "You told me he couldn't sign a contract and acted like he had your soul in a jar. You told me you've been keeping him since before I was born. You told me to put up with his shit as long as no one gets hurt, never mind that people *are* getting hurt and *I'm* the one they come after for it since they can't get you. You said to believe—"

"I said to believe *me*."

"Well, you believe in him. Guess what? I do too." I throw my arms wide, enough that it strains the wet cloth of my suit. "He's happy. He's happy as a fucking clown."

"Stop it, Anthony."

"Stop what? No, wait. Whatever." I laugh, just once, though it's really not funny. I've laughed at worse. "I can't. It's too late. How does the song go? You'd know it better than I do. *'Once we get in there they—'*"

"I said stop it."

"*'—can't drag us'* and I said stop *what*?" Maybe I do have more laughter left in me. It's plain absurd. I still hear the song under every utterance that rasps against my throat. "Stop believing in him? Stop managing him? You're the one who got me into this. What does it matter to you what I do? Someone has to fucking do it, and you gave me to him. The FBI wants me more than you do. That's about how much I matter to you, isn't it?"

Paul backhands me across the jaw. The slap stings first, and two breaths later the welts from his rings flare and open on my cheek. Apparently being an adult means getting hit like one. I bring my hand up, tap my fingers on the welts. He hasn't hit me in years. I'm not sure it was ever this hard.

"You think I did this because I don't care about you?" Paul keeps his voice low, not that it stops me from hearing it all, clear as a siren. "I gave you the job because I thought you could do it and not get hurt."

Bullshit. "Like *you* didn't get hurt?"

Paul is waiting for me to look at him. I can tell. He stands with his hands in fists at his sides, an angled grimace tightening the whole lower half of his face.

"You think I didn't get hurt?" he asks. "Nik is the reason you don't have cousins."

Oh. Oh, *fuck*.

This isn't silence. The walls reverberate with plastic and metal and heat all sliding into place, and laughter and jokes and everything that isn't here. But Paul stands just as still as I do, until he drops his head.

"It," I start, and it doesn't work. I gulp in air again, try to begin with "He" this time, and that doesn't work either. Nik is the reason I don't have cousins. Nik is the reason Paul is alone. It was never by choice. "*What?*"

"I *can't*," Paul says, "and it's because I broke his rules."

All those years thinking of myself as a burden. All those Christmases alone. All those awkward questions about where our family is and pitying looks whenever we answer. "I thought it was your choice."

Paul shakes his head. "I thought it was yours," he says. "You never seemed to want any of the things Nik offers."

I take far too long to form my mouth into words. "I still don't." It's true. I think. "But someone has to take it."

The sound of Paul's back teeth grinding on the crowns has a rhythm that I can map, notate, form into a riff. The song in my head quiets to assimilate it, and the rain outside bursts through open doors, drums on covered drums. Nik is the reason I don't have cousins. Paul broke the rules, and Nik took his future.

drag us out

"It's too late now," I say. That's all. It's true.

"You don't think I know that?" Paul leans the spike of his umbrella onto the floor, twists it into the corner gap between four tiles.

"You wouldn't have come out here if you did."

Paul glares. I stop rubbing my cheek. I've already found the impressions of the rings. It's not as if they're going anywhere. I should care about how it looks to the crew, about the stupid questions they'll ask and the stares I'll get. I don't. Not after this.

"You don't want me to recall you," Paul says.

"Have you got a better job for me to do?" The fake smirk sears my jaw. So does unwrinkling it.

"No," he admits.

"Then I don't think we have anything to discuss. I'm sorry you didn't have the right idea of who I am before you hired me."

"I think that's your fault as much as mine," he says. "And I'm not sure I didn't." There could be malice in it. There's not. It's the same tone he's used every other time I've disappointed him, the same tone I've always struggled to avoid.

It may have been the wrong thing to learn on this tour, but everything is easier when I don't struggle.

"In that case, let me say something I've wanted to say for years." I smooth down the wet panels of my jacket, fold my hands together, and meet his eyes. "Fuck you."

Paul doesn't hit me this time. In fact, he stands there on two dry legs with a damp umbrella, looking exactly as impotent as he should.

Down the hall, onstage, Nik tests the microphones. His count starts at one and the mic picks him up at three.

This is a test. He's been testing me as often as I test him, hasn't he?

"Enjoy the opening." I leave Paul where he stands. His breathing has a beat to it, it always has. It's at odds with the song in my head, so I tune it out. There's work to do. Instruments to dry. Fans to spare. An asshole of a god to appease.

"Anthony," Paul says. Not hello, not good-bye, not *I'm sorry*.

I should feel vindicated. I don't.

MAY 17, 2012

San Francisco is preserved exactly as I left it, in an eternity of sitcoms and dramas and romanticized narratives of someone else's Oz. It's not my place and never has been, but you don't live somewhere for seven years without taking *some* comfort in its familiarity when you return, and I might as well have locked the city in a closet for all the difference six months has made.

Ha. Closets. So funny I'll never laugh again.

Laurie strolls into the Starbucks on Market Street right on time, also looking exactly as I left him: more or less like an extremely short Viking, except with no bloodstains and a floppy canvas fishing hat instead of a helmet. He spots me and trundles over, apologizing to both people whose stools he bumps on the way (in two different languages), and lightly punches me on the shoulder.

"Welcome back!" His accent is always stronger the first few days after he switches countries, and considering that English is his fourth or fifth language, it's probably a good thing that I can hear every nuance in his voice now, even over the canned Starbucks soundtrack of freshly oiled espresso machines and half-indie cover bands. "Thank you for arranging the meeting."

"Sorry it has to look like a drug deal," I say. "I'd get something to drink here if I were you. It costs twice as much at the hotel."

"Yes, ha, thank you!" Laurie takes two steps away, which puts him squarely in line without bumping any more stools, and I follow, iced Black Eye in hand. "Are you going to campus to say hello?"

"Monday," I answer. "There's too much to do this weekend."

"Oh, I understand. Are you full manager?"

"I may as well be."

Laurie laughs, then places his order while I wait. It's a quick fill, so we don't have very far to go, and a few minutes of small talk later we're back on the curb.

We're barely a block from the hotel, but Laurie has a great deal to talk about and conveys an enormous amount of information in what little time we have. *Music and the Moving Image* is in two weeks, and Laurie's presenting, even though his findings aren't as organized as he'd like them to be and, as usual, he's having trouble cutting the paper down to panel-size in English. The Finnish version went over well three weeks ago, he says. I didn't think it would be this awkward to hear about someone's work: I knew there'd be a measure of jealousy, and there is, in the same place the rest comes from, but I expected to feel a bit more actual concern.

Not that I don't care about the national Complaints Choirs as indicative of a new global cultural tradition; I could care more, and I could care less, but the words themselves are a faint buzz like static, or sand in ostensibly washed spinach.

I've finished my coffee by the time we get to the hotel parking lot. Laurie's still working on his, and has to switch hands with it when Nik comes out of the tour bus door, arm outstretched to give Laurie a firm shake.

Nik preens and says, "Hey."

Wait. No. He doesn't. It's "*Hei.*" I can tell the difference.

Laurie brightens up like his ancestors just set a monastery on fire, and proceeds to interrogate Nik in Finnish. I don't speak the language for shit, but I pick my own name out somewhere in the first couple of sentences, and a few words I've known Laurie to shout when he drops textbooks on his foot. I should be as surprised as he is. I'm not.

Nik grins at me over Laurie's shoulder.

He says "thank you" in two languages at once. I know. I hear them both *at the same time.*

That would have been terrifying months ago, even weeks ago. Now, fear takes far too much effort. It's easier, much easier, to wait until the two of them to go inside, then to sit down on the asphalt and call Elise. It's just language. Compared to the FBI riding my ass and me fucking Dionysus in his, it's nothing.

"You're back!" Elise trills before she even says hello. "Welcome back!"

"Nik and Laurie are having their interview," I say, and don't get the chance to add *in Finnish* before Elise laughs and applauds.

"That's great! Also, Julia says hi! And Yuki, sorry. I left them in the library, but I'll tell them you did too. Do you know yet if you'll have time to meet up with everyone?"

"I'm still planning to drop by on Monday." It depends on Nik, which is annoying, but I'm sure that Elise of all people understands. She's worshipped him for years, hasn't she? Technically she has seniority. And yet *I* am Dr. Anthony Brooks, High Priest of Dubiously Legal Fuckery, not her.

"Perfect! Oops, sorry. They can still hear me in the library, so I should stop. And go back. If I don't get done with this paper, I definitely won't have time to come out this weekend and everything. It'll be so great to see Nik! And you. You know what I mean."

"I do." That isn't a lie. But I end the call before Elise's enthusiasm gets her into any more trouble.

By the time Laurie extricates himself from the bus, the shadows stretch into the street. Nik follows Laurie out, and Laurie waves paper, and I watch from the asphalt. It's pretty obvious that Laurie is clutching a handful of tickets and waivers, having difficulty deciding which hand to shake Nik's with again. Nik, for his part, apparently finds it so amusing that his Finnish sounds more like laughter than language.

I wonder if I'll get sunburned from sitting here so long.

"Anthony!" Laurie hollers, waving me over, then decides to just bridge the gap on his own. "Thank you so much for this—Nik has given me tickets and I am going to bring the whole department tomorrow night! Elise was trying to get some before, but now that Nik has given us them free I am sure more people will come! You did not tell me Nik spoke Finnish!"

"I didn't care," I say, even though *I didn't know* is more appropriate, if equally true.

Laurie laughs, and finally decides which hand to shake Nik's with. He says a contextually recognizable "see you later" in Finnish, and then waves, steps over me on the ground, and scurries off.

Nik looms, eclipsing the sun. "You have cool friends."

"They're colleagues."

"Can't be colleagues if you don't work with them anymore."

"Fuck you." It feels somehow hollow, the equivalent of, *Sure, you can take that chair.*

Nik smiles, reaches down a hand to help me up. That's hollow too.

When I don't take his hand, Nik waves it, like Laurie waved the papers. "I want to meet the rest," he says. "You never talk about them."

"They're none of your business."

"Guess not," Nik says, "since they don't seem to make you happy." He rubs my scalp. There's too much hair there now, enough to foster sweat. Nik strokes slowly, like he's testing it, like everyone else who's wondered at its half-texture in the past.

When they were my friends, did they make me happy? Did I even let them? I sucked entertainingly at *Rock Band*, passed on advice about dealing with undergrads, groused about Google invading the city and professors with no boundaries and my lack of a future. They listened. They shared. *You don't live somewhere for seven years without gaining some measure of comfort and familiarity.* Comfort. Familiarity.

Nik's going to take those too.

Concert's at ten, opening act's already on, and Lorenzo should have been at the venue fifteen minutes ago. He isn't answering his phone. This is my job.

I bang on the door of his and Thierry's hotel room. Another bang answers me, a distant echo.

"Well, someone's in there," I say, loud enough to count as an admonition. "Come on, Lorenzo, a thousand people are waiting on you."

Another answering thud.

Fine. I didn't want to be a jerk about this, but I do have a master key card. I warn him, "I'd better not get an eyeful for this," and go in.

Lorenzo is crumpled in the corner of the room like yesterday's underwear. The AC whistles and throbs out of time with the way he's beating his head against it, one cool smack after another. Muffled by Lorenzo's hoodie, the impact sounds uncannily like windshield wipers gathering hail. There's blood. His forehead is spattered like a Rorschach test, the mirror image of the impact on the AC vents.

I probably stand in the doorway, staring, *listening*, for a few seconds longer than I should. Lorenzo looks up, diagonal from the angle of his chin, his face hard and eyes hollow, and says, in Spanish, "I told you it was starting."

I dial 911.

"I don't know," I say for the fortieth fucking time in the last hour, "I don't know," and the forty-first. "I've called everyone I trust and everyone they've told me I could trust. Everyone's out."

Sydney's breath is like a thumbtack pressing the wrong way. "You're trying to tell me there isn't an available keyboardist in San Francisco."

"No, I'm trying to tell you there isn't an available keyboardist in the entire Bay Area who can get here in the next half hour and is worth what he'd ask us to pay him."

"You're lying," Nik says from the greenroom couch.

"Shut up and let me—"

Wait.

Once, when I was five and a proud half, I had the kind of fall that children have and parents fret about, off the monkey bars at the community park, six feet to the ground. I don't remember falling, or what happened after, since I was alternating between shock and unconsciousness until the doctors actually put me under. But I do remember waking up in the papoose board they used to make sure I didn't move my head. It restrained everything—arms, legs, hips— with industrial Velcro bands no five-and-a-half-year-old could break, not even one screaming his head off, terrified that he was already dead.

Nik and Sydney chatter excitedly, one in each ear, and I'm just as motionless as those old doctors would have wanted.

"That's right," Sydney says. "I can't believe we didn't think of this before."

"Right in front of his face," Nik drawls. His voice carries, echoes, warps. Fuck. They want me to play. Lorenzo's in the hospital, and they want me to play.

"And it's fine for tonight at least, he's probably got a handle on the music by now—"

"Yeah, it's in his head." Nik takes my phone. That joke was horrible. I say nothing. "He'll do it," Nik goes on, then adds, half to me, half to Sydney, "and if he wants the chords he can read them. You can read chords, right?"

I don't answer. But yes. Yes, I can.

"Use Ultimate, they're closer to right than 911Tabs. You'll be able to hear when it's wrong." Nik palms my back. I can't even stabilize myself against leaning forward. Everything tilts. No resistance. Nothing. "That takes care of here, and then we've got time to find someone new by LA."

"Perfect," Sydney says.

I would say no if I could do anything but listen. *No, it's not perfect. No, this isn't what I'm here for. No, this isn't my life.*

Of course it is.

Nik folds his fingers over mine and presses the phone back into my hand. "Trial by fire," he says, too cheerful for my ear to handle. "Guess this time you *have* to play."

"Or what," I manage.

Nik shrugs, traces his fingertips between my knuckles. "Don't find out. This'll be fun."

"Fun," I repeat.

"Fun." Once more, Nik pats me on the back. "Go change. I haven't played in a suit for half a century."

I have done a great many things in my life that I considered terrifying at the time. I've pulled myself back up after slipping off a fourth-floor balcony. I've called the cops from a pay phone. I've defended my dissertation in front of Taruskin and a jury of my betters. Objectively, I know this unrehearsed performance of music I don't even like with a god I hate at the head of the band would have scared the life out of me as little as a month ago. In fact, I'm certain it's just as fearsome as advertised, under the giddy rush of adrenaline that's moving my body in spite of it all.

But the music is easier than I thought, and whatever the reason, I'm not paralyzed with fear. I follow along with the set list and chords in front of me on Deon's iPad, racing the music. Honestly, it's more like *Guitar Hero* than musical collaboration, which is a blessing, abhorrent as it sounds.

Everything else is harder. I may be at the back of the stage, on level with Mona, but that doesn't stop me from seeing the crowd. Evidently I'm not a complete hack, because they're still dancing, still scraping at the footlights and screaming Nik's name and singing along. And the faces in the crowd that I *know* don't help at all—they flash like ghosts or significant items in dreams, one f-stop brighter than the animated horde. There's Laurie and Yuki on the edge of the pit, glasses shining like the smartphones behind them; Chuck, clearly convinced to enjoy the beer, hanging back in line of sight; Elise and Julia dancing madly with the rest, euphoric and wild. Elise looks happier than I've ever seen her, and that's saying something, considering. She's changed her hair, it's a natural red now instead of hot pink. She must be done with comps by now. Good for her.

I can't let myself think about her any more than that. The first set's nearly over, and the hardest song so far is coming up. Yes, *that* song. I keep an eye on Nik to wait for the cutoff. The neck of his guitar lifts, flares the same gold as his hair, and I watch it fall, time the cluster in the left hand with the nod of Nik's pins. If I'm right about when to cut off, I don't hear it over the cheers and shrieks in the crowd. It's confirmation enough, so I can relax for now, and I drain the bottle of water next to the keyboard in four enormous gulps.

I wonder how Lorenzo is.

Mona leans over from the drum kit. "Do you know that redhead out front?"

If Mona hadn't pointed, I would have asked *which*, but it's pretty clear, since Elise is draped on the lip of the stage, pawing at Nik's bootlaces like a cat. Mona must have seen me watching her earlier. She catches my eye and waves, squeals my name like she'd rather touch me than even Nik. That's disturbing.

I flick my fingers at her like I'd wave if I had the time, and tell Mona, "Yeah. Why?"

"Totally my girl-type," Mona says, "that's all." Well, that's less disturbing. Elise would be ecstatic to know.

At the front of the stage, Nik rolls his shoulder, reseats the strap of his guitar. That's a cue, and I ready the list of phrase lengths, clip it to the corner of the iPad with the stand light. I have to give Lorenzo credit for having all this memorized or at least being in-tune enough with Nik and the others to fake it. I have neither such luxury, but I've made the music work so far and I'll make it work now. *Trial by fire.*

The introduction belongs to Nik, not that anyone could tell from how the audience laps it up. I listen only as much as I have to, keep my eyes on the list and my toes tapping the pedal. Every stressed beat since the introduction is *without measure*—

—and it starts. Music erupts, onstage and off where the speakers blare it double, and shit, I have to force myself to keep up. Three in seven, one in six, three in seven, two in eight and one in four, seven, six, seven, eight. With all these numbers I can't process the words. It doesn't matter. I keep counting: two of seven, one of six, five of three, one of eight, an endless pulse on the eighth note that Deon and I keep steady while Nik sends the treble soaring. There aren't notes, just clouds of chord that change when I make them, and the dissonances of Nik's guitar and voice over the rest, and the song in my head—a framework without a frame.

The second verse isn't the same as the first. But it's easier. There aren't patterns, but there are augmentations, diminutions, expansions of the chords that Nik laid out and I played a minute and a half ago.

Development. Exposition, then development. Sonata form.

Form.

A pang stings at the base of my brain. I'd reach up to touch the soreness on my skin if my fingers weren't needed on the keyboard. Sonata form. I could be wrong. I might be wrong. Fuck this headache. Nik would tell me that I can see whatever I want to see, it doesn't matter. Nik would tell me to play, to stop thinking and play.

Nik *is* telling me to play. Fuck him.

I try. I follow the numbers, the absence of pattern laid out on the list. The stinging in my skull filters into a menthol coolness, like putting weight on a limb that's fallen asleep. The music spreads through me, and the changes come easier, simple shifts of my fingers from black to white and back up, clusters and chords I can anticipate and meters that shift and wind but not so strangely anymore.

I've got this. I can listen. So I do.

Listening blacks everything else out. My fingers find the keys without sight. My ears pick up the cues on their own. No, not my ears: just the bones in them, and then my knuckles and toes and the fissures between the fused plates of my skull. I *play*—pounding feet have replaced Mona's drums in my ears, shouts have replaced Nik's singing, and it doesn't stop me.

Elise is shouting the loudest of all, wild and inarticulate, like an animal dancing over prey.

Elise.

The backs of my eyelids are walls of veined red. I force them open. Light hits me, slices through the sound.

Elise is dancing, if it can be called that, the nexus of the pit. Her hair is caked to points with beer and sweat, dark as scabs. Her smile is red, not just at the lips but the teeth. Her smile breathes for her.

It's Elise. Elise Morgenstern. Elise Morgenstern. Ethnomusicologist, PhD track at UC Berkeley. Scholar of popular music and of television scoring, wrote her master's thesis on *Boardwalk Empire* and flew out to New York for the first time last year to interview the writers. Never backs down from an argument. Marginally more likely than me to get a job after graduation. Loves her work, and her life, and music, and wonders how I can love mine at all.

My fingers leave the keyboard.

She can't belong to Nik. He wants her, and *she can't belong to Nik*.

The music resists me, tangible, cloying the air. I crash into the nearest amp, duck past Thierry, get to the edge, and throw Elise my hand and maybe, maybe, I tell her *no*.

She looks at me like I'm the one who's lost his mind, and what a pity, don't worry, I can come too.

No. No, I can't.

The song ends, everywhere but in my head. The dance ends, everywhere but Elise, and she's still thrashing and screaming when security drags her out.

And Nik, over my shoulder, looks and sounds two breaths from beating me to death with his guitar.

My hotel room has a mirrored closet. I have been staring into it since I went to hang up a jacket I didn't have, however long ago that was. I'd smash it if the damage fees wouldn't come directly out of my pay. Clearly Lorenzo had the right idea.

Sirens whirl in my ears with the song, even though the ambulances are gone. For all I know it could be someone else getting taken away, someone entirely unrelated to this fiasco. I could check on my phone. God knows Julia and Laurie have sent me enough texts. But my phone is on the end table, and I'm not touching it no matter how many times it buzzes.

I can't blame Nik for this, even if Nik's going to blame me.

I hear his feet and heart pounding down the hall a full minute before he slams the door open like he expected it to be locked. I didn't lock it. I can't lock him out, so why should I try? The hinges strain. I turn away from the mirrored closet, and brace myself since it's too late to dodge.

This time, Nik definitely hits first. His fist pummels my chest, and I hurtle into the mirror. It cracks. *I'll pay for that.* That thought is somehow more present for me than the pain. I'll pay for that, and it'll cost money, and money matters more than how I feel right now, especially since aside from the pain, I'm not feeling much of anything. I might deserve this.

"Asshole," Nik snarls. "You spiteful little asshole, I *trusted you.*"

"Great way of showing it," I manage. Breathing is difficult, but words, words are easy, they're just sounds strung together through time after all.

That earns me another slam into the mirror. It still only cracks. They must coat this glass with something safe. My arms beat against the mirror like they're not mine anymore. I really should be more concerned. Is Nik enjoying this? Am I supposed to? How does enjoyment work, anyway?

"She was mine," Nik says, too low.

"People aren't yours." It's only a fact.

"They are if they give themselves to me, and they're not yours to take." Nik shakes me, and this time my head clips the mirror. I need to shave.

He should probably stop hitting me. As much as I deserve it, he should stop. I get my hands clamped over Nik's wrists on the second try and wrench down. There. Better. "She had other things to be."

"Ask me if I care." Before I can, Nik drags me along the mirror and throws me into the room proper, against the desk. The vertex takes me right below the navel, knocks the wind out of me. Placards topple and fall, advertise room service I'll never get to use. "Go on. She gave herself to me. She loved me. Ask me if I care what else she was!"

Once I can catch my breath, I gather myself up from the desk. Nik's eyes are bloodshot around the gold, the same as that night in December when I hit first.

I remember how Nik fought back, and what Nik wanted. It should sicken me. It might, under everything else.

I don't hear silence. Just white noise.

"Fine." The word doesn't quite make it out of me. I cough, settle what little air I can find in my throat, and try again. "Fine. I took her from you. Here." I step into his space, offer my hand. My voice is still mostly cough. Whatever. I'll jerk him off and be done with this bullshit.

Nik's eyes brighten nearly to the gold of the irises.

I uncurl my palm, lower it. "What better proof can you get that I believe? That's what you really want, isn't it?"

Nik looks from my hand to my face with what can only be amusement snaking through the shadows in his cheeks. This works, goddamn it, *giving in works*. He reaches behind himself and swats the door shut, trails his fingertips along the fissures in the closet mirror on his way to me. It's his right hand, the hand with longer nails.

They're gray today, a matte dark gray with pale nicks and chips from shredding.

One nail scrapes along the television screen, on level with my eyes. I take it, clamp my fingers over Nik's, leave the nails exposed.

"You want the worship I stole from you," I say. "I get it," and bring Nik's fingers toward my mouth, slide my teeth against them. He usually likes this. Whether I do or not doesn't really matter.

I can't keep my eyes open, but hearing the shift in Nik's breath is enough to help me keep track. It echoes, puts the song to rest while the rest of the sounds move on. I wish this didn't work. Nik's pulse is as fast as ever, faster with the thin walls of my mouth to counter it. I trace down to the joints with my tongue, let my hands see to everything else.

Elise would have wanted to do this. She'd have jumped at the chance, not knowing what it meant. But she doesn't *have* to know what it means; no one else should. That's my job. No one has died on this tour, and if this is what I have to do to keep that true until I can get out of this mess, then I'll do it. And it's what Nik's wanted all this time, after all. If he's won, he's won. I am the High Priest of Dubiously Legal Fuckery. There's nothing I can do about that, nothing I *should* do about that, and as soon as Nik has what he's after, this'll stop.

Nik nudges his fingers deeper, doesn't apologize. I bare my teeth, but there's not enough anger in it to make the gesture more than a stretch, a twitch. It gets easier. It all gets easier. Pushing Nik onto the bed is the easiest thing in the world, a scale, a drill, a basic progression. I get his jeans undone, tug them down.

I don't look. His voice is enough to tell me what I'm doing right.

He holds on to my shoulders and neck, harder than I would ordinarily allow. I just take it as a signal and work my hand faster. There's something not quite right, maybe my fingers aren't at the ideal spread or there isn't enough sweat between them, but that's no reason to stop. This is work. Without the song in my head, I count the seconds in steady quarter notes. The count is regular where Nik's hips and breath aren't, where he's ragged and struggling.

Funny, I used to enjoy making Nik struggle.

I could laugh. The walls of my throat move, but no sound comes out.

Nik curses, bites down on his breath, fucks my hand. I stop listening, at least to that: there's a siren somewhere down the road from the hotel, a cooking show on the television next door, a guest struggling with her room key two doors down, a shower knob turning in the room below. There are a thousand things to hear that aren't silence—

—and then there aren't. The room is empty, just like the concert hall in Chicago.

Nik thrashes, shoves me aside. His nails catch on my bottom teeth, and he rolls off the bed.

My eyes flash open, just before Nik braces himself against the television.

Nik's not hard. Flushed and pissed off, but not hard.

Whether this room was ever silent or not, it isn't now, because I start laughing. I can't help it. It's not even real humor, just the dark disbelieving laughter that I reserve for when I'm so far up shit creek that the backup is explosive. I sit up, hang my head in my hands, and let the rest ride it out.

"Let me guess," I say. "This doesn't usually happen."

I expect to get hit for that, but the punch never comes. Nik drags himself to the edge of the bed, lashes out with one arm, and folds over, head to his knees. I think he says, "Shut up," but I can't really hear it.

"I made the god of pleasure not enjoy himself enough." I let my arms fall to my sides, wipe the sweat off on my thigh. It's only sweat. "I should be proud." And I should: it could mean a lot of things, and most of them are good, and all of them have to do with having some power, some stake in this, some *self* in this. "But you know what I feel?" I tell Nik, truly: "Absolutely nothing."

Nik looks up, seething, teeth as white as his eyes should be. He stands and zips his pants up, then glares down; first into the scant space between us, then into my eyes.

Sound returns to the room all at once, and the song pounds back into my head like a jackhammer. I feel *something*. I'm not sure what, but for a moment it's powerful enough to make my heart threaten to burst out of my chest, and then it's gone, leaving only the song behind. Nik's glare wavers like tears might come, or blood perhaps. But I blink, and it's back to how it was: unnatural, but expected.

"Is that better?" he asks.

I roll my eyes. "Better." That's not an answer.

"Why doesn't it make you happy to believe in me?" His voice is like gravel, like a pebble in a running shoe with only blocks to go.

"Because I don't want to," I say.

There's more to say, and not saying it doesn't bring the silence back, but at least it drives him to the door. "You're not worth it," he snaps, "you're not worth anything." He elbows the mirror, slams the door, leaves me where I sit.

The room isn't silent even after that: once he got into my head, the song wouldn't get out.

At checkout, just after my morning run, I pay for the damaged mirror out of pocket, no questions asked. I'll dispute it with Paul later. Maybe.

It's not as if I need the money for anything else.

I'm not going across the bridge to Berkeley. In fact, I'm fairly certain that no one expects me to now, except Laurie, and Laurie won't say anything if I don't. So I get on the bus with everyone else, most of whom are still half-asleep, and shut myself in my bunk.

On the one hand, I've protected hundreds of people from Nik's bullshit on this tour. If they've wrecked their résumés, that's their business, but it hasn't cost anyone their lives. On the other hand, Jonas is my fault, not Nik's. The riot in Chicago was completely unconnected to Nik. Elise is . . .

I can't blame her for it. I can't. Which leaves me.

My phone rings the moment I close my eyes. I answer the call, wishing they could still be closed. "Good afternoon, Detective."

"Good morning, Anthony," Lansing says. Her tone isn't *correcting* me, not exactly, just a joke about time zones that isn't funny. "I don't have to ask how things went last night."

"I don't suppose you do." Well, now that I know what this is about, I can close my eyes again. I sink into the mattress, less than I want to.

"Where is Lorenzo Santos, Anthony?"

"Saint Francis Memorial Hospital."

"Are you sure?"

"I placed the call myself and watched them put him in the ambulance."

"Then Saint Francis ought to have his name on record and a body in a bed."

Outside the curtain and two bunks down, Mona sleeps, snoring gently into her pillow. I don't get to sleep, not now, not seemingly ever. "There are multiple records that I placed the call. The 911 operator definitely recorded me. The hotel cameras picked up the arrival of the ambulance and everything else."

"I don't doubt that you did your job," Lansing says. "But I think it's strange that you didn't follow up on his condition."

"I was swamped."

"I understand that. And where is Elise Morgenstern?"

It takes me a little longer to say, "I believe they moved her to Alta Bates." The mental hospital, not the physical one. She's in a padded room, and it's my fault.

"From?"

"Saint Francis."

"Yes, she's there, and her name is on both records. Strange, that you followed up on her but not Lorenzo."

Again. I think there's a place past Hell, because I just dug myself deeper.

"Perhaps not *that* strange, since she's a friend of yours," Lansing goes on. "I'm sure she'd appreciate it. From her comments on your blog, she seems like she'd be grateful to you. I'm sure you'll speak with her as soon as it's permitted. But I'm more concerned about Lorenzo's whereabouts."

"As far as I knew, he was still in the hospital."

"And who assured you of that? Your uncle? The lawyers? Nik?"

For a moment, my heartbeat is louder than Mona's snoring.

"Anthony," Lansing says, level and cool, "I believe you're an intelligent young man enduring distasteful circumstances, and I sympathize. I know how hard it is to carve out a place for yourself in the world. And I know I haven't given you a reason to support me as concretely as your family and your employers have. So it truly pains me to say this. If you continue to withhold information from me and my investigative staff, I will have no choice but to consider you an accomplice to Nik's crimes, and when we have uncovered sufficient proof of them to arrest him, you will likely be suspect."

Something in my throat explodes, like a running blister. "Why not just get him for illegally crossing the border?"

"Because he's an alien of extraordinary ability."

What? "If you're trying to bring aliens into this—"

"I mean he has an O-1 Visa. He's legally *from* Canada. Don't change the subject, Anthony."

Well, that explains a few things and completely cocks up others.

I wonder if this mattress could swallow me whole and leave no evidence.

"I encourage you to consider your position before we speak again," she says, and I still can't bring myself to respond. Well, nothing I don't say can be used against me in a court of law.

But they'll try. That's the worst part.

I'm not even sure when she hangs up. By the time I can bring myself to look at the screen of my phone again, there's no record of how many minutes it took.

B eethoven's Bagatelle in A minor is overplayed and overrated. It's also unwieldy as hell on the galley keyboard.

I play it anyway. I should care about the weak keyboard action, the uniform sound quality, the complete inability to contour and dynamic in a piece that relies wholly on the contrast between loud and soft. I don't. I plunk out the notes in perfect time at the same colorless volume. It's a drill. It's nothing more than a drill, like this is nothing more than a job. Drudgery. It's all drudgery. Hell and drudgery. Because if I let myself think of it as anything else, I become *part* of it, and the job becomes me, and I'm not just an accomplice, I'm a partner in crime. Dr. Anthony Brooks, High Priest of Dubiously Legal Fuckery, Prophet of Self-induced Extortion, and Seer of Bullshit.

"Whoops," someone says from the galley entrance, "didn't know I wasn't the only one called in."

I look up. I don't know this person—lady, rather, though her voice is the kind of softened-higher that isn't quite falsetto. But she's dressed in an interview blouse with her microbraids swept off her face, and she's carrying a nondescript black binder—scores and references. I understand all I need to. She's here to audition for Nik. To replace Lorenzo.

"You were." I get up from the keyboard. "If you want to practice before Nik jams with you, you can go ahead."

"You're not here for Nik to hear you?" She wipes her brow with a flair too genuine to be dramatic. "Phew. You're real good. I haven't played '*Für Elise*' since high school." She doesn't pronounce the German, says it like "fur." And yes, it was for Elise. "Why aren't you auditioning?"

"I'm the manager," I say, then correct, "acting, acting manager."

"Ha, guess that pays a little better." She offers her hand. Her nails are filed down, short enough that the gold shatter polish is pointless. Her spread is almost as wide as mine, probably an easy eleventh in the right at least. "I'm Ida. Hope this isn't the last you hear of me."

"Anthony," I tell her. "I'll go tell Nik you're here."

"So you're not the one doing the hiring?"

"I'm not sure he cares whether I like you or not," I say with complete seriousness.

Ida laughs. By now, I'm aside from the keyboard enough that Ida can get behind it, and she sits down, pulls the stool in closer, turns an experimental jazz chord. She bites her lip and adjusts the volume a little higher, then plays the same chord, which turns out to be the first of several, and it takes me a couple of seconds to recognize Jelly Roll Morton's "The Crave" since I haven't heard it in so long and she's improvising over the bass. She's good. Not better than me, just different. Confident.

"That your usual style?"

"More or less," she says without missing a beat. "Love Nik's stuff, don't get me wrong, but my heart's, well, here." She plays a chromatic flourish in the right hand straight out of the Cool School, without measure.

Nik's going to like her. Good.

And as if the thought or the music summoned him, he's there when I turn around to head up the galley stairs. His eyes don't even flick toward me, but then, his ears are what matter now.

Ida keeps playing for a full minute, long enough to change the rules. Nik blocks my way out, but not consciously, and I only get the opportunity to leave when Ida finally notices who else is listening.

"Oh," she says, "shit. I was just warming up."

"No." Nik steps down to her level in one strangely fluid glide. "Play."

Ida grins, and does as Nik says. He stalks into the galley, grabs one of the guitars off its stand and improvises a line over her accompaniment. That's all it takes for both of them to start going off, and Nik's smile, bright as lens flare, tells me clear as day to stop worrying about where we'll find Lorenzo's replacement. She's here.

She's here, and we can get on the road to LA tomorrow night without me having to play again.

My phone goes off, on vibrate in my pocket. I take it out and leave Nik and Ida behind, bringing the phone into the light.

Sydney has texted, *New mask arrival.*

Show it to Nik as soon as you can, ask him which wall he wants it on.

And tell him his phone's out of memory.

The mask in question is full-faced, a smooth sallow bronze with a metallic finish. It's frozen in an expression with narrowed eyes and a slit of a mouth, just wide enough to breathe through, and the lips are rounded in a way that suggests the space behind them is hollow. All the shining parts are finely engraved with whorls like fingerprints, except for two patches: a red smear on the brow like a Rorschach test, and a thick section over the forehead and the right eye, draped dark blue like the curve of a hood.

Or of a University of Michigan hooded sweatshirt.

Lorenzo. On the wall. With all of the others that Nik's kept.

The phone keeps vibrating in my hand. Sydney sends photos of the mask at other angles, profile, three-quarters, reverse. Down in the galley, Nik and Ida play, and the sound treads the same tracks as the song that *will not leave.*

O f course there are cops in the hotel parking lot in LA. There are cops everywhere in LA. Sometimes they're even where they're supposed to be. So when the bus pulls up to the concierges and starts to unload, I just nod at the four uniformed LAPD (three of whom are drinking iced coffee) and head in to the hotel for check-in.

"No," I tell Sydney on the phone, "Mona and Ida are both cool with it, and Gen's been sleeping with Thierry anyway, so they might as well get a king size and save us the space."

"Excellent," Sydney says. "So just see if they'll shuffle things around at the front desk. If they give you any trouble, I've got screen caps of the prices on the website from when I booked the place. I'll send those over right now. What about you? Do you still need a room of your own?"

The air conditioning of the hotel lobby washes over me, as audible as anything else and almost as chilling as the thought of sleeping with Nik now that I know what I know. Then again, I've kept that up in spite of everything else. What's so different about now? "Yeah, or I could share with Deon or one of the crew. I don't want to cost us any more than I have to."

"You're entitled."

"It's still polite to refuse."

"Keep the room of your own, Anthony, and get some sleep. You sound like you need it."

Sure, spend three hundred dollars a night so I can keep up the illusion of having any dignity, I don't say aloud. I stand aside, let a concierge wheel by a rack of the band's luggage, and glance out the automatic door as it shuts.

Shit. I'd almost forgotten what Detective Lansing looked like. But there she is, right in the path of the air conditioning. The automatic door snaps shut behind her, a sound effect that illustrates the quirk of her eyebrows.

"Good afternoon, Anthony," she says, twenty feet away. I shouldn't be able to hear it.

I stay as I am, waiting for her. Sydney, in my ear, asks where I've gone. Nowhere. In circles. Hell. Michigan. *Lorenzo.* "Sorry, they're calling me." I don't wait for a good-bye.

Lansing approaches, says, "Good afternoon, Anthony," again, this time close enough that I'm meant to hear it, meant to respond.

"Good afternoon, Detective." My phone pings. Sydney must have just sent those screen caps. I pocket the phone. Lansing doesn't get to see those. "I take it this isn't a coincidence."

"Air travel is complicated even for the law." It's not meant to be a joke—her face is serious as stone. "It's easier to go direct from New York to Los Angeles than it is to go to San Francisco. I'm sure you remember."

"I do."

"And I thought, as long as I am coming out here, I may as well address my concerns with you in person."

"I warn you," I say, because nothing else is firing, "I have work to do."

"So do I." She gestures to the couches in the vicinity of the hotel piano. Escape is a vain hope, but I still check the hotel doors.

They stay closed, even though Nik is standing right against them, close enough to touch.

"It's all right," Lansing says. Whispers, really. Never mind that I hear everything louder than I should. "You can talk. If you talk, I can protect you from him."

The perfect response to that comes to me as easy as a cadence. "Bullshit."

It occurs to me, watching Lansing's face contort as she sits, slow and with the support of the arm of the couch, that she might be taking offense at my honesty as much as at the sentiment itself. "I'm sorry to hear that. If you explain, perhaps I could allay your concerns."

That is also bullshit.

I sit, not on the couch but on the chair beside it, and lean my elbows onto my knees. "You're recording this conversation."

"I am."

"Will I be able to walk away from it?"

"That depends on what you say. You're still not under arrest, Anthony. But the less you say, the more suspicious you look."

"Somehow I think the converse isn't true."

"That depends on what you say. If you insist that revealing any information at all would incriminate you, I can only assume that you're doing something criminal."

"Are you just here to threaten me?"

"Hardly. I threatened you over the phone. I'm here to appeal to your rational sensibilities." She leans one hand on the arm of the couch, tilts forward enough to look me in the eyes. "Don't ruin yourself for him. The only people with arrest records who can get jobs in academia are political prisoners."

I won't take this, and don't waste a moment getting to my feet. "Then it's a good thing academia's already decided not to hire me. Good afternoon, Detective."

She rises too, but not as quickly, and I've turned my back on her. I get in the waiting line for the front desk, suffuse my ears with the murmur of a dozen conversations I'm not part of.

Lansing's already threatened me, figurative Sword of Damocles and all. She can't arrest me if nothing else happens on this tour. They can't prove anything about Lorenzo. They can't take Elise to court. And they can't hurt me any more than Nik has, unless I let them. So I won't.

"Good job," Nik says, looming behind me in line like a backward conscience.

"I didn't do that for you," I say. I hope that's true.

In the comments to the entry posted to asbrooks.com on May 16, 2012:

LaurentTErikssen
Texts aren't going through. Did you changeyour phone?

LaurentTErikssen
Trying again today. Nik mentioned that the wireless on the bus was spotty sometimes. The schedule says youre in Las Vegas now, it shouldn't be spotty there. Are you all right?

CrossBridge
Everything okay out there? Did you change your phone?

juliamei
Hey. I know you must be busy from the tour but I don't think my texts to you are going through, so I'll just give you the update here. Elise got your card last week and she says thanks. She's doing a little better, but they won't let her make phone calls or go online just yet. Anyway, you should keep us up-to-date. Are you still playing keyboards for Nik or did you find a replacement?

> **breakingnecks**
> no there's a new one, check youtube.com/hjkINFS3s8

> **juliamei**
> Thanks, did you see Anthony at that concert?

breakingnecks

no baldy, not by the hair on my chinny chin chin

juliamei

Okay according to the schedule you're in Omaha now, if you're there. It's been almost a month. Seriously, answer your phone.

DontFret

Hey! Sorry to butt in, but I figured I should tell you he's okay. I totally forgot about the blog, we're busy as hell, so I guess he's just not updating. Been a little quiet, but we're all kind of frayed, it's about a hundred degrees down here every day and dry as hell since Vegas and we're all a little crazy. But Anthony's okay and I'll make sure he calls you back to prove it. This is Deon, by the way, the bassist. Are you one of the Berkeley people?

juliamei

Thank god. Yeah, I'm, well, the username says it. Hi! And thanks for the comment, I was really starting to get worried. Also, nice to meet you.

DontFret

Don't blame you, after what happened. I'm guessing you're the Chinese one from up front. Is your friend okay? The redhead, I mean.

juliamei

Yeah, that was me. Chinese-Canadian, though. I'm surprised you remembered!

Elise is getting better. She's going to take next semester off, maybe all of next year, but they're letting her postpone her fellowship funding until 2013 so she'll be able to come back if she's ready. If Anthony calls, I'll pass on anything he wants to say.

DontFret
I'll make sure he calls, I'm sure he wants to, he was beating himself up about Elise, not that he wanted us to see it but I know.

And of course I remembered you. You're hard to miss even from up there. Wish Anthony'd introduced us, but I guess it couldn't happen that night.

He's in the galley, I'll go down and make him call you right now.

> **juliamei**
> You're a gentleman.

> **DontFret**
> Can I ask him for your number?

> **juliamei**
> I don't mind at all.

JUNE 15, 2012

J ulia answers on the second ring. "Thank god you're okay."

"Guess no news isn't good enough news," I say, with a perfunctory, "Sorry I've been out of touch." It's an understatement. But they shouldn't get any nearer to this than they have to, and the tour's already passed through, so that's it. No nearer.

"Sorry I've been badgering you."

"You haven't." The galley isn't empty: Deon's entering Julia's number into his phone, he thinks he's so smooth; Genevieve's reading her Kindle in one corner; and Ida's stretched out next to me on the couch doing her nails—but it's not as if I can't hear Julia perfectly. "I haven't looked at the blog since that post."

"And my texts?"

I don't care enough to lie about that. "They've all come through. I just haven't been able to deal with them." That is also an understatement.

"Elise liked your card."

I stare out the galley window at the street beside the parking lot. Omaha is surprisingly metropolitan. There would be things to do if I had time before tonight's show. I don't. I don't even think I want to. I just want this to end. This, for a nonspecific definition: the tour, the job, my life.

"Anthony?"

"Still here."

"You know she doesn't blame you," Julia says, as if it matters.

"She doesn't know enough to blame me."

"What, it's actually your fault?"

Nik's outside the bus. He wasn't before. I can hear him crossing the street, can hear the sharp intake of Americano through a straw and the clink of half-melted ice accommodating to its new confines, can hear the whip of Nik's hair, longer than it was last week, in the reciprocal wind of traffic.

"No," I lie. "Guess it wasn't."

"So you don't have to blame yourself," Julia says, a melodic line over the drone of everything else. "Elise got a little too into it. She gets a little too into a lot of things. Remember when Bear McCreary gave that lecture, and she walked into the gamelan and tripped and broke the gangsa on her belt spikes?"

I do remember. If I could dredge up a vestige of the schadenfreude I felt back then, I'd probably feel better about it now. Between hearing everything and feeling none of it, I've got automation down. Clearly, transhumanism is next. "Right."

"She's Elise," Julia says, "it's what she does. If she didn't overdo it, she wouldn't be her. So don't blame yourself. You just invited the rest of us, so she got excited and it's taken her longer than usual to cool down."

"So she believes that?" I ask, incredulous. "She thinks it's *her* fault?"

Julia doesn't fall silent, but then, nothing falls silent.

"I didn't think so." I'm not exactly speaking loudly, but Ida looks up from her nail polish, quirks her ears.

Julia protests, "No, it's not about blaming *anyone*."

"What is it about? Nik?"

"She's not supposed to talk about Nik."

To anyone but Lansing, at least. As if I didn't know. "Why, because it's not *his* fault? Is it really better for her to blame herself instead of him or me?"

"Nik can't do that to people," Julia says.

The buzz in my skull of *don't say that, no one should say that*, is almost as loud as Nik himself, like an engine through the walls of the bus. But I say nothing. The FBI could be tapping my phone, for all I know.

"Elise made a choice," Julia says. "Even if Nik's music does have power, even if it inspires her that much, it's still just music. She still has to hear it and interpret it. Don't forget, Anthony, I was there too. And I was dancing. I don't know if I felt the same pull Elise did, but I definitely felt something, but it didn't compel me to do what she did. She's Elise, Anthony. That was at least as much her as the music. Nik couldn't make her do anything she didn't want to do."

The song in my head isn't music anymore. It's laughter. Meterless laughter, at the cosmic joke for which I am the punchline.

"So please don't blame yourself," Julia says. "It's just music."

I mean to say, *You don't know what you're saying.*

"You don't know what music is," comes out instead.

In the parking lot, Nik crushes plastic in his palm, an empty cup where there used to be ice and coffee. The sound is like a shot or a scrape, and only I seem to hear it properly.

"Okay," Julia says, tentatively but still at peak clarity in my ear. "I understand what you're saying, and I know you're busy and stressed out. Thanks for getting back to me. I'm sorry I had to hound you across platforms."

"No problem," I lie. Lying gets easier. Everything gets easier.

"Just keep me posted, okay? I know I can't make you update the blog, but don't completely ignore my texts."

"All right."

After a moment of, again, not silence, I sign off the call.

Ida scoots over, blowing on her nails. They're marble this time, teal over platinum. "What was that about?"

"Your predecessor," I lie. Yes, easier.

"Right," Ida says. "What happened to him?"

My shoulders chill and crack. "If Nik hasn't told you yet, it's not my place to."

Nik is at the top of the galley stairs, wiping condensation off on the front of his thighs. I don't look more than I need to, but he's got Ida's full attention now.

"Don't tell me," Ida says, nails clicking together, "there's a massive scandal and you're saving it for the press."

Nik laughs. It's for my ears as much as Ida's. "The press makes itself. I just make music."

It's more than that, and I know it but have nothing left to say.

JUNE 30, 2012

S o far, Wichita is the easiest stop yet, probably because I've stopped giving a fuck.

Not that the audience is following the rules, since there aren't any: Kansas is about as depraved as everywhere else the tour has stopped, just with different school colors discarded on the floor and different drugs trading hands in the same concrete corners. There isn't an appreciable difference in the number of people who dance like they're having sex as opposed to the number who have sex like they're dancing. Even the smartphones are similarly dispersed, on Nik, on the dancers, on me—the owners of said phones waiting for me to do something worthy of archival on the internet. I probably will, by their definition. It doesn't matter. Unless Lansing arrests me, it's the only way I'll ever be recognized in life, now. This is my job. This is what I do. This is who I am. Maybe that's why things are so easy. Maybe I was supposed to be here all along.

I remember when that thought sickened me.

Nik makes music. The band supports him. The world strains to accommodate the sound. I define the boundaries of that world, what few boundaries there are. It sounds almost important when I think about it like that.

"Hey, asswipe," someone says, over music I can't listen to anymore, "I've been looking for you."

"I'm sure you have," I say without turning around. Probably another amateur videographer.

The music is loud enough that no one hears me, except maybe Nik, who likely doesn't give a shit. So it comes as no surprise when the same person behind me says, louder, "I said I've been looking all over for you," and follows it up with the word they keep banning *Huckleberry Finn* for.

"And I said I'm sure you have." I reach up and pat some sweat off the back of my neck.

Someone, presumably that same someone, grabs me by the wrist and yanks me around. Said someone turns out to be a man, white, a little younger than me, with the kind of T-shirt one would designate exclusively for keg stands because it hasn't been clean since the first time. It's hard to get a clear look at his face because of the light behind him, most of which is coming from smartphones held by people who look about as obnoxious as this one.

"You still policing our concerts?" the guy asks, like he already knows the answer.

"It's my job." Something's passively familiar about this. One of the assholes from my blog, maybe.

"Says you."

"Says Nik."

The guy reaches into his pocket, hands off his phone and wallet and chains to one of the people behind him, and cracks his knuckles. "Let's see what Nik has to say about this."

I would ask *About what?* if it weren't blindingly obvious, curled into a fist, and headed straight for my nose.

Fighting is easiest when you don't fight back.

I dodge but not enough, and the guy's fist slams into my cheek, skidding on the faint trace of stubble. I remember reading somewhere that bruises lead to ingrown hairs. It's a strange thing to think about when there's another swing arced straight for my face, and maybe I shouldn't be thinking anything.

"C'mon," the guy snarls, somewhere over the music, not part of it, not here. "Police this."

It should be funny. Nothing's funny, least of all the pain in my jaw and, now, my chest. Ribs are stronger than they look. Most bones are stronger than they look.

"C'mon, hit me back and I'll put it on the fucking internet. How's that, asshole?"

This guy really shouldn't ask rhetorical questions. They're taking up space in my ears, and the swelling inside is shoving them right back out. I'm almost surprised to hit concrete instead of flesh.

I feel the music through the floor and shut my eyes to listen.

It stops.

Not to the point of silence. Damn it, I was looking forward to silence. Seems like I'm right about Nik, he can't create silence, just stop the music. That isn't funny, though I could laugh if the muscles that control it weren't swollen and sore, but the music indeed stops. There's only noise now, murmurs and protests and shuffling feet and the microphone-amplified thud of someone tearing through the crowd, and I would hear all that even if I weren't trying to listen.

"Just getting rid of an eyesore for you," the guy huffs, his tone too shaken to be entirely self-satisfied.

"Thanks, but no thanks," Nik says.

I open my eyes, tilt up from the concrete to see. And I do it just in time, because once Nik grabs the guy by the chin and hefts him up, pulls him in so close that the guitar still slung over Nik's shoulder is crushed between them, I can't see much of anything.

"You having fun?" Nik asks.

The guy gibbers his answer.

"Not enough, hmm?" Nik nonchalantly tucks a strand of hair behind his ear. It's black again as of this morning, sucks in the light of the iPhones surrounding him. "Don't worry. I can help."

Paul's voice breaks through the song in my head: *Nik is the reason you don't have cousins.*

Nik smiles, tightens his grip on the guy's jaw. The guy's body shakes like someone just called *clear* and jolted his heart. His eyes roll back, his mouth slacks open. The fly of his pants catches on the strings of Nik's guitar, and Nik smirks, glances down between their bodies.

"Nik," I choke out before I can cut the breath off. "Nik, stop it—"

"I'll deal with you later." Nik doesn't even look away from the guy, lifts him a little higher off the floor. "You, though. You didn't come here just to fuck with my manager, did you? You came here to have fun."

The guy's back arcs since his hips have nowhere to go. I drag myself up from the floor. "Nik—"

"You should have come here to *listen to me.*"

The guy groans, pleads, grits his teeth in a way that's far too familiar. Nik drops him, and he curls up on the concrete, knees toward his chest, hands and wrists fumbling. The phones capture everything, shining in accusatory rectangles on my face as they cross over it toward the man futilely grinding against the concrete, and Nik glowering down at him with eyes like molten coal.

There should be silence. There should be reverent silence, with Nik at the heart of it. Instead, there's security, and applause and jeers and demands for Nik to get on stage, static from the amplifiers and stalled breath.

I get my hands off the concrete, then stand up from there.

"What the fuck were you doing?" Nik asks, still not on his way back.

It's not a rhetorical question, even though he should already know the answer.

I say it anyway. "Nothing."

"I thought you were going to say, 'Your job.' Maybe that's because up until now, you were doing it."

The cameras are still going. I close my eyes.

My job is to protect people from you, Nik. You're right. I'm not.
I can't.

JULY 1, 2012

T he bruises formed hours ago. By now, they're an ashen purple in the lighter places, almost black in others. The ones on my face are particularly dark, and since I made the mistake of shaving, they stand out like sections of ocean on a map in the yellowed fluorescence of the hotel bathroom. They aren't like last time, with Uncle Paul's rings imprinted on my jaw like growths: this guy, whose name turned out to be Dan Thieme, wasn't wearing any rings, and fists leave more consistent marks than backhands.

They took Dan off in a cop car, not an ambulance.

It's out of my hands now, so it doesn't bear thinking about. Neither do the bruises, really. They'll be awkward to sleep on, but that's what painkillers are for, and if those don't work, I'm sure someone in the band has something stronger.

No. There's too much in my head right now. If I force it down and sleep around it, it'll burst in the night. Maybe literally. Weirder shit has happened. Weirder shit *is* happening, to me. *This is my life.*

So never mind that it's three in the morning, never mind that the source of this unmedicated headache is one hundred percent *me* and the welts on my ribs sting no matter how I move; I pull on a shirt on my way out the door, don't bother with shoes or anything that's not already in my pockets.

The hotel lobby has a piano, and that piano isn't Nik's, and I will play it and get all this ridiculousness out of my head if it kills me.

Nik said I'd know if he was trying to drive me insane. I still don't.

There's no one in the lobby, not even a security guard. I've learned to spot the cameras but don't care since these ones are just security, no one's holding them, no one's here. I sit down at the piano, push up my sleeves, and put my fingers on the keys. Instead of doing scales, I shut my eyes and breathe, deeply enough that if I dove into water I could choose never to surface.

Chopin's "Ocean Étude" is one of the hardest pieces I have ever played, but that's what pours out first, and once it starts it's too late to stop. That's the kind of piece it is, breakneck sixteenth notes soaring up and down in sixths and octaves, the melody all but slammed on my thumb at the bottom of each swell. It's impossible to hold back with a song this fast and this loud.

So I don't.

Waves tower and crash as the music demands. The pedal thuds at the beginning of every measure with every melodic note, until the hinge of my right ankle is sore from forcing it and my left foot is biting a print into the carpet too deep to vacuum out. The ocean can't be created with just fingers; it needs hands, upper arms, my shoulders and my seat, and the blood drilling under my skin, the breath I can't hold anymore.

If I can't drive the song from my head—the laughter and the pain and the *absence* and everything I've been shunting aside for the past six months—if I can't drive it off, I'll drown it out.

Sweat stings the corners of my eyes, cakes the shirt to the back of my neck. The gaps between my fingers ache, stretch sickly and cracked. The waves roll, threaten to snap the hammers and strings and the walls of the resonator, as much sound as music. There isn't a difference, not right now. There might not be a difference ever again.

A red void sears my eyes. I open them, since my hands aren't enough.

But the étude races to an end, so fast that I almost forget the chord that resolves it all. Almost. I drive my hands into the keys, hold them hard until my knuckles can't push back.

The pedal and the hammers click into place, resonate in every hollow, inside and out.

"I knew you could play," Nik says.

I surprise myself by not letting go of the keys, not startling, not turning aside. I simply say, "I didn't play it for you." It feels like the truest thing that's broken past my lips in weeks.

Nik laughs. "I accept it anyway. It's mine."

"No, it's not. Not unless I give it to you. Not everything is yours, Nik."

To Nik's credit, he doesn't vocally disagree immediately. He comes closer, but I don't turn around, don't even search out Nik's reflection in the sheen of the piano. For all I know, or care, this might just be a hallucination brought on by stress and headaches and the time of morning. Hell, it might be fucking *Fight Club*.

Some of the keys are still depressed, some of the strings are free. Nik's voice triggers the overtones, fills the piano with the diluted impression of a C major chord. "Why can't you be like that all the time?"

"Like what?"

"Like you were just now. Focused. Happy."

"You think I'm happy."

"I think you *were* happy."

"That's not who I am."

"Happiness isn't something you are. It's something you choose. You like choices; you make them all the time. You make the *same* choices all the time and turn them into rules. Why not choose to be happy?"

"You mean why not choose you."

Nik says nothing, scratches his jeans with one longer nail. Nothing echoes.

"Because I can make more important choices than that," I say, whether it's what Nik wants to hear or not.

Nik scoffs. "You're not making those either."

"What, you don't want me to work for you anymore?" I let off the keys, laugh, sort of, not hard enough for sympathetic vibrations. "Choose to be happy. Ha. Sure. You want to dry me out and hang me on your wall. I get it."

"*No.*"

That one word gets the reverb that I missed. The piano rings with it. The glass doors ring with it. Everywhere surrounding me rings with it, but I'm a congestion of noise and I can't feel it. Silence. Silence on the inside.

What the fuck is *wrong* with me?

I turn. Nik looks almost normal. "Then what the fuck do you want?"

"Don't destroy yourself for no—"

"Let me guess," I cut him off, "that'll hurt even worse than lying about you."

"That's not why."

"Do I care why?" The venom in that question surprises me almost as much as the volume. "Do I look like I care why? Do I look like I care about *anything*? Fine. *Fine*, you got what you wanted from me: you got my worship and you got me to play and you got me to change my fucking career and now I'm giving you the rest. Here's the rest, Nik. Here's the rest." I swivel back toward the keyboard. "It's yours—"

He takes me by the wrist before I can touch the keys. I don't care enough to swat him off. It's only my right hand. I have another.

I play with my left. It's not that no sound comes out: the hammers click and strike the strings, just low popping sounds like rain on a roof or cracking bone. But the strings don't vibrate. There's no pitch, no melody, just the piano as percussion.

"Is this what you want me for? Ha. Stop trying." I sigh, brusque enough to almost turn into laughter. "You'll never create silence."

Nik's grasp tightens, too suddenly and too painfully to ignore. But my left hand slams into the keys, and they sound again, a cluster of pitches just barely in tune. Nik wrenches me around, and oh, *this is it*, but instead of shoving me against the keyboard he pulls me up and forward, almost to my feet.

"Anthony," he whispers. "Anthony Brooks."

It should matter much more to me that this is the only time Nik's called me by name since we met. It should matter that he's calling me by it here, now, in the softest and darkest part of his voice. A month ago, maybe an hour ago, I would have been gratified beyond belief to hear Nik plead, doubt, want.

It's too late.

"Since when have you cared what you call me?" I ask.

He doesn't answer, just lets go.

I sink back down to the bench, wring out my wrist, stare at it even after I've confirmed that yes, the blood's still flowing. "I meant what I said."

"Sounds like," Nik agrees, the edge back in his tone.

I know exactly how long he stands there, watching me, waiting for something I'm not interested in giving. There is an analog clock behind the registration desk, and the second hand ticks sixty-one times. I count, because my mind is otherwise empty. It works. My bruises sting at the same pulse as the ticking clock. My breath divides the beats into groups of four, evenly matched. I blink every two. My hands settle on the leather cushion, the right a little more swollen than the left, with the crests of Nik's nails around the wrist.

I don't feel like playing anymore.

JULY 19, 2012

New Orleans is less desolate than the internet makes it out to be. That's not to say it's paradise, but it's not particularly mind-blowing in either its ruin or its recovery, at least not to me. The view from the galley is eliciting the same lack of reaction as Houston, as Dallas, as Wichita. Something will hit me when I have to leave the air conditioning, most likely. Once we get to the hotel. Until then I regard the scenery with level apathy.

Besides, Ida and Deon are ecstatic enough for everyone else. Well, alternately ecstatic and moved, then enthusiastic again to compensate for being moved. With a little more staging, it could be funny. It almost is, with me listening to Dvorak's *New World Symphony*. There's something inherently humorous about that piece. Perhaps I played the abridged version too many times as a four-year-old.

It's only sound, to drown out and confuse other sound. Nothing has been music since Wichita. God, I should be angry. I should be *something*.

After a bump in the road, Ida waves me over excitedly. I take an earbud out to be polite, not because I need to.

"Quick, gimme your phone! Can I take a few pictures?"

I hold it up, letting one of the earbuds dangle.

Ida laughs, but does wait for me to pop the other earbud out before taking the phone off my hands. She fiddles with the buttons on the side, brings up the camera function, but taps the screen one time too many and jumps from Take to View.

"Cool mask!" she says. "Is it yours?"

The chill in my shoulders is more than just the AC. On the one hand, fear, finally. On the other hand, the first shoe just dropped.

"It's Nik's," I answer.

Ida squints down at the phone, whatever photo she meant to take apparently forgotten. "No, for real, I've never seen anything like it. When's it from?"

I don't feel compelled to answer that.

"Let me see," Deon says, coming away from the window. His face washes tense before the phone is even in his hand. He mutters a half-conscious curse, and stares.

"Guys?" Ida looks between us. "There's something I don't know, isn't there."

"No, ha," Deon lies. Deon can't lie for shit. "It's just creepy, Nik's got a whole wall of them."

"Bullshit." Ida looks down at the phone, then up again.

"No," I say, "it's true. Nik does have a whole wall of them."

New Orleans passes by outside the windows. No one's taking pictures anymore. Ida stops looking at the phone, and her focus darts between the two of us. Deon at least has the presence of mind to look nervous. I'm not sure how I look. Relieved, maybe.

"Where is he?" Ida asks.

Deon almost gulps. "Where is who?"

"Nik."

"Upstairs," I answer, because I always know. It's my job.

I think I'm about to lose my job.

"I'm taking your phone," Ida says, already on her way out.

I want to protest that I probably have to start looking for replacements now, but that would be the worst possible thing to say.

Their conversation takes almost two hours. I only overhear the first fifteen minutes and the last four. The bus arrives at the hotel, and I take care of check-in, borrow Deon's phone to call Sydney and the venue and make arrangements for later, and oversee the unloading of the luggage. Deon mills around awkwardly for a while but then retreats up to his room with his phone, which leaves me nothing to do but reacquire mine or bask in the hundred-and-fifteen-degree downtown heat. If not for the smog over the parking lot, I'd feel like a lizard in the sun.

There's work to do, not that I care, but I reenter the bus on principle. The residual effect of the air conditioning lingers, a concession to Nik and Ida.

"It ain't my place to stop you," Ida is saying. "But I can choose to go, and I'm choosing to go."

"But you believed—"

"I still do. I believe in you and your music. But I don't have to give myself to it like that. I worked real hard to get this body the way I want it. So I'm gonna live in it."

I put my hand to the nearest wall, stop breathing. I can tell just by listening that Nik stops too. And there isn't silence, not at all, not with cars wheeling outside and the engines still cooling down and mosquitoes battering the windows, but no one says anything for a while.

Is that even possible? *Can* she go?

Ida laughs, uneasily, and gets up from the bunk. "You can call me in to jam anytime, cover for whoever you need. But I won't stay."

"All right," Nik says. "You sound pretty sure about that."

"I'm more than just pretty sure. I know it's not for me."

So that's it. She's going. All but gone. Already taking her postcards off the wall and heading downstairs to grab her suitcase. I wish I could follow.

I ask from the end of the corridor, "Will you be okay for money?"

"Probably not," Ida admits, with a grin that tends toward a grimace at the corners. "But I'm used to it by now."

"That's fair," I say.

Nik says nothing. He hasn't gotten up from the bunk, hands tented into talons on the mattress. Even though half of his expression is hidden behind the sweat-stuck points of his hair, I know that the smile is fake. I know the hallmarks of disappointment far too well.

Ida offers her hand. I take it. "Are you sure you can't give us two weeks' notice?"

She laughs—it's still audibly shaken—and pulls me into a hug. "I don't have a contract," she says. "And even if I did, I know I can't play for you tonight. Not knowing this."

I nod, turn my face into her shoulder. "Don't go to the cops."
Don't go at all.

"I won't."

She puts my phone straight into my hand. Lorenzo's mask still stares vacantly out at me, refreshed a dozen times by twitching fingers.

Ida sidesteps me on her way out of the bus, and doesn't say goodbye to Nik.

It's still not silent, even after she goes. Nik's breath slows but deepens, and if it weren't for all the cushions and curtains, it might echo.

I fold my fingers over the phone. "I'll find someone," I say, so Nik doesn't have to tell me to.

Nik glares at me. In the shadows, his eyes are an ordinary light brown, the irises as pale and sober as they deserve to be.

JULY 20, 2012

I t should have been easy. Like everything else is by now, it should have been easy. There are thousands of musicians in New Orleans, half of whom are starving, any of whom would jump at the chance to play backup for Nik for a night. Some who would crave the permanence of a position, an escape, a breakout chance. Some who came to this city thinking it would be one thing and now want nothing more than to get out. Some who are dealing with the same crap I dealt with a year ago. I could walk into any bar in any quarter and walk out with Ida's replacement, temporary or otherwise.

Instead, I spend the morning and afternoon staring at the listings on my phone, discarding every single pianist, notes unheard.

I don't want to subject anyone else to this. No one else should have to put up with Nik. No one else should have to burn out her life on him. And as long as I do, no one else has to.

I really am the Seer of Bullshit. I see it, and I spew it.

Sydney texts me: *Found someone yet?*

I text back: *It's taken care of.*

And after doing everything else I have to do, I show up in the greenroom in jeans and an undershirt, with a freshly shaved head.

Mona looks up from her iPad and whistles at me. "Too hot for a suit!"

I shrug. "Looks like."

Gen echoes her cheer, and the rest of the band looks up. "I'll say! What's the occasion?"

"There isn't one." If I'm going down fighting, I should look the part.

"Guess we're all just lucky." Mona laughs, reaches up from the couch, brushes her fingers on my biceps. "Man, I feel like I've never even seen your arms."

It's probably true, but I just shrug again, get out my phone to check the time. The opening act should be finishing up any minute now.

"Sucks about Ida; she was cool," Mona goes on. "So, who's covering?"

I put the phone back in my pocket. "I am."

"Like fuck you are," Nik says in the doorway behind me.

I don't turn around. "There's no one else. I'm doing it."

"No."

"Fine, then you're one man shy. I hope none of your fans mind canned music."

It is predictable, almost comically so, when Nik grabs me by the shoulder and turns me around. The soles of my shoes skid on the tile, screech. I hold my ground.

I've endured worse glares from Nik. I'm not even sure that "endure" is the right word here. They're just eyes. They can't make me feel ashamed.

"You can't," Nik says. "We saw how well that worked last time."

"And it won't happen *this* time, because this time I don't give a shit."

"You think I want someone who doesn't give a shit playing my music?"

"I think you want your music played."

"And you proved you can't play it."

"And you're lying through your teeth, Nik. I can play. And I will."

"And you'll die," Nik says.

If I didn't know better, I'd think Nik was *surprised* that he said it. He said it, aloud. If the FBI is tapping this shit, there, there's the motive it wants. There's Nik's confession.

All I have to do is prove it.

"You care more than I do," I say without a second thought.

Nik lets me go. "No. I don't." He snarls, swipes something off the table beside me, and heads for the greenroom door. "Fine. Do what you want. See you up there."

Dionysus is telling me to *do what I want*. It's funny in a staid, protracted way, like a missed opportunity, a comeback only realized an hour after the insult.

On the couch, Thierry fiddles with his Kindle, whistles through his teeth. "Awkward."

"No shit," Mona says.

It's quiet enough in here now that I can parcel out the distant sounds of the opening act, the crowd, the techs backstage, the noise, everywhere but here.

I'll be done soon.

Genevieve swings her feet off the coffee table and brushes some dust off her pants. "I should get to the booth."

"Yeah," Thierry says, and stuffs the Kindle into his back pocket as he follows her out.

Mona watches them go, and doesn't stay much longer herself. She has a little more to clean up, actually puts a cover on the iPad and tucks it under her arm before clearing her drink from the table. "I'll put this on the keyboard for you. See you back there." She gives me a little tilt of her jaw. There's hesitation in her smile. I might be sorry, somewhere.

That leaves Deon, leaning on the minifridge. He looks down at the floor, cricks his neck, taps his fingers on the vertex of the fridge. Whatever he was planning to say, he chuckles instead, and keeps his eyes down, passing closer to me than he probably means to.

Or not, because he puts his arms around my shoulders and holds me close.

It's strange; I don't know where to put my hands. I didn't know when Deon kissed me six months ago, and I don't know now. The longer the hug goes on, the more I think I might have to decide. Outside, the opening act finishes up, to a fair amount of applause, but I'm sure that Deon doesn't hear it at all.

I could hug him back. It might fix a few things. But as soon as the thought crosses my mind, Deon lets go. He sidesteps me on the way out the door.

I check my phone one last time, and leave it on the greenroom table.

It may be July twenty-first by now. I don't know. I'm keeping track of sets, not time.

Three in seven, one in six, three in seven, two in eight and one in four, seven, six, seven, eight. I play. It's not following now, it's *playing*, throwing myself on the mercy of the band. No one's complained. The crowd is louder and nearer than ever, crushed to the lip of the stage. I thought they were like maggots in the wounds of a corpse once. I don't think so now.

I don't think at all. I play.

Second verse, not the same as the first. Four in seven this phrase, one in eight, three in seven, two in six, expansions and diminutions and augmentations of themes I'm just beginning to understand. How did Lorenzo pick it up? How did Ida learn so quickly? The audience is another voice, crowding mine out, thickening Nik's voice with octave overtones, second and third and fourth partials, more out of tune than in. Their feet follow Deon and Mona, their breath is in counterpoint with Thierry's, and everything autonomic belongs to Genevieve.

It's not a song anymore; it's a setting, and I'm not part of it. I'm outside, forcing myself in.

This song ends, and there's no cue, no hint what's next. Nik's guitar melody explodes into a cadenza, soars through the speakers and suffuses my bones. I lift my hands from the keyboard, wipe the sweat off my forehead before I remember that I have no sleeves. I remember the heaviness in Lorenzo's voice when he said, *"It's starting."* I don't feel that or anything like it, not yet.

Maybe Nik's full of shit after all.

This song bleeds into the next, and I concede to it, support it, play along. The chords scroll by on the iPad clipped to my keyboard, and I use them, track with my hands and half-intuitive textures. No one's called me out yet. No one's looked at me for cues. No one's glanced at me from the dance floor, not without a smartphone in front of their eyes. It's safer up here than it is down there. Maybe they don't even recognize me. Or care. If I were them, I wouldn't care.

Nik sings. The words don't make it back here, but the tones do, and those are what matters. I play without listening. Hearing is enough.

Something clicks in my inner ear. It sounds, and feels, like a knuckle one notch beyond a crack.

I can trace the words now, layered over from the crowd, in a legion voice, like a choir mimicking a tuning orchestra. I stall, come in late on the next change. I bring my fingers down again. Another click. If the break weren't inside me, I'd think something's wrong with the instrument. I play through it, count, keep up, no time signature changes this time but the arpeggiation is getting faster. It's that *Vertigo* augmentation, from when Dina Marshall tried to fly and died. I didn't think it was part of this set.

Someone in the audience might try to fly. There's no one there to stop her tonight.

Words, again. They're still not in Nik's voice. The tune's there, but I can't see the lip of the stage beyond a red and gold smear: Nik working the crowd, not looking back. I shouldn't look, I have to follow the chords, but they're starting to come on their own now, changes I've memorized or maybe just know.

I know the song. That's almost enough on its own.

This song spirals, augments out and diminishes in, opens and locks. My fingers shift from chords to tremolo to arpeggio and back again, right and left in opposite directions. They slide to the extremes of the keyboard and down, thicker, the clusters denser than I've heard in this song before. I like it. It makes the music better, truer, even if there aren't rules. I remember Ida and Nik jamming in the galley, how a jazz progression became something Nik could impress himself on and not sound out of place, not at all—

Another click. Louder, this time. It's less like air and more like stone.

Contribution. It's a strangely coherent thought in the face of this music. *Contribution to a living situation.*

Nik doesn't want my support. He wants *me*.

Forget re-creating the song from the chords. That's not Nik's music. That's a template. No wonder it doesn't sound the same: it's not the same, it's not supposed to be the same. It's supposed to be a framework for the eventuality of music. No wonder Nik doesn't discuss his work: it *changes*.

Fine. If that's what he wants, if that irreverence is what he wants, I'll give it to him. It'll be the last thing I do.

I can't see Mona or Deon, and they have the beat, but I don't need to see them; it's reverberating through the stage. Thierry has the chords. It doesn't matter. I don't have to play the same ones. The words are gone but Nik's voice is the guide— No. It's not about guiding, supporting, reinforcing. I don't care. I've been saying I don't care for weeks now. It's about time I believed it.

I might as well be alone on this stage, with the audience lapping at my ankles.

Wait.

They dance. They're not dancing to Nik. If I'm playing like this, then they're dancing to me. They hear *me*, not Nik, and I give them something to dance to. Music. *Mine.* I wish that I could see it or at least the look on Nik's face. They'll dance whether I tell them to or not, all I have to do is play. Keep playing. Play anything. *Play.*

The keyboard has keys for the entire band.

Somehow, I have enough hands to play them.

The song in my head isn't equally tempered, and yet the tones come out correct. Correct: the right sounds at the right volumes at the right time in the right order, for a definition of "right" that's—Whose? No one's. Music's. Mine. Sound instead of sweat. Instead of breath. Instead of blood; I don't feel blood anymore.

I open my eyes on black instead of red.

The stage isn't gone, I just can't see it. The white footlights and overheads must still be there, they're burning me. The wires are there, insulated electrical fires just waiting to spark and spread. The band is there, maybe, maybe not at all, maybe just their sounds, weaving in and out of mine, not counterpoint, just coexistence. Distant coexistence, like planes circling a command tower, waiting for clearance to land.

I expect to hear the voice of God. Or *a* god, maybe. And yeah, Nik is singing somewhere, but not to me.

With me— No, *against* me.

My hands are moving, going through forms, but I can't see them either. That's fine. I don't have to watch them to make this music; I've heard enough since it infected my mind, in unwinding zippers and sirens and ragged breath. The keys blur together, silver ambiguities between the black and white. I play those too, glide my fingertips over them. They sound in the shadow as much as the touch.

Heat swells in my ears, leaks out, curls down my neck. Oh. I do still have blood. The music must feel crowded. I was planning on giving up that part of myself anyway.

The edges of the keyboard fragment, crumble, erode. That's fine too. I can still find them. I prove it, fan out my fingers and let the sound come through. No instrument. No intermediary. It's for the best; I'd just get blood between the keys. I know how hard it is to get it out.

Get it out.

Get it out. You put it there so get it out.

There's another click. This time it's not in my ear or my knuckles; it's there, at the base of my skull, the hollow place where the song lurks.

It cracks.

Sound tramples me, peels back my skin, tears at the muscle underneath. I can't laugh, not with the music crowding it out of my mouth, but the impulse is there all the same.

I turn it into a counterpoint for the song. Without measure, like Nik's—

—No. Like laughter. When has real laughter ever had meter?

I stop. The music doesn't.

They're not dancing to music. I'm not *playing* music. They're dancing because they chose to dance. That's what Nik is. That's what Nik's giving them. That's why they fall to it, why they snap, why they give up. I've said all along that this wasn't music, and I'm right. It's half of that and more than that. Nik is what he says he is: is all the creation and none of the rules.

And I'm not what I say I am. I am more than putting music into words. Words are rules. *I make the rules.*

But it's not the rules themselves that make the music.

An abyss of pure, unfettered creation surrounds me, fills me. I trace my hand through it and something responds, resists but responds. It cracks but doesn't crumble, like automotive glass, and makes no sound.

There could be silence on the other side.

I can reach it. I can create it.

Cheers bore into me like a headache. They aren't for me, they're for Nik, but I hear them all the same. My eyes are burning in the floodlights—I must never have closed them. The plastic face of the keyboard is spattered with blood. It's fresh. It's mine. There's not as much in me as there was a second ago, but I can still smell it, hear it pounding in my heart.

I'm not dead.

I laugh. Whatever sound I make is drowned out by the cheering, but all the right muscles are moving. I lean on the keyboard, and an equally tempered cluster rings out, dissonant but clean, each individual note as clear as if it were marked on a page.

I'm not dead. The FBI is going to kill me. I keep laughing.

People have stopped cheering to point. Murmurs diminish the music. Smartphones record. Someone takes my shoulder and pries me away from the keyboard. It's Mona—she's closest—and she whacks her hip into one of the amplifiers, drags me into the wings. It's not hard to hear her, but I can't quite string the sounds together. That's what it means to hear it all at once.

She sits me down, leans my cheek against the wall. I stare out at Nik, at the way his expression changes when Mona gets on tiptoe, whispers in his ear.

Nik's eyes are as raw and exposed as I feel.

He doesn't even look at the crowd, just unslings his guitar and shoves it into Mona's arms. One blink, and he's looming over me, a shadow and a heat as pervasive as the music seconds ago. I blink back, I think. That would explain why the world goes dark until he fills it again.

He touches my cheek. His fingers come away stained.

We both stare at Nik's fingers. Nik's mouth hangs open, his breath close enough to twist with mine. I should say something. I might. I don't hear it.

Nik presses his fingertips to his lower lip. *Shh.* It's more than that, but that's what I hear, and I breathe it in, keep it, watch Nik walk back out onto the stage and leave me.

I think I just gave him more than he asked for.

In the footlights, my blood is like rust on Nik's skin, under his fingernails. Nik picks up his guitar again, waves one arm back to the rest of the band, telling them without words that this isn't for them.

The crowd stills.

Nik plays.

It's strange, stranger than it should be, to have to strain to hear. It could be like Chicago—but no, everyone around me is doing the same. Nik's eyes are shadowed but his fingers aren't, and they work slowly on the strings, in and out of the lights. I remember the sound that flooded out of me, and I feel it again in a surge of pain through his arms and chest. This is mine. This is my silence.

He's just using me because he can't do it on his own. I see that now.

Nik's melody is so faint, slow, clear, that I can't let anything contest it. And in one moment of listening, I know I'm not the only one. Everyone in this hall is holding still, trying not to breathe. No dance. No echo. Madness, but the quiet creeping madness that comes with reverence.

In the moment after Nik lifts his hand, the guitar strings vibrate down to stillness, and a room of a thousand people is silent, truly silent.

I listen, take in the silence as long as I can, as long as it lasts. It's mine. He didn't create it, he called it out of me, plucked it out like a splinter.

Then sirens slice through it, a pattern I know far too well. I should go and deal with them. I stand up. They're here for me after all.

... They can wait. I'll just ... sit here, and they can wait ...

JULY 22, 2012

Somehow my alarm has synched with my heartbeat. I reach out to turn it off, whack my arm on something cold, wince, and curl back up. The alarm keeps beeping. So does my heart. I listen to both for a full minute before it adds up that the beeps are at quarter equals eighty, not sixty.

I open my eyes, and cringe at the crusted whites and pale blues of a hospital room.

Looks like I got an ambulance instead of a cop car.

I laugh, and it hurts to laugh, but the thought's too hilarious to stop.

"Stay down," Paul says.

I do the exact opposite: sit up, get a look. Paul is on his way from a chair by the window. I'm not sure which side of the hospital I'm on, but the sun is squarely in the center of the glass, unobstructed until it gets to Paul. But once he's at my bedside there's enough of a reprieve from the light to see him clearly, from his knuckles folded on the bedrail to the harried expression on his face.

Not disappointed, though. Just drawn, afraid, old.

I hold tight to the rail as well, my hand an inch from Paul's. It hurts to breathe, let alone to speak. I do both anyway. "Sorry."

Paul glances down and lifts his hand. I start to pry my own away too, but Paul's comes down to cover it.

That's funny too. "So. Were you right?"

"About what, Anthony?"

He doesn't read minds. I specify, "About whether he could hurt me."

Paul curls in on himself a touch, but nods. "Yes. I am now."

Which means you weren't then. Which means I wasn't *this*, then. "What the *fuck*."

"Watch your mouth," he starts—and then laughs, just a little. A rare smile. I don't see that often. "Never mind. I don't get to tell you what to say."

"No, but you do get to tell me what the fuck that all was." It might be the IV drip, but I'm smiling back. "Am I . . . like him? Are you?"

"No," Paul says.

"Then what am I?"

That rare smile takes on an ironic twinge when he answers. One word. "Mixed."

It means something entirely different than it used to. Well, everything does, now.

And then the rest of the implications hit. Mixed, and Paul isn't, which means my father isn't, which means—

"Mom," I whisper. Another word that doesn't mean what it used to.

4G4V3BR00K5. Agave Brooks. Nik knew her name, enough to lock his wireless with it.

Paul nods.

The heart monitor skips a beat. "Is she even really dead?"

"I don't know how it works," Paul says. That smile is long gone, and I don't blame him for that at all. "I'm sure she'll come back. Nik wasn't always Nik. You know."

I do know, don't I.

I have time. Maybe I always did. "You regret giving me this fucking job, don't you."

"Only if you regret taking it," Paul says.

I look down at the foot of the bed, then out the door. "You know what?" I answer, question or not. "I don't."

"**G**ood evening, Anthony," Lansing says from the door.

"I thought visiting hours were over." I'm suddenly a little short of breath in spite of myself. I sit up straighter, even though the cot is already at that vaguely comfortable obtuse angle like an old reclining chair, and I put my book in my lap. Lansing pulls up a chair; she looks just as old as Paul, just as hard-eyed, sitting in the same place. I can hear her blink, breathe, swallow.

"They make an exception for us." She seems oddly small from the height of a hospital bed. "So."

"So."

She takes out her recording device, makes sure I see her turn it off. There could be others, I know, but they wouldn't provide court-admissible evidence. This isn't about that.

"Do you usually get information out of inpatients?" I'm surprised I've got the energy for such a pointed tone. She deserves it, though.

She doesn't smile. "Survival has a way of making you want to live."

The IV stings the back of my hand, distended around the needle. I flex my fingers, feel the skin strain. "I'm still not sure I survived."

She smiles indulgently. "We can protect you from him."

"Bullshit. Once you're in, you can't get out." I shut my eyes, try to listen between them. "If I'm going to help you, you're going to do more than just protect me."

That, apparently, makes her smile—the same kind of tense relief that she must wish wasn't amusement. "Of course. We'd be glad to. I'm sure we can help you get a teaching position under a new identity. Academia is one of the safest places for witness protection."

"But it's not the place for me."

She nods. "We'll figure something out."

"You also have to know," I say, and it takes all the breath I've got, "that even if I talk, I don't know if you can do anything to him. He's got more power than you think. Telling you might give him some. He's started over before. He can still do what he does as someone else. And I don't know if you *should* stop him, let alone if you can."

To her credit, Lansing considers this, but doesn't seem to have an answer waiting. She looks down at the recorder, thumbs the power button but doesn't press it down, and nods again, this time as much to herself as to me. "I understand. But my objective is the same as it's been from the start: to keep him from ruining anyone's lives. That includes yours. I'm not expecting miracles from you. Just help. And we can help you too. He's not the *only* one who's started over." She smiles, almost, and lets that sink in. "We all do what we have to if we want to adapt."

We all. We.

"I'm one of you now," I say, just because I need the clarification. "Aren't I."

It isn't a question. But she answers it anyway. "Yes. You're more than you were."

"And is it his fault?"

"Anthony, it's not about *fault*."

"Says the detective."

"What you are isn't about fault. Only what you did, or what was done to you. Not what you are."

Both of those are relevant: not just what he did to me, but what *I* did. It isn't easy to admit, and even after I take a breath and get ready, the words take too long to come. "I'm not just a victim. I walked into this. I knew something was wrong and went along with it anyway."

"That doesn't mean you're as culpable as he is."

I blink.

"The thing about contracts is they make someone responsible." She taps her fingers on the bedframe. "You signed it, so you think it's you. He didn't—am I right, that he didn't?"

"Yes."

"So you think it's all your responsibility. And you're partly correct. You are at fault for walking into this without completely understanding what you were getting into. And you're at fault for everything you chose to do, even withholding information from me, because yes, you chose to do it. But you are not to blame for anything Nik did."

"What happened to charging me as an accomplice?"

"Are you an accomplice?"

"I don't know."

"If you don't know, you aren't."

The heart monitor may have just skipped a beat.

"Nik was using you. Yes, you let yourself be used. I think I told you before: you're an intelligent person enduring distasteful circumstances. Endured, I should say. You didn't get out as soon as you wanted to, but you did what you thought was safest for you at the time, and you can blame yourself for not doing *enough* all you like, but it's more important that you found the strength to get out. You asked me earlier if I would consider you an accomplice. My answer comes down to this: would you defend yourself if we put you on trial?"

"I don't know," I admit.

"Then until your answer is clear, you're your own judge."

I knocked out Jonas in self-defense. I had no idea what was going on with Lorenzo, whether I *should* have known or not. Elise threw herself on Nik's mercy, and my only crime against Dina Marshall was getting there too late. But *I* was in this for myself at first, not just in fear of my life. I kept Nik on the road just to keep my head above water, and spread his music to thousands of people *knowing* what he is and *believing* what he is, and I still don't know all that he was using me for.

Ignorance isn't a crime, but negligence is. I'll be sifting through the space between them for as long as I live and picking out any kernel of truth I find. It's gray and uncomfortable and complicated, like sanity, like sobriety.

But if I have the chance to go on, I'll take it.

Lansing's hand hovers over mine. It looks more like a signal for *stop*, at first, but I catch her eyes, and she tenses her forehead as if to ask, *Is this okay?* I nod, and she folds her fingers over the back of mine.

"If you never want to see him after this, we can make that happen," she says. "In exchange for your cooperation I can promise you that you will not be arrested and will not stand trial, under this name or whatever new one you take, for anything pertaining to your contract with Nik, unless someday you collude with him again. Is that acceptable?"

It's not perfect. But it is acceptable. I can move on from that, I think. I can do more. Apparently I have a lot of time. "Then I have two other terms."

"Yes?"

"Don't tell Uncle Paul. He'll believe what he wants to believe."

She snickers. "That's fine. And the other term?"

"Will I have to pay off my student loans under the new name?"

"Yes."

"Then take whatever's left over after that from my account. I want you to put it toward Elise's and Jonas's recovery." I'm never going to see Elise again, but it's the least I can do to make sure she gets back to where she wants to be.

"Done." She nods, and lifts up her recording device, thumb over the power button. "Are you ready to talk?"

I breathe, just barely out of time with the monitors. "No. But it's better for me if I do it anyway."

"After all the hell you've put yourself through, I'd have to agree."

"I've never thought that Hell was the kind of place you went *through*. There, fine. Out the other side, no." I scoff at the thought, but a smile comes to my lips without me quite wanting it to.

"You wouldn't be the first," Lansing says, gray eyes glittering.

"Yes, but Orpheus never had to deal with this shit."

Lansing's laughter isn't metered either. That's less startling than the fact that she's laughing at all, and the sound reverberates on the window, the tile, the monitor screens.

Meterless or not, I could transcribe it.

All through the interrogation, there's a song in my head. It's not the one Nik put there—and it may not be a song exactly, but it's definitely music. Illustrative music, a buzz in the strings, low and distant and quiet, with pervasive woodwinds just as soft but octaves higher. I could score this scene. I might, when there's paper on hand.

SEPTEMBER 8, 2012

There is surprisingly little to pack.

I can't—won't—take all of the books with me. Most of my winter clothes can stay as well. Not all of them, since I may have to travel again, but at least half of them can go wherever the FBI wants them to go. Everything else can be replaced, or belongs to Nik.

So it only takes two suitcases and one box. I'm more amused than perhaps I should be, but this makes it easier to believe those movies and plays where one symbolic suitcase is all someone needs to walk out and shut the door. There isn't much you can take with you.

I might not even have to make two trips. I just stack the rolling suitcases and balance the box under one arm, shoulder my way into the hall, and leave that room behind for good.

"Leaving so soon? You only just got here," Nik says, arm out to block the hall. His hand is spread between two masks, one pink and gold and one stark black and screaming, and he's smiling, as cutting as ever. He's not supposed to be here. If the police escort waiting for me downstairs saw him, they'd have detained him, and if he was in the apartment when I entered, I'd have noticed by now. As usual, the rules do not apply to him.

It doesn't matter.

"Get out of my way," I say.

"What's the point? You'll only come back."

"You have to let me go to test that out. So get out of my way."

He doesn't. But his smile tightens, toward a smirk or a grimace, I don't care. "And you were just starting to enjoy yourself."

"Yeah," I say, sarcasm thick as stone, "that was an amazing hospital stay. I can't wait to go back. *Get out of my way.*"

"You wanted silence. I gave you silence. You were happy."

"I thought *I* gave that to *you*."

The first time I scored a point against Nik, it was a pointless battle about books belonging on shelves. It turns out I was right about what dejection looks like on him. His fist thuds against the wall, which is less of a punch and more pushing off, and I back into the suitcase but hold on and don't trip.

I was right. And he has to know it. "I did. You needed me for that. You can't do it alone. So you had to get it from me. You proved you could do it, great, but *you needed me*. So don't pretend it was some grand gesture to win me over."

"You went to *her*," Nik snarls, "didn't you."

There is nothing to say to that but, again, "I did."

Nik rams himself against the box, and I don't brace myself in time. I trip backward over the suitcase like a playground bully planned for me to fall, but I don't hit the floor, and I don't drop the box. I just clip my shoulder on the doorjamb instead.

"I'm sure Paul will protect you." Hell, I'm so pissed off that it's crossed over into amusement. "That's what he's here for, isn't it? But that's his job. Not mine. I don't work for you. I didn't sign anything for you. I worked for *him* and my contract is up."

"And you think the Feds'll help you?"

"It doesn't matter if they do as long as I'm not here."

"You were fine with me before."

"You keep telling yourself that, Nik."

"You were. You stayed."

"That doesn't mean I was fine with it, and that doesn't mean I'll stay now."

Nik laughs, replaces his hand on the wall, doesn't budge one inch. I hold on to the suitcases and the box and keep as steady as I can. I can do this.

"But you stayed," Nik says, around laughter that's as much a menace as it ever was. "Why would you do something you don't want to do?"

He's the god of pleasure. Of course he doesn't understand.

He honestly thought—thinks—that this was what I wanted, because I stayed. He's never felt a conflicting impulse in his life.

No, that's not true. He'd never felt pulled in two directions until that night in New Orleans, when I told him I would play, and he couldn't stop me. Nik was never human. I spent twenty-eight years as one, and whatever the fuck else I become, it'll still be a part of me, and it was never a part of him.

If I'm more than what I was, is he less?

I glower, grit my teeth. "Fine. I wanted to stay. And I got something out of it. But now I don't, and I'm not sticking around to get more."

Nik's teeth flash between his lips, and the grin winds up to his eyes. "So you'll come back when you do."

"No, Nik. I'm not coming back. I've been part of what you do for longer than I wanted to be, and that's it. It's done."

"But you got something out of it, you said so yourself. It means you're in. It means you're mine."

"Cut that shit out. Even if people give themselves to you or whatever you call it, that doesn't make them yours. You keep the mask. That's all you've got in the end. And whatever else you gave me or forced me to face, I didn't sign up to hang myself on your wall."

"Fine. I can take what I gave you away."

"No," I say, "you can't. 'Once it's in there, you can't get it out.'"

Nik's fingers slide one startled inch down the wall. He opens his mouth to speak, and nothing comes out of it. There's no traffic downstairs, no mice in the walls, not even the hiss of halogens overhead. Only silence. And it can't last, but it's *mine* to begin and end, not Nik's.

"You said it yourself from the start," I say, and my voice is the only sound in the world right now. "Beethoven. Shostakovich. Cage. *Ida*. People have walked out on you and lived." And I'm kicking myself to say it, but it's true: "There's always been a way out. I just haven't had the balls to take it. I do now. *Get out of my way*."

There's barely enough room for Nik to stand aside. For a moment, I think he's not going to bother. But Nik flattens himself to the wall opposite the masks, and I drag the suitcases and heft the box, and I do not look back.

On the way out, I take in every mask on the wall, one last time. None of them are mine, and that's what matters.

ENCORE
MAY 15, 2013

"We don't have a studio orchestra," the producer explains as we head down the hall. No one in this industry ever seems to stand still. "I don't know how big an ensemble you're used to, but our budget doesn't necessarily account for—"

"I didn't think I'd need one, from the shooting script." I manage to keep up. "Not with the atmosphere you're going for."

The producer laughs. "That's good to hear! But from your demo I assumed you had a group of your own that you worked with."

"No, that's all sampling and electronic manipulation. Except the piano," I correct, "that's me."

"Good, good. We do have a pianist on call, to play the nightclub scene, and she's getting a band together if you need something live. But it's good that you're working with a budget in mind."

"I'm used to it," I say, with better humor about it than I thought I could muster. This will be a good gig. I've had a few in the last two years—a few not-as-good ones, of course, but this one won't suck.

The producer laughs with me and cuts ahead, opening the door to what turns out to be a recording studio, glass walls, mixing board, and all. "Good, good, a few of you are here. Am I interrupting?"

"There's no red light," Ida says, and one flash of her eyes says plain as day that she recognizes me. I didn't think she would, since I have hair now. But she's reinvented herself before, and I can trust her with this, with myself, my power, my new life.

I don't wait for the producer to introduce me. I reach forward, give her my hand. "Seth Harper." It has a ring to it. Every time I say it I know I chose well. I wonder who she was before, whether she thinks her new name is as right as mine. She probably does. "I think I've just been hired as your composer."

Ida takes my hand, shakes it once. "I'm Ida," she says, just like the first time. "Nice to meet you, Seth. Looks like I'm playing your music on-screen. Hope this isn't the last you hear of me."

"It won't be," I say. "And it's not the last you'll hear of me either. So come on—let's get ourselves heard."

Dear Reader,

Thank you for reading Erica Kudisch's *The Backup*!

We know your time is precious and you have many, many entertainment options, so it means a lot that you've chosen to spend your time reading. We really hope you enjoyed it.

We'd be honored if you'd consider posting a review—good or bad—on sites like **Amazon, Barnes & Noble, Kobo, Goodreads, Twitter, Facebook, Tumblr,** and your blog or website. We'd also be honored if you told your friends and family about this book. Word of mouth is a book's lifeblood!

For more information on upcoming releases, author interviews, blog tours, contests, giveaways, and more, please sign up for our weekly, spam-free newsletter and visit us around the web:

Newsletter: tinyurl.com/RiptideSignup
Twitter: twitter.com/RiptideBooks
Facebook: facebook.com/RiptidePublishing
Goodreads: tinyurl.com/RiptideOnGoodreads
Tumblr: riptidepublishing.tumblr.com

Thank you so much for Reading the Rainbow!

AnglerFishPress.com

AN IMPRINT OF RIPTIDE PUBLISHING.

ACKNOWLEDGMENTS

It takes an orchestra to play a symphony; I had no idea at the time, but it takes about as many people to realize a book.

Like most compositions in my life, this one started with my wife, Abbi, perpetual sounding board, expert blocker, indispensable tool patrol, and cheering section. Then came my brother Rick, whose feedback was crucial in finding the right people to publish *The Backup*. The indefatigable P. Hansen introduced me to the Riptide staff; Meg, Ray, Bec, Chuck, Aria, Dead Emily, and Racheline cleaned up my early drafts so that Caz, Sarah, Alex, and Rachel would have something to read. After more edits than I can count, Amelia and Chris put the book out there with Jay's chilling cover, and L.C. made sure that it was as beautiful inside as well as out. And, of course, I must thank my family for its enduring support.

And those are just the people who *know* they helped. I'd also like to thank the Metropolitan Transit Authority—yeah, I know, most of the time they don't deserve it, but since I do most of my writing and editing on their trains I ought to give credit where it's due. Though she probably doesn't care if she's mentioned, my dear friend Jenn is responsible for getting me started writing in the first place, and for at least one of the fondly disparaging remarks about Pittsburgh. And Dr. Mann's mnemonic device about Pete from the Street and Phil from the Hill is replicated here without his knowledge; I owe him, Harold Meltzer, Dr. Pisani, Dr. Libin, Dr. Nisnevichaya, and Dr. Jacobson for hours of debate on which composers Nik has fucked.

As far as I know, Richard Taruskin has no idea that he's graced these pages with his Apollonian magnanimity. Then again, he knows about the Rite of Spring riots . . .

ALSO BY ERICA KUDISCH

What Aelister Found Here
Substitution Cipher

ABOUT THE AUTHOR

Erica Kudisch lives, writes, sings, and often trips over things in New York City. When not in pursuit of about five different creative vocations, none of which pay her nearly enough, you can usually find her pontificating about dead gay video games, shopping for thigh-high socks, and making her beleaguered characters wait forty thousand words before they get in the sack.

In addition to publishing novellas and short stories, Erica is responsible for the BDSM musical *Dogboy & Justine*, and serves as creative director and cofounder of Treble Entendre Productions.

She also has issues with authority. And curses too fucking much.

Facebook: facebook.com/Erica-Kudisch-497785360383751

Twitter: @EricaKudisch

Instagram: @hardhandmaiden

Enjoy more stories like
The Backup
at AnglerFishPress.com!

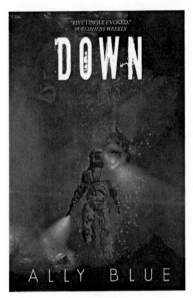

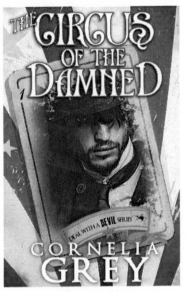

Down
ISBN: 978-1-62649-259-2

The Circus of the Damned
ISBN: 978-1-62649-166-3

CPSIA information can be obtained at www.ICGtesting.com
Printed in the USA
LVOW10s1521050216

473888LV00004B/332/P

9 781626 493711